The Grey Storm

by Lee Knafa

THE LIVERPOOL EDITING COMPANY

First published in Great Britain in 2019
Copyright © Lee Knafa 2019
Cover design: Bodhi Design - www.bodhi-design.co.uk
Editing: Matthew McKeown - www.liverpoolediting.co.uk

This book is a work of fiction. Any references to historical events, real
people, or real places are used fictitiously. Other names, characters,
places and incidents are products of the author's imagination, and any
resemblance to actual people living or dead, events or locales is entirely
coincidental.

ISBN print: 978-1-9993005-2-4
ISBN eBook: 978-1-9993005-3-1

Lee Knafa
The Liverpool Editing Company Ltd

The Grey Storm

Chapters

INTRODUCTION

It was a clear morning on 1 September 1939 when the German training ship, Schleswig-Holstein, anchored in Danzig harbour and, after receiving the code words 'Weiss' and 'Fall,' [1.] opened fire on the Polish garrison at Westerplatte. The Schleswig fired its deadly salvo at point-blank range and without warning, causing massive confusion. This single action signalled the beginning of war.

That initial attack was swiftly followed by air strikes on roads, rail-ways, bridges and airfields, and then, finally, came a land invasion. On the German side, some 60 divisions were committed, led by Field Marshal Gerd von Rundstedt's Army Group South. Six other armies supported von Rundstedt: General Siegmund List's 14th army, General Walter Reichenau's 10th army, General Johannes Blaskowitz's 8th army, General Gunther von Kluge's 4th army, General Kucher's 3rd army in East Prussia, and General Fedor von Bock's Army Group North. The opposing Polish forces consisted of the Narew group in the north, facing East Prussia, under the com-mand of Major General Czeslaw Mlot-Fijalkowski, comprising two infantry divisions and one cavalry brigade. Also facing East Prussia was General Emil Przedrzymirski's Modlin army, backed up by two reserve divisions.

At the base of a huge tract of land known as the Polish Corridor, which separated Pomerania from East Prussia, was General W. Bortnowski's Pomorze army, made up of five infantry divisions and one cavalry brigade. The next formation in the south was the Poznan army, under the command of General Tadeusz Kutrzeba, which stood in the Poznan salient and had a reserve force of two Infantry divisions. In the central sector, along the Polish-German frontier, stood the Lodz army, under the command of General Juliusz Rommel, who had four Infantry divisions and two Cavalry brigades. Facing Silesia was the Cracow army, commanded by General Antoni Szylling, with seven infantry divisions and one cavalry brigade, supported by a mechanised brigade. Covering the southern border was the Carpathian army, under the command of General Kazimierz Fabrycy, which had two mountain brigades, supported by the Tarnow reserve force, consisting of two Infantry divisions. The Prusy army, which acted as a general reserve, was just south of Warsaw and was commanded by General Stefan Dalp-Biernacki, and contained eight infantry divisions, one cavalry brigade and one tank brigade. A thin screening force was left to cover the dangerously long Polish-Soviet frontier.

Although the Polish army fought bravely, it was no match for the well-trained and ultra-disciplined Wehrmacht, and fell under the weight of the mighty German's merciless advance after only five weeks of fierce fighting. The Warsaw fortress of Modlin capitulated on 27 September 1939, before the conflict was brought to a close on 6 October, with German casualties totalling 8,082 killed, 27,278 wounded and 5,029 missing. The Polish suffered losses of 70,000 killed, along with an estimated 130,000 wounded and 90,000 escaped.

As the German Reich continued to grow, more and more rein-forcements were needed to help police the new territories. In early November 1939, Josef Herzog, a second lieutenant from Berlin, arrived at D Company HQ in Karlowitz, Breslau, fresh from the Kriegshule Academie in Leipzig, West Germany.

1. White and Case.

PROLOGUE

January 1919. Grossman Clinic, Madgeburg, East Germany.

Huddled around a table in a darkened room, with only a dimmed light on the patient, a doctor and his female assistants struggle to deliver a baby.

Although the doctor tries not to show it, there is fear in his eyes, and a nurse responds by swabbing cotton across his drenched brow with a gloved hand. He steps back from the table and pulls away his mask after thirteen hours of nothing but hot, stale air.

He instructs the nurse to administer more oxygen to the patient, and then asks for forceps. The tension rises with each puff and grunt, and then suddenly, the doctor announces that he can see the baby's crown. Dispensing with the tools, he instead uses his bare hands, plucking the youngster from its mother like a pea from its pod. The doctor holds the trophy up high, but rather than the joy and elation that normally follows a successful birth, there are gasps of shock before the room is plunged into silence.

The Grey Storm

CHAPTER ONE

The open-topped scout car, a gift from the fleeing Polish army, pulled up sharply with a long squeal outside D Company HQ. Stiff from the long journey, Josef alighted awkwardly from the vehicle. As he stood up to straighten his crumpled uniform, he heard a thud behind him, swiftly followed by the noise of a revving engine. He turned slightly, looking over his right shoulder and seeing that his small, bulky brown leather suitcase was lying on its side in the middle of the road.

'Danke!' he yelled after the scout car, as it pulled away quickly. He leaned into the road with his hand raised in the air, but the driver had already turned the corner.

He collected his suitcase and turned to face the main entrance of the building. In front of him lay three large sandstone steps that led up to a double set of dark brown varnished doors, guarded on either side by two smartly dressed sentries, each stood with mauser rifles tucked neatly into their right sides. They wore slate grey steel helmets, and field grey tunics with neatly pressed grey trousers that disappeared into their shiny black leather boots. The guardsmen were shaded overhead by a long, narrow red brick balcony, with a decorative white wrought iron grating that extended along its full length. On either side of the balcony hung impressive red swastika flags that fluttered gently in the soft morning breeze.

As Josef climbed the steps and reached out his hand to turn the ornate brass door handle, the sentries snapped to attention and lifted their rifles, bringing them to rest in front of their chests. Now, this is the life, he thought with a grin, as he passed through the gigantic main doorframe.

'Ah, Pech,' Weise said by way of greeting, 'You're probably wondering why I've sent for you, no?'

'It did cross my mind, sir,' Pech replied. 'Why the urgency?'

'This new officer I'm expecting this morning,' Weise said.

'Herzog, sir?' Pech asked.

'Yes, Herr Leutnant, Herzog,' Weise said with slanted eyes. 'What do you know about him, Pech?'

'Well, sir, all I can tell you is that he's a twenty-year-old unmarried zweiter leutnant, straight out of kadett schule. Is there a problem, sir?'

'There could be, Pech. There could well be.'

Josef entered cautiously into the busy foyer, finding to his surprise that it was most grandiose. In the main hall hung a collection of small crystal-shaded lamps that were evenly spaced along semi-circular dark blue walls, complemented by a large and magnificent chandelier that was suspended from the centre of a lofty white ceiling. Uniformed personnel rushed across the highly polished floor, entering one room and then dashing back out and into another, all the while carrying files or clutching large briefcases. He stepped forward almost unnoticed and stood himself near the left wall, at the foot of a wide white-stoned staircase that curved up sharply and joined a T-shaped landing. He scanned across to his right and spied a curious looking obergefreiter [1.] sitting behind an enclosed wooden counter, reading some kind of document while sipping from a white china mug.

Weise carefully opened a long brown file and then slapped it down hard onto his desk, pointing at it furiously. 'Take a look at that, Pech,' he shrieked.

Pech gently rotated the file around until he could read it. 'Mein Gott,' he gulped, 'ein schwarz!' [2.]

'Genau!' [3.] Weise barked back. 'Tell me, Pech, is this some kind of joke by the high command?'

'I'm afraid not, sir. I would take this very seriously if I were you, Herr Hauptmann.'

'Kannich helfen sie, Herr Leutnant?', the obergefreiter grunted. The lance corporal clearly wasn't quite sure what to make of this exotic gentleman, and stared at him with deep curiously.

'Oh, yes,' Josef replied, and clicked his way across the glossy brown-tiled floor. As he neared the counter, he could not help but notice the obergefreiter's disability. A thin purple scar ran down the left side of the man's face, starting from his ear and ending at the jawline, while the left arm of his field grey jacket was pressed flat against his side and neatly tucked into his bottom pocket. On his right arm, below the shoulder, was a downward-pointing chevron with a single cluster in the middle, denoting a man of at least six years' service. 'I have an appointment at ten o'clock with Herr Hauptmann Weise, Herr Obergefreiter,' he whispered.

The lance corporal continued to stare.

'Was ist los, Herr Obergefreiter?' Josef asked.

'Tut mir leid,' the lance corporal said. 'I've never seen eine schwarz offizier before, sir.'

'Well, you have now. Confirm mein appointment bitte.'

'Jawhol, Herr Leutnant,' the obergefreiter replied curtly, while lifting the heavy receiver from the black Bakelite telephone on his desk.

'What are you going to do about this Herzog fellow, sir?' Pech asked nervously.

'I don't know offhand,' Weise admitted. 'I could do with more time to think.' Suddenly, the phone rang, and he snatched to answer it. 'Ja, ja, send him up,' he mumbled frustratedly, 'but tell him to wait outside.'

'Jawhol, Herr Hauptmann, I will send him up right away!' the obergefreiter said, before slamming the phone down and looking at Josef. 'Right,' he growled, 'what you do is take the stairs here, turn left on the landing and then it's the third door on your left. You must wait outside until you are called for, verstehen?'

'Yes, danke, Herr Obergefreiter,' Josef nodded, checking his wristwatch. It was 9.50am. He tucked his peaked visor cap firmly under his left arm and made his way up the steps towards the landing, running his right hand along the top of the black wrought iron railings that framed the grand staircase. Once he reached the first floor he paused for a moment, and then turned left onto the landing and walked slowly along the narrow corridor until he arrived at the third brown door, which had the name 'Hauptmann Weise' written on it. He sat himself down on a long wooden bench that was positioned opposite Herr Weise's office, and quietly waited to be called.

'Well, Pech, he's here,' Weise sighed, 'and it seems we have no choice but to go along with this ridiculous charade. I want you to give him the worst duties possible, and then hopefully, after a week or so, he'll realise his mistake and ask for a transfer.'

'Yes, sir,' Pech replied.

'OK then,' Weise said, 'I suppose you'd better wheel him in, eh?'

'Yes, right away, sir,' Pech answered sharply, and turned towards the door.

Josef sat motionless on the hard bench, knees firmly together and with his peaked visor cap placed neatly on his lap. He glanced along the hallway, noticing a large, brown-framed portrait of the Fuhrer hanging precariously from the cracked beige-coloured wall to his right. It depicted Hitler sitting at a table, wearing a light brown tunic with a black Iron Cross suspended just below the left breast pocket, and matching trousers and black boots. His left hand was on his thigh, while his right arm rested on the table in front of him. His face was grotesquely pale, as though to further emphasise the funny little Chaplin-esque moustache stuck under his nose. He had cold, black piercing eyes that seemed to be watching the leutnant, like a suspicious sentry.

He heard a door creaking slowly on its hinges, and turned to see a tall man wearing a Wehrmacht uniform standing in front of him. 'Morgen, Herr Leutnant,' the man said, 'Hauptmann Weise is ready to see you now. Would you follow me please?'

Josef nodded, and then settled his cap on his head before marching smartly into the office, stopping just short of a large desk where a man who he took to be Hauptmann Weise sat with his face obscured by a large brown file.

'Nehmen de platz, [4.] Herr Leutnant,' Weise said, peering over the top of whatever it was that he was reading. 'The man standing next to you is Herr Oberleutnant Viktor Pech. He will be in charge of your new training, and you will answer directly to him. Never question his orders, verstehen?'

'Yes, of course, Herr Hauptmann,' Josef coughed, hoping to disguise a furtive glance at Oberleutnant Pech. The man was tall, slim and good-looking; in his early thirties and very well dressed, with jet-black hair cropped short and stylishly backcombed. He wore a black Iron Cross first class on his left breast pocket, and just above that was a small red and black ribbon, which slanted downward from his tunic button and disappeared behind the front hemline of his jacket, signalling that he was also a recipient of the Iron Cross second class. He stood silently at Josef's side, staring at him with a constant grin on his face. This gave Josef the immediate impression that he was to be the puppet, and Pech the puppetmaster.

'Well, Herr Leutnant,' Weise spoke after a period of silence, 'I have read your record, and quite frankly I'm not that impressed.' He frowned as he lowered the file, and then dramatically slapped it down onto the desk.

For the first time, Josef had a clear view of his new commander. Weise's face was round and ruddy, and his greying-brown hair was showing signs of receding, in addition to being thin on top. His uniform was heavily decorated, and he wore the Knight's Cross around his neck. Below his left breast pocket hung the Iron Cross first class, and beneath that was an oval-shaped, solid silver Wound Badge, issued only to those who had been severely injured in battle.

'What am I supposed to do with this chap, eh, Pech?' Weise asked, turning swiftly to the oberleutnant. 'I ask for seasoned officers, and what do they send me but a damned monkey!'

Josef sat mortified on the edge of his chair, but he was determined to maintain his composure.

'Not to worry, sir,' Pech answered, still sporting that annoying grin. 'We will make him.'

'Or break him, eh, Pech?' Weise chuckled. 'Anyway, getting on with the business at hand, could you tell me a little about yourself,

Herr Leutnant? For example, how did you come to join the Wehr-macht?'

'Well, sir, I've always wanted to do soldiering since I was a small boy. It's a man's job, and you get to see the world, sir. Mein vater paid for me to attend militarisch schule, and has supported me all the way, sir.'

'Ah, yes,' Weise nodded, 'about your vater, Herr Leutnant. It says in your file that he is of Afrikan descent.'

'Yes, sir, that is correct.'

'So, tell me, how did your vater come to live in Deutschland?'

'Well, I'd have to go back a fair bit to explain that, sir.'

'That's quite alright,' Weise smiled, 'we have plenty of time. Please, enlighten us.' He leaned forward with interest.

Pech also seemed intrigued, as he pulled up a chair and sat down to listen.

Still perched on the edge of his seat, Josef clasped his hands together and broke into a huge smile. He knew that he finally had them where he wanted them. 'Mein vater,' he began, 'served as a sergeant with der Kaiser's Imperial Army when Deutschland colonised Namibia in nineteen-four. After serving for two years, he was shipped to Deutschland and stationed in the Rhineland, where he met and eventually married mein mutter. Later that year, they moved to Berlin, where they still live to this day. I think that's about it, sir.'

'Not quite, Herzog.' Weise corrected, 'You forgot to mention the royal connection.'

'Royal connection?' Pech blurted out, unable to contain his surprise.

'I didn't think it important, sir,' Josef blushed.

'Not important?' Weise laughed, practically beaming. 'It's not every day that we receive Royalty at D company, eh, Pech?'

'No, it's not, sir,' Pech answered, mouth agape. 'Please tell us more, Herzog.'

Sensing a more cordial atmosphere now, Josef relaxed back into his chair. 'Mein vater is an Afrikan noble,' he went on with his remarkable story. 'A Duke by European standards, you might say.'"

'Hence the name, eh?' Weise said.

'Sir?' Josef asked.

'In German, "Herzog" means "duke," does it not?' Weise said.

'Why, yes,' Josef confirmed, 'mein vater is the son of the chieftain of Namibia, and it was because of his hereditary wealth that he was allowed to enter Deutschland. It's also how he was able to pay for mein education at militarisch schule.'

'So, that must make you a viscount by German standards, surely?' Pech cut in.

'To be honest, I've never thought about it, sir.'

'So, where does your loyalty lie, Herzog?' Weise eyed him suspiciously. 'With Deutschland or Afrika?'

'Why, Deutschland of course, sir,' Josef replied without hesitation, indignant at the supposition that it could be anything but. 'It's the only country I have ever known.'

'I'm glad to hear it, Herzog,' Weise said, closing the file on his desk. 'Well, I don't think there is anything further, unless you have something to add, Herr Oberleutnant?'

'No, sir,' Pech shook his head, 'I think you've covered everything.'

'Very well, Herr Oberleutnant,' Weise said. 'Show him to his accommodation, and then brief him on his new duties.' His darting eyes met Josef's. 'I will be keeping a close eye on you, Herr Leutnant.'

'Yes, sir. Thank you, sir,' Josef replied enthusiastically, while rising to his feet. Both he and Pech stood to attention and saluted their commanding officer, before marching stiffly out of the room.

1. Lance corporal.

2. A black man.

3. Precisely.

4. Take a seat.

The Grey Storm

CHAPTER TWO

'I think the old man likes you, Herzog,' Viktor laughed, as they made their way out of the main entrance.

'Oh, well, at least I'm getting off to a good start, then,' Herzog replied, as they cleared the three large steps outside D HQ. 'Don't you think, sir?'

'Yes, very much so,' Viktor grinned. 'He likes young boys.'

'I don't follow you, sir?'

'It's rumoured that he's a homo!'

'A what, sir?'

'A homosexual. You know what one of those is, don't you?' Viktor was of course perpetuating a vicious, and false, rumour that had been started by Herr Vance Meyer, a disgruntled junior officer who had wrongly assumed that a recent plea for divorce from Weise's wife, Frau Rosa, following ten years of childless marriage could only mean one thing: the man was sweet! Meyer had successfully put two and two together and come up with five. 'Ha, don't look so worried, Herzog. The "War Council" will protect you.'

Herzog stopped at the roadside, and Viktor walked up alongside him. It had stopped raining now, and the sun was desperately trying to breakthrough the fluffy grey clouds. Occasionally, a few rays of light would escape and reflect off the corrugated roofs of the barracks that lay ahead of them. Herzog filled his nostrils with the fresh damp air, evidently glad to be free of Weise's stuffy office.

Viktor raised his arm and pointed across to the other side. 'Come, on,' he said amiably, 'it's almost lunchtime. I'll take you to the officers' mess and you can meet the War Council. I can't wait to see the looks on their faces,' he giggled.

'What is the "War Council," sir?' Herzog asked, wearing a confused look on his face.

'You'll find out soon enough,' Viktor beamed.

The two men navigated their way across the staggered traffic, which consisted almost entirely of heavy trucks, staff cars and tanks. Once safely across, Viktor led them through a gap between two huge wooden buildings.

'Just a little further, Herzog,' Viktor said.

'OK, sir,' Herzog replied.

'Hey,' Viktor said over his shoulder, 'you can call me Viktor when we're not on duty.'

'Oh, yes of course,' Herzog smiled, 'Viktor.'

'Here we are,' Viktor said, rubbing his hands together, 'just around this corner. Follow me.'

As they turned the corner, Josef looked as though he couldn't believe his eyes. In front of them, separate from the other buildings, was a shabby wooden hut that had been hastily painted combat green. On the front door was an incongruous white plaque which read, Offizier Messe. It was a far cry from the luxurious surroundings of officer training school, Viktor knew. 'Don't worry, Herzog,' he chuckled, sensing Josef's disappointment, 'you'll get used to it soon enough.'

Josef followed Viktor into the makeshift mess and, once inside, began to intently survey the interior. There was just enough seating capacity for approximately twenty officers, with two long tables pushed together in the centre of the hall, surrounded by hard brown Bakelite chairs. The brown ceiling rose to a steep point, supported by church-like beams that ran the full length of the hut. Next to the inner doorframe ran a long, narrow shelf holding numerous square metal containers filled with a variety of foods, such as boiled ham, boiled vegetables, soup and so forth.

'Take a plate, Herzog,' Viktor said with a smile. 'It's self-service here, you know.' He leaned over a container and began scooping up food with relish.

The incoherent background chatter of the smoke-filled room faded into a low mumble, as all eyes fell on Josef. Some officers looked shocked and whispered furiously to their colleagues, while others simply stared out of curiosity at this odd little black fellow wearing a Wehrmacht uniform. Suddenly, a giant of a man rose up from his chair and began walking toward the new arrivals. He was at least six-foot tall, and must have weighed around 110 kilos! He had an unusual appearance; his ginger hair was cropped and his face was pale and freckled, and he was now stood towering over Viktor.

The ginger beast placed a huge hand on Viktor's shoulder and squeezed hard with sausage-like fingers. Sporting a grin as large as his body, he asked, 'Who's the monkey?'

The words were at first met with complete silence, and then by a huge roar of laughter from all around the mess hall. Josef became furious and reacted quickly, still sore from the comment made by Hauptmann Weise earlier. 'Now listen here, you-' he began, but was cut off before he could finish.

'Sit down and shut up, Uri!' Viktor bellowed, putting an end to the laughter. 'I'm sorry, Josef,' he said, turning and softening his voice. 'He didn't mean anything by it, really. Here, try this,' he slapped down several pieces of hot meat onto Josef's plate, 'brathanchen und bratkartoffeln. [1] Sehr gut, ja?' [2]

'Ja, danke,' Josef replied, despondent, but forcing a smile. There was one good thing to come out of it all, though. Viktor had called him by his first name. Maybe things will get better as the day rolls on, he thought.

'OK,' Viktor said, patting Josef on the back, 'I'll now introduce you to the War Council. Follow me.'

The War Council, Viktor explained, was a nickname given to a group of rowdy young lieutenants who, when off duty, were often loud and occasionally drunk! He himself was their appointed leader, being the most senior officer among them. 'Sitzen hier,' he ordered, pointing to an empty chair as they arrived at what was to be their table.

Josef stepped forward as instructed, and could not believe his own misfortune. Sitting in the next chair along from his was none other than the ginger beast!

'Ja, ja, sitzen,' the beast said, a piece of veal swinging from his mouth.

'Right then,' Viktor said, wringing his hands together, 'now that we are all seated, gentlemen, and I use the term gentlemen lightly,' he paused, as a cheer of approval rang out instantly around the table. 'Alright, alright, settle down. Now, you've probably already noticed that we have a neu boy on the team. He is Herr Leutnant Viscount Josef Herzog.'

'Herzog?' the ginger beast belched. 'That's a funny name for a chimpanzee!'

Almost immediately, the whole table erupted into laughter.

'That's enough, damn it, Uri!' Viktor barked. 'I've already warned you once, and I won't tell you again!'

Uri rolled his eyes and slumped back into his chair like a naughty schoolboy, as Viktor rose to his feet and tapped on the side of his glass with a thin silver teaspoon.

'Gentlemen,' he addressed the room, 'I would like you to toast our neu freund in the usual way.'

The other officers stood swiftly. 'Herzlich willkommin, [3] Herr Leutnant Herzog!' they sang in unison, with their cups of tea held out in salute.

'Danke, mein Herren,' Josef whispered back, feeling quite over-whelmed and more than a little embarrassed. The Germans love heraldry and royal connections, he knew, and the fact that he was a viscount helped to quickly assimilate him, not only into the War Council, but also into the Wehrmacht, which was top-heavy with Vons and Ritters.

'I shall now introduce you in turn to the War Council,' Viktor giggled. 'You've already met Herr Oberleutnant Uri Voss, haven't you, Josef?'

'Why, yes, h-hello Uri,' Josef stammered, producing a nervous smile.

'Nice to meet you, mein schwarz prinz,' Uri replied, slapping Josef heartily in the centre of his back.

'And over here,' Viktor said, indicating a well-groomed and handsome man, with blonde hair that was a bit longer than army regulation, 'is Herr Oberleutnant Philipp Grinburger. His vater is a general in die Wehrmacht, you know.' Philip had a kind, friendly face, and nodded warmly by way of greeting. 'And next to him,'

Viktor continued, guiding Josef's gaze with an outstretched arm, 'is Herr Oberleutnant Erich Heiter. His vater is chief of police in Baden Wurttemberge.'

'Ja,' Uri cut in, 'the black forest. You two should get on like a house on fire!'

Once again, the table exploded into laughter, only this time Viktor joined in. 'I'm sorry, Josef,' he said, trying to control his chuckling.

'It's alright, Viktor,' Josef answered with a huge grin.

'And last, but by no means least,' Viktor said, 'this man here is Herr Leutnant Egon Binde. His vater is of no real importance, and being that he is of the working classes, how he became an officer is a total mystery to me.'

'Hey, watch your tongue,' Egon replied in mock indignation. 'I'll have you know that mein vater is essential to the war effort. Somebody has to drive the damned trains, you know. You're such a snob, Pech!'

'Oh, and never forget the War Council's secret motto, Josef,' Viktor said. 'And what's that, Viktor?' Josef asked.

'Zusammen immer, [4] of course!' Viktor yelled, turning to the rest of the group.

'Ja, zusammen immer!' the War Council roared back, as they banged their cups against the cluttered table.

Josef imagined a possible friendship between Egon and himself, due to him being the most unassuming of the War Council. Egon was quite heavily built, with a large round face that always appeared flushed. His uniform was untidy, and there were specks of gravy down the front of his jacket, but perhaps his personality would eclipse his physical appearance.

'Come on, prinz,' Uri spluttered, his mouth full of potato, 'tuck in. It's gut stuff. It's funny, I don't know how you and I have come this far.'

'What do you mean?' Josef asked.

'Well,' Uri pondered for a moment, 'let me put it to you this way. We're both mongrels, aren't we?'

'I think you mean we're both of mixed race, don't you?'

'That's what I just said, didn't I? Look, you and I are the same. We're both outsiders. Mein mutter is Russian and mein vater a German. Did you not think that I was the butt of all jokes when I first enlisted?'

'No, Uri, I didn't.' Josef realised that he had another potential friend in the unlikely form of the ginger beast. He relaxed back into his chair, feeling quite at home in his new surroundings. Maybe life in the regular army won't be such a bad thing after all, he thought, while looking around at his new comrades.

Viktor leaned in close to Josef, whispering into his ear, 'When we finish here, I will show you to your new duties. Herr Hauptmann Weise has ordered me to give you harsh assignments, and I must obey him. However, they will not last for very long. You're on night watch for the rest of the week, and you will aslo oversee the latrine duties. Show willing and do your best, no matter how difficult it may seem to you at the time, verstehen?'

'Of course, Viktor,' Josef whispered back.

'Now remember, in here we lark about, but outside it's business as usual. I'm your senior here, second only to Herr Hauptman Weise, so when I say jump, you jump, verstehen?'

'Yes, Herr Oberleutnant,' Josef stiffened.

'Relax, Josef,' Viktor laughed, 'we're not outside yet.'

Josef blew the air out of his cheeks, and wondered how long it would take before he got used to the situation.

'I think Viktor really likes you, Josef,' Uri giggled.

'Oh, do you think so?' Josef replied, feeling quite flattered.

'Oh yes, but I'd watch your arse if I were you!'

'I heard that, Uri,' Viktor snapped over his shoulder, having been facing the opposite way. Everyone around the table laughed. 'OK, Josef,' he said, 'when you have finished your meal, I will show you to your neu office and resting quarters, and then I'll introduce you to your men.'

'That sounds great,' Josef said. 'Thank you, Viktor.'

1. Roastchicken and roastpotato.
2. Very good, yes.
3. A warm welcome.
4. Together always.

CHAPTER THREE

Viktor unlocked the door to Josef's new office and passed him the keys. 'Here we are,' he smiled, hand extended as he offered Josef the chance to enter first.

Josef opened the door fully and walked slowly inside. The room was large, with bare floorboards and a musty odour. A naked light bulb hung from the centre of its cracked off-white ceiling, and the magnolia walls looked to be in need of a good painting. Directly opposite him was a long wooden table, with a brown tubular-framed Bakelite chair tucked in neatly behind it. A long single wooden shelf ran across the back wall, displaying three dust-covered books at one end, and what looked like an old toy or mascot at the other. Above the shelf was a small dirty window, decorated on both sides by tattered blue curtains. To the left of the door was an old black radiator that rattled continuously, and on the wall was a large, dog-eared military propaganda poster, which read in bold print at the bottom: JOIN THE MARCH FOR FREEDOM. Above that was a menacing portrait of a helmeted Wehrmacht soldier, brandishing a mauser rifle in one hand and performing a beckoning gesture with the other.

'Well, what do you think?' Viktor asked, licking his lips in anticipation.

'Not bad, Viktor,' Josef answered unconvincingly. 'Not bad at all.'

'Come on, I'll show you to your quarters. While you're getting settled in, I'll get a telephone fitted in your neu office, OK?'

They made their way to Josef's new sleeping quarters, where they both stood silent for a few moments at the door, until Pech broke the silence by saying, 'What are you waiting for, a fanfare? You have the keys, man!'

'Oh yes, I have the keys,' Josef giggled as he fumbled in his jacket pocket, producing the keys and then rattling them into the lock, which turned with a crack. The door sprung open suddenly. 'Hey, I like it,' he declared, scanning the room. 'I could really do something with this place.'

The room was a bit of a mess, with some of the previous occupant's junk left scattered about, but overall it was far better then he had expected.

'Right, Josef,' Viktor said, 'I'll leave you to crack on with it. I'm going to get your phone line connected now, so give me a ring from your neu office when you have finished here, and then I'll introduce you to your men, OK?'

'OK,' Josef agreed. 'Thank you, Viktor.' He took off his jacket and boots and rolled up his sleeves to make a start, and it seemed like only a few minutes had passed when he heard the heavy stomping of boots outside. Before he knew what was happening, his door was flung open and Egon was standing in front of him, red-faced and breathing heavily.

'Josef,' Egon panted, 'Josef, stop what you're doing and get dressed!'

'Calm yourself, alter junger,' [1] Josef laughed. 'Where's the fire?'

'This is no joke,' Egon insisted. 'We have a briefing in ten minutes, so get your boots on – now!'

'Alright, but first tell me what the hell is going on?' Josef struggled to get into his jacket, before fastening his broad black leather belt and holster around his waist. 'Damph! Damph! I can't find mein boots, Egon!'

'Here, let me help you look for them. I'll bring you up to speed as we go,' Egon puffed. 'We have to get to briefing room number two. Herr Major Lowe is about to give- hay, here they are. I've found them!' he bellowed, holding the boots high in the air.

'Nein, nein, they're brown boots, you fool,' Josef chided jokingly. 'They probably belonged to some old Luftwaffe pilot!'

They shared a loud laugh, until Egon noticed something pass the small side window that gave him pause. 'Oh no,' he mumbled, 'we're in for it now. Here's Pech!'

'Why are you two still here giggling like schoolgirls?' Pech demanded, popping his head through the open doorway. 'Get yourselves off to the briefing room right now!'

'Jawohl, Herr Oberleutnant,' they both said, stifling their sniggers.

Oberleutnant Erich Heiter spied his opportunity, and pulled Viktor Pech to one side for a private chat. 'How long have we got this Herzog fellow for?' he asked.

'I've no idea,' Viktor shrugged. 'Why do you ask?'

'Well, me and the lads don't want to work with him,' Erich said.

'You and the lads?' Viktor asked.

'That's correct.'

'Egon and Uri seem to like him, and as for me, I felt the same as you before I got to know him.'

'So, you're saying that you like him, too?'

'Believe it or not, I actually think that Herzog could be an asset to us.'

'Viktor, everyone's laughing at us. We need to get rid of him!'

'That decision can only be made by Herr Hauptmann Weise. Until then, you'll have to get used to him.'

'The lads won't be happy about this.'

'The lads?' Pech repeated, eyes narrowing. 'Are you sure it isn't just you who has a problem with it?'

'Look, it's nothing personal. I think he's a nice lad, but being a viscount is not enough. The men will never take orders from a Negro, and they will never follow him into battle. You must know this?'

'How can I know this when he hasn't been given a command yet?'

'He's got to go, Viktor.'

'Listen to me. While he's here, he's a member of the War Council, and we look after our own. Got that?'

'When things start to fall apart, I promise not to say, told you so.'

'Look, I will pass your concerns onto Herr Hauptmann Weise, but I don't think that it will make any difference.'

'Thank you, Viktor.'

Josef and Egon crept into the back of the crowded briefing room, crouching low, but still they were spotted.

'Glad you could make it, gentlemen,' a voice growled; it was Major Lowe. He was standing on a small stage at the front, pointing with a thin cane at a large map of Poland, which was suspended directly behind him. 'Right then, let's begin again shall we?' he said, looking down at Hauptmann Weise, who was seated on the front row of officers, nervously fondling the Knight's Cross around his neck. 'As you all know, two of our units came under attack this morning.'

'Attack?' Josef whispered in alarmed voice. 'What does he mean, "attack?"'

'That's what I was trying to tell you,' Egon muttered. 'Now, shut up and listen.'

'They happened almost simultaneously,' the major said, pointing at two large red circles no the map. 'Here, on the outskirts of Odra, and here, just outside Olenica. We believe our units took fire from the remnants of the Polish army, who have banded together with local Partisans. I have received orders from our neu Gauleiter, Herr Arthur Greiser, to eliminate all insurgent activity within the two zones shown here. We do not have the facilities for prisoners here, gentlemen. I need you all to remember that.'

'Gut Gott, Egon,' Josef exclaimed. 'did you hear that? They want us to kill them all.'

'Yes, I heard,' Egon answered, 'but for Gott's sake, keep your voice down!'

'What about the Geneva Convention, Egon?' Josef asked. 'It was created in to stop this sort of thing from happening!'

'Don't get involved in things you don't fully understand, Josef,' Egon said. 'You're still raw, just fresh out of College. Best to keep your mouth shut.'

Josef could see that Egon was uncomfortable with this subject, but before he could apologise, a voice rang out from the row in front. He looked ahead to see an officer with short blond hair turning around to glare at him. In sharp contrast to Leutnant Grinburger's friendly Aryan face, this man's poster boy features were most aggressive.

'You school children are all the same,' the man sneered. 'All wind and piss, with books and theories coming out of your arses! I would listen to what your freund says, you spineless bastard!'

Josef bristled. 'Hey,' he fired back, 'you can't speak to me like-'

'I told you to keep your voice down, didn't I?' Egon hissed, pulling Josef in close. 'This is a neu war we're fighting, Josef, with neu methods. You must either get used to it or be destroyed by it. There's simply no other way.'

Reluctantly, Josef turned his attention back to the front of the room, where Major Lowe was still giving his address. 'Hauptmann Weise will lead the attack on Odra with Herr Oberleutnant Pech and Herr Leutnant Voss, while I will command at Olenica with Herr Oberleutnant Heiter and Herr Leutnant Herzog.'

'Did you hear that, Josef?' Egon gasped. 'That's you!'

Panic set in as Josef began to understand what all of this meant. His heart quickened and the palms of his hands began to sweat. 'Egon, what am I going to do?' he said. 'I have never experience combat!'

'That's precisely why you've been chosen, alter junger,' [1] Egon gulped.

'We will be leaving immediately,' Lowe concluded. 'Any questions? No? Alright then, all commanders get your men and equipment assembled in the courtyard. That will be all.'

A voice from the front row shouted, 'Aufstehn!' [2] and everyone present stood to attention, as the major marched down the middle isle and out through the door.

1. Old chap.
2. All stand.

CHAPTER FOUR

Josef looked to Egon as they made their way out of the briefing room. 'This is it, then,' he said. 'Death or glory, eh?'

'You're quite mad, do you know that?' Egon laughed. 'You could get injured or even killed out there!'

'Ah, you're the one who's mad if you think that a bunch of old farmers and conscripts could be any match for a well-trained army like ours,' Josef said.

'Oh, but of course, I forgot that we're the Master Race, aren't we?' Egon replied sarcastically. They began to share a chuckle, but were quickly interrupted.

'Moment bitte,' Herr Hauptmann Weise said, beckoning them over to one side. He looked very angry. 'If either of you ever pull a stunt like that again, I will see to it personally that you peel potatoes the rest of your miserable lives. You'd better pray I don't get it in the neck from Herr Major Lowe, because if I do, your stay with me will be very uncomfortable indeed. Now, get your men to fall in behind the trucks, with full packs.'

'Full packs, Herr Hauptman?' Egon asked, his ruddy face a mask of shock.

'Yes, that's right,' Weise answered with a grin, 'full packs. You're going to be out there for quite some time.'

'It's the wrong time of year to be stuck outdoors, Egon,' Josef said, as Weise went stalking off, 'in this weather we're likely to freeze our nuts off!'

'Ah, but it's death or glory, isn't it, Josef?' Egon giggled, just as Weise was doubling back towards them with another body in tow.

'I wish there was more time to get you acquainted with the men, Herzog,' Weise said, 'but this is what war is like – you have to improvise. This is Herr Feldwebel Walter Schmidt,' he indicated a soldier who had come up alongside him, 'he will look after you. He is very experienced in combat conditions.'

'Hello Company Sergeant Major,' Josef smiled, as he extended his hand.

'Die Herr Major has, as you already know, put Herr Oberleutnant Erich Heiter with you,' Weise said.

'Oh yes,' Josef yawned, 'a nice bloke, sir.'

'Stay awake while I'm talking, Herzog,' Weise snapped, distinctly unimpressed. 'Anyway, he's a gut man to have around if things turn nasty. He, too, has been instructed by me to look after you. The overall command belongs to Herr Major Lowe, so do whatever he tells you to do and never question his orders, verstehen? Now, get your men loaded onto the trucks.'

It was 3.30pm when the convoy of green canvas-covered trucks began to pull out of D Company HQ. The sky darkened and the rain began to fall, lightly at first, but with the threat of it worsening. Josef was placed in the warm, comfortable cab of the third truck alongside Schmidt, while his soldiers had to rough it, all hunched up in the back. Major Lowe and Heiter were in the first truck, which led the convoy through the heavy steel gates of the compound, past two helmeted sentries wearing winter great coats and holding their schmeisser automatic machine pistols in combat position. The wind picked up as they weaved their way across the open countryside, and occasionally an icy gust of wind would lift up a loose flap of canvas and bite deep into the men that were huddled tightly in the back, singing old marching songs to help pass the time.

'Have they been treating you well since your arrival in Poland, Herr Leutnant?' Schmidt probed.

'Oh, I can't complain, Schmidt,' Josef said. 'They're a gut bunch of lads, aren't they?'

'Yes, sir,' Schmidt concurred, 'they're Wehrmacht, the very best. But... may I ask a personal question, sir?'

'Please, fire away.'

'Have you not found it, well, difficult, sir?'

'Difficult? In what way, Schmidt?'

'Erm... being black, sir. Well, you're not really black, are you? You're more brown than black, sir, if you know what I mean.'

'I think I catch your drift, Schmidt.' Josef laughed. 'The Political policies of our country make it easier to live in the military rather than as a civilian.'

'I don't understand, sir,' Schmidt frowned.

'Well, you may not know this, Schmidt, but there has been a massive sterilisation programme organised back in Germany.'

'Sterilization programme? I still don't understand, sir.' Schmidt repositioned himself, trying to get more comfortable.

'What I'm referring to is the special selection of people considered non-Aryan, such as people of Afrikan or other foreign races. By the end of nineteen thirty-seven, half of all mixed-race children had been treated at some point by Nazi doktors, and at least two hundred had disappeared into camps.'

'I knew nothing of this, sir. It's hard for me to believe that such things could happen in our modern society.'

'Well, believe it, Schmidt. A close freund of mine told me how a group of SS men came to his house and woke him up at six AM. They took him by staff car to the local hospital, where a man wearing a brown SA [1] uniform under his white coat carried out an operation on him, making two small incisions around his testicles, and using very little, if any, anaesthetic while doing so. He was then returned back to his home when it was over, as though nothing had happened.'

'That is all quite remarkable, sir. Who on earth would organise such a programme?'

'The programme was put together by the leading geneticist, Herr Dr Eugen Fischer,' Josef muttered the name disdainfully.

'May I ask you another personal question, sir?'

'Sure, go ahead.'

'Did they get you, sir?'

'No, of course not. That's what I've been telling you. Mein vater put me into kadett schule before they could get to me. The army saved me. I owe everything to the army. Without its protection, Gott knows what might have happened to me. How much farther until we reach our sector, Schmidt?' Josef asked, checking his wristwatch. It was 4.30pm, and beginning to grow dark.

'Erm, another two hours I think, sir,' Schmidt estimated.

Both men relaxed deeper into their seats and sat quietly, rolling with the bends and turns of the bumpy narrow road. Wiping a small round hole in the steamy side window, Schmidt looked out over the fading countryside and said, 'I love the open spaces – the ploughed fields and the fresh air. Did you know that I was a farmer before the invasion, sir?'

'Why no, Schmidt, I didn't.'

'Oh yes, mein family have been involved in the business for generations. I will go back to it when this is all over.'

'Well, don't quote me on this, Schmidt, but I think it could be some time before you do. I have heard of plans to extend our flag into other countries. If the rumours are true, you could be away for quite some time.'

'Ah, this damphed war! I thought we'd had enough after the last one,' Schmidt glanced furtively at Josef, seemingly worried that he had spoken out of turn. 'I'm sorry, Herr Leutnant, I didn't mean that. I'm just a bit tired is all. I'm sure that the Fuhrer knows what he's doing.'

'Yes, of course, Schmidt,' Josef said, recalling his own personal experience of what can happen when one talks in a defeatist manner. 'Tell me, Schmidt,' he decided to change the subject, 'what's the Polish soldat like in battle?'

'What's he like? Hmm,' Schmidt rubbed his chin, 'he's a very brave fellow the Pole, that's for sure, but he's not too clever.'

'What do you mean, "not too clever?"'

'Well, let me put it to you this way. When we first engaged them in battle, they would make old cavalry-style charges on horse back. Can you believe that?'

'That's quite extraordinary, Schmidt. I had no idea.'

'Well, it's true, and that was the stupidity. But you see, there was also the sheer bravery of these men, too. Unfortunately, they were commanded by old, out-of-date fools, who would bring them on in the same old way, and then we would send them off in the same old way. Madness – bloody madness. We should be arriving at our sector any minute now, sir. So, stay frosty.'

The trucks squealed to a halt, and the drivers jumped out of their cabs and ran to the rear of the vehicles, releasing the bolts from the heavy green tailgates and letting them fall with a bang!

'Up, up, up!' Schmidt shouted, as the men sprang from the tailboards like paratroopers jumping from a plane.

'Schmidt, Herzog, you will organise the men and equipment,' Heiter ordered, 'but first, I want an OP [2]. One there, another one there and also give me one here,' he pointed as he spoke. 'And when you have finished that, meet with Herr Major Lowe and myself in the CP [3.], OK?'

'Jawhol,' both men replied with a salute. Josef and Schmidt began hurriedly organising the men and their equipment into position, checking munitions, food and medical supplies.

'OK, Josef, that's that,' Schmidt said, as he surveyed their handiwork. 'Now come with me to the CP, and when we get there, let me do all the talking, OK?'

'Yes, you do all the talking, Schmidt,' Josef eagerly agreed. 'I'm still learning, after all.'

They walked towards an area covered by trees, where they found an improvised dugout surrounded by sandbags.

'Right, come on, Herr Leutnant,' Schmidt beckoned him on, 'let's see what the major has got planned for us, eh?'

Both men had to duck slightly as they entered the CP, since there was little headroom in the tent, which was dimly lit by small kerosene lamps that hung from the thick, damp wooden beams overhead. There was a fresh, earthy smell about the place, and it was quite claustrophobic. At the far end sat Major Lowe, with Oberleutnant Heiter standing over him, clutching a handful of documents.

'Ah, it's gut to see you, Schmidt,' Lowe said, greeting them with a broad smile. 'And I see you've brought the neu boy with you, eh?' he laughed heartily. The major was in his late-forties, slight of build and with jet black hair, probably dyed, and his face, though sharp, bore friendly features. Like Weise, he was heavily decorated, sporting both the Knight's Cross and Iron Cross First Class. 'How are you finding it, Herzog?' he asked Josef.

'Oh, I'm finding it all very exciting, sir,' Josef answered, 'and I'm learning a hell of a lot from Herr Feldwebel Schmidt, sir.'

'Gut, gut, that's why we put you with him,' Lowe nodded. 'You could do a lot worse. Now, I have asked you both here because there is something that I want you to do for me. Heiter will explain,' he turned to light a long, fat cigar.

'Danke, Herr Major,' Heiter grunted. 'We want you to take a couple of men and do a recon [4] of the surrounding area. We must learn the enemy's positions, so that we can launch an attack come first light. Who would you like to take with you, Schmidt?'

'I will take Herr Leutnant Herzog, Privat Steg and Gefreiter [5.] Griff, if that's OK with you, sir?'

'Yes, all excellent choices,' Heiter agreed. 'OK, get going, Schmidt, and report directly back to me once you're done. I'll then process your findings before going over them with Herr Major Lowe.'

'Right away, sir,' Schmidt said with a wink.

1. Sturm Abteilung (terrorist militia)
2. Observation post.
3. Command post.
4. Reconnoitre.
5. Corporal.

CHAPTER FIVE

'You'll have to keep an eye on Steg, Josef,' Schmidt warned. 'He's a gut man, but he has a big mouth on him at times. He was once an unterfeldwebel, [1.] but was busted to privat after his drinking got out of hand. However, he's a first rate soldat. Gefreiter Griff, on the other hand, is as steady as a rock. A family man with a wife and two kids. Very dependable and won't shy away from combat, so you have a gut experienced crew that will look after you if we should meet with trouble, OK?'

'That's great,' Josef said, 'but tell me, Schmidt, are we expecting trouble tonight?'

'No, of course not,' Schmidt said reassuringly. 'Hey, you're not frightened, are you? I can always get someone else to take your place, you know.

'No, no, it's alright, Schmidt,' Josef insisted. 'Don't bother your-self.'

'OK, Herr Leutnant. I was only joking, by the way,' Schmidt laughed. 'Come on, let's collect the men and make a start. Oh, and bring your field glasses with you.'

'Field glasses?' Josef asked. 'Whatever for? It's black as tar out there!'

'That's right, but you may still need them. Trust me.'

They collected the rest of the men and made their way through a nearby thicket, which brought them to a small clearing with a modest hill on the other side. The men scrambled up to the crest of the hill, allowing them an unrestricted view of the countryside below, and Schmidt scanned across the open space very carefully. To their left ran a long narrow hedgerow that stopped just short of a dense coppice, which lay directly ahead. To their right was a flat open field that disappeared around the back of the coppice.

'What do you think, Steg?' Schmidt whispered.

'I don't like it, sir,' Steg grunted. 'That coppice is where I would be if I were the enemy.'

'I have to agree with Steg,' Griff added.

'What do you think, Herr Leutnant?' Schmidt asked Josef, inviting him to join the conversation.

'Well,' Josef said, 'I can't see any movement.'

Schmidt silently gestured with his finger toward Josef's neck, prompting the young leutnant to slowly move his hand up his chest until he felt the leather case that contained his field glasses.

'I think I'll try the field glasses, Schmidt,' Josef said, receiving the message. 'We have gut moonlight, so I may be able to spot something.'

'Sehr gut, Herr Leutnant,' Schmidt smiled.

Josef slowly panned his binoculars from left to right, calling out what he could see to his men. 'Nothing behind the hedgerow, lads, and the field on the right is flat with on cover, but wait – wait! I see movement! There's something moving in that coppice. Here, take a look.'

He passed the glasses to Schmidt, who carefully adjusted the lenses and looked deeper into the dense tree line. 'You're right, Herr Leutnant,' he said. 'There is indeed activity in the coppice. We should check the other sectors and then report back.'

'Yes, of course,' Josef agreed, 'but first, let me take a grid reference, and then we're on our way, OK?'

'OK, but make it snappy,' Schmidt grumbled. 'If we can see them, that means they can see us.'

'Well, men, what did you find?' Heiter asked, folding his arms.

Josef responded by unravelling his grid map and pushing it towards a small flickering table lamp, where he, Heiter and Schmidt could lean forward and study it.

'These three sectors are clear, sir,' Josef explained, indicating with his finger, 'but this one has definite activity.'

'Ah, and this is the sector with the forest, ja?' Heiter asked.

'Coppice, Herr Oberleutnant,' Josef chirped cockily.

'You have done well, gentlemen,' Heiter said. 'I will present this to die Herr Major, who will then draw up a battle plan to be executed at first light, so get some food and rest, because you'll be busy in the morning. Guten nacht, gentlemen.'

Josef and Schmidt both saluted and walked out.

'I'll give you a shout around five-thirty AM, Josef,' Schmidt said, as they were about to go their separate ways.

'OK, Schmidt,' Josef said. 'I'm going to get something to eat before I turn in. I'm starving.'

'OK, but remember to stay frosty. Somewhere out there is the enemy.'

'I will. Guten nacht, Schmidt.' Stay frosty, Josef thought. That won't be difficult. It's bloody freezing!

He found himself a nice, thick tree trunk and sat down with

his back against it. He then pulled a heavy grey woollen blanket over himself and broke off a big chunk off his bread stick, which he dipped hurriedly into the thick, hot soup, which steamed up from his shallow tin cup like water from a boiling kettle. As he looked around, everything seemed still and quiet, except for a lone sentry who was pacing up and down the perimeter with a rifle strapped across his back. He was bent double with the cold, and would occasionally stop to blow on his naked hands while stamping his feet. Josef lit a cigarette and looked at his wristwatch; it was 12.30am. He smoked the thin white stick halfway down before stubbing it out and deciding to bed down for the night. He placed his empty tin cup to one side, and then pulled the warm blanket over his shivering body as he began to drift off into sleep.

He was awoken by a gentle kick to his side.

'Come on, Herr Leutnant, it's five-thirty,' a voice said. 'Time for breakfast.'

Josef slowly opened one eye, and looked up to see a dark figure standing over him.

'Wake up, sleepy head,' Schmidt laughed, 'There's a war on, you know, and we don't won't to be late now, do we?'

'Yes, yes, Schmidt,' Josef replied groggily. 'That just wouldn't do now, would it?' He rubbed at his eyes as he struggled to his feet.

'After we have eaten, I will take you to the CP. Herr Major Lowe wants to go over the battle plans he has drawn up.'

'OK,' Josef yawned. 'When is the attack due to start?'

'All will be explained at the briefing, Herr Leutnant.'

Schmidt took Josef to a truck nearby, and they climbed into the front cab for warmth. Schmidt then opened a tin and spooned half its contents into a metal cup, which he then passed to Josef, along with a piece of dried black bread. 'There you go,' he said.

'Breakfast.'

'Schmalz?' Josef gasped.

'Yes, what's wrong with that?' Schmidt asked. 'I always eat schmalz back in die heimat!'

'But we're not in die heimat, Schmidt, we're in Poland – and I've not eaten this since I was a child!'

'Well, that's all there is, so eat it.'

Copying Schmidt, Josef put two fingers into his cup and scooped out the thick chunks of lard that contained bacon pieces and fried onions. Schmidt watched closely as Josef forced it down his gullet, knowing that it would be his last meal until after the battle. After breakfast, they made their way through the bustle of troops and equipment to the CP, where the morning's briefing was about to take place.

'Ah, morgen Herzog, morgen Schimdt,' Lowe bellowed as they entered. 'Please, help yourselves to some kaffee before we begin.'

Josef eagerly grabbed a cup and filled it with rich, black steaming liquid, pausing to sniff the beautiful aroma. He cupped both hands around the large beaker for warmth and began to slowly sip at its velvety contents, savouring each mouthful. He looked at the wall and saw an improvised map, with many lines, arrows and crosses drawn onto it. Oberleutnant Heiter was standing on the opposite side of the bunker, next to the funkmeister [2.], talking quietly into a telephone receiver that was held to his ear.

'Now, gentlemen,' Major Lowe called for attention, 'please gather round and I will take you through the plan.'

Josef and Schmidt both stepped forward, followed closely by Heiter, who had just finished on the phone.

'Have you sent the report to HQ, Heiter?' Lowe asked.

'Yes, Herr Major,' Heiter answered. 'I have explained your plan to Herr General von Waldmann, and he is very happy with it, sir. He also gave me a short message for you, saying simply, "gut jagen."' [3.]

'Ha, ha,' Lowe slapped the table in delight, 'das alt fuchs [4.]. He would love to be here among the smoke and fire. Anyway, let's press on, shall we? Timing is crucial in this operation, gentlemen. There must be total surprise.' He moved towards the wall map, pressing his finger to a previously marked point. 'This is where Heiter and I will be, behind the hedgerow, ready to move after the first attack, which will be launched by you, Herzog. You are now kompaniefuhrer, what do you think about that?'

Josef was stunned at the news, but managed to recover himself quickly. 'It's an honour, sir,' he said, 'thank you. I will not let you down.'

Lowe turned to Heiter, chest puffed out, and said, 'Did you hear that, Heiter? The lad reminds me of myself when I was a young officer, eager to get blooded. It's only once you're blooded that you become a man, eh, Herzog?'

'That is correct, sir,' Josef replied, somewhat unconvincingly.

'Your task is to be the hardest of all, Herzog.' Lowe frowned. 'It's your job to engage and distract the enemy with a full-frontal assault, so that Schmidt can outflank them on your right. He will make his way across the open land, and then attack and cut off any retreating enemy. This attack will trigger Heiter and I into a charge along the hedgerow, in a classic pincer movement. Now, because you are new, I'll offer you two suggestions. Firstly, never stop for a wounded man. The medics will follow up and take gut care of him. Secondly, never waver once you've committed yourself to an attack. You must keep up the pressure, OK?'

Josef cleared his throat and nodded. 'I understand, Herr Major.'

'One last thing, Herzog,' Lowe said. 'Use stealth when moving over the hill. Once you're on the other side there will be little cover, and the only protection for you will be darkness. Now, ready your men to attack as soon as the natural light allows you to see the individual trees in the line. It will be light very soon, so get yourselves into position. Oh, and gut gluck, gentlemen.'

The men stood and saluted before quietly exiting.

'I don't know whether I can pull this one off, you know, Schmidt,' Josef confessed, once they were far enough away from the CP. 'It's all moving a bit too fast for me.'

'Don't worry, Herr Leutnant,' Schmidt said, 'I have taken measures to help you.'

'What kind of measures, Schmidt?'

'I have selected the best men out of the unit and placed them all with you. Steg and Griff you already know, and the rest I can personally vouch for. Once the shooting starts, they will automatically do what they are trained to do. All you have to do is lead them and avoid getting killed. It's simple really,' Schmidt gave a huge belly laugh.

Josef and his men scrambled over the hill as quietly as they could, and then settled into a long line at the base unnoticed. He looked through his field glasses to his left, where he saw Major Lowe's men taking up position along the hedgerow, and then panned to the right and spotted Schmidt's unit crouched on the edge of the field. He checked his wristwatch; it was 6.30am and growing light.

'Who's that lad over there, Steg?' Josef asked, nodding towards one of his men. 'The one with the headphones.'

'Oh, that's Funkmeister Monke, sir,' Steg answered.

'Well, tell him to send a message to Herr Major Lowe,' Josef said, 'telling die Herr Major that we are in position and ready to attack.'

He pulled the brim of his grey cap down over his eyes, and forced his fingers into his brown leather gloves while quickly scanning along his line of men. They all looked a bit edgy, but they didn't lack for confidence.

A thin layer of mist hovered just above the damp grass, and the leaves on the tall oak trees sat motionless in the eerie atmosphere. The birds began to sing their morning songs, completely oblivious to what was about to happen, and Josef realised that he could now make out the individual trees in the tree line. He checked his men one last time, asking them, 'Now, manner, alles klar?' [5.]

'Jawohl, Herr Leutnant!' they replied in unison.

He nervously pulled out his heavy new Luger pistol from its shiny black leather holster, before looking across to Steg and saying, 'Your best support.' Steg gave a quick nod, and Josef rose to his feet and give the command, 'Aufstehen!'

The men stood as one and cocked their rifles, guns and machine pistols. Some of them pushed stick grenades down the sides of their boots, while others tucked them neatly under their tunic belts.

Josef filled his lungs with the fresh morning air, and with a thin stream of vapour pouring from his mouth shouted, 'Now, manner, advance mit mich!' [6.]

The soldiers advanced in a steady line, with all eyes firmly fixed on the trees ahead; the distance from the starting point to the coppice was about the length of a football field. Josef looked to his right and saw Schmidt crouched in the corner of the field on one knee; he had a machine pistol in his right hand, while giving a big thumbs up with his left. They were roughly halfway across the field, and could see the tree line very clearly, when Josef began to wonder if the place was actually deserted. Perhaps the enemy had left quietly in the night, and their advance would be a mere formality.

Suddenly, there was a small white flash from in between the trees, followed by a loud crack. A trooper next to Josef fell face down with a heavy thud, and lay motionless on the cold, wet grass.

'Everybody down!' Steg screamed, but Josef only bent slightly, as he tried to figure out where the shot had come from. 'That means you, too, Herr Leutnant,' Steg shouted, pulling Josef to the ground by his jacket sleeve.

The noise from the single shot had sent the birds squawking from the trees in different directions, as the peaceful calm of the morning was broken, never to return.

'Lie still, Herr Leutnant,' Steg whispered, slowly raising his head, 'while I try to find out what's going on. I see seven riflemen and-' another shot rang out, and a bullet whistled passed his head.

Josef could feel something tugging at his boot; it was Funkmeister Monke, holding a handset to his ear.

'Herr Leutnant,' Monke said, 'Herr Major Lowe wants to know why we are not advancing, sir?'

'Tell die Major that we are advancing,' Josef snapped, 'right now, damn it!' He turned back to Steg. 'Prepare to move your men on my mark, OK?'

'Yes, sir,' Steg said. 'On your mark.'

1. Sergeant.
2. Radio operator.
3. Good hunting.
4. That old fox.
5. All is clear
6. With me

CHAPTER SIX

Steg rolled onto his left side and signalled to the men using hand signs only, before rolling back to Josef. 'The men are ready, sir,' he said.

Josef nodded and checked his watch; it was 6.45am. He awkwardly cocked his pistol, trying desperately to control his shaking hands, and then looked directly at Steg, seeing a face drained of all emotion, with eyes dark and soulless. He raised his arm straight into the air before dropping it swiftly and yelling, 'Folgen mich!' [1.]

The men sprang to their feet and ran forward, screaming like wild banshees as they went. The tree line filled with sparks and smoke as the enemy opened fire and men began to fall all around Josef like swatted flies, but still he kept up the advance through the thick, choking cordite. Suddenly, there came a strange whooshing noise overhead.

'Mortars!' Steg cried. 'Hit the ground!'

Before Josef could react, a deafening bang knocked him off his feet. He lay on his back for a moment, and then struggled to get himself upright as a second bang went off, although thankfully this one was much further away. Despite being a little dazed, he managed to look around and take stock of the situation. The main body of men had successfully pushed through into the coppice, and Major Lowe was now in position behind the hedgerow, waiting for the right moment to launch his attack. This respite was short-lived, however, as he felt a sharp pain in his stomach that dropped him to his knees. He looked down to see that his field grey tunic had turned a deep crimson, and he instinctively knew to begin pressing against the wound with his gloved hands. 'I've been hit!' he called out through the dense smoke.

'Stay where you are, sir!' Steg shouted back. 'I'll get a medic to you as soon as possible.'

Josef glanced around and saw what looked like a leg with a boot still attached to it. He then heard the anguished cries of someone not too far away from him.

'Helfen mich!' a faint voice begged.

Josef mustered all his strength and staggered forward to find a trooper lying on his back, clutching with both hands the bloody stump that was once his leg. He recognised the trooper immediately; it was Monke! A sickly feeling came over Josef, as he realised that he himself was not really injured, but had in fact been struck by Monke's severed leg. 'Lay still, Monke,' he said, 'I'll get some help. Krankentrager! [2.] Krankentrager!' he screamed, but Monke was now going into shock, and he pleaded with Josef not to leave him. 'Alright, Monke, I'll help you, but you must stay calm, OK?'

He tied the jagged stump tight, using his gun belt to stem the bleeding, and then lifted the man onto his shoulder and ran back towards the hill to find help. There, he found two medics kneeling on the damp grass, tending to another victim who had fallen earlier in the battle. 'Here, take care of this man,' he said. 'He's lost a lot of blood already, and I think he's gone into shock. Monke, can you hear me?' he placed a hand on the funkmeister's arm. 'You're going to be alright. The medics will look after you. I must return to what's left of my unit.'

'Yes, I'll be alright, sir,' Monke replied in a half-stupor. 'Danke.'

Josef ran back towards the coppice, zigzagging around the bomb craters and the bodies left strewn across the field. He glanced to his right and noticed that Schmidt and his men had disappeared from their starting point, and assumed that they must have moved around the back to cut off the enemy retreat. He then looked to his left and saw Major Lowe's men advancing along the hedgerow, shooting at random and bobbing up and down like ducks at a fairground. A huge smirk spread across Josef's face, and it occurred to him how peculiar it was that one should have a sense of humour at such a critical time during battle. His men had done well to push through the first line of trees and into the coppice, and as he ran towards the woods he bent down and snatched a Schmeisser machine pistol from the hands of a fallen comrade, and quickly pulled out the long, slim clip to check for bullets. Gut, a full magazine, he thought, as he slammed it back in with the palm of his hand and cocked the weapon. He continued on into the coppice, where he found Griff crouched behind a tree, preparing to throw a grenade into a group of Polish soldiers that were dug in deep and causing problems for Lowe's men, who were attempting to enter from the left.

'Where's Schmidt?' Josef gasped.

'Ah, glad to see you're still alive, Herr Leutnant!' Griff sniggered, as he unscrewed the small metal cap from beneath his wooden-handled stick grenade and pulled on the thin white cord, which dangled underneath. 'Schmidt is over there, to your right, but I think now would be a gut time to duck, sir.' He tossed the grenade high into the air and waited for the loud bang, which was followed by a belch of white smoke that spiralled up towards the heavens. Hot steaming clumps of earth rushed through the trees, as Griff moved to shield Josef from the blast. This was immediately followed by the unholy screams of the wretched foes that could be clearly seen from Josef's position, rolling along the ground in agony, with their uniforms in tatters and the raw flesh hanging from their bones.

'Right, Griff,' Josef said, 'let's finish them off.'

The two men let out primal screams as they leaped from behind their natural cover and charged forward, Schmeissers blazing in all directions. The enemy were forced to abandon their dugout positions and fled even deeper into the coppice. As Josef and Griff advanced, a badly wounded polish soldier rose up from his foxhole, arms extended outward, screaming, 'Christus!'

For Josef, this was a new experience; he had never had a direct encounter with an enemy combatant before, and an air of excitement filled him as they came face to face. The Polish infantryman was no more than eighteen years old, with a fresh white face and a noticeably modern-cut khaki uniform. He wore short brown ankle puttees over tan leather boots, and he was carrying a full field kit, which consisted of a heavy canvas knapsack with brown leather shoulder straps, an ammunition belt, dagger, grenade, water bottle and spade.

Josef couldn't help but think to himself that in another reality, they might have been friends, but the boy was now getting dangerously close, while still holding his heavy 7.9mm Mauser rifle, complete with fixed bayonet.

'Halt!' Josef called out to him. 'Hande hoch!' However, the soldier kept edging closer and closer.

'Shoot him!' Griff shouted.

Josef hesitated for a moment, but then levelled his Schmeisser and fired, only for it to jam! 'Hande hoch!' he implored the youth once again.

The boy ignored his second warning, so Josef let the weapon fall to the ground and quickly drew his service pistol from its holster, and emptied two bullets into the infantryman at close range. The first shot hit the boy in the right shoulder, causing him to stagger backwards, but the second, fatal attempt hit him in the left temple, opening up his head like a ripe red melon. The warm spray of blood hit Josef in the face, forcing him to stop in his tracks and wipe himself clean. He looked down into his open hand, where he noticed small flecks of greyish-pink brain tissue dripping through his fingers.

Filled with both horror and exhilaration, he continued his advance through the trees, looking for his next opponent. The adrenaline was pumping through his veins, as only now did he fully understand what the major had meant when he said, 'You're not a man until you have been blooded.'

He was now a Jager; unstoppable, invincible and ready to cut down anything that stood before him.

'Come on, Griff,' he yelled at the top of his voice. 'Keep up, man!'

'Herr Leutnant, lookout!' Griff shouted after him, but it was too late.

Josef heard a dull thud behind him. It was a Polish hand grenade, and it had landed in between him and Griff. There was a bright orange flash, followed by an immense surge of heat, after which both men hit the ground hard. He looked over at Griff, who was lying on his side and seemed to be moving in slow motion. He was curled up into a tight ball, and although his mouth was moving,

Josef could not hear the words.

'Are you alright, Griff?' Josef called out weakly.

'Nein, Herr Leutnant,' Griff answered. 'Ich habe bauch wunde.' [3.]

Josef rolled slowly onto his back. 'Lie still, Griff,' he said. 'Someone will get to us soon.' He stared up at the clear powder blue sky, and watched as the bough of an old oak tree swayed gently overhead, with its broad green leaves trembling in the early morning breeze. A smile grew on his face as he admired the tree's beauty, but then he had to bite hard as a tremendous surge of pain ran up his legs before radiating throughout his whole body. Everything around him steadily grew darker and darker, until finally there was only black.

1. Well, men, all set.
2. Advance with me.
3. Follow me.
4. Stretcher-bearer!
5. I have a stomach wound.

CHAPTER SEVEN

'Herr Leutnant,' a soft voice spoke. 'Herr Leutnant, wake up.'

Josef slowly opened his eyes, but all he could see was a blurred white figure leaning over him.

'Herr Leutnant?'

He began to focus, and as the grey haze gradually lifted from his eyes, a beautiful young nurse appeared in front of him, as if by magic. She had big round hazel eyes, and her long auburn hair was tied back neatly into a tight bun. She wore a white starched apron over her blue and white striped shirt, which had a large round badge attached to it, bearing the words: Deutsches Rotes Kreuz. A large white hat almost covered her entire head, partly masking her true beauty. She appeared to be in her early-twenties, with a very pale complexion. Her lips were round and full, painted a luscious deep red, complementing her perfect white teeth.

'Am I alive?' Josef whispered.

'Yes, Herr Leutnant,' the nurse giggled, 'you are alive.'

'Where am I?'

'You're in ward B, at a hospital in Olenica. You have sustained a number of shrapnel wounds to your legs, but you're going to be alright.'

As she leaned over him to write on a large wall chart above his head, he noticed a square white badge above her left breast pocket, which gave her name as Hastler.

'Die Herr Doktor will be round shortly to talk to you, Herr Leutnant,' she said, and then turned and made her way over to the next patient.

I've died and gone to Heaven, Josef thought, as he watched the white angel glide across the grey-tiled floor. He raised himself up on his elbows in order to properly take in his new surroundings. To his left were two large white doors with small glass portholes in them, that swung freely back and forth as the busy staff rushed in and out. The doors send gusts of air into the room when they opened and closed, causing the three large green tin ceiling lights to sway gently on the long black cords that held them suspended. It appeared to be a men's-only ward, with ten beds that were spread between eight long windows, allowing strong shafts of sunlight to stream in and reflect up off the highly polished floor. Placed beneath each window was a small, white single-doored bedside cabinet, which not only provided space for personal effects, but also had a side pouch for newspapers and magazines. In the centre of the ward stood a huge black iron heater, spreading its warmth throughout the room. At the opposite end of the room stood a single wooden table, which had been pushed right up against the wall, and on top of which sat a tall white china vase stuffed with brightly coloured artificial flowers. Above the table, ticking rather loudly, was a large round clock with a beige face dial, surrounded by a thick black plastic rim. Its long black fingers were set at 2.15pm. Josef turned to the man in the next bed, to ask if he might borrow a pen, but he was interrupted when he heard a vaguely familiar voice call out, 'Herr Leutnant, is that you?'

Josef turned to face the speaker, who was sitting up in the bed opposite, but he was unable to make out his face, due to it being obscured by a huge domed leg cage. 'Who is it?' he enquired.

'It's me, sir,' the man said, 'Funkmeister Monke!'

'Ah, Monke!' Josef cheered. 'How are you, man?'

'Well, sir, they tell me I'll never play fusball again, but at least I'm alive, and that's thanks to you.'

'Oh, nonsense, Monke. I did what anyone else would have done.'

'I disagree, begging your pardon, sir. Not many officers would have disobeyed die Herr Major's orders not to stop for the wounded, but you did, sir. You saved my life, and I thank you for that.'

'Yes, and thank you for reminding me that I will probably be court-martialled once I get out of here,' Josef laughed. 'Now, if you'll please excuse me, Monke, I've grown somewhat fatigued and need to rest.' He pulled the crisp white sheets over his head, and slowly began to drift off.

'Herr Leutnant, are you asleep?' a voice asked.

Josef peered over the top of his blanket, and noticed that the curtains had been drawn around his bed. A short fat man was standing over him, wearing a white coat that was slightly open, revealing a dark green officer's uniform. He had an old face with a strong, chiselled jaw line, and Josef knew by the colour of the his uniform that he was not Wehrmacht; something which immediately put him ill at ease.

'Hello,' the man said, 'mein naam ist Doktor Schlossman. How are you feeling today?' Schlossmann was an admirer and follower of Dr Eugene Fischer, who in 1905 studied children of mixed race in Namibia, who were the result of German troops having relations with native women. Fischer did not approve of such relationships, and in 1938 suggested that mixed race children be sterilised. In 1924, while imprisoned in Landsberg, Hitler read about Fischer's justification for an Aryan society, and later incorporated these beliefs into his book, Mein Kampf.

'Apart from a little pain, quite well, thank you, Herr Doktor,' Josef replied.

'Sehr gut,' Dr Schlossman nodded, 'I will get Nurse Hastler to give you some painkillers, although I'm surprised you need them, coming from the bush.'

'I don't know what you mean, sir.' Josef said, his suspicions about this man growing stronger.

'Well, how can I put this? You schwarze have a natural resistance to pain. I know this because I have studied your kind before.'

'I can assure you, Herr Doktor, that I feel pain exactly the same way you do!'

Schlossman glared down at Josef, studying him with cold blue eyes. 'We had to dig quite deep into your legs to retrieve the fragments,' he finally said. 'You will be laid up for at least two weeks. Do you have any questions, Herr Leutnant?'

'Yes, I've two questions, sir,' Josef answered. 'Firstly, how long have I been here?'

'You've been here for two days, Herr Leutnant. You were unconscious when you first arrived, but then after your operation you came around briefly before lapsing again. You have a second question?'

'Yes, sir. Another man was injured along with me. Would it be possible to find out if he is here? His name is Griff – Gefreiter Walter Griff.'

'This name means nothing to me,' Schlossman said curtly. 'However, I will check it out. Now get some rest. I will be back later with an assistant, to carry out some tests.'

'What kind of tests, sir?' Josef asked anxiously.

'Oh, nothing too serious,' Schlossman laughed. 'Just a few samples and a quick measurement.'

'A quick measurement of what, Herr Doktor?'

'Nothing to concern yourself about, Herr Leutnant,' Schlossman said irritably, running his fingers through his receding grey hair. 'Just a few genealogical measurements. Quite painless, I can assure you.'

'Genealogical?!' Josef stiffened. 'Sir, I must protest most strongly. I'm a German national, and I demand the same rights and privileges as everyone else here.'

Schlossman reeled back with rage, his face turning red and becoming distorted. He threw open his white coat and placed his hands on his hips, taking an arrogant, provocative stance. Josef's suspicions were confirmed, as he could now clearly see the silver SS runes that were mounted on the doctor's black squared collar tabs. 'You are in no position to demand anything!' Schlossman spat. 'You are a servant of der Third Reich and are thus bound by its laws, sir. And furthermore, if you do not cooperate with me fully, I shall have you shot!'

Josef eased himself back into his pillow and stared straight up at the ceiling, thinking better of getting into a full-blown confrontation with this man.

'So, you're not going to give me any trouble, are you?' Schlossman asked calmly.

'Nein, Herr Doktor,' Josef replied quietly, eyes fixed to the ceiling.

'That's a gut little schwarz boy,' Schlossman sneered. 'I will return at six o'clock, aufwiedersehen.'

Josef slid under the covers and contemplated his fate. After all his father's efforts to keep him safe from the Nazis, it should now come to this. He managed somehow to fall back into slumber, only to be unexpectedly awoken once again.

'Herr Leutnant?'

'Gut Gott!' Josef bellowed, looking over the covers for a second time. 'Can't a man get any peace around here? Oh,' he caught himself, 'Nurse Hastler, please forgive me. I didn't mean to be so rude.'

'That's quite alright, Herr Leutnant,' she said with a dazzling smile, 'we make allowances for the wounded here. Could you roll up your sleeve for me please?'

Josef did as he was asked without argument, knowing that if Nurse Hastler had said, 'Could you please place your neck on this guillotine for me?' he would have done exactly that.

'I'll try not to hurt you, OK?' she promised, as she produced a long, thick syringe from beneath the white cloth that covered the shiny silver tray she was carrying. 'Are you going to be alright with this?'

'Oh yes,' he smiled, 'when you've been in combat, as I have, this seems like nothing.'

'Well, I'm glad to hear that, Herr Leutnant. You wouldn't believe how many people are frightened by needles.' Selecting a vein in the centre of his arm, she squeezed with her thumb and index finger until it stood out proud, and then said with a smile, 'Here we go.'

A sharp burning pain shot up his arm and slammed right into his head.

'Nearly finished, Herr Leutnant,' she muttered, her face a mask of concentration.

The needle went deeper and deeper, until eventually it felt like it was touching the bone, and Josef could only watch on helplessly as the glass tube of the syringe filled slowly with his thick red liquid.

He gritted his teeth and forced a broad smile, but he knew that he could not hold out much longer. He felt powerless to stop the air that was now rushing up his throat, but then just as he was about to let out a blood-curdling scream, the searing pain came to an abrupt halt.

'That's it,' she said, 'all done. I must say, you handled that very well. I've not been doing this for very long, and most of the patients usually give out a damned gut scream!'

'When you're a combat soldier, there's no time for screaming,' he said, trying to clear his throat while he spoke. 'Especially when you're in the field, you know.'

'Mein Gott, it's five o' clock!' she realised. 'I must get the meals ready. See you later, Herr Leutnant.'

'Yes, see you later.'

As he watched the beautiful nurse disappear through the swinging doors, Josef lay back with his arms crossed behind his head, feeling quite smug about himself.

'Hey, Herr Leutnant,' Monke yelled over from his bed, 'I think you're in with a chance there, you know.'

'Ah,' Josef waved him off, 'when you've had as many women as I have, Monke, you quickly lose interest.'

'Yeah, right!' Monke said, before quickly remembering himself. 'I mean, of course, Herr Leutnant.'

They both laughed.

Picking up a magazine to read, no sooner had Josef finished the first page when he heard the sound of a squeaking trolley approaching. He looked up and smiled, expecting to find the lovely Nurse Hastler standing before him, but to his horror he instead saw a short, rounded nurse leaning against a large food trolley in the centre of the room. She had a hard, ruddy face, and thick dark eyebrows that accentuated her hostile frown. On her left cheek was a huge black mole, with two erect hairs protruding from it, and across her top lip ran a thin, light-brown moustache, which made her appear more like an Olympic shot putter than an orderly. She slammed his meal down hard onto the small rickety side table, and then poured some weak-looking tea into a chipped white enamel cup for him, even though he hadn't asked for it!

'Herr Leutnant,' she grunted, pointing to his table.

'Ah yes, thank you, nurse.' he gave a sarcastic little bow, and then slowly lifted the metal lid that covered his plate, revealing a sorry collection of raw vegetables, some small, grey boiled potatoes and a thin sliver of pink ham, which was no bigger than the circumference of his cup. He quickly replaced the lid, preferring to drink the weak tea instead. After managing only a few sips, he looked up at the large wall clock; it was now 5.55pm. He rubbed his chin nervously, knowing what was about to come.

'So, Herr Leutnant, you must have copped it just after me, eh?' Monke shouted from across the room.

'Copped it?' Josef said, snapping out of his daydream. 'Oh, I see what you mean, Monke. Yes, that's right. After I left you, I ran back to mein unit and joined up with Griff. We were making gut progress until a grenade struck us. I've asked die doktor to find out what happened to him, but so far I've heard nothing.'

'Not to worry, Herr Leutnant,' Monke said, 'here's die doktor now. Why don't you ask him again?'

The doors swung open, and through them marched Dr Schlossman and his assistant, who was wheeling a small trolley in front of him that had a white cloth draped ominously over its cargo. Josef swallowed hard as the doctor rushed up to his bed wearing a broad smile on his face; the kind of smile one sees when a hunter bags his pray. Leaning forward, holding a large camera in his hands, he said to the assistant, 'Here's the chap I've been telling you about, Kreisel.' He was practically glowing as he hastily closed the heavy floral curtains around Josef 's bed. 'Did you enjoy your meal, Herr Leutnant?'

'Yes,' Josef lied, 'it was very nice, Herr Doktor. Begging your pardon, sir, but have you any news of mein kamerad, Walter Griff?'

'Oh yes,' Schlossman recalled, 'he was killed in your little skirmish back in the woods.'

'Killed?!' Josef couldn't believe it. 'There must be some mistake, sir. He was alive − I remember him lying right next to me on the grass.'

'Yes, that is correct. However, after you passed out he stopped breathing, and the medics could not save him. This is Herr Doktor Kreisel,' he gestured towards the man who was accompanying him, 'he will be assisting me today.'

'Forgive me, Herr Doktor,' Josef said, 'but how can you just change the subject like that? A gut man is dead.'

'It is the duty of every soldier to die for der Vaterland,' Schlossman replied nonchalantly. 'The best a soldier can hope for is to at least die with honour, and it seems your freund managed to do just that. Now, let's move on, shall we? Did I mention that this is Herr Doktor Kreisel?'

'Herr Doktor,' Josef nodded respectfully to the second man.

There was something different about Kreisel, Josef saw. He was a younger man, likely in his thirties, with wavy brown hair, black-rimmed spectacles and a fresh, well-scrubbed face. He looked at Josef in a kind and sympathetic way, unlike Schlossman, who seemed to view him as nothing more than a lab rat.

CHAPTER EIGHT

Schlossman raised his camera and took a series of quick snap-shots; firstly, a full-frontal of Josef's face, followed by left and right profiles. 'I'll measure, and you will take notes, Kreisel,' he ordered. 'Could you pass me the small gauge please?'

Kreisel pulled aside the white cloth that was covering the trolley, revealing a truly gruesome assortment of instruments. Every muscle in Josef's body tensed, as he braced himself for Gott knows what!

'We have a high quality specimen here, Kreisel – a man of nobil-ity,' Schlossman remarked, as he began the examination. 'Write this down, will you? Afrikan male, aged twenty years. Height, approx-imately five-feet and two inches, of lean, muscular build. Mutter, German. Vater, Afrikan. Eyebrows, fifty-four-point-nine-three millimetres. Ears, sixty-four-point-four-three millimetres. Nose, thirty-six-point-two-five millimetres. Mouth, fifty-two-point-eight-three millimetres. Chin, forty-two-point-two-one millimetres. Jaw, one-seventeen-point-two-four millimetres. All teeth are present, with only two fillings. Could you pass me the large gauge please, Kreisel?' He fiddled with the device a moment. 'And finally, the head. That's two hundred and three millimetres by one-two-seven-point-nine-two millimetres.'

Josef's eyes burned red and his fists began to clench. A single tear rolled slowly down his cheek, and his bottom lip began to quiver. This had to be one of the most humiliating experiences of his whole life.

'Interesting,' Schlossman said, hovering over him like a hungry nit nurse, staring down at his scalp. 'Kreisel, come look at his head. Notice the sloping forehead, and see how flat the back of the cranium is. These are all typical characteristics of the common chimpanzee.'

As if sensing Josef's next move, Kreisel shook his head slowly from side to side, indicating that he should say and do nothing.

'Well, that wasn't all bad was it, Herr leutnant?' Schlossman asked rhetorically. 'I will take these figures and process them, while you to take blut and urine samples, Kreisel.' He made to exit, but then paused halfway through the curtains and turned to regard Josef suspiciously. 'You're very quiet, Herr Leutnant,' he said. 'You're not planning on giving me any trouble now, are you?'

'No, sir,' Josef mumbled, head bowed low against his chest. 'I will give you no trouble.'

'Gut, gut,' Schlossman smirked. 'You do remember our last conversation, don't you?'

'Oh yes, sir,' Josef answered, looking up to meet the doktor's gaze, 'I certainly do.'

'Sehr gut,' Schlossman said. 'Carry on, Kreisel.' With that, he disappeared through the curtains, whistling obnoxiously as he left the ward.

'Could you roll up your sleeve please, Herr leutnant?' Kreisel asked politely. 'I need to take a blut sample.'

'I gave blut earlier, Herr Doktor,' Josef complained, 'why must I give it again? Haven't you bastards had enough out of me?'

'Herr Leutnant, I am not your enemy,' Kreisel said quietly, as though mindful of not being overheard. 'Schlossman is what he is, and no one can help that, but if you persist with this negative attitude, you will lose the support of all around who wish to help you. Now shut up and listen, because this is important. We are not all SS here. Some of us actually practise medicine, believe it or not.'

'Herr Doktor,' Josef was confused, 'what are you trying to say?'

'We're going to get you out of here, but you have to play the game. If Schlossman gets the slightest inkling that we're up to something, we'll all be for the firing squad.'

'Herr Doktor, you must forgive me, but this whole thing has been a bit of a nightmare. One minute I'm in danger, and then the next I'm being rescued. It's all quite bizarre.'

'Strange things happen during strange times, Herr Leutnant. There is someone much higher than Schlossman who is very interested in you for some reason. You're not quite out of danger yet, but we're trying to arrange transport to take you back to Breslau first thing in the morning. Once there, you should be safe, since there are no SS doktors at D Company HQ. Your treatment will then continue under regular army supervision.'

'I must apologise, Herr Kreisel, for my rudeness, but it's been a very trying day for me, you understand?'

'Yes, of course. I don't know how I would have reacted if the situation were reversed. Now, try to get some rest, and remember, not a word to anyone. It's not just your skin that's at risk here.' He took the samples and placed them under the plain white sheet that covered the trolley. 'See you in the morning, Herr Leutnant,' he said, as he exited the ward quietly.

Josef lay awake half the night, wondering if Kreisel could really pull off such a bold plan. He knew that if he could get back to D Company HQ, it would be near impossible for Schlossman to reach him, but by the same token, as long as he was still in this hospital, he remained in danger. He finally drifted off to sleep, but was soon awoken by the din of clattering china. It was the shot putter nurse again, bashing down cups and saucers and shouting, 'Tee, gentlemen. Wake up! Wake up!'

The lights came on, shining so brightly that Josef had to shield his eyes for a moment. He glanced over at the big wall clock; it was 6.00am. He pushed himself up onto his elbows and tried to look through the square-framed window opposite, but it was too dark to see anything.

'Tea, Herr Leutnant?' the nurse winked, but remained otherwise po-faced.

Could she be in on the plan? Josef wondered. She had never shown any sign of friendliness before.

'Breakfast, Herr Leutnant?' she asked.

'Yes please, nurse,' he answered, cracking a half-smile.

She neatly laid out two hard-boiled eggs and two rounds of fresh-ly buttered toast, before winking again and loudly announcing, 'For you, zwei ei mit zwei brot. That should keep you going until your next meal, Herr Leutnant.'

What does she mean, "until your next meal?" he thought. Is she referring to Breslau? No, it's not possible. I must stop looking for co-conspirators.

'Hey, Herr Leutnant,' Monke called over, 'how come you have two eggs and I've only got one? Are they fattening you up for the kill?'

'What?' Josef replied, startled. 'What- who's going to kill me?

Where did you hear that, Monke?'

'It was just a joke, Herr Leutnant,' Monke said. 'I didn't mean any harm by it.'

'Yes, of course,' Josef breathed a sigh of relief, 'a joke. I'm sorry, Monke. I didn't get much sleep last night.'

'Ja, tell me about it. I wasn't too gut myself last night. Maybe you need some pain killers, eh?'

Josef knew that if there was going to be any chance of escape, he must calm himself, or else risk exposing everyone around him. He decided to read a book, hoping that it would help pass the time quickly, and ironically, the novel he picked up was about a man who had attempted a daring escape from prison. After reading for a short while, he was interrupted by the sound of a familiar voice, and as he raised his head he was greeted by the sight of Nurse Hastler, looking as beautiful as ever.

'Sorry to disturb you, Herr Leutnant,' she said, 'but could I take your blut pressure?'

'No need to apologise, nurse,' he grinned, 'it's always gut to see a pretty face.' He slammed the book shut and sat up straight, as Nurse Hastler gracefully lowered down onto the edge of his bed.

'Could you roll up your sleeve please, Herr Leutnant?' she blushed, opening a long narrow box and taking out an armband with a thin rubber tube attached to it, which she wrapped around his arm. Once that was done, she squeezed a small rubber ball on the end of the tube, and the armband began to tighten. 'That's not too uncomfortable for you, is it?'

'Not at all. Please, carry on.'

She looked furtively around the ward, and then leaned in close to him and whispered, 'Herr Dr Kreisel will come for you at nine-thirty, so be ready, OK?'

'Yes, thank you,' he whispered back.

'Well, your blut pressure seems fine, Herr Leutnant,' she said loudly. 'I will be back to check on you later.'

'OK,' Josef smiled, 'thanks for everything. You've been most kind.'

She stood and gathered her items from the bed, and then leaned forward and touched him gently on the hand. He looked deep into her large brown eyes, and knew instinctively that she felt the same way he did.

'Gut gluck, Josef,' she said, before turning and walking away slowly, occasionally glancing back over her shoulder as she disappeared through the white double doors.

He stared down at the spot where she had sat, and gently rubbed out the creases with his hand while wondering if he would ever see her again. His heart was heavy as he eased himself back down under the covers, where he lay trance-like until another comment from Monke broke his reverie.

'I think that Nurse has got the hots for you, Herr Leutnant,' the funkmeister giggled.

'You're mistaken, Monke,' Josef mumbled. 'She probably acts that way with everyone.'

'If you say so, Herr leutnant. Hey, when we eventually get out of here, we must go for a drink or something. That's if you don't mind being seen out with a one-legged man, eh?'

'Yes, that's a gut idea, Monke, as long as you don't mind being seen out with a two-legged black man!'

'No problem, sir. We Austrians talk to anyone. It's a very cosmopolitan country, you know.'

'I know exactly what you mean, Monke. I'm from Berlin, and it's like the League of Nations there. We have Chinese, Japanese,

English and Afrikans. Tell me, what is your first name?'

'It's Johan, sir.'

'Funny isn't it, Johan. I've been here almost three days, and I'd never thought to ask your name before now. Oh, I'm Josef by the way.'

'Ah, Josef. That's Judisch, isn't it?'

'You know, I've never thought about it before. I don't think there's a Judisch connection in the family, though. Mein mutter was born an Evangelisch and mein vater a Katholisch.'

Suddenly, the white double doors sprung open and Kreisel appeared. He made a beeline for Josef's bed, closely followed by a porter pushing an empty wheelchair. 'Herr Leutnant,' the young doctor hailed, 'I have come to take you for an x-ray. Are you ready?' He used a clipboard to disguise a thumbs up.

'Oh yes, Herr Doktor,' Josef beamed, 'I'm ready alright.'

'Sehr gut,' Kreisel said. 'The porter will help you out of bed and into the wheelchair, but please don't move yourself. Let him take care of everything.'

The porter carefully folded back the bed sheets and then turned to the wheelchair, slowly lowering the two foot stirrups. He wasn't moving fast enough for Josef, who feared that Schlossman could enter the ward at any moment.

'Here, here, I'll help you,' Josef said, lifting his buttocks off the bed.

'Nein! Nein, Herr Leutnant!' the porter reacted angrily, pushing him back down onto the bed.

'Herzog!' Kreisel interjected sharply, albeit with an understanding smile. 'Let the man do his job. There's no need to panic.'

The palms of Josef's hand were beginning to sweat, and his eyes were fixed on the white double doors.

'There you go, Herr Leutnant,' the porter grunted, as he and Kreisel slid Josef off the blanket and into the wheelchair.

'Herr Doktor, would it be possible for me to say aufwiedersehen to Funkmeister Monke before we go please?' Josef asked.

'Sure,' Kreisel said, nodding to the porter, 'but be quick.'

The porter wheeled Josef swiftly across to the other side of the ward, stopping next to the radio operator's bed.

'I'm leaving now, Johan,' Josef informed his comrade. 'They're transferring me back to Breslau, but I hope that drink offer still stands, eh?'

'Oh, you bet, Josef,' Johan smiled. 'Look, I can see that you're in a bit of a hurry, so I'll just say gut gluck, Herr Leutnant.'

'And the same to you, Johan,' Josef replied with a salute.

They whisked him through the double doors of Ward B, and then along the wide corridor towards the lift, only for the lift door to close just before they could reach it. Josef looked up despairingly at Kreisel, who attempted to reassure him with a forced smile. They watched on in silence as the huge brass finger above the lift door moved agonisingly across the large embossed brass digits: four... three... two... one... finally, it had reached the bottom. Great, Josef thought, now the damned thing has got to come back up again!

He turned to Kreisel, who was now nervously wringing his hands together, and a thin bead of sweat began to slowly trickle down his forehead as he scanned the corridor like a hawk.

Come on, Come on, Josef pleaded, feeling as though his head was about to burst. The finger began to move again. Yes, yes, that's it, one... two... three... four! The bell chimed, and the lift came to a halt in front of them. The porter pulled the first safety gate back with a clunk, and then tried to do the same with the second, but it jammed!

'Here, let me try,' Kreisel said, pushing the porter to one side.

Josef raised himself up using the arm rests and looked down the long corridor, where to his horror he saw Dr Schlossman standing outside Ward B with his head bent forward, apparently reading something on a clipboard.

In his desperation, Kreisel resorted to giving the gate a good kick. 'That did the trick,' he grinned, not realising that the noise had echoed down the corridor and drawn Schlossman's attention. Fortunately, another doctor appeared from inside the ward to ask the SS man's opinion on something. This kept him distracted long enough for Kreisel to slam the wheelchair into the back of the lift and then bang the gate shut. 'Unten! Unten!' [1.] he barked at the porter, who hit the ground floor button repeatedly until at last the lift jerked into life and began to descend.

They arrived at their destination with a bump, and Kreisel immediately prised open the gates and ordered the porter to wheel Josef out as quickly as possible. A green military ambulance, with two large red crosses painted on its back doors, waited outside the hospital entrance with its engine running.

'Well, it looks like this is it, Herzog,' Kreisel said, unable to hide a slight crack in his voice.

'Yes,' Josef smiled, 'thank you, and please thank everyone else involved. I owe each and everyone of you.'

'Nonsense,' Kreisel said, clasping him on his shoulder, 'just get going and look after yourself.'

The doors slammed shut, and he was soon on his way back to D Company HQ in Breslau, where Wehrmacht doctors would assess his condition and decide when best to return him to active duties.

1. Down

CHAPTER NINE

As Josef relaxed on his new bed, he heard a disturbance outside the ward. Before he could ask what was going on, the door burst open and through it came Viktor, carrying a large woven basket full of fruit, quickly followed by Philip and Erich, both wearing huge grins. Viktor sat himself down on the edge of the bed, while Erich and Philip pulled chairs around for themselves.

'How are you feeling, Josef?' Erich bellowed. 'You look like shit!'

'Don't listen to him, Josef,' Viktor laughed, 'you look great. Here, I've brought you something to eat.'

'Thanks, Viktor,' Josef said, eyeing the fruit greedily. 'It seems like an age since I last saw you guys, you know.'

'Well, you've missed nothing,' Phillip said, diving into the basket and picking out the biggest, shiniest apple he could find. 'Everything's the same as it was before you left.'

'Cut the small talk,' Viktor said. 'We heard that you had to be smuggled out of Olenica, is that true?'

'Yes, Viktor,' Josef answered sadly, 'it is indeed true. There was an SS doktor there, who thought that he might experiment on me, but thanks to some really decent people working at the hospital, I was transported out of there before he could get his hands on me. Now, I've a question for you, Viktor. How did you and Uri get on at Odra?'

'Well, Josef, compared to you we got off lightly,' Viktor said. 'The enemy gave up almost immediately and we suffered only minor injuries, but we always knew that your mission was more dangerous. Herr Major Lowe could have transferred you to the Odra campaign, but he wanted to test you in battle. A test that you passed with flying colours, I might add.'

'Yes, and did you know that you're to be nominated for the Iron Cross?' Erich spluttered, while biting into a banana.

'No, I didn't,' Josef said, taken aback, 'but it's certainly a nice surprise. It's about time I had something to fill that empty space below the breast pocket.'

'So, Josef,' Philip interrupted, 'How were the nurses in Olenica compared to the ones here. Sexier?'

'Yes,' Josef said emphatically, 'and more freundlisch. Not like that blonde nurse over there,' he indicated with a slight nod of his head. 'She never talks or smiles whenever she's near me, and always tries to avoid helping me if she can get away with it. I think it's because I'm schwarz!'

The three officers turned and looked in the nurse's direction, and then back at one another in embarrassment. A silence fell around the bed.

'What's wrong, fellas?' Josef asked. 'Is it something I said?'

'He doesn't know, Viktor,' Erich said. 'You'd better tell him.'

'Tell me what, Erich?' Josef was becoming increasingly concerned. 'Viktor, what's going on?'

'That nurse you're referring to,' Viktor said under his breath, 'have you looked at her name badge?'

'Name badge?' Josef said. 'What are you talking about? I've just told you that she won't come near me, so how could I read her name badge? Now, for the last time, Viktor, what the hell is going on?'

'Her name is Frau Griff, Josef.' Viktor said quietly.

'Griff?' Josef said, needing a moment to put two and two together. 'Wait, you mean she's Walter's wife? Mein Gott!'

'Yes,' Viktor confirmed, 'that's most likely why she's been avoiding you.'

Josef groaned. 'She blames me for Walter's death, doesn't she, Viktor?'

'Don't be ridiculous, she's just a little raw at the moment,' Viktor snapped, but then quickly softened. 'Look, Josef, there's one thing you must never do when you're an officer, and that is blame yourself for the loss of a komrade. It can destroy your confidence and affect your ability to lead. I should know, because it has happened to me before, so take my advice and don't dwell on what happened. I'm sure she'll come around eventually,' he hopped off the bed and stood straight. 'Right, lads, we better get going. The doktor tells me you should be back with us within a couple of days, Josef, so take it easy and we'll see you soon, eh?'

'Yes, thanks for coming, fellas,' Josef said. 'It was really gut to see you guys again, and thanks for the fruit, Viktor – or what's left of it at least.'

Josef lay back on his bed and stared up at the ceiling. His mind was recalling the recent battle. Could he have done more? Could he have done better? What would become of Monke, and how would he adjust to life as a one-legged civilian. He also worried for Griff's wife; how would she cope on her own with two young children? He felt that it was because of his lack of experience that Corporal Griff was dead. If he hadn't insisted that they charge deeper into the coppice, Griff might still be alive. Too many things were going around his head, like why didn't he listen to Major Lowe's advice not to stop for the wounded? By stopping for the wounded, he allowed his men to get ahead of him, causing him to lose sight of Sergeant Major Schmidt and Private Steg. He also missed Nurse Hastler, and wondered whether he would ever see her again. Although their time together had been brief, he had developed deep feelings for her; feelings that he had never experienced before. Could these feelings be what other people refered to as love? he wondered. Surely not. Is it even possible to fall in love so quickly?

After three days' bed rest on the clinic, the army doctors decided that Josef was fit enough to return to duty and released him back into his unit. Upon his return to D Company, he was immediately ordered to the office of Herr Hauptmann Weise.

'Ah, Herzog,' Weise greeted, 'come in. It's gut to have you back. Please, nehmen de platz. I hope you are fully rested after your terrible ordeal in Olenica?'

'Oh yes,' Josef replied, 'thank you for asking, sir.'

'Now,' Weise said, moving quickly past the opening pleasantries, 'as you may already know, Herr Oberleutnant Heiter and Herr Major Lowe have nominated you for a citation. What normally happens is that once you're nominated for an action or actions, it first has to be confirmed by three witnesses, whose independent statements are taken and compared. If the statements match, which I'm sure they will, an application can be made and you then receive your laurels within five to eight weeks, depending on red tape of course. However, because two senior officers witnessed your deeds, we may forego the usual bureaucracy, which means you should receive your Iron Cross First Class and Wound Badge within two weeks. How does that sound to you?'

'That sounds excellent, sir.' Josef grinned.

'OK, now let's get down to business. There is another reason why I sent for you today, Herzog. Herr Major Lowe and I think that you should be given another command as soon as possible, but it won't come into effect until the new year.'

'What will I be expected to do in the new year, sir?'

'Herr Greiser, our new district leader, has plans to repatriate the Judisch communities in the district of Lodz, either back to Israel or to the island of Madagascar, and it will be your job, along with several other officers from D Company, to organise the rail transportation of those deportees. But, as I've just said, it won't come into effect until after Christmas. Any questions?'

'Yes, sir. You say these people are to be deported, but why?'

'It's quite simple, Herzog. Our government has decided that all Polish Juden are to be considered illegal immigrants, and must therefore be removed from this land, but you don't need to worry about all that until after Christmas. Any more questions?'

'No, sir, you have answered everything.'

'Very well, that will be all,' Weise said by way of dismissal, only to remember something just as Josef was at the door. 'Oh, and Herzog, the information discussed here today is not for anyone other than officers, verstehen?'

'Yes, sir,' Josef nodded, 'understood.'

CHAPTER TEN

Josef returned to his office with the intention of catching up on the paperwork that had been mounting on his desk since his enforced absence. He had not been seated long, however, before he heard a low tapping at his door.

'Enter,' he called, but the knocking persisted. 'Yes, please enter!' he called again, this time more assertively.

The door slowly opened, and a young soldier stood nervously in the doorway, with his head lowered and his cap rolled up in his hand.

'Private Schmout, isn't it,' Josef said. 'What can I do for you?'

'Well, sir,' Schmout mumbled, 'I haven't been feeling too gut lately, sir.'

The other soldiers didn't like Schmout, Josef knew, because he was always complaining about things. He was a small-framed chap with a pale, weasel-like face; the kind of face you would never tire of punching!

'Don't hover in the doorway, Schmout,' Josef said. 'Come in and sit down, man. Now, what exactly is the matter with you?'

'It's the pains, you see, sir,' Schmout explained. 'The pains, they're horrible.'

'The pains? Could you be a bit more specific, Schmout?'

'Well, you see, sir, it's the pains. They're in my stomach, sir.'

Josef looked at his watch, and then at the mound of papers on his desk. It was 3.10pm, and he had to get through at least half of the documents before getting himself ready for the dance that was to be held later that evening. 'Look, Schmout,' he said, picking up the phone. 'I'm going to send you back to barracks for some rest, OK? Hello,' he said into the receiver, 'could you get me Herr Feldwebel Schmidt please?'

'You know, sir,' Schmout suddenly brightened, 'the pains aren't so bad now. Maybe if-'

'Oh, be quiet, Schmout!' Josef cut him off, returning to the phone. 'Hello, is that you, Schmidt? It's me, Herzog. Yes, it's gut to hear your voice, too. Yes, I'm out of hospital and I feel great. Now listen, I've got one of your men here, a Privat Schmout. He says he has stomach pains, so I'm sending him back to barracks. Will you keep an eye on him for me? OK, that's great. See you later.'

The door swung open again, startling Schmout, and in walked none other than the ginger beast.

'Hey, sorry I couldn't see you in hospital,' Uri started, before noticing Schmout. 'Oh, are you busy?'

'No, Herr Leutnant,' Josef said, 'Privat Schmout was just leaving.'

'Yes, sir, I was just going,' Schmout concurred. 'Thank you, Herr Leutnant,' he said, springing up from his chair and scampering through the door.

'What's he come down with this time?' Uri laughed.

'Stomach pains or something,' Josef threw up his hands in exasperation, 'I don't know!'

'Well, you should know,' Uri pointed out, 'you're his commanding officer. Anyway, how are you, man? You look great!'

'I'll feel a lot better when I get through all this rubbish. How come you're never bogged down with this kind of thing?'

'It's a matter of seniority. I'm a full leutnant, and so compared to me, you're whale shit! But don't let that worry you, it could be worse.'

'Oh, and how do you figure that, Uri?'

'Well, you could be a trooper – ha! But seriously, are you coming to the Christmas dance tonight? There's going to be lots of drink and lots of women, so I'm told.'

'Yes, I'll be going, but only if you get out of here and let me knuckle down to some work!'

'OK, I can take a hint. I'll see you later, man.'

After getting rid of Uri, Josef began beavering away at the paper mountain on his desk once again. It was 4.15pm when he next looked up from his labours, just in time for the shrill ringing of the phone to make him flinch.

'Hello?' he answered, 'Yes, Herzog here. What?! OK, I'll see you at the clinic. I'll be there right away.' He slammed the phone down and dashed out of his office, making his way over to the medical clinic, which was not too far away.

'Right, bring me up to speed, Schmidt?' he said upon arrival.

'I went to check on Schmout, as you ordered, and found him lying on the floor of the barracks, complaining that his stomach was hurting. I got some of the lads to bring him here, and now I'm waiting on the doktor for a report. Oh, here he comes now.'

Josef turned to see the doktor walking slowly towards them, clutching a clip board and shaking his head from side to side. 'This doesn't look gut, Schmidt,' he whispered, struggling to disguise half a grin as he faced the approaching physician. 'Well, Dok, what's wrong with him?'

'I don't know how to break this to you, Herr Leutnant,' the doktor replied, still shaking his head.

'Just give it to me straight, Dok,' Josef said.

'Well, how can I put this in layman's terms,' the doctor paused for a moment. 'It's wind.'

Schmidt quickly turned away, trying desperately to suppress his laughter.

'I still don't understand, Dok,' Josef said, confused. 'What do you mean when you say wind?'

'I've given the patient some tablets,' the doktor explained, 'and I have no doubt that after a gut fart he'll be as right as rain, Herr Leutnant.'

'Right, you can leave now, Schmidt,' Josef said, blood boiling. 'I'll deal with Privat Schmout!'

He stormed into the small examination room and barked, 'Get dressed, Schmout. I've got a nice little job for you.'

Moments later, they were both sat in Josef 's office, sorting through the various piles of paperwork. In some instances, Josef dictated letters to Schmout, but he mostly had him filing documents into a rusty metal cabinet. They soon reduced the backlog, but it was now 5.30pm.

'OK, Schmout,' Josef said, 'that will do for today. Tomorrow, I'll cook up something nice and juicy for you.'

'Oh, are we having a meal tomorrow, sir?' Schmout asked hopefully.

'Nein, you fool,' Josef yelled. 'Work! I'm talking about work. Just get out.'

Having sent Schmout scurrying down the corridor, he switched the lights off and locked up his office, before heading to the living quarters to press his uniform in preparation for the big night ahead.

Josef laid out the various parts of his uniform, ready to iron, across his single bunk bed, but before he could begin, his door burst open. It was Egon.

'Josef!' Egon panted. 'It's really gut to see you again.'

'You too, Egon,' Josef said, crossing the room to shake his friend's hand.

'You know, we thought you had bought it back there in Olenica,' Egon admitted. 'We were told that you got blown up by a grenade.'

'Yes, that's true,' Josef said, 'but fortunately, it wasn't a German grenade. That would have finished me off for sure!'

'Ja, the Poles don't know how to make grenades,' Egon laughed heartily. 'Oh, here, I almost forgot.' He produced a plain white envelope and passed it to Josef, who quickly prised it open. 'It's just a little something me and the lads put together,' he chuckled.

Josef pulled out what appeared to be a homemade card, with a childishly hand-sketched drawing on the front. It showed six soldiers, presumably representing the War Council, all stood around a huge snowman. One soldier had a blacked-out face, with a broad arrow pointing down at his head, and the name Herzog printed above it. At the bottom of the card, written in thick print, were the words Frohliche Weihnacten [Merry Christmas].

'Why, I don't know what to say, Egon,' Josef said. 'Thank you very much.'

'Ah, don't mention it,' Egon blushed. 'Anyway, tell me, what was it like being in combat for the first time?'

'Well,' Josef took a moment to recollect, 'I've got to tell you, it was pretty scary at first. I was shaking so much that I couldn't grip my pistol, and the noise from the mortars was so deafening that I couldn't think straight. But then, suddenly, everything clicked, and the shaking stopped. It was so weird. The lads performed excellently, of course – especially Griff.' His head then lowered at the memory of what happened to Griff, as he began to feel far away.

Egon quicky pulled him back, though, patting him on the arm and saying, 'Hey, it should be a laugh tonight with all those stuffed shirts and their old fraus, eh? Listen, I'll call for you later, OK?'

'Yes,' Josef smiled thinly, 'see you later.'

No sooner had Egon left, allowing Josef to finish off the ironing and begin waxing his black knee-length boots and matching belt, before there was another knock at the door. This time it was the ginger beast.

'Hey Josef,' Uri said, 'I've just overheard that little rat Schmout telling one of the lads what a pushover you are, after you swallowed that stomach gag. What are you going to do about it?'

'Why, that little worm,' Josef seethed. 'I'll think of something, but right now I need to concentrate on getting ready.'

'I understand, man,' Uri turned to leave. 'I'll get off, then.'

'No, wait,' Josef stopped him, 'I'm glad your here. I meant to ask Egon a question earlier, but maybe you could answer it.'

'What is it?'

'How did you get on in Odra, for casualties, I mean?'

'Not too bad, actually. We only sustained two injuries, and the whole thing was over within an hour. We were lucky, I guess. How about you?'

'Seven wounded, including myself, and five killed, including Griff.'

'I was sorry to hear about Griff. You had a hard nut to crack, but at least you're still alive. You've got to be glad about that, man!

Anyway, I'll catch you at the party.'

Without any further interruptions, Josef was able to finish off the waxing in short order. Seeing that it was still only 6.30pm, he hung up his clothes and decided to get a quick bite to eat before the lads called around to collect him.

Once back at his quarters with a full belly, he slipped into his boots and put on his jacket just as Viktor and Egon arrived, bang on time, in their dress uniforms.

'Don't he look a picture, Egon?' Viktor remarked.

'He sure does,' Egon agreed, 'but it's a pity there's no Iron Cross to go with that jacket, eh?'

'Oh, do be quiet, Egon,' Josef laughed, fastening a black leather belt around his tunic. 'Come on, let's get out of here.'

The dance was being held in an annex next to HQ, and was heavily guarded, due to it being considered a great folly to have so many senior officers gathered together in one place at any given time. A guard in full ceremonial uniform opened the heavy brown oak door, which led to a main hall that was brightly lit by three huge chandeliers. The lights were already shrouded in a veil of thin cigarette smoke, which hung just below the ornately decorated white ceiling. There were long, white-sheeted tables that ran the full length of the hall on both sides, cluttered with bowls of fruit and serving dishes offering a selection of cold meats. Waiters dashed from table to table in their short white jackets, pouring glasses of Zekt and Schnapps from small silver hand trays. In the centre of the hall was a large, highly polished wooden dance floor that ran towards a raised stage, which held a group of uniformed musicians who were sat in small semi-circle playing soft background music. The tables were filled to capacity with women clad in expensive silk ballroom gowns and sparkling jewellery, flanked by men sat in their dress uniforms, proudly sporting their gongs and ribbons.

A funny little chap, wearing a black claw hammer coat and a starched white shirt, approached the officers and led them to a table that had been reserved for their party. Already seated were the other War Council members, Philip, Uri and Erich, guzzling greedily from the bottles of Zekt so generously provided by the waiters. Without warning, they all stood to attention and raised their glasses, as Philip stepped forward and proclaimed loudly, 'To the winner of die Eiserns Kreuz, erste klasse, Herr Leutnant Herzog. Huah! Huah! Huah!' they all chanted together, while stamping their feet on the bare wooden floor.

Sensing that the whole room was watching him, Josef dived for the nearest seat, but before he could sit down Uri grabbed him and, pulling over a chair and beating it with his shovel-like hands, said, 'Prinz, sit next to me, man.' He poured the bubbly into a glass, over-filling it and sending white froth cascading across and over the edges of the white linen table. 'Get some of this down you!'

'You really are a troglodyte, do you know that, Uri? Viktor laughed.

'Ja, whatever you say,' Uri shrugged. 'Hey, Prinz, come on,' he gestured towards the full-to-the-brim champagne glass, 'drink up, and I'll order us another bottle.'

Josef raised the glass to his lips and began to sip, but then he noticed that sitting opposite was Major Lowe and his wife. The major was signalling for him to join them. 'Would you excuse me a moment, gentlemen?' he said, as he shuffled along the chairs towards a point where he could stand. 'I must speak with die Herr Major.'

As he squeezed past Uri, the big man got him in a friendly headlock. 'Screw die Herr Major!' the ginger beast bellowed. 'You're with the War Council now. Everything else comes second!'

'Let him go, you big dope,' Viktor intervened. 'Go on, Josef. I'll deal with this monster,' he laughed, picking up a loose bottle. 'Here, Uri, have a drink.'

Uri loosened his grip to make an exaggerated lunge for Viktor's bottle, and Josef took the opportunity to make his escape.

'Here's the lad I've been telling you about, Marta, dear,' Major Lowe said to his wife, as Josef approached their table. 'Come, Herzog, nehmen de platz.'

Josef bowed his head a little, saying with a nod, 'Herr Mayor, Frau Lowe.'

'I liked the way you handled yourself back in Olenica, Herzog,' Lowe said. 'We have need of more officers like you if we are to push on through Europe, as der Fuhrer has hinted.

'Why, thank you, Herr Major,' Josef was flattered.

'I also heard about your lucky escape from hospital, Herzog,' Lowe added. 'Quite brilliant, I thought.'

'Yes indeed, sir,' Josef said. 'I have a lot of people to thank, but unfortunately, I may never see them again.'

'Oh, I don't know about that,' Lowe grinned. 'There's one of them sitting not far from us right now.'

'Sir?' Josef asked, confused.

'Look over there,' the major said, indicating the next table, 'see?'

'How nice to see you again, Herr Leutnant,' a melodic voice came from the direction in which Lowe was pointing.

Josef could not believe his own eyes. He paused for a moment, and then loudly exclaimed, 'Nurse Hastler?! What are you doing here?'

'Oh dear,' the nurse said, feigning upset, 'it sounds like you're not pleased to see me, Herr Leutnant?'

'On the contrary, Fraulein,' Josef insisted. 'I'm very pleased to see you.'

'Please, come and join us, Herr Leutnant,' she said, patting an empty chair next to her own. 'I would like to introduce you to mein parents.'

After politely asking to be excused by the major and his wife, Josef headed over to the Hastler's table, where he stood to attention while waiting to be introduced.

'Herr Leutnant,' Nurse Hastler began, 'I would like you to meet mein vater, Herr Oberst Rhone von Hastler.'

'Herr Oberst,' Josef nodded respectfully.

'And this is mein mutter, Frau Elke.'

'Frau Elke,' Josef smiled, as he leaned forward and kissed the back of the older woman's hand.

'Please, sit down and make yourself comfortable Herr Leutnant,' Fráu Elke spoke warmly. 'We've heard so much about you, Viscount Herzog.'

'Thank you, Frau Hastler,' Josef sat down next to Nurse Hastler. 'It is a great honour to meet you, and may I say, your daughter is most fortunate to have inherited her mother's looks.'

'Oh, what flattery,' Frau Elke giggled. 'I think I'm going to like this young man, Rhone!'

'Indeed, mein dear,' Herr Hastler said. 'So, Herzog, how is your vater. Well, I hope?'

'You know mein vater, sir?'

'I should say so,' Herr Hastler laughed, 'he served under me back in Namibia. He was the best damned sergeant major I ever had – he could really whip those men into shape. He must be very proud of you.'

'I hope so, sir.'

'I believe you're to be awarded the Iron Cross, eh?'

'That is correct, sir,' Josef answered. 'Truth be told, I'm very excited about it.'

'Yes, quite,' Herr Hastler said. 'You know, I can still remember the feeling when I first received the Iron Cross, but of course that was many years ago now, you understand? Ha!'

'He means many, many years ago, don't you, darling?' Frau Elke chuckled. 'Anyway, enough talking shop, Rhone. Let's talk about you, Herr Leutnant. Are you married or single?'

'I'm single, Frau Hastler.' Josef replied.

'What?' she said incredulously. 'A handsome young man like you? How could that be?'

'Well, I'm just waiting for the right person to come along,' Josef said, glancing at Nurse Hastler as he spoke, 'if you know what I mean.'

'You know, I quite fancy a waltz, Rhone,' Frau Elke turned to her husband. 'Don't you?'

'Not really, dear,' Herr Hastler frowned. 'You know I've got two left feet.'

'Nevertheless, I would like to dance please,' Frau Elke insisted, rolling her eyes towards the dance floor, as though hinting that the young ones should be left alone.

'Oh, yes,' Herr Hastler winked, catching her drift, 'I would love to dance, dear. It was nice to meet you, Herzog.' He got up from the table and took his wife by the hand, leading her gently away.

An awkward silence fell upon the table, with Josef nervously tapping his fingers in time with the music while staring out into the crowd.

'It's lovely here, isn't it, Herr Leutnant?' Nurse Hastler said, finally breaking the ice.

'Yes, it is,' Josef agreed. 'Oh, and please, call me Josef.'

'Alright, but only if you call me Monika.'

'Monika. What a beautiful name. Tell me, Monika, how did you come to be here tonight?'

'Well, mein vater is based here. He is one of the senior commanders at D Company, didn't you know?'

'No, I didn't. You see, I'm not yet familiar with the higher echelons, but I've no doubt that in time I would have met him. Tell me, if he is here, why are you in Olenica?'

'Well, I'm very fortunate in the fact that the job allows me to travel all over Poland, working between different hospitals. It's all quite fun, actually.'

'Where do you plan to be in the new year?'

'I'll probably be going to Poznan in the new year. There's a big army base there, you know. What about you? Will you be getting a posting in the new year?'

'There's something in the pipeline, but I've not been fully briefed yet.' Josef sat in thought for a moment, and then said, 'I owe everything to Dr Kreisel, you know. It's because of him that I'm sitting here talking to you now.'

'Oh, and what makes you so sure that it's Dr Kreisel you owe everything to?' she asked.

'Well, he got me out, didn't he?'

'No, it was me, you idiot,' she burst out laughing.

'You?' Josef gasped.

'That's right, and don't look so surprised! Dr Kreisel only played a small part, as did some of his staff, but it was I who got you out by using mein vater's influence and position. I got him to issue the order for your transfer back to Breslau.'

'Mein Gott, I had no idea. Please, accept my deepest apologies, and thank you very much.'

'It was nothing, but I must tell you, Dr Schlossman had some pretty nasty things lined up for you, and we were all very worried indeed. I can't believe that a man such as Herr Schlossman, who is sworn to protect life, could so easily want to take it away.'

'Yes, I agree, but then we are living in strange times, Monika. The world seems to have gone mad. I believe there is a terrible storm coming. A storm so great that it will engulf us all.'

'Oh, please stop it, Josef, you're frightening me.'

'But of course, forgive me. Would you do me the honour of a dance?'

'Yes, that would be nice, though I hope you dance better than mein vater!'

They shared a laugh as Josef escorted her to the dance floor.

At the War Council table, the lads from D Company were having a right old time, and steadily getting drunker and louder. Uri was arm-wrestling with Philip across the bottle-strewn table, and Viktor was arguing with Egon over old battle tactics. Erich was enjoying a moment's peace as he lit a long cigarette, when he looked up and noticed Josef in the middle of the dance floor, accompanied by a woman.

'Hey, look, fellas!' Erich alerted the others. 'Josef is dancing with some gorgeous brunette!'

'I don't believe it,' Uri chirped, 'the lucky devil.'

Unfortunately, it wasn't just the War Council that were taking an interest in Josef. He was also being observed by a small group of SS officers, who were stood to the right of the stage. Viktor locked onto them right away, and became very concerned for Josef's safety.

CHAPTER ELEVEN

'Listen up, lads,' Victor said, interrupting the revelry, 'one of you needs to go over there and get Josef.'

'Get Josef?' Egon belched through a mouth full of ham. 'Are you crazy? He's having the time of his life. Leave him alone, man.'

'Listen to me,' Viktor implored, 'the SS [1.] are watching him. I think he might be in danger.'

'Ah, screw the SS,' Uri blabbed, as he downed another glass of bubbly.

'Hold on,' Philip said, squinting his eyes to get a better look,' Viktor could be right. Do you know who those guys are? The one on the left, wearing the black eye patch, is Hauptsturmfuhrer [2.] Hants Wohlner. He's with First Panzer Corp, Totenkof Division. I don't know much about him, but the one in the middle is Sturmbannfuhrer [3.] Ernst Lunder, and he's with First Corp Leib Division. He's a right bastard, I'll have you know, and an ardent Nazi. The one to his right is Oberstrumfuhrer [4.] Zeig Ulricher, and he's with Third Panzer Das Reich Division. You don't won't to be in their gunsights if you can help it, fellas, let me tell you.'

'Ja, I'm really frightened,' Uri snarled, getting unsteadily to his feet. 'Why don't we all go over there and beat the shit out of them right now.'

'You're drunk, Uri,' Viktor said, pressing him back down into his seat. 'You just sit tight, OK? I'll go and get Josef myself. As for the rest of you, climb on top of Uri if you have to. I don't want him running around loose in here.'

Victor made his way through the crowded dance floor until he found Josef, and then tapped him on the shoulder and asked, 'May I cut in?'

'Certainly, Herr Oberleutnant,' Josef said, looking decidedly unimpressed. 'Maybe I'll see you later, Fraulein Hastler?'

'Yes, Josef, that would be nice,' the young lady replied.

Viktor could tell that Josef was angry with him, but still he bowed out gracefully and headed back to rejoin the War Council.

'Hey, what's got into Pech, cutting in on me like that?' Josef asked, as he arrived back at the table. 'Is he jealous or something?'

'Believe it or not, Josef, he's trying to save you,' Erich explained. 'There's a group of SS over there, and they seem most interested in you.'

'Ja, and I'm going over there to crack some skulls,' Uri slurred. 'Who's coming with me?'

'No need, mein big freund,' Josef said with a wave of his hand. 'I can fight my own battles, you know.'

Before anyone could think to stop him, he turned and started walking casually towards the SS officers, forcing a nervous grin across his face as he went. The SS men stood proud and brazen, looking like a murder of crows in their smart black uniforms, and they each stared in disbelief at Josef's audacity as he approached.

'Guten abend, mein herren,' [5.] Josef said cautiously, 'may I introduce myself.'

'No need,' Hauptsturmfuhrer Wohlner replied testily, 'we already know exactly who you are. You're the hero of Olenica, but then where is your Iron Cross? Surely, all heroes must have an Iron Cross, mustn't they?'

'That is correct, Herr Hauptsturmfurer,' Josef said. 'The paper work will be completed quite soon, I believe.'

'That may be so,' Obersturmfuhrer Ulricher interrupted, 'however, as much as I don't want to piss on your parade, a little black bird tells me that you won't be getting it.'

'Oh, and how so, Herr Obersturmfuhrer?' Josef said, fighting to maintain a calm exterior, but before the obersturmfuhrer could respond to the question, the sturmbannfuhrer stepped forward.

The sturmbannfuhrer was a fine figure, as befitted an SS officer of his rank, with a strong, chiselled jawline and clinical eyes of deepest blue. His white-blond hair was smartly gelled back and neatly trimmed into his neck, and the air around him was filled with the sweet sickly aroma of his aftershave. He was heavily decorated, wearing the Knight's Cross with an oak leaf cluster around his neck, supported on his right lapel by the silver bullion SS runes, or lightning rods. Above his left breast pocket ran an impressive row of multi-coloured ribbons. Directly beneath the ribbons was a round, solid gold party badge, beneath which was an Iron Cross First Class. On his upper-left arm was a wide, red swastika band, and below it, just past his elbow, was the Leibstandarte Cuff title, which comprised a one-inch thick band, with the words Adolf Hitler embroidered on it in silver bullion. He held in his hand what looked to be a small chain of black beads, which he rotated through his fingers as he became more agitated.

'Enough of this stupid talk,' the sturmbannfuhrer barked, glaring straight into Josef's eyes. 'You are an insult to that uniform, and you don't belong here! No matter how they dress you up in fine clothes and call you a viscount, you're still just a gorilla in a monkey suit. You should be happier in a tree than at a dance, don't you think?'

'Is that so, Herr Sturmbannfuhrer?' Josef said coolly, with his arms folded in a sure manner. 'You know, I find that it is you, sir, that is most offensive in that black uniform. Your kind are not liked by the Wehrmacht, and you will never be fully accepted here.'

'I think you should leave while you still can,' Haupsturmfuhrer Wohlner snapped.

'Oh, and who's going to make him,' a gruff voice came from behind Josef, 'you?'

'Ah, Uri Voss,' Wohlner growled, 'the Russian. Now, the set is complete. With every monkey comes a banana, eh, mein herren?'

The three SS officers burst into laughter, and Uri, now visibly enraged, pulled back his right arm to take a swing at Wohlner, only for Viktor to intervene just in the nick of time, grabbing him by the shoulders.

'Ah, here you two are,' Viktor said jovially, nodding to the SS men, 'the lads have been looking everywhere for you. Would you please excuse us, gentlemen?' He quickly herded both Josef and Uri back to the table where the rest of the War Council were sitting. 'What the hell did you think you were doing there?' he demanded. 'Have you both gone completely mad?'

'Oh, calm yourself, Viktor,' Uri waved away the complaints, 'it's only a couple of Nazis. You should have let me crack them one!'

'Yes, that's about right for you, isn't it, Uri?' Viktor said accusingly. 'Just a quick slap around the head, and everything's alright, eh?'

'Come on, Viktor,' Josef said, 'don't be so hard on him. He was only trying to help.'

'Oh, shut up,' Viktor replied. 'It's because of you that we're all in this mess!'

'What are you saying?' Josef asked. 'Are you suggesting that if I were white, everything would have been OK? Is that it? Well, I'll just bid you all guten nacht, gentlemen.'

'No, that's not what I meant,' Viktor said, but Josef was already getting up to leave. 'Josef, come back, damn it!'

'Now look what you've done,' Uri said. 'I still say you should have let me belt them one.'

'Shut up, Uri!' The whole table shouted in unison.

'Why did you let that schwarz scum and the Russian talk to you like that, Herr Sturmbannfuhrer?' Ulricher asked. 'You should have pistol whipped the pair of them!'

'Ruhe, [7.] Ulricher,' Sturmbannfuhrer Lunder said sternly, 'both Herzog and the Russian will be taken care of, all in gut time.'

'And when that time comes, Herr Sturmbannfuhrer, may I have the honour of the kill, sir?' Ulricher said.

'Of course,' Lunder smiled, 'once I'm given the order, you may indeed have that honour for yourself.'

1. Shutz Staffeln (Protection squadron)
2. Captain.
3. Major.
4. First Lieutenant.
5. Good evening.
6. Leibstandarte (Personal bodyguard)
7. Hush.

CHAPTER TWELVE

The following morning, Josef was sat at his desk in his office, sifting through his troops' mail, when Uri suddenly burst in.

'Prinz, why did you leave so early last night?' Uri asked. 'The party was just starting to warm up. You know that Viktor meant no harm, don't you? He thinks very highly of you, and would never knowingly offend.'

'Yes, of course,' Josef said, 'you're right. It's just that I've never experienced racism in such a crude form before. It's only since I've been in Poland that this sort of thing has happened to me.'

'Surely, you must have known that the SS would act this way towards you. They hate me just as much as they hate you, and you know I make no secret of my feelings toward them.'

'Yes, I suppose Viktor was right. I should never have approached them. It was quite stupid of me, don't you think?'

'Just put it down to experience. Anyway, this is what I really came here for.'

Uri held out a large yellow envelope, which Josef accepted from his bucket-sized hands. The letter was addressed simply, in bold handwriting, to Herzog. D Company. Josef could smell the sweet aroma of perfume as he slowly prised open the letter.

'Who's it from?' Uri asked, as he hung over the desk.

'I don't know until I open it, you idiot,' Josef laughed. 'Give me some space, will you?'

'Alright, alright, cease fire, man!' Uri said, backing off with his hands in the air. 'Hey, did I tell you that it was hand delivered this very morning?'

'No, you did not.'

'Well, who's it from?'

As Josef fumbled with the letter within, a small black and white photograph fell to the floor. He picked it up quickly. 'Why, it's from Monika,' he gasped. 'I mean, Nurse Hastler.'

'Ah, Nurse Hastler,' Uri crooned. 'What does she say in the letter?'

'She's invited me to a New Year's Eve party, which is to be held at the Hastler's private residence!'

'Ha, I'm sorry, man, but you're on duty all over the Christmas period. Mein Gott, how unlucky can a guy get, eh?'

'Actually, it says here that mein duties for that period have been waived, by order of Herr Oberst Rhone von Hastler. Ha!'

'Bastard! You've got more lives than that cousin of yours, the black cat!'

'Oh, shut up and get out. I'm very busy, you know.'

'Ja, right. I'll see you later, you lucky son of a bitch! Wait until I tell the lads about this one, man.' Uri slowly left the office, scratching his head and shaking it from side to side, muttering, 'Wait until I tell the lads about this.'

Josef leaned back in his creaky old chair and put his feet up onto the desk, and looked at the small picture of Monika. She was sat in a long-backed chair, in semi-profile, with her beautiful long auburn hair draped over her shoulders. A large diamond necklace covered the nakedness of her neck and cleavage, but the black and white photograph failed to do justice to her silky white skin, nor did it display her lovely royal blue silk party dress, with it's elaborate tucks and folds. He held the photograph close to his face, intently studying its every detail, but his concentration was soon broken by a loud knock at the door. He quickly replaced the letter and photograph into the envelope, and then tucked it smartly into the top draw of his desk. 'Yes, enter,' he called, as he removed his feet from the desk and straightened his uniform.

'Sorry to disturb you, Herr Leutnant,' Schmout said, as he entered the room.

'Oh no, not you, Schmout,' Josef despaired. 'What is it this time, sore ears?!'

'No, sir,' Schmout said earnestly. 'I've heard a rumour about a training exercise scheduled for this afternoon. Is it true, sir?'

'You know more than I do, Schmout,' Josef said. 'How did you come by this information?'

'I overheard a couple of NCOs [1.] talking, sir.'

'You were eavesdropping more like. Now look, Schmout, I know nothing of such an exercise, and even if I did, what's it got to do with you exactly?'

'Well, you see, sir, I was hoping to be excused if there was to be an exercise, because I keep getting dizzy spells, sir. It's quite scary, sir. One minute I'm standing, and the next I'm hitting the floor.'

'Yes, well, if there is to be an exercise, I can assure you that you'll be attending, because if you don't, it will be the floor of the military prison you'll be hitting, verstehen?'

'Jawhol, Herr Leutnant!' Schmout shouted, jumping to attention.

'You're supposed to be at artillery training this morning, aren't you?'

'Jawhol, Herr Leutnant.'

'Then snap to it, and on the double. That should clear your head, eh?'

'Jawhol, Herr Leutnant.'

Clearly sensing how annoyed Josef was with him, Privat Schmout ran out of the office in double time, slamming the door behind him. As the sound of the hypochondriac's footsteps faded, Josef leaned back again and reopened the letter, first sniffing it, and then reading it again very slowly with a broad smile, while clutching Monika's photograph in his other hand. The old black telephone on his desk began to ring faintly, showing its age, and he quickly picked up the receiver before it croaked its last breath.

'Hello,' he answered, 'Herzog speaking.'

'Herzog,' the voice at the other end of the line said sternly, 'Weise here.'

Instinctively, Josef sprang from his desk and stood to attention. 'Yes, Herr Hauptmann, how may I help you, sir?'

'Report to mein office at ten o'clock sharp. That is all.'

'Yes, Herr Hauptmann.'

Josef heard a click as the line went dead. He began pacing up and down his office with his hand on his chin, wondering what Weise could want with him. He sounded quite angry, he thought. He looked at his wristwatch; it was 9.10am. He ran a trembling hand down his face, telling himself that it was probably nothing to worry about, and then returned to his desk, collecting the letters that he had sorted earlier and making his way out of the office, to deliver the mail to his men.

When Josef arrived at Weise's office, he was surprised to find Uri waiting outside the door. 'What are you doing here, Uri?' he asked.

'I think we're in trouble, Josef,' Uri said sullenly. 'Shall we go in and find out?'

Josef tapped lightly on the door.

'Enter!' came a shout from within.

Josef carefully turned the handle and gently pushed open the door.

'Please take a seat, mein herren,' Weise said, gesturing towards the empty chairs placed in front of his desk. 'There are two reasons why I have called you here this morning. The first is to say that there will be a training exercise later this afternoon in Namyslow, which will involve two units from D Company.' He got out of his chair and walked over to a large wall map, which he used to indicate positions with a pointed finger. 'Herzog, you will lead a simulated attack here in sector seven, along with Feldwebel Schmidt, and then proceed to take the marker from this ridge here. Meanwhile, you, Voss, will try to stop him. You're the enemy for today, verstehen?'

'Verstanden, Herr Hauptmann,' Uri answered with a nod.

'This will take place at two PM,' Weise said. 'Now, it's a two-hour drive from here to where these war games will take place, so I want you and your men ready to move as soon as this interview is over. Any questions, mein herren?'

'Just one, sir,' Josef stammered uncertainly. 'Why now, sir? It's Christmas?'

Weise and Uri looked at each other, and then both began laughing loudly.

'What the hell has that got to do with it, Herzog?' Weise chuckled, grinning broadly. 'You're a soldat, not a tourist. You know, Herzog, in the Great War, our men still fought bitter battles even though it was Christmas.'

'Yes, I know, sir,' Josef replied, 'and I think it was most ghastly, too. Everything should stop for Christmas. It only comes once a year, sir.'

'You know, Herzog, you really are a wit sometimes,' Weise shook his head. 'I never know when to take you seriously. Anyway, let's get to the second reason why I've asked you both here. I have before me a written complaint from an SS Sturmbannfuhrer Ernst Lunder, regarding two officers from D Company who, allegedly, made violent threats toward him and two other officers at the Christmas dance last night. Now, would either of you know anything about this?'

'If I may speak first, sir-' Josef began.

'No, Herzog,' Weise cut him off, 'I would rather Herr Leutnant Voss speak, since he is the more senior of you.' He turned to Uri. 'Well, Herr Leutnant Voss?' he leaned forward with his hands firmly clasped together, wearing a sickly smile. 'In your own time, Herr Leutnant.'

'Well, sir, it's all quite simple really,' Uri explained. 'You see, it was the Nazis who started it, sir.'

'Now just a minute, Voss,' Weise said. 'You know I'm on your side in this matter, but you must refrain from using that sort of language.'

'What, Nazis, sir?'

'You see, there you go again, damn it,' Weise sighed. 'I must warn you, Voss, that your official statement will be recorded, and if it reads the way you're saying it now, you will probably find yourself standing in front of a firing squad before the investigation even starts. Do I make myself clear?'

'Jawhol, Herr Hauptmann,' Uri said, sucking his teeth and lowering his head.

'Now, let's start again, shall we?' Weise suggested.

'It was the SS officers that were looking for trouble, sir,' Uri said.

'Josef only went over to introduce himself because they seemed to be very interested in him.'

'Excellent,' Weise said. 'You see, you can conduct yourself properly when you have to, Voss. Now look, you two have got me into a right mess here, and it's going to take some considerable thinking in order to get you both out of it. I think it best that you both leave now, while I formulate a plan. Get your men and equipment together, and we will discuss this further once you reach Namyslow.'

Both Josef and Uri stood to attention and saluted before making their way out. Then, as they reached the door, Josef felt compelled to turn back towards the desk. 'Herr Hauptmann,' he said, 'will this incident affect mein nomination for die Iron Cross, sir?'

'Of course not,' Weise said. 'Now get yourself and your men to the appointed sector, ready for the battle simulation.'

'Yes, sir, right away,' Josef replied, and then added, 'May I ask why you are attending the exercise this afternoon, sir?'

'I'm attending because I'm one of the marshals that will be monitoring your progress,' Weise answered. 'Herr Major Lowe will be there, too, and he will be watching you very closely indeed, Herzog, so be at your best at all times. He expects a lot from you, for some reason. Now get going.'

Josef and Schmidt loaded their men and equipment onto two heavy, ten-wheeled trucks, and then started the two-hour journey towards Namyslow, in the Opolskie region of Poland.

'Everything looks straightforward enough, Schmidt,' Josef said, as they approached their destination. 'I can make out the red marker on the second ridge. Can you see it?'

'Yes, Herr Leutnant,' Schmidt confirmed, 'and I can also see someone standing not too far from it.'

'Here, pass me the field glasses, Schmidt, and let me take a closer look,' Josef said, peering through the lenses. 'Ah yes, I see him. It's Hauptmann Weise, wearing a white marshal band around his helmet. He's got a clipboard in one hand and something else in the other – I think it's a stopwatch. There's another marshal just coming into view, from behind one of those trees down there.'

'Do you want me to position the men, sir?'

'No, not yet, Schmidt. I need to survey the area first. There's nothing between us and the ridge, but there's a small group of trees to the left that concern me.'

'Flashbacks to Olenica, sir?'

'Oh, you just had to bring that up, didn't you?'

'Well, sir, it's not that dissimilar. Flat open land in front of us, open land to the right, save for a few bales of hay and some vo-gelscheuchen, [2.] and to the left some trees and scrub land.'

'I suppose you're right,' Josef acknowledged, as he turned up the magnification on the field glasses. 'What time is it now, Schmidt?'

'One-twenty PM, sir,' Schmidt said, checking his watch. 'Is there something wrong, Herr Leutnant?'

'Yes, Schmidt, there's something very wrong. I'm seeing a strange object in between those trees down there, and there's movement in that scrub you mentioned. Mein Gott!'

'What is it, sir? What do you see?'

'It's a tank! The crafty devils. It's well-camouflaged, but it's there alright. Here, have a look for yourself, Schmidt.'

'Yes, I can see something, but if it's a tank, why can't I see its kanone, Herr Leutnant?'

'You can't see the mussel, Schmidt, because it's a Stug Three Ausf A. [3.] It has a snubnose, seven-and-a-half-centimetre Howit-zer kanone, and is used as a tank buster, or artillery gun. It's ideal for an ambush, but it may prove to be to our advantage.'

'How so, sir?'

'Well, you see, Schmidt, this particular model is fitted with a fixed turret, which requires the whole tank to turn and take aim. If we can disable the tank, it's kanone will be limited, giving us a fighting chance when we make the dash across its path. Oh, and by the way, it has no fixed machinegun, which means the gunner has to open the hatch and fire from the turret, and when he does, I expect you to take him out.'

'Understood, Herr Leutnant. I must say, I'm very impressed by your knowledge of our field weaponry.'

'It's standard training at college. Now, let me have one last look at our surroundings. I figure that Uri and his men are hiding in that scrub, and are ready to launch a surprise attack. As for your vogelscheuchen, they are soldaten.' [4]

'Soldaten?! How can you know that, sir?'

'Because I can see the shapes of their rifles lying in that long grass next to them, and I won't be surprised if those bales of hay suddenly spring to life once we go charging out into the open, but I'll deal with them when the time comes, which will be very soon. It all goes off at two PM, doesn't it?'

'That's correct, sir. It's now one-fifty.'

'OK, this is what I want you to do, Schmidt. Take two men with you and disable that tank.'

'Yes, right away,' Schmidt hesitated for a moment. 'But, how do you want me to do that, Herr Leutnant?'

'I want you to approach the tank from the rear. Once there, you'll see two small exhaust pipes. Fill them, quietly mind, with as much damp earth as you can, and then give me a thumbs up signal. Don't use the radio, because I don't want the enemy to intercept our transmissions. Once I come charging across the open land, the tank driver will start his engine, wanting to turn the vehicle for the best firing position, but it will stall, giving me a chance to make it to the ridge. You'll then knock out the tank crew and attack the scrub, and I'll deploy some of my men from the main attack body to assist you once we're passed the tank position. Then, another small group will peel off to the right, to take out those vogelscheuchen and suspect bales. We, the main body, will carry on and take the ridge and the marker, verstehen?'

'Sounds gut to me, Herr Leutnant.'

'OK, it's nearly time. Make sure all your men put on their light green helmet bands, so that we know who's who when we get into a scrum with the enemy, who, I'm told, should be wearing red headbands. Now get going… Oh, and one more thing, it's gut to be working with you again, Feldwebel Schmidt. Gut jagen.'

'Yes, and you, sir,' Schmidt said, as he and his men began to scramble down the embankment and make their way towards the trees.

Josef looked behind him, where he could see Major Lowe standing up in the back of his staff car, with a pair of binoculars glued to his face. From his position atop the small hill, he had a perfect view of the manoeuvres. Josef glanced down at his wristwatch; it was 2.00pm. He heard a loud whistle, and observed a green flag being raised by a marshal who had suddenly appeared from behind the trees below. He quickly moved his men into position, and waited nervously for Schmidt's signal. 'Come on, Schmidt,' he said aloud to himself, while squeezing hard on his field glasses, 'what's keeping you?'

Finally, Schmidt came into view, waving his right thumb high in the air.

'OK, lads,' Josef breathed a sigh of relief, 'move at a nice steady pace, and then when I shout go, run like the devil himself is at your heels.'

The men formed a loose skirmish line, with Josef taking point. All was still. So far, so good, he thought, as they neared the tank position. He looked to his right, and noticed that small openings were beginning to appear in the bales of hay just as he got in line with them. He could now clearly make out smooth black machine gun barrels protruding through the small square hatches that were now fully opened. The silence was was then broken by the roar of a tank engine, but no sooner had it started up than it began to splutter and stop. Choking off the exhaust pips with mud had worked, and Josef smiled to himself as he observed Schmidt climbing onto the turret and tapping the machinegunner on the shoulder, and then pulling him out of the tank headfirst.

As much as he was enjoying the amusing sight of Schmidt grappling with gunner, Josef knew that there was no time to waste. 'This is it lads,' he shouted, 'go, go, go!'

1. Non-Commissioned Officer
2. Scarecrows
3. Sturmgeschutz 111
4. Soldiers

CHAPTER THIRTEEN

The men dashed ahead as ordered, but were suddenly engulfed in clouds of white smoke as mock mortar bombs exploded next to them. Josef looked towards the tank, where he could see bright red flames emanating from its stubby short canon, as it belched out another wad. His suspicions regarding the lifeless vogelscheuchen were proved right, as they each transformed into fighting soldiers, grabbing their rifles from the long grass and firing at will. The mounds of hay had also come to life, turning into machinegun nests and spitting out red tracer bullets that ripped across the men's path.

'Right flank, engage the machinegun nests,' he shouted at the top of his voice. 'The rest of you, folgen mich!'

The main body advanced towards the ridge as planned, but then red-banded helmets started to appear out of the long scrub, firing frantically in all directions.

Ah, I see Uri has decided to join us at last, he laughed to himself. 'Left flank, engage the scrub,' he called out. 'The rest of you, onto the ridge, mit mich!'

Everything was going like clockwork, and he could see the red marker quite clearly; it was almost within his grasp. The main body had taken a pounding from the mortars and the crossfire, but he still had five men around him, which was more than enough to do the job. Nothing can stop me now, he thought.

They scrambled up the front of the ridge, and once at the top, he could see Hauptmann Weise standing next to the red marker with a broad grin on his face. Josef smiled back at Weise, certain now that victory was at hand, but as he reached out to seize the red marker, Weise's expression changed dramatically.

'Stop, Herzog,' Weise said, placing his hand on Josef 's chest. He put his other hand to his ear, to better hear a message that was coming through his headset. 'Something has gone wrong.'

'Wrong?' Josef asked, bemused. 'What do you mean, sir?'

'Just stay where you are for a moment,' Weise ordered, 'I think someone has been injured.'

Josef and his men stood in silence, as they waited for further instruction.

'Ja, ja, OK,' Weise said, pressing the earphone close to his head. 'One of your men has been injured, Herr Leutnant. I'm sorry.'

'What?' Josef felt sick to his stomach. 'Who is it?'

'I don't know at this present time,' Weise said, 'but we'd better get down there and take a look, eh?'

As they neared the bottom of the ridge, they could see a crowd of men gathered in the thick scrub. Josef pushed through to the front, where he found Private Schmout lying unconscious on his back, covered in blood from the waist down.

'Oh no,' Josef cried, 'what the hell happened here, Schmidt?'

'Well, Herr Leutnant, I think he was too close to die nebel minen [1.] when it went off,' Schmidt offered. 'It's a bit of bad luck, sir.'

'Bad luck?' Josef was incredulous. 'More like incompetence,

Schmidt!'

'Watch what your saying, Herzog,' Weise frowned. 'Accidents happen all the time in training exercises. This is most unfortunate, but there it is.'

'They don't happen on my watch, Herr Hauptmann,' Josef replied. 'Schmidt, get a medic here immediately! Herr Hauptmann, I would like to speak with Herr Major Lowe, if that is permitable, sir?'

'Yes, of course,' Weise cleared his throat. 'He will want a full report on this anyway, so we may as well go now.'

As Josef and Weise approached Major Lowe's grey open-topped staff car, they found that its engine was running, while the major sat in the back wearing his heavy full-length black leather coat, which was fastened up to the neck. A thin stream of vapour poured from his mouth, as he wrestled his hands into the field grey gloves on his lap.

'Ah, Herzog,' Major Lowe greeted, 'you didn't disappoint me, mein mann. That was a first-class manoeuvre. First class.'

'Thank you, Herr Major,' Josef said solemnly, 'but I'm afraid that one of my men has been injured, sir.'

'Yes, I witnessed everything from up here,' Lowe said, 'most regrettable. I expect a full report on this, of course, once we're back at HQ.'

'And how should that report read, sir?' Josef asked.

'I don't follow you, Herzog.' Lowe replied.

'Well, sir, should I include in the report that Privat Schmout's injuries were caused by negligence?' Josef said.

'Now that's enough, Herr Leutnant!' Weise interjected.

'No, no, that's alright, Herr Hauptmann,' Lowe raised a conciliatory hand, 'let him finish. You were saying, Herzog?'

'Well, sir, it's your responsibility, your duty, to ensure that this exercise is run in a proper manner,' Josef explained, 'and I have a man on his way to hospital because of your failure to-'

'I think I've heard enough from you now, Herr Leutnant,' Lowe cut him off, clearly vexed as he rose to his feet. 'You come to me, like a black puppy, yapping in my face about responsibility and duty! What would you know of these things? You're only just out of nappies, for Gott sake! So far, I've shown you a great deal of sympathy and support, Herzog, but I must warn you that you're overstepping the mark here. Now, get back to HQ and write out that damned report. I want it on my desk as soon as possible, verstehen?'

'Jawhol, Herr Major,' Josef stood to attention. 'May I be allowed to see to the injured trooper first, sir?'

'Yes, of course,' Lowe allowed, 'but make sure I get that report, and make sure you give only the facts. I want no passion, just the facts, alles klar?'

'Yes, sir,' Josef saluted, 'crystal clear.'

Once formally dismissed, he turned and walked away.

'I must apologise for his behaviour towards you, Rudolf,' Weise said, as he watched Herzog march back towards the trucks.

'Nonsense, Ralf,' Lowe replied. 'I only wished we had a few more like him. Did you notice how concerned he was for the welfare of his trooper?'

'Yes indeed,' Weise said, 'and his leadership skills are excellent, too. He shows a gut sense of his surroundings, and he knows how to use them to his advantage. Maybe we should promote him. What do you think, Rudolf?'

'Well, let's see what he puts in his report first, eh?' Lowe grinned.

'Yes, of course,' Weise laughed, 'but on a more serious note, what are we going to do about this SS sturmbannfuhrer?'

'Who, Lunder? Oh, I wouldn't worry too much about him, Ralf. He's just another jumped up Hitler Youth boy scout.'

'That may be so, Rudolf, but he has an appointment with me for tomorrow afternoon. He'll want to know what form of a punishment I've handed Herzog and Uri, following their conduct at the dance last night.'

'Hmm,' Lowe took a moment to consider. 'Ralf, could I ask a favour of you?'

'Why yes, what is it?'

'Will you allow me to be present at this meeting of yours tomorrow afternoon? There are a few things I would like to say to Lunder, Major to Major, if you know what I mean.'

'Yes, why not,' Weise smiled. 'That should prove most interesting.'

'Well, Schmidt, how is he?' Josef asked.

'I've just spoken with the surgeon, Herr Leutnant,' Schmidt answered, 'and he feels it may be necessary to remove Schmout's right foot.'

'Mein Gott!' Josef said. 'Is there anything else you're not telling me, Schmidt?'

'And possibly his testicles, sir,' Schmidt admitted.

'Gott damph!' Josef shook his head. 'He didn't want to go on this exercise, you know, but I forced him into it. Damph stupid of me – damph stupid!'

'I think you're being too hard on yourself, Herr Leutnant. You could not have foreseen this outcome, and it was your duty to ensure that everyone involved should attend the exercise, sir. It's just bad luck is all, sir.'

'You know, Schmidt, I'm getting sick of hearing the phrase, "bad luck!"'

'I understand, sir, but you know, sometimes those pips can lay heavy on the shoulders.'

'Yes, you're right as always, Schmidt. We were so close to success, too.'

'Well, as far as the Herr Major was concerned, it was a complete success, sir.'

'Ha! Is that what you call it? I never got the marker, and one of my men may lose a foot and Gott knows what else!'

'Maybe you should get some rest, sir. It's been a very long day.'

'Yes, I do feel a little tired. I'll be in my quarters, writing my report for the Herr Major, but keep me fully informed if there are any new developments with Private Schmout.'

'Yes, of course, sir. Now, would you please go and get some rest?'

1. Smokebombs.

CHAPTER FOURTEEN

Sturmbannfuhrer Lunder straightened his smart black uniform before knocking on Hauptmann Weise's door. Upon being invited in, he entered with his right arm fully extended, announcing his arrival with an enthusiastic, 'Heil Hitler!'

'Heil Hitler,' Weise replied in kind. 'Please, nemen de platz, Herr Sturmbannfuhrer.'

'Why thank you, Herr Hauptmann,' Lunder said, sitting himself down. 'I must say, I'm a bit surprised to see you here also, Herr Major Lowe.'

'Oh, I was just passing and heard that you were having a meeting with Weise,' Lowe said. 'I hope you don't mind me sitting in, Herr Sturmbannfuhrer?

'Not at all, Herr Major,' Lunder replied.

'Excellent,' Lowe said, 'but can we first dispense with the formalities of rank, and address each other by our first names, Herr Sturmbannfuhrer?'

'But of course,' Lunder agreed. 'Please, call me Ernst.'

'Very well, Ernst,' Lowe smiled. 'I'm Rudolf and this is Ralf,' he said, indicating Weise. 'Now, if you would please take over, Ralf, seeing as this is your interview.'

'Yes, thank you, Rudolf,' Weise said. 'Well, Ernst, what can I do for you?'

'Oh, I think you know why I'm here, Ralf,' Lunder said. 'I need to know what action is to be taken against the two officers I wrote to you about, Herzog and Voss.'

'Well, Ernst, I have decided that due to the circumstances, I shall give each officer a verbal warning.'

'A verbal warning?' Lunder exclaimed. 'Is that it?'

'Yes, that's it,' Weise said. 'What else did you expect, Ernst? Do you think that maybe I should clap them both in irons for such a trivial offence?'

'I think that striking a fellow officer is more than a trivial offence, sir!'

'Gentlemen, if I may cut in,' Lowe said. 'You know as well as I do, Ernst, that no officer was struck, and I do happen to agree with Ralf 's decision. No real harm was done now, was there?'

'I agree that no physical harm was done, Rudolf,' Lunder conceded, 'but from a command point of view, they disrespected both myself and my officers in public. I don't need to remind you both that I'm Leibstandarte, [1.] personal guard to der Fuhrer, and as such I have a reputation to uphold. I can't have a jungle bunny rearing up to me in that manner. It's just not on, you know?'

'Ah, so now we get to the real root of the problem, eh, Ernst?' Lowe raised his eyebrows.

'I'm sure I don't know what you mean, Rudolf,' Lunder replied, running the small ring of black beads that he carried through his fingers, as he felt his stress levels began to rise. His doctor had recommended that he should always use these 'worry beads' in times of great anxiety, as he attempted to recover from a nervous breakdown suffered a year ago, which was believed to have been brought on the strain of trying to advance himself up the ranks. Unlike many other SS officers, who either bought their position or were promoted because they were old party members, he had been required to earn his status.

'Oh, but I think you do, Ernst,' Lowe suggested. 'It now appears that only one of our officers truly offended your honour, and that is Herr Leutnant Herzog. Would you care to explain why this is so?'

'Look, Rudolf, you know as well as I do that we can't have these schwarze running free amongst us,' Lunder said, 'and as for allowing them to give orders to our men, well, I mean, it's just too ridiculous! Our lads will never follow, let alone take orders from, a primate, will they? We are masters over them, not them over us!'

'I'm not here to debate Darwin's theories,' Lowe said stiffly, 'but I am here to talk about two of our officers. Now, as for Herzog, he has proved himself a capable and reliable young man whose men will follow him into battle, as you well know, Ernst. And I must warn you that in the Wehrmacht, we look after our own, and nothing that you may feel or think will ever change that fact.'

'With respect, Rudolf, you and your kind are romantic old fools, and will be swept aside once we have grown to our full potential,' Lunder countered. 'I just cannot believe how men of your calibre can support this schwarz ziege. [2.] Did you know that he escaped the mass sterilisation program back in Berlin?'

'No, I did not,' Lowe said, 'but what of it anyway, Ernst?'

'What of it?' Lunder cried indignantly. 'Well, I'll tell you what of it. At the Christmas dance, he openly flirted and danced with a white woman, for Gott sake! Can you imagine what would happen if he were to mate with one of our own? He would bastardise our race!'

'You make him sound like an animal, Ernst,' Lowe snapped. 'I would remind you of the face that he is an officer of the Wehrmacht, sir.'

'Oh, I can see that this is a complete waste of time,' Lunder said. 'I must go now, and make a full report on this most unproductive meeting.'

'May I ask to whom you are making this report, Ernst?' Lowe asked.

'I can't reveal to you his true identity at this present time,' Lunder answered, 'but I can tell you that Mr X is a powerful man. A very powerful man indeed.'

'Ha!' Weise chimed in, making no attempt at hiding his amusement. 'Secret identities and code names. This is all very cloak and dagger stuff, isn't it, Ernst?'

'Ralf, I can assure you that this is no joking matter,' Lunder warned. 'When Mr X gets this report, you and your country club freunde won't be able to save your little schwarz boy! I bid you both guten tag, mein herren. [3.] Heil Hitler!'

He leaned forward and snatched his black visor cap from Weise's desk, and then jumped out of his chair and dashed for the door, slamming it loudly behind him.

'He's like something out of the funny papers, isn't he?' Weise chuckled, once he was certain that Lunder was out of earshot.

'I wouldn't write him off so quickly, Ralf,' Lowe said darkly. 'He's unnerved me for some reason. We must be ready to give Herzog our full support.'

'Oh, come off it,' Weise laughed. 'You're not buying into all that "Mr X" rubbish, are you?'

'Let's just say that, for now, we should keep a close eye on Herzog.

Humour me on this one please, Ralf.

'Hey, that idiot has really got you rattled, hasn't he?'

'Hmm.'

'Hello Herr Doktor,' Josef announced himself on the surgical ward, 'I've come to see how Privat Schmout is getting along?'

'Oh yes, Schmout,' the doktor said.

'Well, Herr Doktor, how is he?' Josef asked.

'Not too bad, actually. We managed to save the foot, but I'm afraid he will walk with a limp for the rest of his life.'

'Well, that's gut news – about the foot, I mean.'

'Yes, of course, although you do know that his military career is now over, don't you?'

'Yes, that is most unfortunate. What about the other thing, Herr doktor?'

'The other thing, Herr Leutnant? What do you mean by that?'

'You know, the other wound he sustained.'

'Oh, you mean his testicles. We were only able to save one, but he'll still be able to have children, don't worry.'

'Thank Gott for that. May I speak with him, Herr Doktor?'

'Yes, but not for too long, you understand? He's on Ward C, third door on your right, OK?'

'Danke, Herr Doktor. I promise it will only take a minute.'

Josef walked slowly towards Ward C, lingering just inside the doorway as he scanned each bed. The ward was busy, with nurses tidying up dinner plates and serving cups of tea to the patients, who were all sat upright in their beds. He thought back to the time when he himself was in this very same position, but then quickly put the memory out of his mind and focussed on finding Schmout, who he spotted in the fourth bed on the left. Josef stepped forward and began navigating his way through the dinning trolleys, while

Schmout remained totally unaware of his presence, seemingly lost in the book he was reading.

'Hello Schmout,' Josef said, 'how are you feeling?'

'Herr Leutnant,' Schmout looked up from his book, 'what a surprise. I wasn't expecting anyone. Please, sit down.'

'Thank you,' Josef said, taking a seat at the bedside. 'I'm glad to hear that your operation went well.'

'Oh yes, a complete success. The doktors say I can still have kids, thank Gott!'

'Yes, quite. Look, Schmout, I'm sorry this had to happen to you, truly I am, but you see, I had no choice. You had to attend the exercise because-'

'I don't blame you, Herr Leutnant. It was an accident, that's all. It could have happened to anyone.'

'Well, I'm still sorry, Schmout. Listen, if you should need anything, anything at all, you only have to ring me at my office, OK?'

'Thank you, Herr Leutnant, that's very kind of you. Oh, did you know that I'll be leaving the service, sir?'

'Yes, the doktor told me. I'm very sorry to hear that, Schmout.'

'It's not all bad, sir. I was a tailor before the war. I'll just have to go back to doing that.'

Josef stood up awkwardly from his chair and extended a hand to Schmout. 'Well, I wish you all the luck,' he said warmly. 'It was a pleasure to serve with you, Privat Schmout.'

'And you too, sir,' Schmout smiled. 'Aufwiedersehen.'

They shook hands, and then Josef turned and walked away quickly without a backwards glance. The guilt was still weighing heavily on his mind. First there was the loss of Griff and the injury to Monke, and now Schmout was facing an early discharge. Maybe I'm not really officer material after all, he thought. It was all beginning to take its toll on the young leutnant. He retreated back to his office and sat with the lights out, leaning back in his old creaking chair and closing his eyes, before being disturbed from his meditations by the sound of his phone ringing.

'Hello,' he answered with a sigh.

'Hello, is that you, Josef?'

'Yes, and to whom am I speaking?' he asked, barely cognisant of the fact that it was a woman on the line.

'It's me, Monika.'

'Oh, Monika, just a moment,' he said, fumbling for the lamp switch, and knocking an empty teacup to the floor in the process. 'Monika, it's gut to hear your voice.'

'Is everything alright there?'

'Oh yes, everything is great. So, what's happening with you?'

'Nothing much. I've just had to sit and listen to mein vater's music, and it was so boring that I decided to give you a call.'

'So, you only call me when you're bored, eh?'

'Ha, you can be silly sometimes. No, I'm ringing to see if you may be free to attend mein vater's New Year's party tomorrow night. Are you?'

'Yes, I'm free, and wild Polish cavalry charges couldn't keep me away from you, mein liebling.' [4.]

'Well, I'm glad to hear that. Shall we say, oh, eight o'clock?'

'Yes, eight o'clock it is, then. I look forward to seeing you again,' he paused to consider his next words carefully. 'I've missed you, Monika.'

'I've missed you, too. So, eight o'clock, then?'

'Yes, now say gutten nacht and put the phone down.'

'No, you put it down first.'

'OK, I'm putting the phone down now. Are you still there?'

'Yes, will you please put it down?'

'OK, putting it down right now. Gutten nacht, mein liebling.'

'Gutten nacht… Josef, are you still there?'

'Yes, ha. Look, this is getting ridiculous. Now, after three we both put the phone down, OK?'

'OK, but let me count.'

'Ok, you count.'

'Eins, zwei, drei…'

1. Only this elite group of guards were permitted to wear the words 'Adolf Hitler' on their cuff titles.

2. Black goat.

3. Good day, gentlemen.

4. My darling.

CHAPTER FIFTEEN

'Pass me the boot polish, would you, Egon?' Josef asked.

'Why all the fuss?' Egon said, handing him the bottle. 'It's a party, not a parade, you know.'

'I'm told there will be some pretty high-ranking officers there tonight,' Josef said, 'so I must look my best.'

'Hmm, nothing to do with that brunette then, eh?' Egon eyed him sideways.

'Well, maybe a little,' Josef laughed, hearing a knock at the door. 'Hey, get that for me, would you? I've got polish all over my hands.'

Egon ambled over towards the door, and then stiffened when he saw what was on the other side. 'Scheisse!' he gasped. 'What's happened to you?'

'Are you just going to stand there or are you going to let me in, you dope?' boomed a voice from out in the corridor.

'Egon, who is it?' Josef called, looking up from his boot polishing. 'Mein Gott,' he said, when Egon moved out of the doorway, 'Uri, what's happened to you?'

'Is there an echo in here or something?' Uri said, stalking into the living room. 'I've been roughed up a little, that's all.' He was sporting a cut lip and a bruised left eye, and his uniform was in tatters, with black soil marks covering his knees and elbows.

'Who the hell did this to you?' Josef demanded. 'Tell me, and we'll go fix them right now.'

'You're in no position to fix anyone,' Uri crashed down onto the couch. 'You're only half-dressed, man! They'll be well gone by now anyway.'

'Egon, will you talk to this dumb ox,' Josef said, exasperated. 'You might get more sense out of him.'

'Alright, I'll tell you, Gott damn it,' Uri threw his arms up. 'I was jumped on my way over here.'

'Who attacked you?' Egon said, putting his hand up to stop Josef from interrupting.

'Let's just say that there were four of them, and they were wearing black uniforms.'

'SS?' Josef asked, leaning forward.

'That's correct,' Uri replied. 'They said that they were delivering a message.'

'A message?' Josef said. 'But to whom?'

'To you, Prinz,' Uri sighed. 'They said that next time it would be you.'

'We have to report this to Weise immediately,' Egon said.

'No, Egon,' Uri waved away the suggestion, 'they would only deny it.'

'Then what are we supposed to do,' Egon said, 'just let them get away with it?'

'No, of courses not,' Josef said, pacing up and down. 'If it's me they want, it's me they shall have. Pass me mein pistol and gun belt.'

'No, Josef,' Egon protested. 'Uri, don't let him do this, it's crazy.

We must report it to Weise, I tell you.'

'Oh, shut up, Egon,' Uri said dismissively. 'We should have done this back at the dance. Here, Prinz, now let's go crack some skulls.'

'No, you stay put,' Josef said, 'I think you've had enough for one evening, don't you?'

'Ja, OK,' Uri conceded, 'but remember to keep your left up, ha!'

'Wahnsinn!' Egon lamented. 'Alle Wahnsinn! [1.] I'll have nothing to do with this.'

'It is noted, Egon,' Josef said, 'but at least wish me luck, eh?'

'No,' Egon shook his head, 'I want nothing to do with it.' He turned his back and stood with his arms folded, pretending to look out of the small window.

Josef shrugged and strapped on his gun belt, before simply nodding to Uri and leaving. He made his way along a row of dark green blockhouses, towards two freshly painted grey wooden huts that housed a newly arrived division of Waffen SS truppen, under the command of General SS Albrecht von Froder, der Panzertruppen first SS panzer corp. Approaching cautiously, he could hear the men inside laughing and joking about how they gave 'the Russian' a damned good kicking. This infuriated Josef, causing the red mist to descend in front of his eyes. He strode purposefully into the smoke-filled room unnoticed, as the rowdy crew drank and played cards.

'I believe you have a message for me, mein herren?' Josef said loudly.

The room fell silent, save for one soldier who giggled while swigging away at a bottle of Schnapps.

'What a surprise to find you here, Herr Obersturmfuhrer Ulricher,' Josef smirked.

'You know, you really shouldn't have come here, Herzog,' Ulricher said, thumbing through his cards, 'but seeing as though you've taken the trouble to join us, we really must welcome you properly. Heinz,' he called out, 'would you care to offer Herzog your hand?'

Heinz Bulmann was a 6'3" Waffen SS feldwebel, who must have weighed in at at least 110 kilos, if not more. Slowly rising from his chair, he seemed to keep growing until his head almost struck the thick wooden beam that supported the ceiling. He lumbered towards Josef, rolling both shirtsleeves up to his elbows and wearing a sardonic grin on his grimy face, showing off yellow-stained teeth that were pitted due to constant cigarette smoking and poor dental hygiene. His greasy brown hair was cropped short, and stood up at the ends like a hedgehog's back. He extended his hand and said, 'Pleased to meet you, Herzog.'

Unsure of Heinz's intentions, Josef took a few steps backwards and rested his right hand on his black leather pistol holster.

'Oh, forgive me,' Ulricher interrupted, stopping Heinz dead in his tracks. 'Please, let me take your gun belt and pistol, Herzog. We wouldn't want anyone to get seriously hurt now, would we?'

'Nein, danke, Ulricher,' Josef declined. 'I'd rather hold on to it a little longer, if you don't mind?'

'As you wish,' Ulricher said, 'but know this. In here, we fight as men, not women.'

Josef could not help but rise to the challenge that Ulricher had laid down, even though his instincts were telling him otherwise. 'Perhaps you're right, Ulricher,' he said. 'The belt does feel a little heavy on mein waist.' He unfastened the gun belt and placed it not too far from reach on a nearby table, in case he ended up needing it.

Heinz began to approach him once again, but this time there was no smile on his face. Josef gulped nervously and steadied himself, flinching as he felt the wind rush past his head as Heinz dealt him a glancing blow. He managed to dodge the next one, but as he regained his balance a blow to his chest sent him careering backwards, and despite his best efforts he crashed onto the floor with a heavy thud. This prompted an immense roar of excitement from the watching SS, who were now baying loudly, like wild animals, and shouting, 'Kill him, Heinz! Kill him!'

Stunned by the force of the punch, Josef could do nothing except look up helplessly as Heinz brought his hammer-like fist down towards his face. He closed his eyes and waited for the impact, but then nothing happened, and everything fell quiet. Slowly opening one eye, he found to his amazement that Heinz's fist was suspended just inches away from his face, held firm by Uri's giant, trembling fingers.

The ginger beast winked at Josef, and then turned his head toward Heinz, saying, 'I think you should pick on someone your own size, don't you?' He punched the enormous feldwebel in the stomach, sending him staggering backwards into the now silent crowd. 'Quick, Prinz,' he said, 'grab a chair or something. We're going to have to fight our way out of here if we want to stay alive!'

Furniture began to fly through the air and tables were overturned, sending beer bottles and playing cards crashing to the ground. Windows were smashed, and very soon the military police were on the scene, batons drawn. Josef just about managed to land a punch on Ulricher's chin during the melee, sending him sprawling in a most undignified fashion, before the military police got a chance to arrest him.

1. Absolute madness.

CHAPTER SIXTEEN

'Hey, you did well tonight, man,' Uri grinned. 'I liked the way you handled yourself back there. Not bad for a baboon!'

'Ja, right,' Josef sighed, 'all I've done is land us both in jail. It's not exactly what I'd call a victory, you know.'

'I disagree,' Uri said. 'Those apes won't mess with us again in a hurry, I can tell you that.'

'Oh, what a mess,' Josef dropped his head into his hands. 'Monika must be wondering what's happened to me.'

'Ah, she's just a piece of skirt, man. Forget about her.'

Before he knew what he was doing, Josef sprung to his feet, shaking with rage, and grabbed Uri around the neck, pinning him up against the damp cell wall. 'Don't you ever talk that way about Monika,' he screamed, 'got it?'

Uri simply peeled back Josef's hands with effortless ease, before picking him up and throwing him onto a grotty single bunk bed that was pushed up against the opposite wall. 'OK, calm down,' he said, nonplussed by the attack, 'I meant no harm, man. Gott, you're a gutsy little bastard, I'll give you that much.' He placed a paw-like hand to his stomach. 'Hey, do you think we'll get something to eat in here?'

'I don't believe this,' Josef said. 'I've just tried to throttle you, mein life and possibly mein army career is in tatters, and all you can think about is food! I tell you, Uri, you're not human, do you know that?'

'Yes, I know. That's what those SS bastards tell me all the time. They keep saying that the Russians are subhumans and are not to be trusted. I tell you, Prinz, things have steadily got worse for me since Russia invaded Poland in September, and now I hear that they've just launched an attack on Finland. This can only fuel more distrust.'

'But why? The Russians are our allies.'

'That is true, Prinz, but Hitler and Stalin are ice cold with each other, and I fear that the two of them will probably go to war one day.'

'Oh, surely not,' Josef said, beginning to feel guilty. 'Hey, I'm sorry about what I said, about you not being human. I meant nothing by it, you know.'

'Ah, it's OK, mein schwarz Prinz,' Uri smiled. 'I don't know how we have lasted this long.'

'Yes, so you keep saying, Uri. Everything will turn out alright, though. Together always, eh?'

'Ja, zu zammen immer, of course. You're shipping out to Lodz tomorrow, aren't you?'

'Well, that was the plan, but after all this I'm not so sure.'

'You worry too much, that's your trouble.'

'Maybe you're right. Do you think they'll allow us to survive, Uri?'

'Who?'

'The state – the system, you know.'

'You mean the Nazis? Sure they will. We're Germans, aren't we? Shush, someone's coming. I hope it's food!'

'Achtung! Prisoners, stand clear,' the guard bellowed, slinging his rifle over his shoulder. He struggled to unlock the door with his large heavy keys, until finally the rusting iron door swung open with a loud creek and a bang.

'Are we having something to eat?' Uri asked the guard, holding his bulging paunch.

'Nein,' came the sharp reply, 'you have visitors, now stand back!'

With the door now fully open, Weise, Egon and Monika appeared.

'You know, Herzog,' Weise said, 'Herr Major Lowe told me to keep a close eye on you, and up until now, I didn't know what he meant.'

'Oh, Josef, I was so worried when you didn't show up tonight,' Monika cried, 'are you alright? Oh, mein liebe, look at your face, it's all swollen!'

'Why, Monika, you look stunning,' Josef said, arms outstretched.

'Gott, what sentimental crapp,' Uri mumbled.

'You pipe down,' Weise warned, 'or else I'll have the gaoler keep you here all night. Can't you see that the girl is concerned?'

'Sorry, Herr Hauptmann,' Uri said. 'Why, don't they just make a perfect couple?'

'How did you know where to find me?' Josef asked, wrapping his arms around Monika.

'All credit must go to Egon, Herzog,' Weise said. 'He was the only one who had the sense to come and get me from the party. I've spent the last hour and a half arguing to get you both released, so come on, let's get a move on. I believe you have a party to attend, don't you?'

'Yes,' Josef beamed, 'thank you, sir.'

'You'd better hurry and put on a fresh uniform,' Weise said, 'you look a mess. Uri, get yourself back to barracks while I escort Fraulein Hastler to the party. Egon, you go along with Josef, in case he should run into any undesirables on the way back. I don't think I can bail him out of here a second time.'

'Jawhol, Herr Hauptmann,' Egon saluted.

'Herzog, you still look a mess,' Weise said disapprovingly, catching the young leutnant as he entered the Hastler's party. 'You could have at least got rid of that swelling under your eye! Anyway, you're here now and that's all that matters. Now, straighten up that uniform and go and present yourself to the Hastlers, and for Gott sake, don't mention to anyone where you've been tonight.'

'Jawhol, Herr Hauptmann,' Josef replied. 'Thank you for springing me tonight. Again, I must ask, will this affect mein nomination for die Iron Cross, sir?'

'Ah, I'm glad you mentioned that,' Weise said, taking him by the arm. 'Look, step over here for a minute, would you?' He led Josef over to a quiet corner of a secluded study. There was a look of sadness on his face. 'I've got some bad news, I'm afraid. Your nomination for die Iron Cross has been turned down. I'm sorry, Herzog.'

'Turned down?' Josef was aghast. 'But how can this be? With respect, sir, you said the last incident would not affect my nomination, and surely tonight's incident has happened too soon to have contributed towards your decision?'

'It was not my decision to make,' Weise said, 'nor was it Major Lowe's.'

'I don't understand, sir. If it were not you or Mayor Lowe, well then, who?'

'I don't know, Herzog. You must believe me.'

'Sir, you must know something. I beg of you, please tell me.'

'Look, all I can tell you is that the order to stop your nomination has come from a very high level, and so there's nothing I can do about it. I know this is hard for you, but you must put it to the back of your mind.'

'Put it to the back of my mind?' Josef's head was swimming. 'Oh my, what am I to tell mein parents, sir? They were so happy for me.'

'Pull yourself together, man,' Weise snapped. 'You're an officer in die Wehrmacht, and if you survived Olenica, you can survive this.' He placed both his hands on Josef's shoulders, and the leutnant froze, remembering what Pech had told him when he had first arrived at D Company, but then he realised that it was nothing more than a fatherly embrace and relaxed.

'Now, get yourself out there,' Weise said, nodding back towards the party. 'Monika will be wondering where you are.'

'Monika,' Josef remembered why he was there in the first place, 'yes, of course.' He stood straight and composed himself.

'That's the spirit, man,' Weise said. 'Oh, and Josef, Major Lowe and I will stop at nothing until we get to the bottom of this terrible affair, trust me. Now, try to enjoy yourself tonight, because you travel to Lodz in the morning, remember?'

'Yes, sir. I will try.'

CHAPTER SEVENTEEN

General SS Albrecht von Froder's HQ, Poznan, Western Poland.

Sturmbannfuhrer Lunder was sat at his desk in a high-backed, studded black leather chair, poring over documents detailing the mass deportation of the Poles and Polish Jews. His superior, Gauleiter Greiser, had drawn up the plans, with the intention of using Hans Frank's General Government as a racial dumping ground, in order to cleanse his own district. However, Frank had already written directly to Hitler himself to complain about this, in a move to block Greiser's decision, but thus far had received no serious response from Berlin.

The phone rang.

'Hello?' Lunder answered.

'Heil Hitler, Herr Sturmbannfuhrer,' came a familiar voice. 'It's Ulricher here, sir.'

'Heil Hitler, Ulricher. Was ist los?'

'It's Sapphire, sir.'

'Yes, and what of Sapphire, Ulricher?'

'He came to our barracks this evening, sir, and busted up the place. I think he broke my jaw, Herr Sturmbannfuhrer.'

'You know, I thought you were speaking oddly. Have him arrested immediately.'

'He was arrested, sir, but Herr Hauptmann Weise had him released about an hour ago.'

'Oh, and where is he now, Ulricher?'

'We've had reports that he is at the Hastler's New Year's Eve party, Herr Sturmbannfuhrer.'

'You're telling me that Weise had him released so that he could attend a party?'

'That is correct, Herr Sturmbannfuhrer.'

'This beggars belief. OK, Ulricher, leave it with me. Heil Hitler,' Lunder said, ending the call and then dialling for the operator. 'Hello, this is Sturmbannfuhrer Ernst Lunder. Get me Herr Oberst Hastler's residence… Ja, ja, I'll hold, danke.'

'Josef, you look as white as a ghost, if you don't mind me saying,' Monika giggled. 'Are you alright?'

'Yes, I'm alright,' Josef said. 'It's probably just the day's events taking their toll on me, that's all.'

'Why don't I believe you?' she said. 'Something's wrong, I just know it. Please tell me.'

'I'm fine, Monika,' he insisted, somewhat irritably, 'please don't fuss. Let's go and mingle. You were about to introduce me to some of your freunde, weren't you?'

'Hmm, OK,' she eyed him suspiciously, 'but you will tell me later, because I'm like a dog with a bone. I won't let it go.'

'OK,' he laughed, 'it's a deal. Thank Gott I'm not married to you,' he said, prompting her to turn on her heels and stride away. 'Hey, come back,' he called after her, 'it was just a joke!'

'Rudolf, there's a phonecall for you,' Hastler yelled over the din of music and chatter. 'You can take it in mein study.'

'Oh right, thank you, Rhone,' Lowe said, before bowing slightly to his group. 'Please excuse me for a moment, mein herren.' He snatched a tall, thin glass of fizzing Zekt from a passing waiter's shoulder tray and made his way over to the study, where he found a bulky black phone sitting on a small, highly polished brown corner table. 'Hello?' he said, lifting the heavy receiver to his ear, 'Lowe here.'

'Heil Hitler, Herr Major. This is Lunder speaking.'

'What can I do for you, Ernst?' Lowe asked.

'Is it true that Hauptmann Weise released a prisoner from custody tonight, so that said prisoner could attend a New Year's Eve party, Herr Major?'

'Well, it's not quite as colourful as you make it sound, but yes, that is correct. Is there a problem, Ernst?'

'Yes, sir, there is. You have released a man who has not only assaulted a fellow officer, but also caused considerable criminal damage. Could you explain this to me?'

'Look, Ernst, you must surely know there are always two sides to every story, and I don't intend to explain Weise's decision-making to you. Now, unless there is anything else, I have a party to attend.'

'Nein, Herr Major, there is not. You have made yourself quite clear. Heil Hitler!'

'Heil Hitler.'

Lunder slammed the phone down hard, and then picked it straight back up again and began dialling a long series of numbers. 'Heil Hitler,' he greeted the person at the other end, 'Lunder here. We have a problem, sir. It's Sapphire. He's making lots of trouble for us. I need to know, am I clear, sir?'

'Nein, Lunder, you are not clear,' came the reply.

'I hear you, sir, but you don't seem to underst-'

'Nein! Nein! You are not clear. Don't ring me here again unless it's absolutely necessary. Heil Hitler!'

Click.

'Josef, I would like to introduce you to a member of the family,' Monika said, as they approached a tall, thin and gaunt-looking gentleman with receding grey hair 'This is Herr General Otto von Waldmann. He used to bounce me on his knee, didn't you Uncle Otto?'

'Oh, you're embarrassing the young leutnant, Monika,' the general laughed, offering his hand. 'Pleased to meet you, Josef.'

Josef clicked his heels and stood to attention. 'Herr General,' he bowed slightly, 'it's an honour to meet you, sir.'

'I've been hearing a lot about you,' von Waldmann said.

'All gut I hope, sir?'

'Oh, indeed,' von Waldmann said, 'I've already heard talks of promotion in the corridors of power. Keep it up and you never know, you could soon be sitting in a general's chair.'

'Oh, you flatter me, sir,' Josef blushed, 'but I think not.'

'You really shouldn't put yourself down, von Waldmann said. 'There's lots of room upstairs for positive thinkers, you know.'

'Well, we must be moving on, Uncle Otto,' Monika interrupted. 'Oh, Josef, look, there's mein mutter und vater. You must come and say hello. I told them I was going to meet you at your office because you were working late on a backlog of paperwork, so you must keep to that story.' She gave von Waldmann a big hug and then linked arms with Josef, turning him towards her parents and saying over her shoulder, 'We will talk with you again later, Uncle Otto. Come along, Josef, let's get mein parents out the way first. There are lots of other people that I have to show you off to before the night is done.'

'You make me sound like a prized dachshund,' Josef frowned.

'Oh, don't be so surly, Josef,' Monika playfully scolded him. 'It's New Year's Eve, for Gott sake. Loosen your gun belt a little and let some oxygen get to your brain.' She suddenly stopped and did an about-turn, having spotted something out of the corner of her eye. 'Oh, this is mein beste freund Irma Lang, Josef. I've been telling her all about you.'

Irma was a tall, attractive, twenty-year-old blonde, who had known Monika since their time at nursing school, where they had become inseparable. Monika had used her father's position to make sure that they were always posted to the same hospitals in Poland. Like Monika, Irma was single and had never had a real boyfriend, although she desperately wanted one. Monika often told her that she was too forward with men, and that she scared them off with her boyish manner.

'I'm very pleased to meet you, Irma,' Josef said, extending his hand.

'Likewise, Herr Leutnant,' Irma giggled, offering her own hand in return. 'Would you mind if I took a photograph of you and Monika together, Herr Leutnant?'

'Not at all,' Josef said, 'and please, call me Josef.'

'OK, Josef,' Irma said, readying her camera. 'If it's not too much trouble, could I ask the both of you to stand over there, in front of the fire place? I think it would make a great back drop.'

'You'll have to excuse Irma, Josef,' Monika said, 'she thinks that she's a professional photographer!'

'It's certainly no trouble,' Josef insisted. 'I think that in front of the hearth is a gut idea,' he said with a wink.

While Irma struggled to square up the heavy black concertina camera, Josef and Monika positioned themselves in front of the grand old mantelpiece, which had a large rosewood clock in the middle of its broad shelf, supported on either side by tall silver candle stick holders, complete with flickering candles. The open fire roared fiercely, as its bright red flames licked around the freshly placed logs that crackled quietly beneath the general chatter that filled the room. Josef straightened his tunic and placed his visor cap neatly under his left arm, and Monica ran her slender hands down the front of her pretty party dress and checked her hair.

'Are you quite ready?' Irma asked impatiently.

'Yes, I think so,' Monika replied

'Why don't the two of you move closer together?' Irma suggested. 'Go on, Josef. She won't bite, you know,' she smiled wryly.

They linked arms and stood straight, in what was a slightly wooden pose. The camera clicked and the large bulb popped, sending out a flash of white light which made Josef wince. The moment was now immortalised forever.

'Right, let's move on,' Monika said. 'I think Irma has taken up enough of our time.'

'Oh, charming,' Irma pouted. 'I do hope you'll have time to look at the photograph when you get it, Monika.'

'Don't be so catty, Irma,' Monika said. 'I'm sure that one day you'll have a man of your own. Come along, Josef. I think I've just caught sight of mein mutter.'

Major Lowe and Hauptmass Weise were sat in quiet contemplation on a large burgundy leather sofa in the Hastler's study, with each holding a fat, smouldering cigar in one hand and a large glass of cognac in the other.

'I'm telling you, Ralf, we need to keep a closer eye on Herzog,' Lowe said, breaking the silence.

'Yes, but surely, you're not suggesting that the lad is in any danger from Lunder, are you?' Weise asked.

'Like I said to you before, there's something that unnerves me about that man. Also, he seemed to give up far too easily when we had that phone conversation earlier. Very strange.'

'Lunder is a high-ranking officer. It's inconceivable that he would do anything to harm Herzog. I think you're overreacting, Rudolf, I really do.'

'You may be right, but don't forget what happened to Uri tonight. I think this is just the beginning of things to come. I want you to find out what you can about this Mr X. You have freunde in the Abwehr and SD, [1.] don't you?'

'Well, I know a few people, yes.'

'Use them, and then report your findings back to me. I'm sure if you dig deep enough, you'll find that Herr Doktor Schlossman's name pops up somewhere in the middle of all this.'

1. German intelligence agencies.

CHAPTER EIGHTEEN

'Step out onto the balcony, Josef,' Monika smiled. 'We're about to let in the neu jahr, and I want you close by.'

Josef glanced at the large clock on the mantelpiece; it was 11.55pm. They somehow managed to squeeze themselves onto what was quite a substantial-sized balcony, and Josef began to fear that it would not withstand the combined weight of all the guests, as more and more people tried to find space for themselves. He and Monika stood close together, holding hands as they gazed out into the blue-blackness that had descended over Poland. Small white lights flickered from tiny houses that were interspersed across the rural landscape, punctuated by a few car headlamps along the winding country lanes that split the vast Polish countryside.

'Isn't this romantic?' Monika said.

Josef looked into her dark brown eyes, entranced as her thick, long auburn hair was picked up and blown gently across her pale face by the cool night air, causing her to slowly rearrange it with those slender, elegant fingers.

'Yes,' Josef agreed, gently sliding his hand around her tiny waist and pulling her in close, 'it is very romantic indeed.'

The guests began counting down with the clock, 'Zehn… neun… acht… sieben… sechs… funf…'

'Glucklich Neu Jahr,' she said, looking up at him with a brilliant smile.

'Glucklich Neu Jahr,' he replied.

'Vier… drei… zwei… eins…'

Car horns beeped and church bells began to ring out; the black sky erupted into a kaleidoscope of bright colours, as the fireworks exploded and cascaded down in all directions. The guests inside the house and out on the balcony began singing loudly, as hundreds of thin streamers descended onto their heads. Josef placed his arms around Monika's shoulders and laughed as they looked into the mad crowd, who were now jumping up and down.

'Would you do something for me?' Monika asked.

'Yes, of course,' Josef said. 'What is it?'

'Once everyone has gone back into the house, would you kiss me?'

'Why, mein liebling, nothing would give me more pleasure.'

They waited patiently for the last few stragglers to file back into the main room of the house, and then turned and faced each other, holding hands. The night air was cool and still, and the noise of the fireworks began to fade away, with only the occasional pop in the distance. It was now 1 January 1940. Monika looked straight into Josef's eyes, and without blinking simply said, 'Well?'

He grinned, before carefully brushing her hair to one side with the back of his open hand, and then gently taking her behind the neck and pulling her slowly towards him. As they drew nearer to each other, he smiled nervously, but she continued to look intensely into his brown eyes, with her bottom lip beginning to quivering a little. Their faces were now so close that they could feel each other's breath on their skin. She hesitated a little, but he kept moving forward until his lips were pressed firmly against hers. She began to slide her delicate hands up his back, stopping at his shoulders and embracing him tightly, only to suddenly pull away and walk quickly to the front of the balcony, holding herself like someone who had just caught a chill. She stood silently for a moment, looking out into the dark blue night, before finally turning back around to face him.

'So, you're travelling to Lodz in the morning?'

'Yes, that is correct,' he answered, 'but it will only be for a couple of months, until the SS units are firmly in place, and then it's all over for us – the Wehrmacht, I mean.'

'Yes, I know. Mein vater has told me all about it, but what becomes of you after Lodz?'

'To be honest, I've not given that much thought. Is that why you have gone so cold on me?'

'If you get posted abroad, this whole evening has had no meaning, has it?'

'Oh, mein liebling, you mustn't think like that. Of course, this evening has meaning. How could you possibly think otherwise?'

'I'm not stupid, Josef,' her voice cracked a little. 'Everyone knows what soldiers are like. Once you're abroad, you will forget about me and find someone else.'

'Mein dearest liebling, from the very first time that I looked into your beautiful eyes from that hospital bed, I just knew that you were the only one for me. Whenever you approached, mein heart would race so fast that I thought it was going to explode!'

'Oh, dear,' Monika touched her cherry red lips with the tips of her pale, thin fingers, and then began to blush.

'For Gott sake, woman, you saved mein leben. Distance means

nothing when you love someone, and I give you my word as an officer of the Wehrmacht that if I'm posted abroad, I will see to it that you join me immediately.'

'Don't be silly, Josef. Unmarried women are not allowed to travel abroad with officers, and even if they were, they would be considered loose women!'

'OK, then I'll go to your vater this very minute and ask for your hand. Will that satisfy you?'

He took her by the arm, intending to lead her back into the house to help him locate Herr Oberst Hastler, so that he could ask him for his daughter's hand, but she pulled him back gently onto the balcony and then turned away from his gaze.

'What's wrong?' he asked in a low voice.

'Do you really think that this romance can work?'

Josef placed both hands on her milk white shoulders and gently spun her around to face him, looking deep into her eyes. 'This can work,' he said, searching every feature of her face. 'This will work, but you must believe it. Do you believe?'

'Yes, I believe, but mein parents may take some convincing, don't you think?'

'Your parents are decent people and care only for your happiness,' he smiled, as he lifted her chin. 'I promise you that everything will be alright.'

'I hope you're right.'

'I know I'm right.'

'Do you think we could try that kiss again?'

'Why, certainly, mein liebling,' he grinned. 'Nothing would give me more pleasure.'

CHAPTER NINETEEN

Josef arrived two minutes late for the morning briefing at Hauptmann Weise's office. Oberleutnant Erich Heiter and Oberleutnant Philip Grinburger were already there.

'You're late, Herzog,' Weise said reproachfully.

'Yes, sorry, sir,' Josef replied. 'I had a late night.'

'I know,' Weise said, 'I was there, remember? When I say eight, I mean eight. Maybe if you concentrated more on soldiering instead of womanising, you might actually get somewhere!'

Grinburger burst out laughing.

'That wasn't a joke, Grinburger!' Weise flared. 'Right, let's just get down to it. The reason I'm sending you all to Lodz is for the purpose of repatriating our ethnic Germans coming in from the Baltic states, as well as resettling our Polish Ethnic Germans who live here.'

'What is a Polish Ethnic German, sir?' Josef asked.

'That's a gut question,' Weise answered, 'and I'll try to explain it as simply as I can. The Polish Ethnic German is a person who has lived in the sections of Poland that belonged to Germany since before the Great War. These areas were quickly claimed back after our defeat, and now it's time to put things right again. The order to reclaim the lost territories has come direct from der Fuhrer himself, as part of his lebensraum [1.] initiative. We have already started organising some one hundred-thousand Poles into the Lodz area.'

'Don't you mean Polish Jews, sir?' Grinburger offered.

'Alright, Grinburger,' Weise acceded, 'we've organised Polish Jews into the Lodz district, thus making vacant thousands of properties that need to be filled.'

'Where exactly do we all fit into all of this, Herr Hauptmann?' Josef asked, puzzled.

'Well,' Weise took a breath, 'it will be the job of Herr Ober-leutnant Heiter to organise the house keys and maps for the Ethnic Germans, while you and Grinburger help relocate them to their new properties. You will both be, in effect, the welcome wagon, as the Americans would say. Now, there will be a lot of lost and confused people arriving in the district, so endeavour to make them feel re-laxed and assist their every need. Once you arrive in Lodz, you will all be placed under the kommand of Herr Georg Siltz, who I know personally. He's the Standortkommandant [2.] in Aleksandrow, and a first-class officer, I might tell you. He will supply any additional help you might need, Erich, so don't be afraid to ask. This could turn out to be a big operation. Once the Ethnic Germans have been rehoused and are settled in your job is done, and you can all return back to base. Any questions, gentlemen?'

'No, sir,' the three officers collectively mumbled.

'Right then,' Weise smiled, 'all that's left to say is gut reise.'

Popelwitz Train Station, Breslau. 9.30am

'Is that our train, Erich?'

'Yes, Josef.'

'Are we late?'

'No.'

'Then why is it moving?'

'Quick! Grab your gear and run like hell,' Erich screamed at the top of his voice. 'Hey, somebody stop that train, damn it!'

Philip, being the most athletic of the three, reached the last carriage in time to hurl his kit bag through the small open window and grab the door handle, which he used to haul himself inside. 'Here, give me your hand, Josef,' he said, reaching out to assist his two slower comrades.

'Thank you,' Josef said, sucking in air. 'Come on, Erich,' he turned to see Philip reaching out again, 'you can make it. Grab hold, man!'

'I didn't think I was going to make it,' Erich said, panting heavily, as he was pulled into the carriage. 'Let's go find our seats.' Still wheezing, he led his troop down a long, narrow corridor, stumbling with the motion of the train and struggling to keep his kit bag up on his shoulders. He stopped abruptly, fumbling in his pocket until he produced a ticket. 'Here we are, lads, C3. Come on.'

Erich slid back the large, wooden-framed glass door to reveal an empty carriage, and they carefully placed their bags onto the netted shelves overhead before deciding upon seating arrangements. Josef sat himself down on the left side of the carriage, next to the window, and lit a cigarette. Philip also opted for a window seat, dropping down opposite Josef, and Erich sat beside him. Josef shielded his eyes as the strong morning sunlight broke into the carriage, forcing him to winch slightly. He continued smoking in silence, his attention caught by the beautiful rolling countryside.

'What do you say to a cup of tea in the dining car, lads?' Erich suggested, rubbing his hands together.

'Sounds gut to me,' Philip answered. 'How about you?'

'Ja, gut idea,' Josef said, 'let's go.'

They squeezed past the odd passenger as they made their way along the narrow corridor, until their journey was abruptly halted by a short, tubby man wearing a tight black waist coat, with a silver fob dangling from the right pocket. He wore a black peaked cap that was much too small for his head, and he had positioned himself in the centre of the isle with his right hand open, as if expecting a gratuity.

'Fahrkarte bitte?' the inspector demanded.

'Do you have the tickets on you, Erich?' Philip asked, laughing loudly.

'Yes, they're here somewhere,' Erich said, searching his pockets. 'Moment bitte.'

The inspector was growing increasingly agitated, as he had to keep moving to one side to let the other passengers through, and Philip's incessant giggling wasn't helping matters.

'You'd think that they would have given us military passes, eh?' Josef said, in an effort to break the awkward silence.

'Ja, and who do you think you are, General Rommel?' Philip spluttered.

'I've found them!' Philip declared triumphantly. 'Here you are, Herr Inspektor.'

'Ja, ja,' the inspector said impatiently, thumbing through the tickets. 'OK, gut.'

'Did you see the face on him?' Josef laughed, as they finally moved beyond the pint-sized tyrant. 'You know, I do believe he thought we were stowaways.'

'Who cares what he thought,' Erich said. 'Come on, lads, I'm parched.'

The dining room wasn't too crowded, and they were able to find an empty table halfway down, on the right. As the three men rolled down the narrow walkway, they found themselves having to constantly apologise to other passengers as they either knocked off women's hats or clocked gentlemen on the backs of their heads. One particularly grouchy man was heard to say, 'Damned Wehrmacht, can't even walk straight. Wouldn't last two minutes in der Kreigs Marine!' after Josef inadvertently cuffed him around the ear.

'Well, that wasn't too bad now, was it?' Erich said, fighting to hold back his laughter as they took their seats. He then stuck his hand high up into the air, clicked his fingers and shouted, 'Waiter, drei tee bitte!' much to the annoyance of the other passengers.

'Do you think that we might also have a bite to eat?' Philip asked.

'Certainly,' Erich said, 'what would you like?'

'Oh, just some toast and marmalade.'

'And you, Josef?' Erich said.

'I'll have the same as Philip please.'

Once fully nourished and refreshed, the three officers returned to their empty carriage to relax..

'So, why are we really being sent to this Lodz place, Erich?' Josef asked. 'Surely, this Hauptmann Siltz fellow must have other men at his disposal?'

'Ah, now that's where you're wrong,' Erich said. 'Let me explain, and remember that what I'm about to tell you is not to be repeated, verstehen?'

'Verstanden,' Joef nodded.

'All of our forces are to be redeployed from Poland for the forthcoming battle in Europe,' Erich said. 'We are soon to attack Belgium, Holland and, I have it on gut authority, France. That's why the Waffen SS are following so closely behind us here. Once they take over, we can leave this Gott-forsaken place. You have no idea of how much I hate this damned country.'

'What's wrong with Poland?' Josef said. 'It might be a little chaotic, but I quite like it here.'

'Hmm,' Erich responded, 'and do you know why it's so chaotic? No, you don't, so I shall tell you. It's like this. You have us here in western Poland, which is run by Gauleiter Arthur Greiser. Then, you have eastern Poland, known to us as West Prussia, which is run by Gauleiter Albrect Forster. Finally, we have the General Government, which is run by Gauleiter Hans Frank. Are you keeping up with me?'

'Well, it's a nice geography lesson,' Philip remarked, 'but I'm sure Josef knows who all the Gauleiters are. What's all this got to do with the chaos in Poland, though?'

'Well, if you'll shut up and listen, I'll tell you,' Erich said sharply. 'Now, Frank doesn't like Greiser, because Greiser keeps sending around fifteen thousand Jews a month to Frank's General Government, but Frank tolerates Greiser because they are both getting a share of the loot.'

'Mein gott,' Josef gasped, 'are you saying that these men are robbing the Jews?'

'Shush, keep your voice down,' Erich hissed, 'I haven't finished yet. Now, in turn, both Frank and Greiser hate Forster, because Forster is Germanising en masse in his Prussian district without fully checking his population for Jewish ancestry. So, Frank complains to die Reichfuhrer SS Heinrich Himmler, who in turn complains to Forster, but Forster ignores Himmler and continues to Germanise en masse, leading Greiser to complain directly to der Fuhrer. However, der Fuhrer has yet to respond to Greiser's plea for intervention.'

'Gott, this is so confusing,' Josef shook his head. 'Look, Erich, I may seem a little dim for asking this, but what do you mean when you say Germanising?'

'Well firstly, you're not dim,' Erich reassured him, 'you've just been kept in the dark. The information you are now hearing has only been made available to senior ranking officers, but I'm telling you now so that you and Philip may better prepare yourselves for what you're about to experience in Lodz.'

'This is all beginning to sound like a bit of a horror story to me,' Josef admitted.

'Yes, but hold on,' Erich said, 'it gets worse.'

'You mean there's more?' Josef cried. 'My head is starting to hurt!'

'Oh, just be quiet and listen,' Erich said, 'this is important. All Gauleiters have been given orders directly from Herr Himmler to Germanise their own districts through a careful selection process. Firstly, they're to weed out Jewish Poles from ethnic Poles, and then those ethnic Poles are to be told that they will be Germanised and must forget their own language, and speak only German from now on. All Polish arts, literature and music are to be removed, and all Polish monuments destroyed. All male ethnic Poles who are young enough and fit enough are to be drafted into die Wehrmacht. Any Poles considered unfit for Germanisation are to be deported back to Germany, to form part of the labour force for our agriculture pro- grammes.'

'You've told us of the ethnic Poles, Erich,' Josef said, before lower- ing his voice, 'but what of the Jews?'

'Well, all I can tell you is that, as we speak, the Jews are being sent to camps all across Poland. There are an estimated three hundred camps being built to accommodate them.'

'That's all well and gut, but what happens to them once they're in the camps?' Josef asked.

'I'm told that they are to be processed, and then dispatched to munitions factories and the like,' Erich explained.

'This doesn't sit right with me,' Josef frowned. 'How are we going to keep a thing like this from getting out, and what about the human rights implications?'

'The Jews don't have human rights,' Philip sniggered, 'and as for any of this getting out, as you put it, I don't need to remind you that until we sat down in this very carriage, we were both in complete ignorance of the situation.'

'I suppose you're right about the secrecy,' Josef conceded, 'but they're people first and Jews second, and they do have the same fundamental human rights as everyone else.'

'Not under German law,' Philip countered, 'and the law is the law.'

'Well, I think that's a pretty damned poor excuse, Philip, and you know it!'

'Gentlemen, please,' Erich interjected, 'arguing among ourselves isn't going to solve anything. Josef, you know what your trouble is? You think with your heart and not with your head, and that will land you in hot water one of these days if you're not careful. As for you, Philip, you need to learn to think before you speak. Now, I suggest we all try and get some rest. We've still got a long journey ahead of us.'

'You're right, of course, Erich, and I apologise,' Josef said. 'It's just that Philip appears to be an SS wolf in Wehrmacht clothing!'

'OK, OK, pipe down now,' Eich said, easing back into his seat, 'and both of you, get some rest. That's an order!'

1. Living space.

2. Garrison commander.

3. Good journey.

CHAPTER TWENTY

'Hurry up, Mony,' Irma said, checking her watch, as she and her friend were taking a quick, unauthorised tea break in the hospital canteen before returning to ward duty, 'if we don't get back soon, someone is going to notice that we're missing. You're such a slow drinker!'

'Don't rush me,' Monika replied. 'Stab Nurse Encke has run the legs off me this morning, so I'm going to make sure that I enjoy this cup of tea. Oh Gott, don't look now, but here comes Anna.'

Anna Frantzen was a heavily built auxiliary nurse with a full, round face, who had travelled with them to Poznan as part of the nursing entourage from Breslau. She was a recent divorcee, who now hated all men with a passion, and Monika and Irma would occasionally joke about how her thick eyebrows would meet in the middle of her forehead, or how her lipstick looked like it had been applied with a paint brush.

'Hi girls,' Anna said, pulling up a chair alongside them, 'do you mind if I sit here?'

'Not at all,' Irma said, staring into Monika's eyes with a smirk on her face,

'but we're not staying long. We must get back on ward duty very soon.'

'Oh, that's no problem,' Anna said, 'I only wanted a quick chat with Monika about her neu mann freund.'

'He's not mein mann,' Monika said defensively. 'We're just gut freunde, that's all.'

'Gut freunde?' Anna said doubtfully. 'That's not what I heard.'

'Oh, and just what have you heard?'

'Well, I was told by a reliable source that you seemed more than just gut freunde when you were both stood on the balcony on Neu Jahr's Eve,' Anna said, taking a sip of her tea.

'Ah, and what else did this reliable source tell you?' Monika pressed.

'I was told that he's,' Anna paused, 'well, you know, schwarz.'

'Yes, that's correct, he's eine schwarz leutnant in die Wehrmacht. Is there a problem with that?'

'Well, that depends on your point of view, doesn't it?' Anna said diplomatically.

'And just what is your point of view?'

'Well, I couldn't let someone like that touch me. It gives me the shivers just thinking about it!'

'What do you mean, "someone like that?" You make him sound like a monster, which he's not,' Monika said, face flushed with anger. 'He's a kind and gentle person, and you know what, Anna, I really pity you, because you're obviously someone who has never known love. I think you're really pathetic. Come along, Irma. We must be leaving now.'

Monika violently pushed the flimsy canteen table into Anna's stomach, as she got up and caused the crockery to rattle loudly. She then stormed out of the room, with Irma following quickly behind.

'Monika, slow down,' Irma called after her. 'What's got into you? She's just a jealous cow, that's all.'

'Leave me alone,' Monika said over her shoulder, 'I'm going out to get some fresh air.'

'But what will I tell Stab Nurse Encke if she asks where you are?'

'Oh, I don't know. Just tell her I've gone to the toilet or something.'

Running along the wide, busy corridor, dodging the walking wounded and porters pushing wheelchairs, Monika arrived at three flights of stairs that led to the main entrance of the old hospital. She took shelter on the top step, seeing that it had started to rain heavily below. It seemed like she had only been stood there a moment before hearing a voice say, 'Fraulein Hastler, is that you?'

She turned quickly to find a tall, slim officer in a smart black SS uniform standing before her, clutching a small bunch of drooping wet flowers in his left hand.

'I'm sorry, sir,' Monika replied, 'but I'm afraid you have me at a disadvantage.'

'Oh, please forgive me for not introducing myself,' the officer said. 'I'm Sturmbannfuhrer Ernst Lunder.' He removed his black peaked visor cap and placed it under his left arm, before stooping forward to kiss the back of her hand. Wiping the rain from his face, he added, 'You probably don't remember me, Fraulien. I was at the Christmas dance in Breslau with some other officers. We were stood by the stage most of the night, listening to the band.'

'Oh yes, I think I do remember you now,' Monika said. 'You were the only gentlemen wearing black uniforms that night.'

'Ha, yes,' he laughed, 'one does tend to stand out in this uniform.'

'Are you visiting someone here, Herr Sturmbannfuhrer?'

'Yes, a freund. He's on the top floor – worse luck. Anyway, Fraulien, what brings you here to Poznan?'

'I was transferred from Breslau. And you, Herr Sturmbannfuhrer?'

'My divisional head quarters are not too far from here, but my job takes me all over Poland. One day here, and the next it could be Warsaw. You know how it is.'

'Yes, indeed. It's the same for me, but I like it that way. Well, Herr Sturmbannfuhrer, if you will excuse me, I must return to my duties.'

'But of course, Fraulien Hastler. Perhaps we could have dinner one evening?'

'I'm afraid not, Herr Sturmbannfuhrer. I have a steady relationship with someone back in Breslau, you understand?'

'I would have been surprised if such an attractive lady as yourself was not already in a relationship, but surely we can still have dinner, can't we?'

'I think not, Herr Sturmbannfuhrer, but it was very kind of you to ask.'

'I understand, Fraulein Hastler. Aufwiedersehen.'

CHAPTER TWENTY-ONE

'Josef, wake up,' a voice said, 'I think we're here,'

Josef awoke to the sight of Philip sitting with his face pressed up against the carriage window. He waited for his eyes to fully adjust, and then looked down at his wristwatch; it was 5.30pm. He stood and joined Philip at the window, and they watched as a narrow grey platform began to appear underneath the train. They came to a violent stop, rocking them slightly, as German guards with long trench coats and rifles slung over their shoulders appeared, pacing up and down the platform in between the civilians that waited to board the train.

'Where's Erich?' Josef asked.

'He's gone to die toilette,' Philip said, 'he'll be back in a minute. Listen, before he comes back, I just want to say sorry for what I said earlier.'

'Ah, forget it. We can't agree on everything, can we? If it's true what Erich says about this place, then I think our wits are going to be tested to their limits, don't you?'

'I'm sure you're right, Josef. Here's Erich now.'

'So, you're awake at last, Josef,' Erich greeted. 'We were beginning to think that you were dead, ha! Well, boys, it looks like we're here. You'd better grab your gear.'

The three officers joined an orderly queue of passengers and filed along the narrow isle towards the train's small exit door, with their cumbersome bags thrown over their shoulders. They emerged out into the dark winter night, and found that it was good to smell the fresh evening air.

'Right, lads, keep your eyes peeled,' Erich said. 'There's supposed to be one of Siltzs's men here to collect us, an oberleutnant named Schlachter – Eckard Schlachter, but I can't see anyone that fits his description.'

'And what is his description?' Josef asked.

'Well, look for somebody with an ironing board stuffed up his back,' Erich said. 'In other words, an ardent Nazi.'

'I think I've just found him,' Philip said.

'Where?' Erich turned to look, 'Where is he?'

'He's over there, to your right,' Philip pointed, 'marching up and down like someone has just turned a key in his back!'

'Yes, that'll be him alright,' Erich said. 'I suppose we'd better go and introduce ourselves.' He started towards the marching SS man, calling out, 'Herr Oberleutnant Schlachter?'

'Ja, Heil Hitler!' Schlachter replied, shooting his right arm out in a salute that stopped just short of Erich's nose. He was very much the model nazi, with cold, deep blue eyes, which were now fixed firmly on Josef, making no effort to hide their disbelief. Schlachter was a product of Ernst Rohms SA, an ex-brown shirt storm trooper, who was transferred over to Hitler's SS after 'the Night of the Long Knives,' when the SA chief of staff, Rohm, along with some of his generals were executed in July 1934 on trumped up charges of treason, and in Rohm's case, homosexuality. Hitler made all brown shirt members swear an oath of allegiance to him, and nearly all of them became SS Officers.

'Heil Hitler,' Erich said, 'we are the party from Breslau, Herr Oberleutnant.   This is Oberleutnant Philip Grinburger, and this is Herr Leutnant Josef Herzog. I'm Erich Heiter.'

'Gut, gut,' Schlachter nodded. 'Bitte, folgen mich, gentlemen. I have a car waiting to take you to your accommodation, where you will rest for tonight. I will then collect you in the morning and take you directly to Herr Siltz, die kommandant.'

The Wehrmacht officers felt like kings as they were ushered into a large, black shiny staff car, complete with red leather seats and a black retractable canvas roof. Schlachter snapped his fingers, and the driver, who was a thin, tired-looking untergefreiter, stepped forward and relieved the men of their bags, which he tucked carefully into the small, chunky boot of the car. They were then driven at speed, with headlamps full on, along narrow streets, where many of the houses had been reduced to rubble during the fighting that had recently taken place, following Poland's brief but bloody resistance. The people moving in and out of the shadows would be mostly old women and young children, since all those of working age had been taken as forced labour.

They pulled up sharply in front of an old ex-Polish army blockhouse in the Aleksandrow district, just outside of Lodz. Schlachter turned back in his seat alongside the driver and announced, 'We are here, gentlemen. Bitte cum mit mich, and I will introduce you to Karl Penau. He is to be your personal guide and advisor during your stay here in Aleksandrow.'

As they entered a small hallway, a little man dressed in full combat uniform jumped to attention, stamping his right foot to the floor. He, too, wore the same tired expression on his face as the untergefreiter who had just driven them there. He appeared to be in his late-thirties, and sported a large, brown walrus moustache, which looked to be well-groomed, and although he was slightly overweight, he was well-built. He greeted them with a loud, 'Heil Hitler!'

'Heil Hitler,' Schlachter replied, before explaining to the Wehrmacht officers, 'This, gentlemen, is Unterfeldwebel Karl Penau, your guide. He will show you to your accommodation, and will attend to your every need. Guten nacht, gentlemen, and I will see you in the morning. Heil Hitler!'

'If you will follow me, gentlemen, I will show you to your rooms,' Penau said, once Schlachter had left them. 'I'm sure you would all like to wash and freshen up.'

He seemed to relax the moment Schlachter exited the building, and soon began to laugh and joke with the Wehrmacht officers. He explained to them that he and the other men disliked the stiff-shirted Schlachter, nicknaming him the Cap, because he was never out of uniform and always on ceremony. He went on to tell how they would laugh and make rude gestures behind his back at every opportunity.

Once they had washed and changed into some fresh clothing, Josef, Erich and Philip joined Penau at the webels' mess hall table for supper, ignoring the tradition of officers never mixing with their lower, non-commissioned counterparts. They eagerly tucked into the thick bread and liverwurst that was on offer, washing it down with several steins of frothy lager.

'Sehr gut, Unterfeldwebel Penau,' Erich remarked, as he wiped the froth from his top lip.

'Please, call me Karl, sir,' Penau replied.

'Alright, Karl,' Erich allowed, 'but in that case, I'm Erich, and these two rascals are Josef and Philip.'

'I'm very pleased to meet you all, gentlemen,' Karl nodded to each of them in turn, 'but I hope you don't think it rude of me if I ask Josef how he managed to get into the regular army?'

'Well, it was very simple, Karl,' Josef answered, 'I just enlisted like everyone else. You see, I found that the Wehrmacht was not overly concerned with the colour thing, but more with the ability to command as an officer. They're very particular about things like that, you know.'

'Yes, I understand what you're saying,' Karl said, 'but you must agree that you are indeed unique?'

'Yes, I do feel rather special,' Josef quipped.

'Enough of Josef 's life story,' Erich said. 'What can you tell me about Herr Kommandant Siltz, Karl?'

'What do you want to know?' Penau asked.

'Well, what sort of a man is he?'

'Siltz is a career officer, who will do whatever he is ordered without question,' Penau said. 'He revels in the suffering of others, whether they are Jews, Poles or even his own men. We think he failed his entrance into the SS – only joking, but he's what you might call a right bastard, you know?'

'It sounds to me like he's the right man for his environment, wouldn't you say, lads?' Erich said to his two comrades.

'Yes, quite,' Philip agreed, 'and we'd better be wary of him if you ask me.'

'Oh, I'm sure that the War Council can handle him,' Erich laughed. 'Don't you agree, Josef?'

'Don't ask me,' Josef put his hands up in front of his chest, 'I'm only a junior officer, remember. It's you who wears the pips.'

'Yes, thanks for reminding me,' Erich said, 'since now, gentlemen, it's time for me to use those pips and order you to bed. We've got an early start tomorrow, so get some rest. I'll see you both in the morning.'

The next morning, Oberleutnant Eckard Schlachter arrived bright and breezy at the former army blockhouse to collect the three Wehrmacht officers, and escort them to their briefing at Herr Kommandant Siltz's HQ in Lodz.

'I hope you all had a gut night's sleep, gentlemen,' Schlachter said. 'I trust that Unterfeldwebel Penau took care of your needs?'

'Yes, he did indeed,' Erich said, 'thank you, Herr Oberleutnant.'

'Gut, gut, Herr Oberleutnant Heiter,' Schlachter smiled. 'Now, if you gentlemen will accompany me, I'll take you to Herr Kommandant Siltz for your briefing.'

Once again, they all climbed into the large black limousine and, in stark contrast to the previous night's break-neck pace, drove very slowly along the battered cobbled streets of the town, and then on to the city of Lodz. Although it was a bit windy, the morning sun shone strongly through broken clouds, giving the officers their first real glimpse of the scale of destruction that had taken place, as towers of rubble stood where there were once fine old buildings and schools, and an assortment of military and civilian vehicles lay burnt-out and rusting along the roadside. This was indeed a strange site for the three Wehrmacht officers, since Breslau had sustained very little damage during the early campaign there.

They came upon a military policeman wearing a grey steel helmet and long greatcoat, who halted the limousine. Around his neck was a long silver chain, supporting a silver-plated gorget [1.] with the words Feld Gendarmere embossed across it. He held up a white paddle and directed horse-drawn carts, tractors and tanks across the road, and then beckoned the limousine forward. Schlachter gestured to the driver that he should pull over next to where a large crowd had gathered in a marketplace. His face had lit up with excitement, like a child's at Christmas, and as he flung open the door of the car and leaped from it, he called for the other officers to join him. 'Schnell, schnell, or you will miss it!' he yelled, as he disappeared into the crowd.

'What's going on?' Josef asked.

'I don't know,' Erich admitted. 'Maybe we should follow him and find out.'

The Wehrmacht officers chased after Schlachter, pushing their way through the crowd until they reached the front, where they found a raised platform with four small wooden steps leading up to it. On the platform was a lofty, square wooden frame, resembling a goalpost, with seven ropes dangling from it. Parked next to the platform was a large green military van, with a loud speaker mounted on its roof from which classical music blurred. Eight armed guards surrounded the crowd, as they stood looking up at seven dishevelled civilians that were lined up along the narrow platform – six men and one woman – each with their hands tied behind their back, wearing a look of resignation on their pale faces as they stood obediently motionless. Josef looked across to Erich and Philip in surprise and horror, as it dawned on him what was about to happen.

A tall, gaunt-looking officer wearing a peaked visor cap pulled down over his eyes, and a long grey trench coat with a black gun belt fastened tight around the waist, stepped forward. He ordered a gefreiter to first tie large stones around the prisoners' feet, for added ballast, and then place ropes around each of their necks, which he tugged hard to make sure that they were tight enough. The officer then looped white placards bearing German slogans about traitors and cowards over their heads, before calmly walking to the edge of the platform and producing from his pocket a prepared statement, which he read out to the captive audience.

1. Small metal breast armour.

CHAPTER TWENTY-TWO

The officer on the platform explained to those gathered that they, too, could expect the same fate if they should step out of line. Josef glanced to his left, and out of the corner of his eye spotted Schlachter, who was almost licking his lips with anticipation, like a hungry man awaiting his dinner. When the officer had finished his brief sermon, he carefully folded the statement and placed it in his large sleeve cuff, before walking slowly to the other side of the stage and, with a simple nod, giving the executioner permission to carry out the dreadful deed. There was a loud, heavy clunk as the platform gave way, forcing the prisoners into a quick descent which stopped just short of the ground below. Mercifully, it was all over within seconds.

The ropes creaked as they stretched to their limit, sending the bodies back up at speed and then dropping them back down again. They seemed to dance a funny jig, like puppets on strings, kicking and twitching before finally coming to rest. The motionless bodies then swung gently in the breeze, like limp fruit on a tree, and their faces had already started to turn a bluish-green, while their tongues swelled and turned black, clenched tightly between their teeth. The music continued to play loudly through the tannoy speakers, as the crowd stood in silent reverence at this ghastly act that was now, thankfully, over.

Schlachter's face was now contorted to the point that he looked like a man who had just been sexually gratified. Josef tugged on Erich's sleeve, and with a look of absolute disgust declared, 'I've seen enough. Let's get the hell out of here.'

Schlachter looked puzzled as he watched the Wehrmacht officers make a quick departure, and ran after them shouting, 'Hey, where are you going? They haven't cut them down yet. You're not squeamish are you, Heiter? I thought you were an infantryman?'

'Yes, you got that right, Schlachter,' Erich snapped, 'which means that I don't kill unarmed civilians in cold blood.'

'Ah, they were collaborators and they deserved it,' Schlachter said. 'Welcome to Litzmannstadt, gentlemen, ha!'

The remainder of the journey was passed in frosty silence, which was only broken when the car stopped sharply outside commander Siltz's HQ, prompting Schlachter to announce, 'We have arrived, gentlemen. If you'll please folgen mich, I will take you to Herr Kommandant Siltz.'

Siltz's HQ was in an old, disused police station on the outer perimeter of Lodz. It looked more like a miniature fortress than a police station, with its large, solid grey-stoned outer walls and thick, heavy wooden and steel weather doors, complete with the obligatory full red swastika flags that hung crackling and fluttering freely in the cold wind. The Wehrmacht officers were left to wait in the narrow corridor outside Siltz's office while Schlachter made sure that his boss was ready to receive them. Suddenly, the door opened and Schlachter appeared with a silly grin on his face, telling them,

'Die Herr Kommandant will see you now, gentlemen.'

They filed smartly into a small dark room, which was filled with the acrid smell of stale cigars, and each of them gave a quick 'Heil Hitler!' before removing their peaked visor caps. They stood to attention in front of a large oak desk, behind which stood Siltz, arms folded and gazing out through the window, until eventually he turned to face his guests. Upon seeing Josef, the monocle dropped from his left eye and swung aimlessly across his chest, as he stood open-mouthed, much to the delight of Schlachter, who appeared to be revelling in his boss's obvious shock. The kommandant was a small man of lean build, and despite being completely bald, he looked a lot younger than his years. He had piercing black eyes and thick, bushy brown eyebrows, with an ash-white, no nonsense face. Recovering his composure, he waved his finger violently at Josef and demanded, 'What the hell is that?'

'Sir?' Schlachter replied, pretending to be oblivious.

'That man standing next to you,' Siltz said, still pointing, 'can't you see? Are you blind?'

'Oh, you mean Herr Leutnant Herzog, sir?' Schlachter asked.

'What?' Siltz spat. 'You mean to tell me that this man is a German officer?'

'That is correct, sir,' Schlachter replied.

'I don't believe you. It's a joke, right? You know, you almost had me fooled there for a minute, Schlachter,' Siltz laughed. 'Now, get him out of that uniform and back into whatever camp you found him in.'

'Herr Kommandant,' Josef interrupted, having heard quite enough, 'if I may speak, sir, I am indeed an officer of the Wehrmacht.'

'Nein,' Siltz said, 'nein, not possible. This joke has gone far enough now. Throw him out Schlachter, and that's an order!'

'I cannot, sir,' Schlachter said. 'With respect, I have to tell you that what he says is true.'

'Just give me a moment and let me sit down,' Siltz said, seating himself behind his desk. 'Herr Oberleutnant Heiter, is this true?'

'Yes, sir,' Erich said flatly. 'What Herr Oberleutnant Schlachter tells you is the truth.'

'Well, this is a new one on me,' Siltz shook his head. 'Negroes in die Wehrmacht. What's next, Chinese in der Luftwaffe? I mean, this is absurd, isn't it?'

'With respect, sir,' Josef said, 'it is you who is absurd! I am not the first, as mein vater served with distinction in der Kaiser's army in Namibia, back in nineteen-four.'

'Ja, ja, enough with the damned history lesson,' Siltz said. 'It would seem that I owe you an apology, Herzog. It's very rare that I make a mistake, but there it is, so let's press on, shall we? You've all been brought here because I need gut officers to help oversee the heavy influx of ethnic Germans entering the Lodz district. Now, I know that you have already been briefed on the situation, Heiter, so I want you and your men to set up operations in der Altes Rathaus immediately. Use whatever men you need to get the job done, but do it quickly, as there are already hundreds of people waiting to be rehoused. Schlachter here will be at your disposal, and will arrange for you to be provided with whatever you may need. Guten tag, gentlemen, and gut gluck.'

As they made their way out of Siltz's office, Josef could hear him quietly chuckling and repeating to himself, 'Ein schwarze in die Wehrmacht, eh?'

All four officers climbed back into the black limousine, and headed at speed towards the Altes Rathaus in Lodz. They raced through the narrow streets, dodging the slow-moving traffic, and within minutes had arrived at their destination, only to discover, to their horror, a long line of shabbily-dressed civilians. The queue began at the top of the steps in front of the Altes Rathaus, and ran down onto the street before disappearing around the side of the huge building. Men, women, children and the elderly, mostly from Ukraine, stood looking visibly agitated, with small scuffles breaking out as people tried to jump ahead. It was a scene of total chaos, which was compounded by the guards, who were simply stood around in small groups, talking and smoking. Exiting the limousine, the officers sprung into action immediately, ordering the guards to take control of the situation, and then pushing their way through the throng and up the sandstone steps that led to the main doors. The people surged forward to meet the officers, waving documents in their faces and complaining about how long they had been waiting. Heiter instructed Josef to pacify the baying mob, knowing that his unusual appearance would bemuse and hopefully calm them down. The plan worked beautifully, with a silence slowly descending upon the crowd as they looked in awe at this slim, young black lieutenant, who was knocking the white guardsmen into shape and ordering them about. He then turned to the crowd and promised them that they would all be seen to in turn, but only if they remained quiet and waited in an orderly fashion.

Once they were inside the grand building, Heiter began to organise what few staff were there, and quickly managed to form an efficient office, before telephoning Siltz and asking for Unterfeldwebel Penau, along with a few more reinforcements, to join them in order to stem the heavy flow of immigrants. Within three hours of their arrival, they had processed some four hundred applicants, ready for Josef to begin loading the ethnic Germans onto trucks and buses, ahead of them being transported to their new addresses.

Most of the houses that they visited looked as though the previous occupants had been emptied out very quickly and violently. Furniture was often left strewn across floors, along with broken glass, china and, on some occasions, blood! On one particularly harrowing journey, Josef had to deliver a family to a restaurant address, as they had been restaurateurs back in Ukraine. However, due to an administration error, the previous owners, who were Polish Jews, were still living and working on the premises. When Josef arrived with the new family, there was utter confusion. The ethnic Germans wanted to move in immediately, but the Polish family insisted on staying, and reminded Josef that they had legal rights, and had lived at the address for more than twenty-five years; they would not budge one inch. Unfortunately, both for them and for Josef, an attachment of Waffen SS were parked nearby and overheard the commotion. A tall, thin SS obersturmfuhrer with a pockmarked face appeared and quickly took charge of the situation, ordering his men into the building while Josef, who was now outranked, could only stand and watch in horror as the SS soldiers kicked and punched the restaurant owner to the ground, and then physically dragged him, his wife and their two children from the premises by their hair, screaming as they went. Once the Polish family were loaded onto the back of the SS transporter, the commanding officer then turned and apologised to the ethnic Germans, telling them that they could now enter the restaurant and officially welcoming them to Poland. He then walked towards Josef with an ugly smirk on his face and said, 'Ah, the famous Herzog.'

'You know me, sir?' Josef said, the surprise evident in his voice.

'Are you kidding?' the officer snorted. 'Everyone knows you. You're the joke of every mess room across Poland. You know, you really do look ridiculous in that uniform. When you get back, tell your commander that next time he should send a man, and not someone from the bush, if he wants to get the job done properly.'

They saluted each other, and Josef remained stony-faced as he reboarded the bus and continued with his passenger drop-offs. He eventually arrived back at the town hall feeling very weary, but was relieved to find that all the people waiting outside had now been processed.

'Here he is, Philip,' Erich announced, as Josef entered the make-shift office. 'I thought we would never see you again. How did it go?'

'It was absolute chaos,' Josef fell into a chair and wiped his brow. 'Please tell me that it won't be like this again tomorrow?'

'I shouldn't think so,' Erich said. 'There was a bit of a backlog when we first arrived, that's all. Anyway, let's get back to our quarters for some hot food and a drink, eh, fellas?'

'Sounds gut to me,' Philip said, collecting his sheets of paper and stuffing them into a tall grey filing cabinet. 'I've got writer's cramp from filling out those damned request forms.'

'Alright, boys,' Erich said to the rest of the men, 'I think we've done enough for today. Karl, fetch the car. We're leaving.'

After a hearty meal, the Wehrmacht officers decided to sit outside the old blockhouse with a few bottles of red wine and enjoy the brisk night air. Joined by Penau and Schlachter, they sat in a line with their backs against the crumbling outer wall, facing out onto the busy street. As they were discussing the day's events, Schlachter suddenly called out to a small, thin man who was stood across the street, dressed in a dark waistcoat and black cloth cap, which he quickly removed and nervously rolled up in his hands as he walked across to meet the officer. He had a drawn, pale face with shadow of a beard, and he was going slightly bald on top.

'Hey Maus, come here, you little worm,' Schlachter jeered, as the man timidly approached. 'Did you get me what I asked for?'

'Uh, I'm afraid not, Herr Oberleutnant,' Maus said, head bowed. 'Nineteen Thirty-Seven Moselle is getting harder to find here, sir.'

'You always disappoint me, Maus,' Schlachter shook his head. 'OK, what about the nylons?'

'Tomorrow, sir,' Maus promised, 'definitely.'

'You're useless, do you know that, you Polak? Get out of my sight, and don't fail me again!'

'Wait!' Josef called out, before Maus could leave. 'Can this man get hold of nylons, Schlachter?'

'So he says, but like all dumb Polaks, he's a damned liar, aren't you Maus?'

'No, sir, truly I can get you what you need,' Maus said pleadingly, 'but you'll have to give me a little more time.'

'Pull up a chair and sit with me, Maus,' Josef said, 'I may need a few things from you.'

'Don't encourage him, Herzog,' Schlachter said angrily. He's just a peasant!'

'I don't care what he is, as long as he can get me what I ask for. Come, Maus, and sit down next to me. I need chocolates and nylons. Now, can you get me these things or not?'

'Definitely, sir,' Maus nodded, 'but as I tried to explain to the Herr Oberleutnant, there is a war on, and things are difficult at the moment, but I will deliver, sir. I always do.'

'Very well,' Josef smiled. 'I'll leave it with you, but please don't let me down, will you, Maus?'

'No, sir,' Maus said. 'You can rely on me.'

'Well, gentlemen, I think I shall retire,' Josef said, as he watched

Maus scuttle off down the road. 'I'm feeling a little fatigued after the day's events.'

'Yes, we'll be joining you shortly,' Erich said, 'and don't worry, I'm sure tomorrow will be a lot easier than today. Guten nacht.'

As it turned out, Erich was very much mistaken, as the following day was no less overwhelming, with more and more ethnic Germans pouring in at an incredible rate, choking up the grand Altes Rathaus like bees around a hive. He pleaded with Siltz for more help, but his request was met with a cold, short response: 'No men available due to army land manoeuvres.'

Once again, Josef and Schlachter collected their passengers and crammed as many as they could into the bus that was parked outside, before heading for the inner-city districts. This was something that Josef had not been looking forward to, as they would be travelling near to the infamous Lodz ghetto that Erich had told him about during the long train journey across Poland. Up until now, Josef had managed to stay out of the inner-city, but this trip would deliver him into the jaws of hell itself.

CHAPTER TWENTY-THREE

Even though it was midmorning and very bright when they approached the northern section of the city, everything seemed to be growing dark around them. The tall, grey towering buildings and long, narrow streets did nothing to help, acting like natural sun blockers as they cast an eerie dark shadow as far as the eye could see. The bus pulled up sharply at the first address, which was a scruffy-looking house with peeling light-brown walls and tattered grey net curtains. As Josef leaped off the vehicle, he could smell a bitter acrid odour that filled the air and irritated his eyes and nostrils. Unbeknown to him at the time, it was actually coming from within the ghetto compound, where prisoners had been reduced to burning their own furniture for warmth, causing black plumes of thick, choking smoke to spiral upwards into the powder blue morning sky.

Wasting no time in reboarding the bus and heading for the second address, he could not believe his eyes when, as they neared the city centre, the bus stopped short of what could only be described as a giant chicken coop. For the first time since arriving in Lodz, he had a clear sight of the notorious ghetto, which was walled off by seven-foot-high meshed fencing and supported by thick wooden beams, cemented into the ground at six-feet intervals. Curled, rusted barbed wire ran across the top of the fencing, which stretched all the way across Krzyzow Street, and ended at a row of old houses that had very recently had their doors and windows bricked up. Local armed police patrolled the fence, marching back and forth with expressionless faces while the people inside the compound clung to the mesh, pressing their ghostly pale faces up against it and calling out for help. Their thin, grimy white fingers protruded through the rusty chicken wire and wriggled in frustration, making for a truly pathetic and depressing sight. Directly behind the prisoners lay broken furniture, bicycles and old mattresses. General domestic rubbish was piled high in the middle of the street, and old women with young children and dogs scavenged among the debris, hoping to happen across a morsel of food. Small groups of refugees huddled around open campfires and talked quietly with their hands in their pockets, all the while being watched closely by the Judischer Ordnungsdienst [1.], who wore black peaked visor caps and beige raincoats tied tightly at the waist by thick, black leather belts, and leered menacingly as they held their long wooden clubs at the ready.

Josef and Schlachter alighted from the bus and helped the ethnic Germans with their luggage, and then presented them with the keys to their new accommodation, along with maps of the local area. As Josef went to reboard, he noticed an old man in a tall black hat standing behind the fence. The man had long grey ringlets that dangled from beneath the brim of his hat, and a thick white beard that rested on his long black winter overcoat, which was buttoned all the way up, with the collar also turned up to keep out the cold morning air. On the left arm of his overcoat was a broad yellow band, and when Josef scanned deeper into the camp, he noticed other people wearing the same markings on their coats and jackets. The old man was beckoning to Josef with an open hand, but the young leutnant knew to ignore it and continued towards the bus. However, as he did so, he heard the old man call out to him in a weak and shaky voice, and against his better judgement, he decided to approach the fence.

'Please, sir,' the old man was calling out. 'Please, I must speak with you!'

'What is it, old man?' Josef asked cautiously.

'You must help us, sir. My wife and I are old and starving. We had to sell the last of our hidden jewellery to the outsiders, and now, with nothing left to trade, we will soon die if we don't get food!'

Outsiders was the name given to the ethnic Poles that were now Germanised and thus free to go wherever they pleased. They exploited the Jews by either purchasing their jewellery at less than half price, or by bartering inferior goods for minks and furs. Many of these outsiders were now growing fatter and wealthier at the expense of the Jews, who in contrast were becoming weaker and thinner by the day.

'What?' Josef said, disbelieving. 'You had to sell all your personal possessions to these people out here?'

'Yes, sir,' the old man said, 'and most of our furniture, too. As you can see, the situation here is only getting worse. They have squeezed more than one hundred and sixty thousand of us into a pocket less than two square miles, sir. Can you help us? You're not like the other officers, I can tell. You have kind eyes. I know you're a good man. You must help us!'

'I sympathise with you, but I'm only a junior officer, and there's really nothing I can do to help.'

'Hey Herzog!' Schlachter cried from the bus. 'Get away from that fence, and do it now!'

'Schlachter,' Josef called back, 'come here and listen to what this man has to say. He needs our help!'

'I said step away, damn it,' Schlachter roared, arms flailing wildly. 'That's an order!'

'But these people are starving, Schlachter!' Josef tried to explain.

'Right, that's it,' Schlachter screamed, bounding over to Josef and grabbing him by his right arm and violently swinging him to one side, while at the same time unclipping his black leather gun holster. He quickly drew his small Walther p38 service pistol and levelled it at the old man's face, cocking the weapon.

The old man looked deep into Josef's eyes and smiled. 'Never let them change you, my son,' he said calmly. 'Shalom.' [2.]

Josef sprung forward, crying out, 'Nicht schiesen!' [3.] but he was too late, as Schlachter squeezed the trigger and fired at point blank range, forcing him to close his eyes and recoil. He felt the familiar gush of warm liquid splashing across his face, and when he opened his eyes he caught sight of the old man falling backwards in slow motion, like a flickering series of snapshots. He hit the stone pavement hard, before finally settling in a crucifix position. There was a small, perfect hole in the middle of his forehead, and a thin red line trickled down the side of his right temple, forming a large crimson halo around his head. The old man's wife dropped to her knees beside him on the cold stone cobbles, wailing loudly as she clutched her black shawl with one hand and shook him by the shoulder with the other. His eyes and mouth remained wide open, frozen in shock, staring up towards the heavens. The people nearby paused for a brief moment, and then continued with what they were doing as if nothing had even happened.

Josef stood in silence, staring at Schlachter, before taking out a white handkerchief from his breast pocket and wiping the old man's blood from his face. Then, as Schlachter turned to walk away, Josef asked him the simple question, 'Why?'

'Why?' Schlachter scoffed. 'You ask me why? Ask yourself why, you stupid bastard. It was you who killed that old Jew, not me. I told you to stand clear, but no, you just had to play the Gut Samaritan, didn't you?'

'There's no justification for what you just did, Schlachter,' Josef fired back. 'You're a murderer, pure and simple.'

'Listen up, Herzog,' Schlachter said, low and menacing, 'because you're neu here, I won't take any further action, but be sure that if you ever disobey a direct order from me again, I'll make sure you swing. Now, get on that Gott damned bus before I change my mind!'

A dark vail of depression washed over Josef. This was not what he had signed up for in military college, and they had never prepared him for this. They had schooled him in military tactics, such as battle formations, jungle warfare and battle plans. He had read privately about the British Concentration camps in South Africa during the Boer War, and knew that between 1900 and 1902, the British had rounded up men, women and children and left them out on the plains in searing heat, in front of the hills where the Skiet Commando were positioned, hoping to force them out of their sniper hideouts, but that the strategy had failed. Whenever criticised over the treatment of the Jews, Hitler himself cited this example, claiming that it was the British who had given him the idea for setting up concentration camps in Poland.

1. Jewish police.
2. Peace be with you.

3. Don't shoot.

CHAPTER TWENTY-FOUR

As usual, Josef and Schlachter spent the drive to collect the others from the Altes Rathaus in complete silence. However, instead of being greeted by the lively banter that typically brightened their journeys back to the old Polish blockhouse, they were met by drained and weary faces, with Erich looking particularly worse for wear as he approached Josef with what appeared to be a scrunched up telegram in his hand.

'Erich, was ist los?' [1.] Josef asked, immediately concerned.

'I'm afraid I have some bad news, Josef,' Erich said. 'There's been a terrible accident back home in Berlin. Would you like to sit down?'

'No, thank you,' Josef stiffened, preparing for the worst. 'What's happened?'

'There's no easy way to say this,' Erich began, running a hand through his hair. 'Sein vater ist tot. [2.] Tut mir leid, [3.] Josef.'

'No, no, there must be some mistake,' Josef said, his voice cracking. 'We spoke by phone on Thursday evening, and he was in fine spirit. You must be mistaken, Erich.'

'I don't have the full details,' Erich explained, 'but I'm told that your vater was involved in a fight at his local beer keller in Wilmers-dorf last night. That's all I know.'

'This whole day has been like a very bad dream,' Josef said, shell-shocked at the news. 'I should return home at once to be with mein mutter. Gott knows what state she must be in.'

'That's all been taken care of. I've booked you a flight to Tem-pelhof Airport tomorrow morning. You will be met there by Herr Neumann. He's your onkel, I believe?'

'Yes, on mein mutter's side.'

'Now, unfortunately, I could only book you on an old Junkers ju fifty-two cargo plane. It was the best I could do on such short notice, I hope you understand.'

'That's alright, Erich. You've done more than enough, and I thank you.'

'Well, I'm sorry your day had to end like this. Let's get this place locked up and go home, eh?'

They returned to the old blockhouse and again decided to sit outside with their backs to the wall, facing out onto the street, as they had done the night before. Josef sat at the end of the row, keeping himself to himself while the others, respecting his privacy, spoke quietly among themselves. They had not been out there long when Maus appeared on the opposite side of the street, standing under a dim lamp with a small brown parcel tucked under his left arm. He spotted Josef sitting alone, and crossed over to speak with him.

'Herr Leutnant,' Maus hailed, 'I have what you asked for, sir.'

'What?' Josef replied, startled out of his daydreaming.

'I have the chocolates and nylons you asked for, sir,' Maus whis-pered.

'Oh yes, of course,' Josef recalled the order he had placed the previous night. 'Please sit down. You are a welcome distraction right now.'

'Would you like to check that everything is to your satisfaction, sir?'

'Yes,' Josef said without looking inside the bag, 'it all looks fine to me. How much do I owe you?'

'These items are on the house,' Maus smiled. 'I was sorry to hear about your loss, sir.'

'You really do know everything that goes on around here, don't you?'

'It's my job to know all things, sir. That's why they call me the Maus. I live in the walls, you know.'

'Thank you, Maus. I appreciate the gift, but tell me, what is your real name?'

'Nobody has ever asked me that before,' Maus laughed, 'but I will tell you, Herr Leutnant. My name is Stanislaw. Stanislaw Marzynek.'

'And my name is Josef Herzog. I'm very pleased to know you. Now, you say you know all that goes on here?'

'Yes, Herr Leutnant – I mean, Josef, that's correct. Why do you ask?'

'I was in the Lodz district earlier today, and it was the most ghastly experience I've ever had. What can you tell me about the place?'

'Well, Lodz is proving a difficult place to get information from,' Stanislaw dropped his voice to a low mumble. 'There's a lot of corruption there, and it goes right up to the highest level, which starts with Hans Beibow, the Getauoverwaltung. [4.] He runs the Lodz ghetto along with his superior, Gauleiter [5.] Arthur Greiser. Beibow keeps a tight rein on the people in his ghetto, and he won't allow them to be taken into forced labour camps for fear of losing the massive profits that he and Greiser make by using them in his textile and munitions factories. Beibow first strips them of their wealth by taking their diamonds, gold and money, and then puts them to work in his own private sweatshops once they have little else to offer. He splits the profits with Greiser, who in return looks the other way as the mountains of people grow to near bursting point.'

'So, that's why the old man gave me the figure of one hundred and sixty thousand in the ghetto.'

'I think it's probably a lot higher than that. These men live like kings and literarily have the power over who should live or die. Beibow treats his subjects brutally, and it is only when they are almost starved to death that they finally escape from his evil clutches and are sent into camps. The daily diet in the ghetto is poor, and that's if they're lucky enough to actually get fed. The Poles receive six hundred and sixty-nine calories per day, while the Jews get only one hundred and eighty-four. This is in stark contrast to the Germans, who, if you'll forgive me for saying, get as much as two thousand-six hundred and thirteen per day.'

'I'm on your side, Stanislaw, so don't be afraid to speak your mind with me. Please, continue. I want to know everything.'

'Very well, I will tell you what I know. A man called Mordechaj Rumkowski, who was elected Judenalteste, [3.] runs the ghetto, while the Germans control the meagre food deliveries that consist of pieces of mouldy bread, thin, weak-coloured soup and rotten vegetables. He and his associates are also responsible for the policing of the ghetto areas using the Judischer ordnungsdienst. They have their own prison set-up within the ghetto, and rule harshly under Rumkowski and his associates, who in turn organise the textile factories and the lists of people that they deem fit for deportation to other camps in Poland.'

'Hold on. What you're telling me is that Rumkowski is collaborating with us, the Germans, by policing and deporting his own people into forced labour camps. Is that what you're saying?'

'Well, it depends on your point of view. To you, he is a collaborator, but he sees himself as helping to save Jews by letting the weak and sick go into the camps, while protecting the fit and healthy by keeping them safe in the ghetto. Don't look so shocked, Josef. You must understand that people do the most extraordinary things in order to survive, and if the situation were reversed and it were you in that ghetto, how would you react?'

'I think I get your point, but it still sounds bizarre to me. How could they do that to their own?'

'Never forget that Greiser can make all these people disappear with a single stroke of the pen. He can cut a throat with a whisper. They're living on a knife's edge, believe me.'

'You know, you speak well for a peasant, Stanislaw. I'm beginning to see another side to you. Stanislaw the philosopher, perhaps, eh? I've heard a lot about this Greiser chap, but I know nothing of Beibow. What's his background? Where's he from?'

'I know very little about this man. All I can tell you is that he's a former coffee importer from Bremen in Germany, and that he's very cruel towards women. It's like I said before, information is getting harder to obtain from within the district.'

'Hmm, Lodz is proving to be a very complexed city indeed. I have enjoyed our talk tonight, Stanislaw. However, I must be up early tomorrow for the flight to Berlin, so if you will excuse me.'

'Yes, of course. We should talk again on your return, eh?'

'Yes, I would like that. I'll see you when I return.'

1. What's wrong?

2. Your father is dead.

3. I am sorry.

4. Ghetto administrator.

5. District leader.

6. Elder of the Jews.

CHAPTER TWENTY-FIVE

It was raining heavily when Josef boarded the old green Junkers ju 52, an ugly and rudimentary large, heavy plane that had a single prop engine on each of its long, broad wings, and a third mounted awkwardly onto its nose. Its fuselage was made of an unusual corrugated metal skin, and it had four large square passenger windows on either side, complete with incongruous thin white curtains that were neatly tied back. This particular aircraft was used more as a transporter than a passenger plane, and therefore the interior was rather Spartan. Fortunately, though, it would be no more than two hours before they were touching down at Tempelhof Airport in Berlin.

As promised, Herr Neumann was waiting for him in front of his old black Volkswagen car.

'Ah, Uncle Peter,' Josef said, approaching the vehicle, 'you've gone greyer since I last saw you.'

'Ja, and you've become a lot cheekier,' Peter laughed. 'How was your journey?'

'Oh, it was a bit bumpy in that old crate, but I'm here now and that's all that matters. How is Mutti bearing up?'

'Well, she's been under a lot of stress, naturally, but the doktor has put her on strong tranquillisers to help her sleep. Your Aunty Freda sits at her bedside and is looking after her. She's in gut hands, so there's no need to worry on that front. Now, get in and let's get going, eh?'

As they began the hour-long drive back to Wilmersdorf, the rain finally stopped, and Josef could not help but notice the heavy military presence on what he once knew to be quiet suburban streets. Long columns of brand-new panther tanks ambled noisily along the roadside, accompanied by canvas-covered army trucks. The people on the streets seemed strangely subdued, and some wore odd-looking yellow stars on the arms and lapels of their long, heavy winter overcoats.

'Is the army on manoeuvres here, Uncle Peter?'

'Nein,' Peter replied, 'they're the reinforcements, deployed to secure our borders. We are in early preparation for war, as you must already know, and our borders are stretched to the limit. They start from Groningen, in the Netherlands, and end at Luxembourg. A massive front to defend, eh?'

'Yes, it certainly is,' Josef agreed, before adding, 'Why is it that wherever I look, I keep seeing people wearing yellow badges?'

'Of course, you don't know, do you? There have been a lot of changes since you were last here. Those badges you refer to are the Star of David. All Jews are required by law to wear them, or face arrest.'

'Ah, so that's why the old man back in the Lodz ghetto wore a yellow armband. Is this what we have sunk to? The branding of our fellow human beings?'

'I'm afraid so. Thousands of Jews are being deported from

Grunewald Station in Wilmersdorf each week, and those who remain are not allowed to ride the streetcars and have had their bicycles confiscated. It all stems from Krystallnacht. You remember that, don't you?'

'Yes, that was when the Brown Shirts came and burned down two hundred and seventy-five synagogues, and destroyed all the Jewish shops and businesses. I'm glad to say I missed all of that when I was at kadett schule, but that was back in November nineteen thirty-eight. I thought it had all blown over now. Why did the Brown Shirts have to do such a thing, Uncle?'

'Well, they did it because of a seventeen-year-old Jewish boy, who went by the name Hershal Grunspan. He shot dead a German diplomat named Ernst von Roth, in Paris, if memory serves.'

'But what would have caused a young boy to do such a terrible thing like that?'

'Well, it's said that he did it because of the way his family had been treated by us, the Germans. Goebbels approached Hitler and asked for permission to release the storm troopers, to teach the Jews a lesson, and Hitler granted it. So, in the early hours they took their bloody revenge, and many people lost their lives.'

'I didn't know that.'

'Not many people do.

'Where are they deporting them to?'

'You mean you don't know?'

'I wouldn't be asking if I did, Uncle.'

Peter laughed and shook his head. 'You really have been living with your head up your arse, haven't you? They're being taken into forced labour camps in Poland, by train, and with little food or water, I might add.'

'So, that's why they're building so many camps there,' Josef muttered.

'What was that? I can't hear you with this damned window being open.'

'Oh, nothing. Just talking to myself.'

'You know, Josef, I find it hard to believe that you know nothing of the Jewish situation in Poland.'

'Well, you're right, of course, but the knowledge I have is only of the Polish Jews, and what I've witnessed happening to them is truly appalling. I've seen them shot and I've seen them hanged in the most horrific manner, and if I were to tell you of what I've heard from mein fellow officers, I fear you would not believe me.'

'Oh, but I would. Look, we will be arriving at your mutter's house shortly, so please don't mention any of this to her or mein frau, verstehen?'

'Of course not. I won't repeat anything of the sort.'

'Thank you, Josef. You're a gut lad,' Peter said warmly, as they pulled up outside the house. 'Come on, let's go in and see your mutter, eh?'

CHAPTER TWENTY-SIX

Josef got out of the car slowly and looked around. They had made good time; it was only 12.15pm. It had been too long since he'd last visited his parents, and everything around him appeared different than he remembered. He collected his luggage from the boot of the car and ascended the four thick stone steps that led him to a wide, four-panelled front door, which had been left slightly ajar in anticipation of his arrival. As he entered the hallway, everything seemed smaller, darker and narrower than before. He removed his heavy great coat and cap, hanging them carefully on the tall, thin coat stand that stood next to the old ticking grandfather clock at the end of the hall. He then walked into the living room, where he found his Aunt Freda sitting in a chair by the large front window, nervously clutching a cup of tea. On seeing him enter the room, she immediately sprung to her feet and ran towards him, arms spread wide, and hugged and kissed him fiercely as she fought back tears.

'Oh, Josef, Josef, you look so healthy,' Freda gushed. 'Stand back and let me get a better look at you. Would you look at him, Peter? He's so smart in that uniform. Your mutter will be so pleased to see you. Come, let's see if she's awake.'

'No, it's OK, Aunt Freda,' Josef said, 'best to not disturb her if she's asleep.'

'Oh, nonsense,' Freda said, 'all she ever does is talk about you. I'm sure she wouldn't be too pleased if she were to learn that you sat down here while she was upstairs wide awake, now, would she?'

'I suppose you have a point,' Josef laughed, 'but first allow me to peek into her room, just in case you're wrong, OK?'

All three of them crept up the stairs, pausing on the landing outside the bedroom door. Josef gently pushed the door open until he could see that his mother was indeed sitting up in bed, flicking through some old family albums. He opened the door fully and stepped inside, and his mother had to do a double take before she realised that it was really him. Dropping her reading glasses and tossing the album to one side, she screamed, 'Josef!' as she tried to leap up out of bed.

'Nein, Nein, Mutti,' Josef said, moving over to the bed and placing his hands gently on her shoulders, 'don't get up, you must rest.'

'Oh, I'm fine. Stop fussing and let me hold you,' she insisted, embracing him. 'Oh, mein baby. I've missed you so much.'

'I've missed you too, Mutti,' Josef smiled. 'Now, please get back into bed before you catch your death.'

'We'll leave you two to get reacquainted,' Freda said from the doorway. 'I'm sure you both have a lot to talk about. Maybe you would like a nice cup of tea, Josef?'

'Yes, Aunt Freda,' Josef replied, 'that would be nice.'

Freda took Peter by the arm and ushered him out of the bedroom, quietly closing the door behind them.

'Mutti, how are you feeling?' Josef asked.

'I'm OK,' his mother smiled, 'don't you worry about me.'

'How can you expect me not to worry? It's such a terrible thing that has happened.'

'Oh, believe me, it hasn't been easy. I've cried every night, but crying won't bring your vater back. He's gone, and we must accept that.'

'I can't accept it, and I can't be calm about it like you.'

'I know that this will be hard for you to hear, but life goes on, it really does. Now, tell me about this young lady that you always refer to in your letters?'

'Well, what can I say? She's tall, slim and gorgeous, and from a wealthy family. I don't know what she sees in me, I really don't.'

'Do you love her?'

'Yes, Mutti. I love her dearly.'

'Does she love you?'

'Yes, I believe that she does.'

'That's good, but it will take more than love to get you both through the bad times that are heading your way, Josef. Do you understand what I'm saying to you?'

'Yes, we both know the risks, but we want to be together.'

'It wasn't always easy for your vater and me, you know.'

'About mein vater – I have to know exactly what happened to him.'

'OK,' she said reluctantly, 'but what I'm about to tell you may upset you a little. Are you sure that you really want to hear this?'

'Mutti, if only you knew what these eyes have seen, you wouldn't ask that question. Please, tell me everything. I can take it.'

'Very well,' she let out a long exhale. 'Your vater left here on Friday night at the usual time, seven-thirty. He met with his drinking freunde in the local beer keller, and everything was as normal as could be until around nine-thirty, when a group of Brown Shirts from the Plattland [1.] showed up looking for trouble. Your vater provided an easy target for them, since he was the only black man in the room, and they started giving him a hard time, asking what he thought of the Max Schmeling-Joe Louis fight.'

'The Max Schmeling fight? That fight took place in June nineteen thirty-eight. It's old history.'

'Yes, but that doesn't matter to thugs just wanting to start a fight. Anyway, your vater simply replied that he was no sports critic, and this sent them into a frenzy. They started to smash beer glasses and upset tables, sending customers fleeing in panic. They then turned their attentions back onto your vater, calling him some really bad names and threatening to kill him, so his drinking freunde decided to join forces and throw them off the premises. That was the end of it, or so they thought.'

'So, you're telling me that mein vater was killed because of a two-year-old boxing match, which happened to result in a black man winning the heavyweight title of the world?'

'Yes, but I haven't finished yet. Your vater finished his drink at around ten-thirty and said guten nacht to his freunde, but on his way home he was ambushed by the same thugs from earlier. With nobody to help him, he was easily overpowered and dragged into a near by alley, where the bastards repeatedly kicked and beat him to death. When he hadn't arrived home by midnight, I became concerned and phoned the polizei. They found his body at around two AM, and asked if would I go down and identify him. It was awful, Josef. I barely recognised his face. He was always such a handsome chap, your vater, but the man lying on that cold slab looked nothing like the man I married.'

'OK, Mutti, don't upset yourself. Everything's going to be alright.'

'No, Josef, it's not. I fear for you in this damned country. I don't know this place anymore.'

'Please, calm yourself. This is a fine country mit gut, gut leute. [2.] Not everyone is bad. Now, try to get some rest, and I'll see you later.'

He gently pulled the bed covers back over his mother and started to creep out of the room, but as he got to the door he heard her whisper to him, 'Josef, for as long as you stay in Germany, and as long as we're at war, I will worry for you.'

He did not reply; he simply stood in the doorway and watched as his mother's head sunk into the soft white pillow. As she closed her eyes and fell asleep, he noticed that all the deep lines of experience on her face seemed to melt away. Suddenly, she was a young woman again, just as he remembered her from when he was a child. After a while, he turned and walked silently down the stairs and into the small kitchen, where his aunt and uncle were sat eating sandwiches at the table.

'Ah, Josef,' Freda smiled, 'I'll make you a nice cup of tea, eh?'

'Thank you, Aunty,' he replied feebly, 'that would be nice.'

'Here, come and have a bite to eat,' Peter suggested. 'You must be hungry by now, lad?'

'Uncle Peter, where are they keeping mein vater's body?' Josef asked.

'He's at the chapel of rest in Albrecht Strasse, but I would advise against you seeing him.'

'Yes, mein mutter has told me how bad he looks, but why is the body not at the polizei mortuary? Is that not customary during a murder investigation?'

'Yes, what you say is correct,' Peter replied nervously.

'Have they already caught the people responsible for his death?'

'They're not going to find anyone, Josef,' Peter said. 'There must be thousands of brown shirts walking the streets of Berlin. It would be like looking for a needle in a haystack, you must know that?'

'So, what you're telling me is that the polizei have closed the case, and are allowing these murderous thugs to roam the streets and probably kill again,' Josef said, his voice rising with anger. 'Is that what you're saying?'

'I'm sure that one day those responsible will get their comeuppance,' Peter said, sounding hopeful rather than expectant.

'And what of German justice, Uncle?'

'German justice!' Peter laughed bitterly. 'Haven't you heard? That's all been flushed down the toilet. Der Fuhrer has cleverly changed the laws, which means that the only justice you're going to get now is Nazi justice.'

'Peter!' Freda interrupted. 'Please keep your voice down. You know we have to be careful when talking about the neu government. They can shoot you for that, you know.'

'Well, I'm sorry, but the lad's right,' Peter said matter-of-factly. 'We've lost our legal system and replaced it with a gutter system!'

'Josef, you look tired,' Freda said, visibly agitated, 'why don't you go to bed? I've put clean sheets on for you.'

'OK, Aunty,' Josef said, feeling both tired and defeated. 'I'll see you in the morning.'

He took himself off to bed, but he could still hear the argument continuing downstairs. His aunt and uncle bickered late into the night, and as much as he didn't like to admit it, Freda was right; speaking ill of the present government was indeed an offence punishable by death. He lay down and closed his eyes, thinking back to the time before he'd left for military school, just over a year ago. It was a warm summer's day, and he'd had to shield his eyes from the strong afternoon sun as he stepped down onto the freshly mown lawn, glowing in his new cadet uniform. His mother, father, aunt and uncle were all sat around a large white garden table, shaded beneath a huge green and white striped parasol. His mother had looked radiant in a beautiful peach summer dress, which flowed over the wooden lattice garden chair, touching the short emerald grass below, as she leaned back and sipped from a tall glass of freshly made lemonade. Everyone around the table had been laughing and joking while listening to an instrumental version of Happy Days are Here Again, which crackled loudly through an old brass-horned, wind-up gramophone that was balanced precariously on a small wicker table next to his father.

He recalled how he had sheepishly made his way across the lawn towards the garden table, to seek his mother's approval of his new uniform, only to be speedily intercepted by his father, who yelled, 'Well, would you look at the cut of him, Gerda,' and chuckled loudly. 'He almost looks like a real soldat!'

'Oh, leave him alone,' his mother had remarked angrily. 'I think you look wonderful, Josef. Don't you agree, Freda?'

'Why yes,' Freda agreed, 'you look very manly, Josef, take no notice of your vater. What do you think, Peter?'

'Hmm, well you know my opinion on the military,' Peter said. 'I think he's making a big mistake.'

'Oh, come on, Uncle Peter,' Josef cut in, 'we all know why you don't like the military. It's because they failed you on your medical.'

'It looks like the lad's got you there, eh, Peter?' his father had laughed uproariously at that.

'Well, I should have known you would side with your own son, Vincent,' Peter laughed, taking a long drag of his stubby cigar and blowing out a thick white cloud of smoke, adding, 'but seriously, I'm very proud of you, and wish you all the success.'

'Thank you, Uncle Peter. That means a lot to me,' Josef grinned, shaking Peter by the hand.

'Look, there she goes again, weeping into her hanky,' his father said, putting an arm around his mother's shoulder.

'I know it's stupid, Vincent, but I can't help it,' his mother said, blowing her nose. 'He's leaving us, and Gott knows when we will see him again.'

'Calm yourself, Mutti,' Josef said, 'of course you'll see me again, and I promise to write you every week.'

'Well, you better,' his mother playfully warned, 'or I'll be on the next train to look for you, ha!'

'Josef,' his mother said, shaking him gently, 'Josef, wake up. There's a telephone call for you.'

'What?' Josef answered groggily. 'What time is it, Mutti?'

'It's nine AM, sleepy head. Now, hurry up and take the call.'

He scrambled out of bed, scratching his head with one hand and fumbling for his trousers with the other, and then wobbled down the steep narrow staircase into the living room. 'Hello?' he said, picking up the heavy black telephone receiver from its place on a corner table.

'Josef, is that you?' came a familiar voice.

'Yes, who's this? Is that you, Monika?'

'No, it's Lili Marleen,' she giggled. 'Of course it's me, silly, what's wrong with you? Have you only just got out of bed or something?'

'No, no,' he coughed, 'how did you know I was here?'

'Well, Oberleutnant Heiter had to notify Hauptmann Weise of your departure, and Weise told mein vater, who in turn told me. Get the picture?'

'Yes, I do now. Anyway, how are you, Monika?'

'Shouldn't I be asking you that question? I'm sorry to hear about your vater. How is your mutter handling it?'

'Oh, she's a tough old lady, but I think this has damaged her somewhat. She puts on a brave face and tells everyone not to fuss over her, but I fear that on the day of the funeral she will break-down.'

'I'm sure she will be alright now that she has you at her side. I wish I could be there with you, I miss you so much.'

'And I miss you. I will be flying back to Poland once the funeral is over. There's no reason for me to stay any longer than that. Mein mutter is in gut hands with Uncle Peter and Aunt Freda.'

'I can't wait to see you again. Oh, and I got the chocolates and stockings you sent me. How did you ever get hold of them? They're like gold dust around here.'

'Ah, let's just say that I have some freunde in high places.'

'Listen, I have to go now, mein liebling, because Stab Nurse Encke's on the prowl, but I'll speak to you soon. Love you – auf wiedersehen.'

Monika carefully placed the receiver down onto the telephone and peered through a small glass window, waiting for her friend Irma to give the all clear. She then slipped out into the corridor, and they both ran off giggling like naughty schoolgirls until, as they turned the next corner, they were suddenly stopped dead in their tracks by a familiar figure.

'Ah, Fraulein Hastler, we meet again,' the man said. 'And who is this beautiful young lady with you?'

'Oh, h-hello Herr Sturmbannfuhrer,' Monika stammered, caught off-guard. 'Uh, this is mein beste freund, Irma Lang.'

'Well, I'm very pleased to meet you, Fraulein Lang,'

'Likewise, Herr Sturmbannfuhrer,' Irma blushed.

'Oh, please, call me Ernst,' he smiled.

'May I ask why you are here, Herr Sturmbannfuhrer?' Monika asked suspiciously.

'Well, you'll laugh when I tell you this, Fraulein Hastler,' he made a show of looking embarrassed, 'but I've come to ask if you would reconsider having dinner with me?'

'Oh, don't be so formal, Ernst,' Irma chimed in. 'Please, call her Monika.'

'Do you mind?' Monika said under her breath, while nudging her friend in the ribs.

'Ah, Monika, what a pretty name,' he said, smiling sickly. 'Well, Monika, are you free, say, tomorrow evening, perhaps?'

'No, I'm not, Herr Sturmbannfuhrer,' she replied curtly. 'Now, if you'll excuse us, we really must be going.'

'Oh, please don't rush off,' he begged. 'I'm sure I can change your mind.'

'I think not, Herr Sturmbannfuhrer,' she said, becoming exasperated. 'As I've told you before, I'm already in a relationship.'

'Ah, but a little bird tells me that your young schwarz leutnant is in Berlin at this very moment,' he said. 'Es das recht?'

'Come along, Irma,' Monika said, 'before we're late for our shift. Guten tag, Herr Sturmbannfuhrer.' She hooked her friend's arm and hurriedly pulled her along the wide, busy corridor, hissing at her not to look back.

'Hey, he's really gorgeous,' Irma grinned. 'If you don't want him, I'll have him.'

'Absolutely not!' Monika said, horrified. 'He's SS, and he gives me the creeps. Promise me that you'll stay clear of him.'

'Why should I? You've already got a mann freund.'

'Well, do what you want, but don't say I didn't warn you. I wonder how he knew so much about Josef?'

'I don't know, but I'll soon find out with a bit of pillow talk, if you catch my drift,' Irma laughed.

'Irma, you are incorrigible, do you know that?'

1. An SA district.
2. Good people.

CHAPTER TWENTY-SEVEN

'Freda, could you answer the front door for me please?' Josef heard his mother shout. 'I'm just finishing breakfast.'

'Yes, of course, Gerda,' Freda replied, before appearing in the living room a few moments later. 'Josef, there's someone here to see you.'

'Who is it, Aunty?' Josef asked, not expecting any visitors.

'It's me, Werner,' he heard a yell from outside, 'you dumb ox!'

Josef grinned. Werner Adejo was an old school friend of his. They had bonded quickly in their early years, due to them being the only two black children in the neighbourhood. Werner was a year older than Josef and, with both of his parents being of African origin, was much darker-skinned. They had grown up together in Wilmersdorf, and were only separated because Josef decided to enter the military academy, much to the dismay of his friend, who worried that he would never be fully accepted by his white colleagues.

'Werner!' Josef called out, 'Come in, mann!'

'Why, you've lost some weight,' Werner said by way of greeting. 'You're like a bean pole.'

'Oh, shut up and sit down,' Josef laughed, indicating a space on the couch. 'Here, have some tea. Gott, how long has it been?'

'Well, it must be the best part of a year since you disappeared into that militarisch schule,' Werner guessed, taking a seat. 'Listen, I'm sorry to hear of your loss. Your vater was a gut man, you know.'

'Yes, he was,' Josef said, bowing his head slightly. 'We bury him tomorrow at three PM. Will you be attending, Werner?'

'I'm afraid not. You know how much funerals frighten me. You know what I'm like.'

'I know, but I had to ask. Let's change the subject, shall we? You look great. What's happening with Willy and the rest of the gang?'

'They're all gone.'

'What do you mean, gone?'

'You know, gone into camps.'

'Militarisch camps?'

'No, concentration camps.'

'No, no, that's not possible, Gott damn it!'

'Josef, your breakfast is ready,' his mother said, popping her head around the door frame. 'Oh, hello Werner,' she smiled, 'it's nice to see you again.'

'It's nice to see you, too, Frau Herzog.'

'You should visit more often, Werner,' she said. 'Just because Josef's not here that often, doesn't mean-'

'Yes, yes, alright Mutti,' Josef cut her off. 'Put my breakfast in the oven please. I'll have it later.'

'Oh, right then,' she said meekly. 'Don't be a stranger, Werner. Come around anytime.'

'Yes, Frau Herzog,' Werner nodded, 'I promise to do just that.'

'Carry on with what you were saying, Werner,' Josef said, once his mother was out of the room.

'Don't you think that you were a little rude to your mutter?' Werner said reproachfully. 'She was only telling you that your breakfast was ready.'

'You're right as always, Werner,' Josef sighed. 'I will apologise to her later, I swear. Now, please continue with what you were saying.'

'OK, well, Willy, Richard, Mark and Larry have all disappeared. The SS came and took them two weeks ago. They're being held at Heigmer, just outside Dusseldorf. I'm the only black Berliner left it seems, apart from you that is.'

'How come they never got you?'

'I was lucky, I guess. Maybe it's because I work at the film studios. They use me for Nazi propaganda films. There's lots of other black people there, too, mostly from the Rhineland.'

'What do you mean by propaganda films?'

'Well, let's just say, for example, that they want to shoot a scene in Africa. All they have to do is recreate it at the Universal Films Aktien Gesellschaft [1.] here in Templehof, by using us, the Afro-Germans, as frightened natives fleeing from the mighty Wehrmacht or Luftwaffe. They make the audience believe that what they have just seen was actually filmed in Afrika, when in reality, it was filmed just around the corner from them. It's so ridiculous.'

'You know, Werner, every time I think I've heard it all, something else crops up. This is quite remarkable. While you're a film extra in Berlin, you're perfectly safe, is that what you're saying?'

'Well, to coin a phrase, you've got the picture, ha! But seriously, yes, when we're in the studios we're safe, but it's not unusual for one or two of us to be picked up on the streets by the Gestapo [2.] after filming, and then taken to their head quarters, never to be seen again.'

'You mentioned that there are other black people at the studio who have come from the Rhineland. What stories do they have to tell, because I know for a fact that there must be at least twenty thousand people of mixed race living there, as a result of the French-African troops that were stationed there during the Great War.'

'Yes, you're right. I'm told from the people at the studio that many of their freunde and family have been taken away and put into camps in places like Neuengamme, near Hamburger, or Stuttdorf. Some have even been taken as far as Bourg Leopold, a former prison in Belgium. A few have managed to escape imprisonment by joining the local circuses, or taking part in small travelling Afrika side shows.'

'This all sounds pretty grim, Werner. I've heard some talk of the Fuhrer wanting to create a master race. Have you heard anything about this?'

'All I can tell you is that they're pulling in anyone who doesn't fit the Nazi profile, whether it's Jews, gypsys, the disabled or even the mentally ill. I tell you, you're better off staying where you are. It's getting more dangerous by the minute out there.' Werner stood and straightened his clothes. 'Well, I've got to run. I'm due on the film set. You know how it is when you're a big movie star.'

'Oh, but of course,' Josef grinned. 'Look after yourself, Werner, and remember, there's no such thing as a coward.'

The funeral of Vincent Herzog was held at Wilmersdorf Cemetery. It was a brief and quiet affair, attended by only a few people: his son Josef, his wife Gerda, his sister-in-law, Freda, and her husband Peter, as well as two of his closest drinking freunde. It had started to rain heavily by the time the two burly gravediggers, with only cloth caps and waistcoats to protect them from the bad weather, rolled up their shirtsleeves and gripped the ropes with their cold, dirty hands.

Both men struggled as they awkwardly lowered the bulky brown coffin into the sodden ground, causing great concern to the family, who looked on in horror as the casket began to rock from side to side, scraping along the narrow, wet clay walls of the fresh grave. Eventually, and after a lot of tugging and heaving, it came to rest at the bottom with a bassy thud.

The women began to whimper and the men quietly wiped their eyes with crisp, white folded handkerchiefs, as a priest stood at the foot of the grave and began reciting from a small brown leather-backed bible, all the while desperately trying to shield the pages from the rain. Josef placed a comforting arm around his mother's shoulder, as she released a small clump of damp earth through her thin, white shaking fingers, allowing the dirt to fall and hit the long wooden box below with a dull thump. The priest stood for a few moments with his head lowered in silent prayer, while the two gravediggers waited with their hands clasped tightly around their shovels, desperate to crack on with the job. Josef watched in fascination as the rain slowly trickled down Father Mant's forehead and then ran to the end of his nose, where it would hang in a large dewdrop before falling onto the open pages of his bible. Finally, Mant raised his head and slammed the book shut, before turned swiftly on his heels and walking away without uttering another word.

At the conclusion of the brief ceremony, Josef made his way to Tempelhof Airport, where he again climbed the metal stairway that led up to the old Junkers ju 52. He paused at the top of the small platform and waved goodbye to his mother, aunt and uncle, and then climbed aboard the aircraft and found himself a window seat, from which he gazed out as the ground rapidly disappeared from underneath him. Easing himself back into his seat, he reflected on all that had happened during his brief stay in Wilmersdorf. He worried for his mother, although he knew that she was safe with his aunt and uncle. He also grieved for his father, who he already missed dearly, but at the forefront of his mind was the fact that within a few short hours, he would be back in the unpredictable cauldron that was the city of Lodz.

1. Public Limited Company.
2. Secret state police.

CHAPTER TWENTY-EIGHT

'Well, look what the cat's dragged in,' Philip shouted, as he walked towards the mess hall table with a stein of frothy beer in his hand. He leaned forward and handed the over-sized drink to Josef, saying, 'Herzlich willkommen, Herr Leutnant. Why don't you grab a seat?'

'Thank you,' Josef said, grinning. 'It's sure gut to see you guys again.'

'So, tell us, what was it like to be back in die Heimat?' Erich asked, pulling up an extra chair.

'Well, naturally it was gut to be back home,' Josef said, 'but I wish it could have been under different circumstances.'

'Yes, yes, of course,' Erich nodded solemnly. 'How is your mutter holding up?'

'It's hard to say really,' Josef admitted. 'She shows very little emotion when she's around me, but I know she's in gut hands and is being looked after. So, tell me, what's been happening in my absence, fellas?'

'Well, almost all the ethnic Germans have been resettled into their new homes,' Erich said, 'which means that we have at least three days off!'

'Fantastisch!' Josef said, breathing a sigh of relief. 'Das ist wunderbar. Anything else?'

'Yes,' Philip interrupted, 'but you're never going to believe it when I tell you. Uri has found himself a fraulein!'

'What?!' Josef spluttered into his beer. 'Uri has a woman?'

'Don't look so shocked,' Erich said. 'We're told that she looks like an old mattress!'

'Oh, I'm sure she can't be that bad,' Josef said diplomatically. 'Who is she, do we know her?'

'No, none of us know her,' Philip said. 'All we know is that her name is Emmy, and according to Viktor's letter, she resembles a Russian miner, ha!'

'Never mind,' Josef chuckled, 'I'm still glad for him. It's about time the big ugly brute found someone. It might calm him down a little. So, any other news?'

'Yes, bad news, I'm afraid,' Erich replied.

'Oh Gott, what is it?' Josef moaned. 'I don't think I can handle anymore bad news right now.'

'Well, it's not that bad,' Erich said. 'We're flying out to Poznan in the next few days.'

'Poznan!' Josef felt suddenly exalted. 'Why, that's where Monika is stationed, at the hospital. I presume I'll be going, too?'

'Oh yes, but there's more bad news still,' Erich lamented. 'We're flying in that old Junkers ju fifty-two that you've just returned on.'

'Hey, that's not a problem, as long as I get to see Monika.'

'Ah, more bad news, I'm afraid.' Erich shook his head. 'Our orders are to take a special consignment to the Warthegau at Gauleiter Greiser's palace, and then head straight back.'

'Oh, come on,' Josef said pleadingly, 'surely you can tweak things a little, eh?'

'There's no way,' Erich said apologetically. 'The pilot has his orders, I'm sorry.'

'Never mind,' Josef said, 'it was worth a try, eh? So, what's this special consignment all about, then?'

'You're not going to like this one,' Erich muttered, getting up and walking away from the table. 'You explain it to him, Philip.'

'Oh, thanks very much,' Philip called after him sarcastically.

'Hey, come on,' Josef said, 'just tell me what's going on.'

'It's like this,' Philip began, 'and don't explode when I tell you, OK?'

'Christus!' Josef exclaimed. 'Will you get to it, man?'

'The consignment consists of gold bullion, and it's our job to deliver it to Poznan.'

'And is that it?'

'That's it.'

Josef shook his head and laughed. 'You know, you had me worried there for a minute. I thought this might be something quite awful. You two should get involved in amateur dramatics, because you're both wasted here.'

'I think you'll find that Philip has left out the most important part,' Erich said, rejoining them with a round of fresh drinks.

'So, I was correct the first time, eh?' Josef said. 'OK, let me have it right between the eyes.'

'It's Jewish gold,' Erich said quietly.

'No way!' Josef slammed his stein down onto the table. 'No way – there is no way I'm having anything to do with this, Gott damn it!'

'You see, I told you he'd blow a gasket,' Philip said.

'Shut up,' Erich snapped, before turning to Josef. 'Look, I wish there was a way out of this, but orders are orders, and ours are that four officers must escort the consignment, and that means you, me, Philip and Schlachter.'

'Oh, not the Cap!' Josef cried. 'Why must he go on this mission? The man's a murderer, and I'll have nothing to do with him or your Jewish gold!'

'A murderer?' Erich said in a hushed voice. 'What are you talking about?'

'Look, I know I should have told you this earlier, but on our first visit to the Lodz ghetto, the Cap shot an old Jew dead, and for no gut reason. The old man had done nothing except dare to ask for our help, and now you expect me to work with that maniac again? Well, I'm sorry, but no.'

'I understand how you feel, and what you have said disgusts me as much as it does you, but we have no choice,' Erich said. 'Siltz wants the Cap on this mission, probably to keep an eye on us, so please don't make me order you to do this.'

'I will not do it, Erich, I'm sorry.'

'You're giving me no choice but to make it an order,' Erich replied.

'I will not go on this assignment, and that's final,' Josef stated firmly.

'Very well,' Erich shook his head sadly. 'Herr Leutnant Grinburger, fetch Unterfeldwebel Penau, and then place Herr Leutnant Herzog under arrest.'

'Erich, no,' Philip protested.

'Just do it!'

'For Gott sake, Josef, just say Yes, man!' Philip begged.

'No,' Josef remained steadfast, 'I will not do it.'

'If you allow yourself to be arrested for disobeying an order, you'll lose everything you've ever worked for,' Philip said. 'Not only your rank, but you will also be stripped of your Iron Cross.'

'Mein nomination for die Iron Cross has been turned down,' Josef replied. How can you lose what you never had?'

'You should listen to what Philip says,' Erich grunted.

Josef leaned forward and placed his hands on his head. He knew that Philip was right; everything he had strived for would be gone in one moment if he didn't agree, and with a low growl he said, 'OK, I accept.'

'Right then, it's settled,' Erich said, getting to his feet and pulling down on his tunic. 'I'll see you gentlemen in the morning. Guten nacht.'

'Phew,' Philip let out a sigh of relief, as Erich exited the mess hall, 'you really sail your ship close to the wind sometimes.'

'Erich would never have had me arrested,' Josef said, taking a sip of his beer, 'would he?'

'Guten nacht, Josef,' Philip said, draining his glass and fastening his coat.

'Yes, guten nacht. Oh, and thanks. I owe you one.'

Erich had decided that he and his men should take full advantage of the quiet spell which followed the last of the ethnic Germans being safely accommodated, having estimated that they would have at least three full working days before the next consignment of tatty human cargo landed on the steps of the old town hall. It was indeed a generous and well-deserved break, but what would they do with this free time? Where could they even go in this Gott-forsaken district?

The first two day were fun, as the officers spent most of their time lounging around the mess hall, drinking beer and playing cards with Penau and his men, but by the third day it had become quite boring. The old blockhouse was beginning to feel more and more like an open prison, and so Josef decided that enough was enough, and strongly recommended that they should break out before they all went mad. Erich agreed, but ultimately opted to use his remaining free time to deal with the stack of paperwork that was building on his desk, while Philip felt that it was far too dangerous to go outside, adding that there were still partisans out there that were loyal to Poland, and who would kill any German on sight if given the chance. Josef ignored Philip's warning, however, and went out for a walk by himself.

It was a dry and bright Tuesday afternoon, and there were many people out and about visiting the shops, bars and restaurants. Josef felt perfectly safe as he explored the area at a relaxed pace, strolling with his hands in his pockets along Wozna Street and browsing the shop windows like any other tourist, much to the surprise of the locals, who stopped and stared in amazement having never seen a black man before, and especially not one wearing a German uniform.

The attention caused Josef to grin like a naughty boy, as he lapped it all up. He eventually reached a crossroads and stopped on the corner, unsure which way to turn. He first looked to his left, down Slawska Street, and then to his right, which was Szkolna Street. He watched as a large brown and beige tram, crowded with passengers, crawled to a halt and let off a handful of commuters, before continuing on its journey. As it passed him, its long black iron mast fizzed and crackled against the overhead power cables. He decided to carry on straight ahead along Wozna, where he eventually came to a tailor's shop with some finely cut suits lined up in the front window. One particular suit, with a dark, striped double-breasted jacket, caught his eye, so he stopped to look. As he admired the item, he pulled out a pack of cigarettes from his top pocket and placed one in his mouth. Striking a match, he leaned forward and cupped his hands to light it when, suddenly, a single gunshot rang out, prompting him to stand erect. He glanced around quickly, but whoever was responsible had already ran off. A crowd of people on the opposite side of the street all stood pointing in the same general direction, presumably after the fleeing assassin.

Josef turned back to look at the tailor's shop, and he noticed a small round bullet hole in the front window, just about where his head had been before he bent to light his cigarette. The reality of the near miss sunk in fast, and he immediately pivoted on his heels and made for the old blockhouse.

'Back so soon?' Philip remarked, as Josef entered the mess hall.

'Yes,' Josef shrugged carelessly, 'there wasn't much to see.'

'Well, never mind,' Philip smiled, 'at least you got some air. Hey, would you like to join me in a game of darts?'

'Sure, why not.'

'Here, take these,' Philip handed him the darts. 'You can go first, if you like.'

'Sure, why not,' Josef shrugged again. With trembling hands, he let loose all three darts in quick succession, completely missing the board each time, and leaving the little arrows firmly embedded into the old plaster wall.'

'Are you alright, alter junger?'

'Yes, of course I'm alright, why shouldn't I be?'

'Well, it's just – and please don't take this the wrong way – you look white!'

'That's very funny. I'm going to bed. I feel tired.'

'Hey, I did say don't take it the wrong way!' Philip called after Josef, but he was already storming out of the mess hall.

Josef knew that he wasn't really annoyed with his friend, and that he was actually angry with himself. Philip had been right; it was indeed foolhardy to venture out into the Lodz district alone. He now understood that he would have to be very careful in future, and he also realised that there was a lot more resentment and hatred towards the Germans than he had anticipated. Once back in his room, he splashed his face with cold water from the old enamel basin beneath the wall mirror, and then stood staring deep into his cracked reflection, thinking long and hard about how lucky he had been. He decided that maybe it would be better to spend the last day of his leave safely hidden behind the thick walls of the block-house after all, and that perhaps he, too, should use this time to catch up on paperwork before the following morning's long journey to the Warthegau.

CHAPTER TWENTY-NINE

A ten-wheeled green canvas truck screeched to a halt and dropped its tailgate with a bang, as six SS sonderkommandos [1.] in full battle dress jumped down onto the wet road and line up, as if ready for parade inspection. Erich stepped forward to address the men, his breath visible in the cold, damp morning air, while Josef, Philip and Eckard Schlachter stood silently to attention behind him. Before anyone could speak, however, the Maus suddenly appeared, seemingly out of nowhere.

'Ah, Maus, glad to see you could make it,' Erich said, greeting the new arrival. 'Line up with Schlachter and the others while I address the men,' he turned to the six sonderkommandos. 'Now manner, alles klar?'

'Jawohl, Herr Oberleutnant,' they muttered in unison.

'OK, let's get going,' Erich nodded. 'Josef, Philip and Maus, in the back of the truck. Schlachter, you're up front with me. Let's move it.'

Josef managed to squeeze himself in between two burly sonder-kommandos, who both greeted him with snarls, while Philip sat opposite, next to the Maus, who was carrying a small green canvas bag on his lap. Placed awkwardly in the middle of the floor was a large heavy wooden casket, sealed by three huge grey padlocks. The Maus sat fidgeting nervously, his eyes firmly fixed on the long box, looking as if he were waiting for something to suddenly jump out and bite him. Josef also could not help but feel the tension that was starting to build in the back of the cramped truck, as it weaved its way along the bomb-cratered roads toward the airfield. He looked over to Philip, who was sat with his hands on his lap, twiddling his thumbs, before giving Josef a half-smile and turning his head and gazing off into the distance. Josef could only sit and wonder how much gold was actually in that box, but the real nagging question was how did the Maus fit into all of this? The truck began to slow down and then stopped, and within seconds, Erich and Schlacter had unfastened the tailgate and let it fall with a clunk.

'OK,' Erich called for attention, 'Josef and Philip, I want you two to supervise the cargo as it's loaded onto the plane. Maus, you come with me.'

As per Erich's instructions, Josef and Philip organised the six sonderkommandos and then helped them unload the casket from the back of the truck. The sonderkommandos looked more like pall-bearers as they heaved the bulky cargo up onto their broad shoulders and staggered towards the Junkers ju 52 cargo bay, where Erich, Schlachter and the Maus were stood waiting.

'Steady, lads,' Erich chirped, doing his best to avoid getting his hands dirty. 'That's it, come on.'

'Thanks for your help, Erich!' Philip growled.

'Don't mention it,' Erich grinned, 'I'm always glad to assist. OK, everybody who is flying, get on the plane, and the rest are dismissed. Thanks for your help, but we can take it from here.'

With their mission completed, the sonderkommando unit saluted Erich and returned to the truck.

Once the plane was safely in the air, Josef decided to ask why the Maus had been invited to travel as part of the escort team to Poznan.

'Well, it's quite simple really,' Erich answered. 'He's the key.'

'I don't understand,' Josef said. 'What do you mean, the key?'

'He is the key to those three padlocks on the casket.'

'I still don't understand. Could you be a bit more specific?'

'It's like this. We don't have the expertise to crack open that crate, but the Maus does. Get the picture?'

'Mein Gott, you're going to rob the gold, aren't you?'

'Not all of it – just some. Greiser can't possibly know how much is really in there now, can he?'

'If you believe that, Erich, you're an even bigger fool than you look. Of course, he knows exactly how much is in there. He's a German for Gott sake, remember? World famous for being meticulous!'

'Hey, he may have a point,' Philip suggested.

'Be quiet,' Erich snapped. 'Can't you see that he's just trying to scare you?'

'Yes, and he's doing a damned gut job of it, too!' Philip replied. 'They'll shoot us all if this goes wrong. Maybe we should abort while we still can?'

'Nein!' Erich insisted. 'Nein, we stick to the plan.'

'Erich, please listen to me,' Josef pleaded. 'No gut can come of this. Just because Greiser's a thief and a cut-throat doesn't mean that we have to be the same.'

'So, you're telling me that when the war is over and you're made redundant by the army, with no future and no prospect of ever getting a job, you'll simply vanish into the ether?' Erich challenged.

'Well, maybe you want to live on your knees for the rest of your life, but not me. We go ahead as planed.'

'You really have been busy in my absence, haven't you?' Josef said. 'You've got it all figured out and that's fine, but don't involve me, OK?'

'You were involved the moment you boarded the plane,' Erich said. 'You're in it right up to your neck, whether you like it or not!'

'So, you're blackmailing me,' Josef shook his head. 'Is this what it's come to?

'Look, Josef, consider this,' Erich said, changing tack. 'You have a recently widowed mutter. How are you going to provide for her? And worse still, if you were to marry Monika, how would you keep her in the manner that she's accustomed to? You'll find that love fades quickly when you're stood in a long bread line, but you have it your way, noble warrior. I'll respect your high moral standards.'

By not joining in, am I breaking with the traditions of the War Council? Josef wondered. And, more importantly, is this the right way to treat some of the few people that have accepted and supported me since my arrival at D Company? There were more questions than answers. What was happening was morally wrong, he knew, but either way, he had to make a decision. He sat and stared for a long time at the bulky box, which was lying in the next compartment. He looked into each of his comrade's faces, starting with Stanizlaw. The gold would indeed help mein poor Polish freund – his need is far greater than all of ours. But then there's that Nazi pig Schlachter. Why should he profit from other people's misery? He looked over at Philip. He's a gut man at heart, and gut people should be rewarded, I guess. Then there was Erich. Could he be right in what he says? Monika is from a wealthy family, and could I really support her on the meagre wage that I get from the army? He was swimming in dangerous water, he knew, rationalising and legitimising his temptation. 'Fine,' he announced loudly, 'I'll do it, but I don't want any of the loot. You can give mein share to the rest of the war council.'

'What?' Erich said, shocked.

'I'll do it, damn you,' Josef repeated. 'Count me in.'

'Gut man,' Erich cheered, 'I knew I could count on you. You're truly a member of the War Council, and we never let each other down. Zusammen immer, eh?'

'Yes,' Josef muttered, 'together always.'

'In the spirit of the War Council,' Erich beamed, 'I grant you two days' leave, so that you can stay in Poznan with Monika. How does that sound?'

'If you think I'm going to say thank you, forget it.'

'Welcome back, Josef,' Philip said, shaking him by the hand and grinning from ear to ear. 'You really had me going there for a minute, you dumb bastard.'

'Well, you know me,' Josef replied, '"In for a mark, in for a pfennig." So, what's the plan?'

'OK,' Erich began, 'firstly, Schlachter will go to the head of the plane and have a chat with Gunther and his co-pilot, keeping them occupied while our gut freund the Maus here picks the locks on that casket. Once he has cracked it open, we'll fill four kitbags kindly provided by Philip, and lay them next to our seats as though they were just ordinary flight luggage. The plane lands, we put our luggage into the transporter along with the casket, which is now somewhat lighter than before, and deliver the cargo to Greiser's Palace. Then, we make a graceful retreat with our kitbags, get back onto the plane and head for Lodz. Once there, we count our loot and decide upon the best way to bury it in our accounts. How does that sound to you?'

'It all sounds faultless, it really does,' Josef said. 'However, how can you be sure that Greiser has no idea of exactly what is in the casket?'

'When you're stealing the crown jewels, you don't stop to take an inventory,' Erich replied. 'Trust me, Greiser has no idea. Now, don't worry yourself any further. Everything's going to work out just fine, OK?'

'I hope you're right,' Josef said, still not convinced, 'because I've witnessed some of our executions, and I don't fancy appearing in one of them. Catch my drift?'

'Ja, ja, I hear you,' Erich waved away his concerns. 'Right, Schlachter, get to the front of the plane and distract the pilots. Maus, into the cargo bay with me. Philip, get the kit bags ready.'

'What about me,' Josef said, 'what do I do?'

'Just sit there and pray that the Maus can pull this off.'

'Oh man,' Josef felt his palms begin to sweat, 'I've got a bad feeling about this.'

'Stay in your seats until the Cap enters the cockpit,' Erich said, craning his neck to see to the front.

'Hey Gunther,' they heard Schlachter say, 'I hope you don't mind the intrusion, but I've always wanted to see what goes on up here. May I come in?'

'Ja, ja, kommen sie, Herr Oberleutnant,' the pilot answered enthusiastically.

'Right, lads, he's in,' Erich whispered. 'Let's go.'

Josef sat rigid in his seat, anxiously looking over his left shoulder. He could see Erich and Philip standing over the crate, with the Maus kneeling in between them, digging through a small green bag. He produced an array of skeleton keys, and began trying them one by one on the chunky grey padlocks in the shaky cargo bay area. Things were not going to plan, however; it was all taking much too long, and Josef began to nervously scan the front of the aircraft, where Schlachter appeared to be getting on quite well with the pilots. Not being able to withstand it any longer, he rose from his seat and walked down the long narrow aisle towards the cargo bay, and once there, he saw that while two of the three padlocks were off, the last one was proving to be a bit of a problem.

'How's it going, chaps?' he enquired, fingers crossed.

'You'll have to ask the Maus,' Philip answered, 'he's the one doing all the work.'

'Well, Maus,' Josef said, 'how goes it?'

'Nearly there, Herr leutnant,' the Maus said, sounding confident. 'Just one more turn, I think,' he let out gasp of exhilaration. 'Got it!'

'Yes,' Erich squealed, both delighted and relieved. 'Well done, Maus. Right, lads, stand back.'

He slowly cracked open the broad, heavy lid of the casket using a small jemmy bar, while Philip, Josef and the Maus all leaned forward and looked in. At first, there was nothing to see, but then Erich pulled back a long, red crushed velvet cloth to reveal a whole cluster of pearl and diamond necklaces, supported by various other precious and semi-precious stones, such as emeralds, jade, amber, topaz and amethyst, all gleaming brightly in the strong sunlight. Carefully brushing a hand over the jewellery uncovered a cluster of gold watches and rings, studded with onyx, sapphire and ruby stones. Some of the rings had thick gold bands and were encrusted in diamonds, while others consisted of solid gold sovereigns. Erich dug a little deeper, until he found the ultimate prize lying neatly at the bottom: twenty long, shiny gold ingot bars, lined up like soldiers and running the full length of the crate.

'Wow!' Philip exclaimed, mouth agape.

'Mein Gott,' Josef mumbled, his eyes large and round.

'How much do you think all of this is worth?' the Maus croaked nervously.

'Who gives a shit,' Erich laughed, 'we're rich! Quick, somebody pass me a bag.'

'This is quite amazing,' Josef stammered. 'I've never seen so much gold and jewellery.'

'Well, when you've finished drooling, do you think you pass me the Gott damned bag?' Erich asked irritably.

'Yes, sorry,' Josef answered flatly, as he reached for a kitbag. 'Here you go, Erich.'

Erich cupped his hands and began to scoop up the treasure, dropping it into a large green kitbag being held open by Philip, who was also on his knees now. Josef and the Maus stood in silent shock a while longer, and then glanced at each other and dived in, grabbing greedy handfuls of loot and holding it high in the air, before letting long, thick strands of pearls and diamonds slip slowly through their fingers and drop back into the crate.

Erich was right, they were indeed rich, but their celebrations were cut short when Josef noticed a dark figure approaching out of the corner of his eye. He whispered an alarm to the others, and Erich immediately slammed the lid of the casket shut, and hurriedly tried to zip up the green kit bags.

'Gunther said we should be landing in about five minutes,' Schlachter said nonchalantly. 'Wow, is that a real diamond necklace you're wearing, Maus?'

'Why yes,' Maus grinned, 'it's nice, isn't it?'

'Schlachter!' Erich hissed. 'What the hell are you doing here?'

'It's fine, Erich,' Schlachter replied. 'The pilots are busy landing the plane. They're hardly going to start walking around now, are they?'

'Hmm, I guess you're right,' Erich allowed. 'Right, grab a bag and start filling it. As for you, Maus, remove that jewellery from around your neck, you stupid bastard! It could have been Gunther walking down that aisle instead of Schlachter, you know.'

'Erich, we've got a problem,' Philip blurted out, red-faced and sweating. 'It's the kit bags. They're too heavy! We'll never be able to carry them. What are we going to do?'

'Hey, he's right,' Josef confirmed, straining to lift his own bag. 'I can't get mine off the floor.'

'Alright, everybody stay calm and let me think,' Erich took a deep breath. 'OK, look, there's no way I'm putting any of this stuff back, so here's what I suggest. Everyone, fill your pockets, vests and underpants with as much loot as you can carry, until your bags are light enough to lift.'

'You've got to be kidding,' Philip scoffed. 'What will Gunther think?'

'What are you talking about?' Erich said sharply.

'Well, first you get on the plane looking like Josef Goebbels, and then you leave the aircraft looking like Herman Goering,' Philip laughed. 'Gunther's not stupid, you know.'

'Well, if you have a better idea, I'm all ears,' Erich paused, but no suggestions were forthcoming. 'No? I thought not, so let's get cracking. I can almost feel the wheels touching the runway!'

1. Special commandos.

CHAPTER THIRTY

The plane came to an abrupt halt at the end of the runway at Wolnosci Airfield, and when its three giant propellers finally stopped and the rear door popped open, the passengers clambered awkwardly down the three metal steps and lined up beside the aircraft. They were soon joined by six Luftwaffe guards wearing light green steel helmets and long light-grey great coats, with rifles slung across their shoulders, as they waited for Gunther and his co-pilot to finish up their work in the cockpit.

'Well, Herr Oberleutnant,' Gunther said, approaching Erich with his hand extended, 'I hope we gave you a gut flight.'

'Yes, thank you, Gunther,' Erich said, accepting the handshake. 'It was faultless.'

'Tell me, Herr Oberleutnant,' Gunther said, 'have you put on a little weight since I last saw you?'

Josef, Philip and Schlachter stood rigid as they looked to Erich, waiting for his response with breath.

'Yes, it would seem so,' Erich chuckled, patting his belly lightly. 'Nothing a little exercise won't cure, though, eh?'

'Yes, quite,' Gunther said. 'Anyway, your transporter should be here at any moment, so if you'll excuse me, I have to perform a few checks on the aircraft. I'll speak with you again on your return flight, Herr Oberleutnant. Guten tag.'

'Ja, guten tag, Gunther,' Erich said, waving the pilot off.

'That was too close for comfort,' Philip exhaled loudly. 'You played a cool hand there, Erich, I'll give you that.'

'Ah, I told you there was nothing to worry about. Come on, grab the bags. The transporter is here.'

Josef turned to see a heavy truck reversing at a snail's pace towards the cargo bay door, as the Luftwaffe guards cradled the long box and lifted it with ease from the plane to the back of the truck. Already nervous enough as it was, his stomach dropped when he overheard one of the guards remark to his comrades that the he didn't understand why six of them had been sent to unload such a light crate. Once the guards were finished, the band of thieves struggled and puffed as they threw their bulging kit bags up onto the back of the truck, with Josef and the Maus tasked with climbing in and sitting among the Luftwaffe men, to keep watch over the treasure. The tailgate was raised and slammed shut behind them, and Erich, Philip and Schlachter took their places in the front cab, as the driver began the long journey to Greiser's Palace.

General SS Albrecht von Froder's head quarters, Poznan

As always, the telephone was ringing.

'Ja, hello?' Lunder said into the receiver.

'Heil Hitler, Herr Sturmbannfuhrer. This is Ulricher speaking, sir.'

'Yes, Ulricher, what is it?'

'You said to keep you fully informed about anything to do with Saphire, sir.'

'Yes, that's correct. What do you have for me?'

'Well, there are two things, sir. Firstly, Saphire has just landed in Poznan with a shipment from Lodz, for Herr Gauleiter Greiser, sir.'

'What? You mean he's here in Poznan?'

'Yes, sir. Also, I thought you should know that the Bear has found himself a neu fraulein back in Breslau. A German personal secretary to Herr Kommandant Siltz. Her name is Emmy Kirche.'

'Hmm, I'm becoming increasingly concerned about the mixing of gut German stock with gutter scum! Something will have to be done about it. OK, Ulricher, you have done well. Keep me informed. I'll have to hang up, there's someone here. Heil Hitler.' He put down the receiver and looked up at the man who had just entered his office. 'Yes, Kapler, what is it?'

'The fraulein you asked for has arrived, Herr Sturmbannfuhrer. She waits outside. Shall I bring her in, sir?'

'Yes, please do,' he said, quickly fixing his hair as he heard his guest approach. 'Ah, Fraulein Lang, it's so gut of you to come. Please, sit down.'

'I had no choice but to come, Herr Sturmbannfuhrer,' she said. 'The car pulled up and your driver ordered me into it. Why all this in the dark stuff? You terrified me!'

'Well, Irma, if I may call you by your first name, I'm sorry if I frightened you. That wasn't my intention. I just had to see you again. I want to know if you would like to have dinner with me tomorrow evening?'

'You mean you've kidnapped and brought me all this way, just to ask me to dinner,' she laughed. 'Would not a simple phone call have sufficed, Herr Sturmbannfuhrer?'

'Oh, please, call me Ernst. Now, in answer to your question, if I had phoned you, would you have said yes?'

'I really don't know, Herr Sturmban- sorry, Ernst.'

'There, you see. I was right to bring you here and ask you face-to-face. So, will you have dinner with me?'

'Well, you must understand that this has all been most disconcerting for me, and I don't know whether I like being second choice, either!'

'Ah, you're referring to Fraulein Hastler. Please understand that I have no interest in her. She's just a pretty child, whereas you're a real woman who I find far more attractive. So, will you have dinner with me or not?'

'Well, seeing that you have gone to all this trouble, how can I say no?'

'Excellent,' he tapped his desk in celebration. 'Shall we say to-morrow evening at seven?'

'Yes, that would be nice, Ernst.'

'Very gut. I'll have mein chauffeur pick you up at seven. I thought we might try that neu German restaurant on Wroclawska Street, what do you think?'

'Yes, that sounds lovely,' she giggled.

'Then it's settled. You will now be driven back to the hospital. I look forward to our dinner date tomorrow evening.'

'Yes, danke, Ernst,' she gave a little curtsy. 'Guten tag.'

CHAPTER THIRTY-ONE

The grey ten-wheeled canvas truck crawled forward, crunching its way up the long, wide gravel path that led to the tree-lined front of Gauleiter Greiser's palace in the Warthegau, [1.] Western Poland. Although it reputedly boasted at least sixty rooms, Josef felt a little disappointed as the main house came into view, finding that it looked nothing like he had imagined. The large powder blue, double-fronted building was more like a stately home than a palace, with its many tall, white square-framed windows and broad white-painted sills. As the truck neared the front entrance, it suddenly veered to the left and headed towards the rear of the building, where the precious cargo was to be unloaded. The officers leaped out of the cab and ran around to the back of the vehicle, unfastening the tailgate to allow Josef and the six Luftwaffe guards to climb down and start unloading. The Maus was ordered to stay with the truck and guard the kit bags until the officers returned.

A white-haired butler wearing a black claw hammer coat quietly opened a heavy back door, beckoning the officers into a small kitchen area. Once they were inside, the butler requested that they first check their weapons, before instructing them to sit at a large wooden table that held four brandy glasses. Next to the glasses sat a large silver platter containing freshly cut meats and cheeses, complemented by a large, round dome of fresh crusty bread. While the officers were making themselves comfortable, the butler began to pour the thin, light brown cognac into the bulbous glasses, filling each of them halfway. Erich was the first to grab a glass, which he proceeded to raised high in the air with a shout of, 'Prost,' but before the drink could touch his lips, the door burst open again and the six burly Luftwaffe guards marched in, carrying the long wooden crate. They passed through the kitchen and into an adjoining room, which was partitioned off by two square-paned double glass doors, through which the officers could clearly see the guards place the box down onto a plush green carpet. Four of the six Luftwaffe men stood around the crate like honour guards at a funeral, with their rifles tucked smartly into their right sides, while the other two positioned themselves either side of a door that presumably led deeper into the house.

'Please, drink up, gentlemen,' the squeaky-voiced butler said. 'Herr Greiser will join you shortly. You may smoke if you wish.'

Once again, Erich raised his glass and said, 'Prost, mein herren!' The other three officers responded in kind, sipping heartily from their glasses. Schlachter leaned forward and tore off a chunky piece of bread, and the others quickly followed suit. However, in their gusto, they had failed to notice the small, balding figure of a man who had appeared in the adjoining room next to the casket. This man wore a smart, light-brown tweed jacket and black trousers, and his face was marked by a hugely receding hairline and thick, heavy black eyebrows. Although likely in his late-forties, he looked healthy and sun-tanned, and yet his eyes were a deep black and soulless. He peered into the kitchen and regarded the officers with a broad smile.

Josef nudged Philip and asked if he knew who the man was, and then began to giggle, saying that he resembled his old school head master. Philip replied with a shrug, before guessing that he was probably the head butler.

'I trust you gentlemen had a gut journey?' the mystery man asked, having moved into the kitchen doorway.

'Ja, danke,' Erich said brusquely. 'More brandy.'

'Why certainly, Herr Oberleutnant,' the man smiled, placing the bottle on the edge of the table. 'Here, please help yourselves, gentlemen. Now, if you will excuse me, I must check the consignment. I trust everything went to plan and that the cargo is in tact, Herr Oberleutnant?'

'Ja, ja, I'm sure Greiser will find it satisfactory,' Erich said. 'Now, be a gut fellow and slide that bottle over here, would you?'

'Erich,' Josef whispered nervously, a sense of foreboding having suddenly washed over him, 'watch your tongue. This man could be Herr Greiser himself for all we know.'

'Don't be silly,' Erich laughed off the suggestion, 'Greiser always wears a full uniform. He would never be seen dead in a jacket like that. I mean, just look at the cut of the man,' he laughed again.

Still smiling, the man leaned across and handed the bottle to Erich, and then turned and walked into the other room to inspect the cargo. He clicked his fingers, and the two Luftwaffe guards that had been stood at the door brought forward a flat set of scales, which they placed down in front of the crate. The other four guards then lifted the crate and placed it onto the scales. Josef looked across at Erich in horror, but he just shook his head slowly, indicating that he was not to panic. One of guards produced a clipboard, and appeared to be comparing the weight on the scale with whatever was written down before him. He seemed puzzled, and called the man in the tweed jacket over to take a look at something. The men at the table stopped what they were doing and listened intently.

'Herr Obergruppenfuhrer, there is something wrong here,' the guard said. 'The casket appears to be at least forty kilos lighter than it should be, sir.'

'Was?' the man roared. 'Was sag sie?' [2.]

'Christus!' Josef gasped, his heart frozen still in his chest. 'That man is Greiser! What are we going to do now?'

'Steady now,' Erich replied calmly, 'don't fall apart on me. Just sit tight and let me do all the talking, OK?'

'You're damned right, you'll do the talking,' Josef hissed. 'I can't believe I let you talk me into this.'

'Herr Oberleutnant, would you come in here please?' the now unsmiling Greiser called from the other room.

'Yes, sir, right away, sir,' Erich said, getting up from his chair very slowly, and then turning and whispering to the others, 'Now, listen up, lads. Stay in your foxholes. I'll get us out of this somehow, I promise.'

'Your name is Erich, es das recht?' Greiser asked, as Erich entered the adjoining room.

'Jawohl, Herr Obergruppenfuhrer,' Erich said. 'Is there a problem, sir?'

'Yes, you could say that. Forty kilos are missing from this casket. What do you know about it?'

'I'm afraid I can't say that I know anything, Herr Obergruppenfuhrer.'

'Can't or won't?' Greiser bellowed. 'Look, son, I didn't get to where I'm today by being stupid. Now, you were personally in charge of this shipment, and stayed with it at all times between

Lodz and Poznan, es das recht?'

'Jawhol, sir, that is correct.'

'So, it is fair to say that only you and your fellow officers could really know what has happened here, es das recht?'

'Yes, sir, that is true, but you must believe me when I say that as far as we are concerned, everything is in order.'

'OK, look, I think we've got off on the wrong foot here. I know what it's like to be on a junior officer's pay, I really do, and I can appreciate how tempting it must be to want to skim a little off the top. So, here's what I propose. Tell me what you have done with the rest of the cargo, and I promise not to have you shot. Now, how does that sound to you?'

It was at this point that Josef turned to Philip and suggested that maybe now would be a good time to make a run for it, but Philip simply reminded him of their last order, which was to stay put. Philip seemed to be convinced that Erich would somehow honour his promise and get them all out of this dangerous situation, and then Schlachter pointed out that there was nowhere to run to anyway, since the Luftwaffe guards would surely cut them down as they tried to cross the massive lawns that sprawled around Greiser's vast estate.

'Your proposal sounds very reasonable under the circumstances, Herr Obergruppenfuhrer,' Erich said. 'However, I cannot accept your most generous offer, as we are totally innocent of the charge that you have brought against us. We have carried out our orders to the letter, but if I cannot convince you of our innocence, I accept that you must execute us like common thieves.'

'What the hell does he think he's doing?' Josef asked, hardly able to restrain himself. 'Has he gone completely mad?' He remembered what the Maus had said to him when they'd sat outside the old blockhouse back in Lodz:

"Greiser can cut a throat with a whisper."

'I don't know,' Philip said, 'but I can tell you this much – we're all dead men.'

'Well, I don't know about you guys, but I'm getting out of here while I still can,' Josef said, resolving to take his chances on the lawns. 'Anyone coming with me?'

'Shush now,' Schlachter said under his breath, 'something is happening.'

Greiser was pacing up and down room, with one hand behind his back and the other to his chin. He nodded to the six Luftwaffe guards, who immediately cocked their rifles and pointed them at Erich. The atmosphere grew tense, and a small bead of sweat began to trickle down the side of Erich's face. Greiser stopped dead in his tracks, turned and looked deep into Erich's squinting brown eyes, holding his gaze for a moment, and then continuing to walk up and down like a restless groom before a wedding. Erich would have known that he had to be steadfast in his resolve, as he would only get one chance at convincing Greiser of their innocence.

Greiser nodded once again to the guards, and they responded by lowering their weapons. With a cheeky, boyish grin on his face, he walked over to Erich and placed a hand on his shoulder. 'I knew I was right about you, Heiter,' he laughed. 'You're a man of honour and a decent fellow. Es ist das schwein, Hans Frank! [3.] He's trying to steal from me, and it's not the first time he has tried it, I will tell you. Please, accept my apologies, but I had to be sure, you understand?'

'Yes, of course, Herr Obergruppenfuhrer,' Erich said, 'but now that you know the truth, would it be possible for mein men and I to be released and returned to Lodz immediately, sir?'

'Certainly,' Greiser said, 'you may leave right away.'

Back in the kitchen, the four officers stood to attention and saluted the Gauleiter, who returned the gesture and then ordered his guards out of the room. The officers collected their side arms from the butler and walked towards the same back entrance they had entered through, trying to appear as casual as possible. As they reached the door, Greiser ordered them to halt. They each stopped, turning slowly and stiffly to face the Gauleiter, with every muscle in their bodies tightening.

'Before you go, Heiter, I have one last question for you,' Greiser said, with a huge smirk on his face.

'Uh, yes, Herr Obergruppenfuhrer, what is it?'

'Do you know that one of your officers is ein schwarz?' Greiser burst into hysterical laughter.

'Yes, sir,' Erich smiled politely. 'Guten tag.'

The officers once again made for the exit, and although their hearts were pounding, they managed to walk out with an air of calm about them. They all decided to travel back to the airfield in the back of the truck with the Maus, so that they could talk freely and organise how best to split and hide the loot. Josef informed them that he did not want any of the booty, and that his two days' leave, as promised by Erich, was more than enough payment for his part in the dastardly deed. He suggested that his share be split among the rest of the War Council back in Breslau, to which Erich agreed. He also asked to be dropped off en route to the airfield, preferring to make his own way to the hospital to find Monika. They all shook hands, and Josef wished them luck on their travels. Erich ordered the driver to pull in behind a green open-topped regular army truck, which was parked up on the narrow country lane, and Josef jumped down onto the hard tarmac, followed by his now lightened kit bag. He waved goodbye to his comrades as they drove off, and then decided to chance his luck with the driver of the regular army vehicle, who was bent over the engine, filling the radiator with water.

He asked if the truck was going anywhere near the general hospital in Garbary, and although the initial answer was No, the driver then offered to make a slight detour, and told him to climb into the cab. Josef rolled up his side window and turned his jacket collar up around his neck. The day had grown colder, and the night was fast approaching.

1. Greiser's private fiefdom.
2. What did you say?
3. It's that pig.

CHAPTER THIRTY-TWO

Josef arrived unannounced at Monika's nursing quarters at around 6.30pm, and although he'd caught her by surprise, she was delighted to see him. Her quarters were a little cramped, but sufficient for a single person. The room was rectangular, with plain, white-painted walls that were bare except for a medium-sized portrait of Jesus Christ, which hung above the single bed on the left side of the room. In the portrait, Jesus stood majestically in his blue and white flowing robes, with his arms held open. His eyes were the deepest, kindest blue, but seemed sad as they gazed down at them. There was a small window at the end of the room framed by brightly flowered curtains, and below it was a brown chest. On top of the chest of drawers were two differently-sized black and white framed photographs; the larger one featuring Monika's parents, while the smaller frame held the picture of Josef and Monika that Irma had taken at the New Year's Eve party.

They sat on opposite sides of the dresser, turned slightly inward, with a tall pink vase of artificial daffodils positioned in between them. Monika's bed was tidily made up with crisp white folded sheets, and had been pressed up hard against the wall. Josef could not help but notice that a small, tatty brown teddy bear with its right leg missing was lying at an angle across her fluffy pink pillow, and the thought of her still having a such an item made him smile. Opposite the bed was a tall, brown single wardrobe, with a long mirror on the outside door which was slightly ajar, partially revealing a rack of brightly coloured party dresses and a neat line of multicoloured shoes.

'Well, I must say, it looks very comfortable here,' Josef commented.

'Yes, I like it,' Monika said, 'but I'm afraid that you'll have to sit on the bed until I can find some chairs.'

'Oh, that's no problem. I'm sure it's quite comfy.'

'Here, let me take your coat and kit bag. You should have called to say that you were coming. I would have been better prepared.'

'Oh, don't worry yourself. It's you I've come to see, not your living quarters. You are right, though, I should have contacted you earlier. Now, come here and give me a kiss,' he said with open arms.

'So, what brings you to Poznan?' she asked, joining him on the bed.

'I had to escort a consignment from Lodz to Herr Gauleiter Greiser's Palace in the Warthegau, for which I was granted two days' leave that I intend to spend with you.'

'Oh, I see.'

'Is there a problem?'

'No, it's just that I'll have to see Stab Nurse Encke and ask if there's someone I could swap shifts with.'

'Please forgive me for being so selfish, but in the excitement of coming here, I totally forgot about your work.'

'Oh, don't be silly, I would have done exactly the same thing if given the chance. Look at me, going on when you must be starved.

I'll run out to the canteen and get you something to eat. What would you like, tee oder kaffee?'

'Uh, kaffee would be nice.'

'Und schinken oder kase mit brot?' [1.]

'Schinken mit brot please.'

'OK, I won't be long. First, I must see Stab [2.] Nurse Encke, to sort out my shifts.'

She gave him a long, lingering kiss before going off to see the staff sister, leaving him sat on the edge of the bed, trying to light up a cigarette. After a time, he got up and walked over to the small window that overlooked the huge hospital grounds. In the middle of the square was a beautiful hedged garden, which had a maze of tarmacked walkways running through it. He could see small groups of hospital patients sitting on long wooden benches in their house-coats, either talking or simply gazing upon the sparse flowerbeds. Then, the door creaked open and Monika entered with a tray of sandwiches and a pot of hot coffee.

'Gut news,' she beamed, 'I've sorted it with Stab Nurse Encke. I explained the situation to her, and she was very understanding.'

'Great,' Josef smiled, 'so we can spend two whole precious days together, eh?'

'Yes. Two wonderful days.'

'Oh, I almost forgot,' Josef said, reaching down deep into his large green kit bag, and producing a small box. 'I've been carrying this around with me since mein visit to Germany.'

'What is it?' Monika asked nervously.

'Why don't you open it and find out?' he smiled.

'It's a ring!' she shrieked. 'It's an engagement ring.'

'Try it on. I had to guess your size, so I hope I got it right.'

'Oh, you got it right. It fits perfectly, mein leibling,' she gushed, and then gave him a long kiss.

'Are you happy?' he asked.

'Oh, very happy. I can't wait to tell Irma. May I tell her?'

'You can tell anyone you want, mein liebe,' he took her hand. 'Where do you see us in one or maybe two years time?'

'I see us together, like now. I see us stronger and more loving.'

'Aren't you worried about our country – about the way they will treat you because of me?'

Unlike Monika, Josef knew first-hand the risks of being in a mixed race relationship, recalling his parents' experiences of being verbally abused or stared at while out in public. Then there were his own experiences of going to school and being shunned by most of his classmates.

'I don't care about how they will treat me,' she insisted. 'I'm with you, and that's all that matters. I hate the Nazis and everything that they stand for. I will never bow down to them, never.'

'I feel as you do,' he said, 'but I still worry about you. If anything should-'

She took hold of his hand and silenced him with another kiss. They then talked for hours, until eventually he realised that it was getting late and suggested that he should leave, knowing it was forbidden for non-hospital employees to stay in the nursing quarters at any time, day or night. She asked him where he would go, and he replied that he would find a hotel room somewhere near the hospital. She told him that he was more than welcome to stay with her for the night, as long as he didn't mind squeezing into a single bed, to which he eagerly nodded his approval, wearing a huge grin on his face as he removed his field grey jacket.

She switched off the light to hide her modesty while she undressed, but he could still make out her perfect hourglass figure in the grey shaft of moonlight that broke through the narrow bedroom window. He began to unbutton his white shirt, and then removed his shoes and trousers while watching her carefully pull down her black figure-hugging skirt, which she then gently stepped out of before throwing off her blouse and standing before him in only her bra, panties, stockings and black high-heeled stilettos.

Now bare chested and wearing only his pink and white striped boxer shorts, he was struck by how stunning she looked in her white lace suspenders and tan silk-seamed stockings. They moved close and locked themselves into a long, loving embrace, and he then took the lead by slowly unclipping the back of her white lace bra and letting it fall to the floor. She reacted by nervously raising her right arm and holding it tight across her small, firm breasts, as he took her by the left hand and led her over towards the bed. He sat her down gently and kneeled before her, removing her shiny black patent leather shoes and placing them neatly onto the floor. He then slowly and deliberately ran his hands up the outside of her thighs, unclipping the white laced suspenders and carefully rolling the thick dark stocking tops down each of her long, shapely legs, before plucking them off her tiny, perfect feet, and then once again running his fingers along the sides of her toned legs, stopping just short of her white lace panties. He looked into her large brown eyes and gave her a long, smoldering kiss. She smiled back at him, and he slowly pulled the panties down over her knees while she leaned backwards across the bed and carefully took hold of her tatty brown bear, placing it down onto the floor next to her shoes. She then lay herself down gently on the bed with her arms stretched out, beckoning him to join her. He lowered himself down on top of her, lovingly brushing the hair from her angelic face before kissing her on the neck and breasts, and then full on the lips. Looking up at him, she said softly, 'I love you,' and soon they were making passionate love.

A gentle breeze blew in through the small open window, making the pretty paisley curtains quiver slightly as the strong moonlight cast a silvery shadow on the plain white wall above them, shimmering as it cut through the trembling branches of the tall poplar tree outside. Josef suddenly raised himself up as he reached his climax, and with sweat glistening on his muscular chest, he slumped down on top of her. She immediately rolled him onto his back and straddled him, and soon she was writhing with pleasure herself. She squealed loudly, her thick hair falling forwards and covering her face. He held her breasts in his hands and began to massage them slowly, sending her into a shuddering orgasm. She lay still for a moment and then rolled onto her side, pulling back her long auburn hair and giving him a huge smile as he reached over the bed to look for his cigarettes. He lit one and lay back, putting his left arm behind his head as he blew smoke rings from his mouth, watching them spiral upwards and dissipate as they hit the ceiling.

'Was that your first time?' she asked. Monika had the sexual advantage over Josef, having had had an affair some eighteen months earlier with an older man, a Wehrmacht officer, but the relationship was doomed to fail. The man had refused to leave his wife and children in the end, even though at the time he'd promised that he would.

'Yes,' he said, 'was it yours?'

'A lady never tells.'

'Of course,' he laughed. 'Das war fantastisch. You're quite a tiger when you get going, aren't you?'

'Oh, stop it, you're embarrassing me,' she blushed. 'So, what would you like to do tomorrow?'

'I really don't know,' he paused. 'If the weather's nice, I'd like to walk with you through that magnificent garten you have out there.'

'Yes, I would love to walk with you, but there's not much to see out there. All the beautiful flowers have gone now.'

'Well, that's to be expected – it is January, after all. Still, weather permitting, that's what we shall do. How's your freund Irma doing these days, by the way?'

'It's funny you should mention her. She was here earlier this evening, but then left to have dinner with an officer who says he knows you.'

'Nobody knows me here in Poznan. Do you know the officer's name?'

'Yes, I remember it well, because he unnerved me so. It's Ernst Lunder. He's a sturmbannfuhrer in the SS.'

'Ernst Lunder?' Josef sat up. 'Gut Gott, what's he doing here in Poznan?'

'He's stationed here, not far from the hospital.'

'What? You mean you know this man?'

'Only because he bumped into me on the hospital steps, and said that he recognised me from the Christmas dance back in Breslau. You look worried, Josef. How do you know this man?'

'Let's just say we have crossed swords in the past. Now listen, you must stop Irma from seeing this man, because he's trouble. Do you hear me?'

'I can't stop her. She's already with him, remember?'

'Damph,' he cursed, running his hands through his hair.

'I'm not her mutter, for Gott sake! Wait a minute, are we having our first argument?'

'No, of course not. I'm just worried for the both of you, that's all.'

'Well, I think that's very sweet and romantic. I quite like the thought of a black knight coming to rescue his damsel in distress,' she laughed.

'Let's hope it never comes to that. Lunder is up to something, I just know it. He's using Irma to get to you, and then through you, he will get to me.'

'Josef, you're starting to scare me. What's really going on between you and this Lunder fellow?'

'I'll tell you everything in the morning, but for now, try to get some sleep.'

'OK. I love you so much, Josef. I just want you to know that.'

'And I love you. Now, go to sleep.'

'Guten nacht, mein liebe,' she said, kissing him on the cheek.

'Guten morgan, mein liebling,' he joked, wearing a big smile on his face as he pulled the sheets up under his chin and rolled over.

1. Ham or cheese with bread.
2. Staff.

CHAPTER THIRTY-THREE

'Yes, enter,' Major Lowe replied to the knock at his door. 'Ah, Ralf. What can I do for you?'

'Morgan, Herr Major,' Weise said. 'I have finally received some information from mein freunde inside the Abwehr. They have confirmed that your suspicions of a conspiracy against Herzog are correct, but there's also a new addition to the file, sir.'

'New addition? What do you mean, Ralf?'

'Well, sir, the name Uri Voss is now here, too,' Weise said, pointing to a sheet of paper he was carrying.

'Voss? Mein gott. OK, read it all out to me.'

'Well, it's a little sketchy to say the least, sir, but here goes. It all starts with Oberleutnant Seig Ulricher. He's the eyes and ears of the operation. It's his job to report every movement that Josef makes to Herr Sturmbannfuhrer Lunder, sir.'

'I knew it. Didn't I tell you?'

'Yes, sir, you did, but there's more. Lunder processes all the information and then passes it on to Herr General Albrecht Froder, who also happens to be a close freund of Herr Dr Herbert Schlossman.

You know, the man who almost dissected Herzog back in Olenica.'

'Ja, ja, but where does Voss fit into this?'

'Well, sir, I can only assume that Lunder has taken a strong dislike to Uri since the incident at the Christmas dance last month, and then there's the matter of the assaults against Ulricher and his men in the SS barracks. Oh, and by the way, Uri and Josef have been given code names Bear and Sapphire, which indicates to me that something sinister is about to unfold, sir.'

'Hmm, curious. You've done well, Ralf. You mentioned Albrecht Froder. Do you think we can safely say that we've found our Mr X?'

'Uh, not exactly, sir.'

'What do you mean, "not exactly?"'

'Well, my sources say that General Froder passes his reports on to someone else, sir.'

'To Mr X, you mean?'

'Genau, sir.'

'Damph! I thought we had him in our sights.'

'I'm afraid that Mr X is to remain a closely guarded secret, sir. Mein freunde in the Abwehr and the SD have tried desperately to get more information, but it seems to be virtually impossible. I'm sorry, sir.'

'No need to apologise, Ralf. The immediate problem is how best to protect Voss and Herzog from these devious monsters.'

'Do you think we should warn Herzog, sir?'

'No, absolutely not. We don't won't to panic him into doing something stupid, like attacking Lunder. That just wouldn't do now, would it?'

'I guess you're right, sir. Uri's not a problem, since he's here and we can keep an eye on him, but how do we guard Herzog?'

'Well, it's not going to be easy, but we must think of something and think of it quickly.'

'What if we were to just bring him back here to Breslau? At least we would have them both under one roof, so to speak.'

'That's one possibility, but I need more options. Leave it with me, and I'll get back to you. Oh, and send a radio message to Aleksandrow. We need to bring Heiter up to speed with the situation. He will have to be our eyes and ears for now.'

'Jawohl, Herr Mayor. I will see to it right away.'

Oberleutnant Viktor Pech called an emergency meeting of the remaining War Council members in his private quarters, to discuss the arrival of a curious wooden box that had just been delivered to him that morning. Leutnant Egon Binde had already arrived, and both he and Pech were now waiting for Oberleutnant Uri Voss, who was running a little late as usual.

Suddenly, the door burst open and Uri fell into the room. 'OK,' he said, panting heavily, 'what's this meeting all about?'

'Where the hell have you been?' Pech growled. 'You're ten minutes late!'

'Had a lot of paper work, man,' Uri said. 'You know how it is.'

'Paper work,' Egon scoffed, 'you can't even read, you dummy.'

'How would you like to read mein fist, you fat bastard?' Uri shot back.

'Alright, pipe down the pair of you,' Viktor said. 'Now, listen up. I received a delivery this morning, and I think you two should take a look at it.' He placed the heavy box in the middle of the floor, and then quickly scanned his surroundings before slowly prising open the lid. Both Egon and Uri gasped as they leaned forward and saw what was inside.

'Well, well, well, what do we have here?' Uri mumbled, pawing at the contents. 'Gold watches, gold rings, diamonds, pearls – wunderbar!'

'Yes, but what does it all mean, Viktor?' Egon asked, looking puzzled.

'Well, according to Erich's letter, which came with the box, it means that we're all rich, and it's all thanks to Josef.'

'Prinz?' Uri asked. 'How does he figure in all this?'

Viktor sat and began to recite the full contents of the letter, which explained everything that had happened from the time the plan was first conceived back in Lodz, to the day the crate was sent to Breslau.

'They've gone completely mad,' Egon grunted. 'We will all be shot for this, you know. We have to give it all back.'

'Ja, right,' Uri sneered. 'Do that, and we definitely will get shot, you idiot.'

'I don't often agree with Uri, but this time he's right,' Viktor said. 'We can't give it back now. The first thing we have to do is hide it somewhere safe,' he looked at Egon.

'Hey, don't look at me,' Egon said, raising his hands defensively. 'Where the hell am I going to hide it?'

'Well, you're the only one with a chest locker,' Viktor said. 'The rest of us only have small footlockers, don't we, Uri?'

'Eh? Oh, Ja, small lockers,' Uri concurred.

'Alright, alright, but only for one night, and then it goes,' Egon grumbled.

'I don't believe it,' Uri said, grinning from ear to ear, 'we're all rich. The first thing I'm going to do is buy the most expensive dress I can find for mein honig, and then I'm going to place this pearl necklace around her beautiful neck.'

'Woah, woah,' Viktor said, interrupting Uri's reverie, 'you're not going to tell her about this, are you?'

'Of course not,' Uri said. 'What, do you think I'm stupid?'

'Do you really want me to answer that question?' Viktor said, shaking his head. 'Look, just think about it for a minute. How are you going to explain the dress and the necklace to her, considering your officer's pay, eh?'

'That's easy, man. I'll tell her mein aunt has just died and left me a shedload of money.'

'No, Uri,' Viktor said firmly, 'you'll tell her nothing, and you'll spend nothing until we have thought this through properly, verstehen?'

'Ah, what's the use of having money if you can't spend it, man?' Uri sulked.

'We will spend it,' Viktor said, 'just not right now. Promise me that you won't breathe a word of this to anyone, please!'

'Oh, alright, but it's going to be hard for me to sit here scratching mein arsch, knowing that I've got a small fortune tied up in fatty's chest locker.'

'Good,' Viktor nodded. 'Now, I want you both to go about your usual business, and once I've worked out a plan for how best to split the loot, I'll call for you. Dismissed.'

The Grey Storm

CHAPTER THIRTY-FOUR

It was late in the afternoon, and Josef had decided to follow through with his idea to take Monika for a walk around the volks garten. He rolled up the collar on his heavy great coat and, taking his new fiancée by the arm, led her slowly along the tarmacked foot path towards a small wooden park bench, which was positioned opposite a large empty flower bed. The sun was sitting low in the greyish-blue clouds, but it still managed to shine brightly. Most of the patients had by now returned to their wards, leaving the garden empty and quiet, but the eerie silence was soon broken when a light aircraft flew high over head.

Josef sat Monika down and huddled up close alongside her, holding her hand. She gave him a peck on the cheek and, looking at the flowerbed, said, 'It's a pity that there are no flowers. I imagine there would be some really nice plants out here in the summer.'

'Yes, it is a pity,' he agreed, 'but look, not all the plants have gone. There's still some crocus and snowdrops,' he gestured with a gloved hand. 'Anyway, we will soon be back in our own country, hopefully in time to see the German blossoms, eh?'

'Oh yes, I do so miss Germany. I often dream of just the two of us living in a grand old house somewhere in Hanover, surrounded by lots of trees.'

'Hmm, curious that you should pick Hanover,' he said.

'Why do you say that?' she asked.

'I say it because that's where your mutter and vater are from. What's wrong with Berlin?'

'OK, you win,' she laughed. 'Where would you like to live?'

'I would live anywhere, just as long as it was with you.'

'Ah, you always say the right things. Do you really think we will go home soon?'

'Why yes, just look at the facts. Der Fuhrer has done what he set out to do. He's claimed Austria, Czechoslovakia and Poland, reuniting all ethnic Germans. Trust me, we'll be back in die heimat before you know it.'

'Well, I wish I had your confidence. I sometimes think that we are on the precipice of total war.'

'All I care about is you. I don't give a damn about the war.'

'Why do you worry so much? I have a powerful family, and I also have you, mein leber,' she giggled.

'It's hard for me to explain, but I believe that there are people out to get me, and I fear that once they're done with me, they will move on to you.'

'What people? Who?'

'I believe them to be SS, but I can't prove it yet.'

'SS? You mean, Lund- oh, mein Gott,' she said, bowing her head and mumbling into her shoulder. 'Don't look now, but here comes Irma with Herr Sturmbannfuhrer Lunder.'

'If that was meant to be a joke, it wasn't very funny,' he said, turning his head and glancing down the long leaf-covered path, only to see that she was right. Coming towards them were indeed Irma and Lunder, walking arm in arm. He couldn't believe his eyes.

Irma was sporting a huge grin, and waving her hand frantically at Monika as they approached. As they neared the bench, Josef and Monika rose to their feet, and Josef saluted the sturmbannfuhrer, who responded in kind.

'Fancy finding you two here,' Irma beamed. 'I believe you already know Herr Sturmbannfuhrer Lunder?'

'Herr Sturmbannfuhrer,' Josef nodded.

'Herr Leutnant,' Lunder smiled back.

'We were just out for some fresh air,' Irma chirped, obviously sensing tension.

'So were we,' Monika said. 'We would ask you both to join us, but there's little room on this bench for everyone.'

'Oh please, don't worry yourselves,' Lunder said. 'We came here to walk, not sit.'

Irma then noticed the sparkle from Monika's engagement ring. 'Oh, mein Gott! You're engaged! When did this happen?'

'Last night,' Monika blushed.

'Congratuliere, Herr Leutnant,' Lunder grumbled.

'Monika,' Irma said with excitement, 'the Sturmbannfuhrer and I are having dinner again tonight.'

'That sounds very romantic,' Monika smiled.

'Yes, well, I thought, what if we were to make it a foursome? You know, with Josef and yourself?' Irma asked.

'I'm afraid not, Irma,' Josef interrupted. 'We have already made other arrangements, unfortunately.'

'Oh, come on, Herr Leutnant,' Lunder said. 'It would be a gut opportunity for the two of us to bury the hatchet, don't you think?'

'Nein danke, sir,' Josef replied, with anger in his voice.

'Oh, come on, man,' Lunder laughed. 'You can't dislike me that much, surely?'

'Sir, I would rather lay in a pit full of snakes than dine with you.'

'Josef!' Irma fumed. 'How could you be so rude?'

'It's alright, meine liebe,' Lunder grunted thickly. 'I've tried to offer you mein hand in freundshciff, and you have refused. That, sir, makes you a fool. Guten tag, Herr Leutnant.' He pulled Irma close to him and then took off at great speed, marching back the same way they had come from.

Monika shouted after her friend, but Irma ignored her and continued walking alongside Lunder. She then turned to Josef and asked him why he had been so impolite.

'I'm sorry, Monika, but the man's a monster,' he said. 'I fear that I have now put you in great danger, too. You don't know what he is capable of.'

'I told you before, I have a well-connected family. He can't harm me, so don't worry, OK?'

Josef gave her a big hug. 'OK,' he smiled.

They walked back to the nurses' quarters, where they were to spend a last passionate night together before he returned to Aleksandrow. She asked when she would see him again, and after some thought he came up with a brilliant idea, suggesting that he throw a twenty-first birthday party for himself back in Breslau. It was only two weeks away, and it would represent a perfect opportunity for the two of them to get together. He explained that his stay in Lodz was coming to an end, and that he would be posted back to D Company well in time for his proposed party. She became very excited at the idea, telling him that she couldn't wait. They made love once again, but this time it was less intense and more relaxed, as they now felt as though they knew more about each other.

The next morning, they got up early and had a light breakfast, and then Josef held Monika in his arms one last time, giving her a long and tender kiss before stepping out into the empty corridor and saying goodbye. He reminded her that she should keep an eye on Irma, and then begged her to go inside and close the door. He made the long, lonely walk down the empty hallway, through the main door and out into the cold dim morning light, and throwing his green kit bag over his right shoulder, he began thumbing for a lift back to the airfield.

CHAPTER THIRTY-FIVE

Josef entered the old craggy blockhouse in Aleksandrow, finding that it was eerily quiet except for a shuffling noise that was coming from the sergeants' mess. He went over to investigate, cautiously opening the brown wooden door that led into the room, and although he could see no signs of life, he caught a whiff of the fresh aroma of piped tobacco as he dropped his kit bag down onto the mess hall table. He peered into the kitchen, where he saw Unterfeldwebel Penau puffing on his old black pipe as he bent over the hot stove, stirring a pan of stew while playing with his brown walrus moustache.

Sensing that someone was behind him, Penau froze momentarily, before dropping his white tin cup and then spinning around to face Josef. He was still suffering from the trauma of a previous battle.

'Herr Leutnant!' Penau sighed in relief. 'You nearly gave me a damned heart attack.'

'I'm sorry, Penau,' Josef laughed, 'I didn't mean to frighten you.'

'It's gut to see you again, sir,' Penau said. 'How was your stay in Poznan?'

'Sehr gut, danke. I really enjoyed the break, but I'm glad to be back. It's very quiet around here this morning. Where is everyone?'

'They're all in Lodz city centre, sir, except Herr Oberleutnant Heiter. He's not feeling too gut this morgen.'

'Oh, I'm sorry to hear that. What's wrong with him?'

'Uh, too much schnapps last night, sir. Would you like some kaffee?'

'Yes please,' Josef said, sitting himself down at a table. He thanked Penau for the steaming hot cup that was soon brought over, and was sipping tentatively from it when the mess room door swung open, and in marched Oberleutnant Erich Heiter, looking more than a little worse for wear.

'Josef!' Erich said, pleasantly surprised. 'You're back.'

'Erich,' Josef nodded, 'we were just talking about you. How are you, man?'

'Apart from a fat head, I guess I'm alright,' Erich laughed.

'Penau has just made a pot of kaffee. Would you like some? It might clear your head?'

'Ja, gut idea.'

'Why were you drinking so heavily last night?'

'Well, I simply decided to celebrate our new wealth, and got a little carried away while doing so. What about you? How was it in Poznan?'

'Es war fantastisch. Thanks for letting me stay.'

'I should be the one thanking you. You went against your principles for the sake of the War Council, and I will never forget that.'

'Zusammen immer, eh?'

'Ja, zusammen immer,' Erich smiled.

'So, what's been happening the past two days?'

'Nothing much. Oh, the Maus has bought himself a brand-new

motorcycle and a new set of clothes. He's quite the dandy, you should see him.'

'Gut old Maus,' Josef chuckled, 'I'm really pleased for him. Anything else happened while I was away?'

'Yes, Uri has reneged on an agreement not to spend the money until Viktor feels it's safe to do so.'

'Ah, so they got mein share of the loot, then?'

'Yes, I carried out your wish and donated your share of the booty to the rest of the War Council, but unlike here, where we are a law unto ourselves, they have to be careful at D Company HQ.'

'Well, what has Uri done to break the agreement?'

'He has gone against Viktor's express wishes not to spend any money, and bought his fiancée expensive dresses and furnished her with some of the stolen jewellery. Viktor says she walks around the base done up like a Christmas tree. Can you believe that?'

'Gut Gott, that doesn't sound too clever, does it?'

'Hmm, since when has Uri ever been clever? Anyway, getting back to business, you may as well have the rest of the day off and start fresh tomorrow.'

'OK, thanks. May I ask what the plans are for tomorrow?'

'Well, I thought I'd send you to collect refugees from the Lodz ghetto, and then transport them to Kolo train station, ready for deportation. I know, I know, but before you say anything, our work here is almost at an end. Herr Major Lowe has ordered us back to Breslau. We leave in two days, and I can tell you, I won't be sorry to see the back of this place.'

'I agree, it's been a complete nightmare. I just want to return to our unit.'

'Yes, well, drink your kaffee and I'll see you in the morning. I'm going back to bed. Mein head hurts.'

After finishing his coffee and having a quick bite to eat, Josef decided that he, too, should get some rest. He thanked Penau for the refreshments and informed him that he would be retiring to his quarters for the rest of the afternoon, and that unless it was absolutely necessary, he should not be disturbed. He entered his room and dropped his kit bag and coat onto the floor, and flopped face down onto his bunk and quickly drifted off. He had only slept for around an hour when he was awoken by Unterfeldwebel Penau, who was leaning over his bed, shaking him by the shoulder.

'Herr Leutnant, wake up,' Penau said urgently. 'There's an important telephone call for you in the office, sir.'

'What? Who is it, for Gott sake?' Josef stammered groggily.

'It's a Fraulein Hastler on the line, sir. She sounds very upset. She says it's very important.'

'OK, OK, tell her I'm coming, Penau.'

Josef sat up on the edge of the bed for a moment and rubbed at his eyes, before getting up and walking at pace to the Webel's office to take the call.

'Monika, was ist los, mein liebling?' he asked, scratching his head and yawning.

'Oh, Josef, Josef,' Monika wailed, 'the most awful thing has happened!'

'Calm down, I can't understand you. Now, what are you trying to say?'

'You were right, Josef! You were right!'

'Right about what?'

'Lunder. Herr Sturmbannfuhrer Lunder.'

'You're not making any sense, Monika. Please calm down and start again.'

'It's Irma, she's been assaulted!'

'Assaulted? Assaulted by who?'

'By Herr Sturmbannfuhrer!'

'You mean, Lunder assaulted her?'

'Yes.'

'Das schwein hunde! This is terrible news. You must inform the authorities at once, and have that monster placed under arrest.'

'No, Irma won't do that. She feels too ashamed.'

'But you must convince her to change her mind, you simply must.'

'No, you don't understand. After their dinner date last night, Lunder invited her back to his quarters, where he sexually assaulted her with a wine bottle!'

'Mein Gott! This is bad, very bad. Look, this is all the more reason why she must report it. He can not be allowed to get away with it.'

'She won't do it. How will it look to the authorities when she tells them that she went back to his quarters of her own free will? They'll paint her as a loose woman and say that she deserved it. I'm really frightened, Josef. What if I'm next! I don't know what to do.'

'Ok, calm down and listen to me. Telephone your vater and get him to use his influence to get you and Irma out of there and back to Breslau as quickly as possible. We are due back in Breslau ourselves at the end of this week. I'll meet up with you at D Company HQ, and from there we can plan a course of action and get that bastard put behind bars where he belongs, OK?'

'Yes, OK. I'll start packing right away. I wish you were here with me.'

'I know, but don't worry yourself. Everything's going to be alright. Just get yourself packed and make your way back to Breslau, mein liebling.'

'OK, Josef, aufweidersehen.'

Now very much wide awake, Josef decided to get dressed and go for a walk to clear his head. He stepped out of the blockhouse onto the busy wet street, and waited at the kerb for a break in the slow moving traffic before quickly crossing the narrow cobbled road and beginning his steady march along Wozna Street. He then turned right onto Szkolna Street, but he had only taken a few steps when he paused to reflect on the near-death experience he'd had the last time he went walking along Wozna Street. He decided to return to the old blockhouse instead, but as he moved to turn back on himself, he heard the sound of a honking horn and was amazed to see the Maus sat bolt upright on his new motorcycle.

'Hello Herr Leutnant,' the Maus hailed, 'I thought it was you. Where are you headed?'

'Stanizlaw,' Josef laughed, 'you do look a little odd on that infernal machine, but it is gut to see you again. I was just stretching the old legs and going nowhere in particular.'

'Good, then jump on.'

'What, on that boneshaker? You must be joking. I'll walk, if it's all the same to you?'

'No, wait. I'll park up, and we can go for a drink and a chat, eh?'

'Yes, but nothing stronger than kaffee, OK? I'm in uniform, which means I'm on duty.'

'There's a cafe just across the road. Will that do?'

'Perfect,' Josef smiled.

Stanizlaw parked his motorcycle up against the butcher's shop front, much to the annoyance of the butcher, who peered at him angrily through the swinging, naked carcasses. He placed his brown leather gloves, goggles and helmet onto the saddle, and then crossed the street with Josef and entered the cafe.

'It's a bit small in here,' Josef grumbled.

'Yes, but they serve the best coffee in town. Come, sit down and I'll order. Two coffees please,' Stanizlaw called over to the counter. 'Would you like something to eat, Herr Leutnant?'

'No, just kaffee bitte.'

'So, how did it go in Poznan, Herr leutnant?'

'Excellent, thank you, and you can drop the Herr Leutnant bit now. The waitress has gone to make the drinks.' Josef opened a fresh pack of cigarettes and placed one in his mouth, before offering another to his companion.

'Of course,' Stanizlaw accepted it gratefully. 'So, Josef, how was it?'

'Oh, it was gut to be with Monika again. I didn't want to leave her, I can tell you. But enough of me, what about you? What have you been up to in mein absence?'

'Well, I've been spending a little of my new-found wealth, and having a right good time doing it, too. People treat you differently when you have lots of money. I've stayed in the best hotels and met some of the most beautiful women Poland has to offer!'

'Ooh la la,' Josef smirked, 'you have been living it up, haven't you?'

'Well, you only live once, so why not, eh?'

'Oh, I quite agree.'

'I hear you'll be leaving us in the next few days. Is that true?'

'Yes it is, and while I won't be sorry to see the back of this Gott forsaken place, I will miss you, mein freund.'

'Same here, Josef. I don't think I'll ever find another German as tolerant as you. I believe you are to escort some refugees from the Lodz ghetto to Kolo Station tomorrow?'

'That's correct. Where do you get all your information from? Is there anything you don't know?'

'Well, I don't know everything, but I can tell you what I do know. The refugees you refer to are not being repatriated to Israel or Madagascar. They're going straight into Chelmno, an extermination camp near East Prussia.'

'An extermination camp? Are you sure?'

'Josef, have I ever lied to you? They say that once you walk into this camp, the only way out is up the chimney.'

'Mein Gott, do you know what you're saying, man?' Josef's voice dropped to a whisper.

'Yes,' Stanizlaw frowned, 'Chelmno is one giant crematorium, which has the capacity to gobble up thousands of people each day. You may liken it to a gigantic factory that churns out corpses by the minute.'

Josef covered his ears with his hands, and with a grimace pleaded, 'Stop, Stanizlaw. I don't want to listen anymore. This whole place disgusts me.'

The Maus ignored his protests and continued to speak. 'It's very important that you do listen, because someone must carry the message. Poland is about to turn onto a terrible page in its history, and there will be need of good people like yourself – people who will stand up and bear witness to the atrocities and testify on the day of reckoning. Believe me, Josef, when this is all over with, there will be a day of reckoning.'

'I agree with what you say, but why me? I'm only a junior officer and of little importance. Who will listen to me?'

'Look, someone has to tell the story, and who better than you, a loyal and respected German officer who tells it like it is? Do you know that as we speak, Nazi scientists are conducting experiments that consist of converting large military vans into mobile gas chambers?'

'You're telling me something I don't know, and that I'm not sure I want to know!'

'This is all part of your re-education, so listen up. They're mostly using ordinary military vans, but I've been told that they are also cleverly disguising one or two of them to resemble commercial vehicles. They put large advertisements and slogans on the side of the vans, so as not to raise suspicion, and then pile as many as sixty to a hundred prisoners into the back of them, before running a rubber tube from the exhaust pipe into a special aperture attached to the underside of the vehicle. The drivers don gas masks, and then drive around for thirty minutes, filling the van with deadly carbon monoxide, and when they're finished, they simply deliver the corpses to the crematoria where the bodies are burned and bones ground to powder.'

'Shush,' Josef ordered, as a small, white-haired old lady, wearing a long black dress and a starched apron, approached the table to refill their empty cups with fresh coffee. She stared at the two men while adjusting the neat grey bun on the back of her head with pale, trembling fingers, but said nothing. Josef quickly lit two more cigarettes, passing one to Stanizlaw, and stalled for time until the waitress had gone. 'Please, keep your voice down,' he said quietly, once the waitress was back behind the counter. 'I swear, these people here can hear every word you're saying.'

'Ah, they already know, but nobody wants to talk about it. Well, I'll talk about it, if you'll listen?'

'OK, I'm listening, but keep it down, or else we'll both be shot! Now, you said they make bones into powder. Then what happens?'

'One of two things. They either tip them into the local river, or use the powder as fertiliser on the farms, but I have it on good authority that Reichfuhrer Himmler feels that this method of killing is far too slow, and is introducing new measures to help speed things up.'

'Hmm, and I assume you know exactly what those new measures are, eh?'

'Unfortunately, I do. Himmler is toying with the idea of turning most of the huge shower blocks at his camps into gas chambers, by converting the shower heads to let out gas instead of water.'

'OK, stop it now. You're really depressing me. Where the hell are you getting all this information from?'

'Believe me when I say this, Josef. You're better off not knowing, because you're in enough danger with what you already know. This is a very big deal here. I'm taking black operations stuff, and on a massive scale.' The Maus dug deep into his pocket and produced a pieces of crumpled yellow paper, and then paused for a moment, glancing furtively around the café. 'They've been building in Germany since as far back as nineteen thirty-three, and are still building extermination camps today.'

'How the hell do you expect me to remember all this stuff?' Josef sighed.

'Don't worry, my friend. I'll send a courier with everything to you, once you're back in Breslau. Only you can bear witness to what has happened here, Josef. I know it's a real shitty deal, but that's just the way it is. If you're a true friend, you'll do this one favour for me. Now, will you do it?'

'Can I have some time to think about it?'

'Yes, of course, but I must know before we leave this café, because I fear it may be the last time that we ever see each other, you understand?'

'Yes, quite,' Josef nodded, 'but first, answer me a question. Why is all of this so important to you?'

Stanizlaw pulled his chair in close, and stubbed out his cigarette before saying in a voice so quiet, it was barely audible, 'I should have told you this much earlier, and for that I apologise. You see, I have Jewish blood running through my veins.'

Josef leaned back in his chair and ran his fingers through his hair, thinking hard for a moment. He took another sip of coffee from the small white china cup, blew the air out of his cheeks and declared, 'Yes, I'll do it.' He gave Stanizlaw his oath as an officer that he would memorise all the events that he had witnessed during his stay in Lodz, and pass them on to the proper authorities once the Polish occupation was at an end.

The two men stood and shook hands, wishing each other all the best in the event that they did not meet again. Josef left the cafe and headed back to his quarters, to rest and prepare himself for the following day's events.

CHAPTER THIRTY-SIX

'Did you have a gut breakfast, Josef?' Erich asked.

'Yes, thank you,' Josef replied, while still chewing a piece of burnt toast.

'Gut, gut,' Erich said with a smile. 'This will be our last job before returning to Breslau. You know what to do, don't you?'

'Yes,' Josef sighed, 'Philip and I are to escort the refugees to Kolo railway station, and then check the manifest before they board the train.'

'That's correct. You do understand that the Cap will be working with you today, don't you?'

'Yes, I understand, but I don't like it. I don't like it one bit.'

'I know that the two of you don't see eye to eye, but it's only for this morning, and just think, we'll be on our way back to Breslau before you know it. Try and get on with the brute as best you can, OK?'

'Yes, OK.'

'Right, the car is waiting outside. Penau will be going with you, and he's promised me that he'll keep an eye on you.'

'Keep an eye on me?' Josef asked incredulously. 'Why?'

'Because you're a hot head, and your mouth is always getting you into trouble, that's why. Now, get going, and I'll see you back here late afternoon. Gut gluck, Herr Leutnant,' Erich said with a broad smile on his face, as he playfully saluted.

Josef gathered his documents and joined Philip, who was already sitting in the back of the staff car with Penau while an untergefeiter sat waiting behind the steering wheel. They started their familiar journey through the narrow, cobbled streets that led them right into the heart of the city, and Josef steeled himself one last time, focussing on the fact that this would be his last mission in Lodz. As they neared the ghetto boundary, they could see at least twenty-five open-topped green army trucks lined up in the road, with masses of people being herded onto the back of them. Women, children and old folk were being hauled up by men that had already boarded, and in the middle of all this chaos, Herr Oberleutnant Eckard Schlachter strutted about like a feathered peacock, bullying and shouting out orders to his heavily armed Waffen SS and police guard.

'I don't know if I can go through with this,' Josef said.

'What do you mean?' Philip asked, looking puzzled.

'I don't think I can work with that man.'

'What man?'

'You know, the Cap.'

'The Cap?'

'Josef is referring to Schlachter, Herr Leutnant,' Penau explained to Philip, unable to hide a grin.

'Oh, I wouldn't worry too much about him,' Philip said. 'We'll try to keep him away from you as much as possible, OK?'

'Yes, and make sure that you do,' Josef frowned.

The officers exited the car, and carefully navigated through the babbling hordes of women that were stood with their arms outstretched and screaming. 'Please!' one of them cried, tugging feebly at Josef's sleeve. 'They have separated us from our husbands and children. You must help us, please!'

Josef and his comrades were forced to raise their arms in a defensive posture, in order to push back the ever-increasing weight of the raucous crowd. They fought their way towards Schlachter, who was standing in front of them, legs apart and with his hands on the tan leather gun belt and holster at his hips. He was wearing his usual sardonic grin as he welcomed them with open arms.

'Ah, mein manner are here,' Schlachter cheered. 'Now we can get things started.'

'Where do you want us, and what do you want us to do, Schlachter?' Philip asked cautiously.

'Well now,' Schlachter said, rubbing his hands together, 'firstly, I want you, Feldwebel Penau, to join the police guard and knock them into shape. They've become sloppy and have allowed some prisoners to escape back into the ghetto, and we can't have that, can we?'

'Prisoners?' Josef asked. 'I thought they were refugees?'

'Whatever, 'Schlachter snarled, 'just take four men with you and make those crazy Jew bitches be quiet. They're worrying the others. Oh, don't look so shocked, Herzog. I can be compassionate when I want to be, you know,' he said with a dry smirk. 'Now, go and maintain order, verstehen?'

'Yes, Herr Oberleutnant,' Josef reluctantly replied.

'Philip, you will come mit mich. I need you to count how many pris- I mean, how many refugees we can get onto those trucks. OK, it's now eight forty-five AM. To your stations, gentlemen, and let's get things rolling.'

In less than an hour, hundreds of people had been boarded and were transported to the train station. Once there, they were shunted out of the trucks and onto the 20 wooden boxcars that were lined up at the platform, where they were to be locked in without sunlight, toilets, food or water. Only when the human cargo was safely locked up could the officers and their soldiers board their carriages, which were luxurious in comparison to the boxcars. Josef joined Schlachter and the other officers in a spacious rail car, with comfortable padded seats and net curtains over each window. Young army waiters ran up and down the narrow isles serving beer, schnapps, wine and brandy to whoever required refreshments, quickly followed by more waiters offering platters of fresh fruit and sandwiches. Josef felt compelled to refuse the hospitality, feeling sick to the stomach at the thought of all those poor wretched souls that were crammed tightly into the cars behind. Instead, he chose to simply light a cigarette, and turned his face towards the huge glass window next to him, through which he stared out silently at the beautiful Polish countryside, trying desperately to think of better times.

At 1.05 pm, the train began to slow down as it reached Kolo, eastern Poland. A sudden jerk woke Josef from a warming dream in which he and Monika were running together through a swaying field of yellow rape. They were laughing loudly as they danced in the hot, dry summer sun, but as his eyes began to regain their focus, he quickly remembered that it was not dry, hot or sunny, but cold, grey and damp, as the rain descended heavily from the murky heavens. He pressed his face up hard against the condensated window, and craned his neck to see what lay ahead of the large, heavy black steam engine, but the white plumes of smoke that spewed out from its thick black funnel was obscuring his view. Eventually, the dark, ghostly shape of a platform began to loom in front, but as the train neared the station it veered sharply onto a narrow siding to their left, before coming to a halt alongside twenty-five shallow, open-topped railway trucks.

'Philipp,' Josef said, the concern evident in his voice, 'what's going on? Why are we not at the station?'

Schlachter cut in before Philip could answer. 'Well, it's like this, mein schwarz freund,' he said. 'The local government doesn't want its dutiful taxpayers to be alarmed by a sudden influx of Jews and gypsies on their platforms. You must understand that Kolo Station is about to become a very busy place, so we have been sidelined to another gallery, if you get my drift?'

'Yes, I get your drift, Schlachter,' Josef said hotly, 'and in future, please don't address me as your "schwarz freund," got it?'

'Come on, Josef,' Philip said, patting him on the back, 'let's get off this old crate and start organising the refugees, eh?'

'Yes, let's go,' Josef agreed. 'There's a foul smell in here, don't you think?'

The two officers jumped down from the train onto the wet gravel, swiftly followed by Schlachter, and were walking back towards the boxcars when they were confronted by a group of dubious-looking sonderkommandos, led by a tall, rugged officer. The space between the two trains on either side of the platform was shadowed, giving the impression of a dark narrow corridor that served to make the motley crew appear even more menacing, but as the two Wehrmacht officers approached, Schlachter pushed himself in front of them and gave a long-armed nazi salute, before heartily shaking the hand of the commanding officer, much to the relief of Josef and Philip.

'Gentlemen,' Schlachter boomed, 'this is mein gut, gut freund, Hauptscharfuhrer [1.] Otto Trubel. We go back a long way, don't we?'

'Yes, Herr Oberleutnant,' Trubel said, 'but without sounding rude, can we press on and get the prisoners out of the boxcars and onto the railway trucks?'

'Ja, ja, Herr Hauptscharfuhrer,' Schlachter nodded enthusiastically. 'Herzog and Grinberger will supervise,' he said, turning to Josef and Philip. 'Well, what are you waiting for? Schnell!' he barked, clearly out to impress.

The officers split themselves into two groups, and Philip gave the order to open the boxcars. This had to be done quickly, as both he and Josef knew that the condition of the refugees would not be good after their long, confined journey, and as the first car was opened, their worst fears were confirmed. A small, fat sonderkommando removed the heavy padlock and then struggled to pull back the large wooden door, allowing a grey haze to rush out and five lifeless bodies to crash to the floor, followed by a massive stampede of people gasping for air. Once released, the refugees showed little regard for their dead compatriots, as they leapt from the boxcar and landed heavily on the urine-covered corpses below. Schlachter quickly drew his service pistol and began waving it in the air, threatening to shoot anyone who so much as thought about escaping. He ordered Josef and Philip to take charge of the situation, telling them to make use of all the guards at their disposal. This meant separating the men from women and the young from the old.

The sonderkommandos were brutal and overzealous in their treatment of the refugees, and were quick to strike any that failed to immediately comply with their orders, using the butts of their rifles as batons, or simply kicking and punching those foolish enough to argue with them. Josef witnessed one soldier grip a young woman by the collar of her coat and drag her over the jagged shale, before dumping her next to the open railway truck and demanding that she get on board, but her condition was weak. Racked with pain, and with her nylons shredded and her legs bleeding badly, she pleaded for mercy, but this only made the soldier even angrier. He responded by kicking her in the stomach, and then training his rifle on her head and firing. The noise of the shot sent a cold shudder up Josef's spine, as he reached the point where he could no longer contain himself. He approached Schlachter and protested in the strongest possible terms, but this only served to make the SS man more determined to crack on with the job, which meant robbing the Jews of any valuables they might have been carrying and stripping them of their furs, along with any other clothes considered to be of good quality, for shipment back to the Reich.

Josef, Philip and Penau had done their best to put the frightened captives at ease, and had almost loaded the last of them onto the train, with only two women still remaining on the gravel path, struggling to remove their coats for the demanding guards. Schlachter and Trubel were stood nearby, engrossed in conversation about who had the better sidearm, with Trubel insisting that his standard issue Luger pistol was far superior to Schlachter's small Walther P38, and suggesting that maybe he should try it out. Schlachter agreed to give it a go, taking hold of the heavy Luger and, without skipping a beat, aiming and firing it at one of the women, who was still in a state of semi-undress while being berated by a guard. The woman flinched sharply, and then dropped to the ground with a heavy thud. Schlachter then cocked the pistol and took aim again, this time zeroing in on the second woman, but Josef dashed across and stood in between them, shouting, 'I've had enough of you, you schwein! Lower the weapon and hand it back to der Hauptschar-fuhrer. Do it now!'

Schlachter and Trubel looked at each other and paused momentarily, before bursting into laughter. Schlachter then levelled the pistol at Josef's chest. 'Well, well, well,' he chuckled, 'if it isn't mein Juden loving freund. Always in my face, and always interfering. Well, this is the last time you'll interfere with me, Herzog. Prepare to join your Juden freunde, because I'm sending you directly to hell.'

Josef stepped back a few paces, settling on a spot where, if need be, he would make his final stand. 'You won't get away with this, Schlachter,' he said. 'If you don't lower that weapon, I swear I'll make sure everyone here knows about your dirty little secret.'

'What's he talking about?' Trubel asked, seemingly intrigued.

'Oh, nothing,' Schlachter said dismissively, 'he's just babbling and pleading for his miserable life. A life that is about to end.'

Just as he was about to shoot, Philip stepped forward and said quietly, 'Shoot him, and I'll give myself up to the authorities and tell them everything. That is, if you don't shoot me, too. But then, I should imagine that killing two officers would require quite a bit of explaining back at HQ, eh?'

Reluctantly, Schlachter lowered the pistol and returned it to Trubel, making out to his friend that it was all just a big joke, and then angrily turning and marching away.

'Danke, alter junger,' Josef said, placing his hand on Philip's shoulder. 'I owe you one, but I don't know if I've done the right thing by saving that woman's life today.'

'How could you say that?' Philip asked, bemused. 'You had no choice.'

'I don't know, Philip,' Josef shook his head. 'Terrible things are going to happen to those people once they reach Chelmno. It might have been more merciful to let Schlachter kill her there and then.'

'How are you so certain about what's going to happen to them at Chelmno?'

Josef's heart quickened, as he realised what he had just said. I must be more careful in future, he thought. A slip like that in front of the wrong person would surely land Stanizlaw in front of a firing squad. 'I'm not certain of anything,' he said quickly. 'Just forget I ever said it, OK?'

Philip shook his head in disbelief. 'You're a constant worry to me,' he said. 'Come on, let's find Penau. We're going home.'

They were soon boarded onto the train, and headed full steam towards Lodz Station. Josef removed his peaked visor cap and tossed it onto the empty seat opposite, and lay back with his feet up, blowing air out of his mouth. He closed his eyes and tried to block out the horrors of what he had just witnessed, but the terrifyingly graphic images remained. Opening his eyes, he began fumbling in his breast pocket for a pack of cigarettes and nervously pulled one out, which, with unsteady hands, he placed into the corner of his mouth and lit.

'Hey, are you alright?' Philip asked, sounding concerned. 'You look like shit.'

'Yes, I'm alright,' Josef said, placing his head in his hands, but then after a short pause he added, 'No, I'm not alright. I think I'm losing it!'

Philip got him to look up by snapping his fingers in the air. 'Waiter,' he called, 'zwei kognak bitte,' he turned back to Josef. 'Now, what's all this about? You're going home, back to Breslau.'

'Yes, but it's not really home, is it?'

'What's got into you? You're acting very strangely.'

'I know, but I can't help it. I've seen too much, too quickly. How many people do you know that have witnessed what we have seen? Tell me, how many?'

'Look, everything you say is true, but you're an officer in die Wehrmacht, which means that you're expected to deal with extreme circumstances. Here, drink this. It will make you feel better.'

Josef accepted a large glass of brandy, taking it in both hands and swigging it all in one go. He wiped his lips with the sleeve of his tunic and slouched back into his seat, feeling totally exhausted. He then thanked Philip for reminding him of his duty, and closed his eyes once more. When he awoke, he found that they had arrived back in Lodz.

'Well, how do you feel now, Herr Leutnant Viscount Herzog?' Philip asked.

'Like a complete arse, Herr Oberleutnant Grinburger. Would you accept an apology?'

'Ah, don't mention it,' Philip laughed. 'Even I gripe sometimes, you know.'

Penau popped his head through the carriage door, and announced that the staff car had arrived and was waiting at the main entrance of the train station. He also suggested that the officers should grab their gear and get a move on.

1. Master Sergeant.

CHAPTER THIRTY-SEVEN

The journey back to Aleksandrow seemed to pass quickly, and they soon found themselves parked outside the old blockhouse, with Erich waiting for them at the door.

'Gut reiser, gentlemen?' Erich asked.

'I wouldn't know,' Josef answered with a chortle, 'I was asleep the whole time.'

'What's tickling him?'

'Oh, it's a long story,' Philip replied. 'Let's just say that he's glad to be going home. Hey, got any schnapps? I could really do with a drink.'

'Sure, follow me,' Erich said.

They entered the mess hall, and were pleasantly surprised to see that Erich had already packed most of their gear into large green kit bags.

'Well anticipated,' Philip said, clapping his hands together.

'Yes, well done, Erich,' Josef echoed.

'Well, as you know, it's because of such anticipation, combined with a higher level of intelligence, that I have attained the rank of

Oberleutnant,' Erich grinned, 'which, Komrad, is something you will never be able to say.'

'Do we really have to listen to this dross?' Philip laughed. 'Just fetch the schnapps for Gott sake, man.'

'OK, OK, I'll get it,' Erich said, 'but if we can be serious for one moment, gentlemen, we don't have much time, so double-check everything.'

'Don't have much time?' Josef asked, pulling off his dusty boots. 'What do you mean?'

'What I'm saying is, a plane is due to land at Wolnosci Airfield within the hour, and its purpose is to fly us back to Breslau,' Erich beamed. 'So, if it's not too much trouble, could you please get your arse out of that chair and get moving?'

'Within the hour?' Philip belched. 'Why, that won't give me time to finish mein drink, let alone shower.'

'Hey, I've got no problem with that,' Josef said, putting his boots back on. 'The sooner I'm out of here, the better.'

'Sehr gut,' Erich said, rubbing his nose. 'Schnell, manner!'

Within twenty minutes, they were double-checked and packed ready for the airfield. Unterfeldwebel Penau shook hands with each of them, and wished them all a safe journey before helping them carry their heavy kit bags to the staff car that was waiting outside. They were then driven off at top speed, and although it was beginning to go dark, they could still clearly see the familiar shape of a Junkers ju 52 sitting on the edge of the airstrip, with all three of its engines running. The car screeched to a halt, and all three officers scrambled out holding onto to their caps, as the wind from the giant propeller blades blew back their long army coats, stretching them out like sails on a ship.

As they neared the plane, Erich shouted at the top of his voice,

'Hey fellas, look. It's Gunther!'

'Gunther!' Philip bellowed, as he clambered up the small metal steps to the plane. 'Guten tag, Gunther. Fancy meeting you again.'

'Ja, guten tag, Herr Leutnant,' Gunther replied. 'It's really gut to see you boys again. Please, get yourselves strapped in and we'll be on our way.'

The officers settled down into their seats, and Erich and Philip gently brushed back their hair with their hands as the engines roared, thrusting the plane forward. They were soon high up in the air, looking down at the airfield that was getting smaller and smaller as they soared into the darkening sky. Once the plane had levelled off, Gunther stuck his head through the cabin door and told them that it was safe to remove their seat belts, and offered them some light refreshments.

'Well, boys,' Erich said, leaning back with a cup of tea in his hand, 'it looks like we've all survived, eh?'

'Nein,' Josef snapped back, 'I think you mean that it's we who have survived, while you sat safely in that damned Altes Rathaus.'

'What are you babbling on about, man?' Erich frowned. 'As the officer in charge, I had to coordinate things from the CP, which just happened to be in the Altes Rathaus.'

'Yeah, right,' Josef grumbled.

'Hey, calm down, the pair of you,' Philip chuckled. 'We've all done our bit. It's just that Josef has done a little more, that's all.'

'You got that right,' Josef said.

'Ja, but it's all behind us now, correct?' Philip said, acting as referee.

'Yes, I suppose so,' Josef said flatly.

'Gut, now let's change the subject. Have you given any thought to where you'll have your birthday party once we're back at the base?'

'Well, not really,' Josef admitted. 'I've been a little distracted since Lodz.'

'Ja, well, that's understandable,' Philip said. 'I assume you're going to invite a lot of people?'

'Yes, there will be the War Council, of course, and a couple of Monika's freunde, too.'

'How about the officers' mess?' Philip suggested. 'It's pretty large, and should easily accommodate everyone.'

'Yes, that's a gut idea,' Josef nodded. 'Do you think you could clear it with Hauptmann Weise, Erich?'

'Oh sure, that won't be a problem. I'll also have a quiet word with Kurt, and ask him to do the catering.'

'Kurt?' Philip coughed.

'Why yes,' Erich said, 'what's wrong with Kurt?'

'He's the army cook, for Gott sake!' Philip cried.

'And?'

'Don't you remember Egon nearly choking on the bratwurst, just before we left for Lodz?'

'Perhaps you're right,' Erich laughed. 'OK, I'll bring in some outside help. Either way, you won't have to worry about a thing, Josef.'

'Thanks, Erich,' Josef said. 'I'm sorry about the way I spoke to you earlier.'

'Ah, forget it, man,' Erich brushed it off. 'Look, I know I wasn't with you on those missions, and If I could have kept you away from the horrors, I would have. But, like Philip says, it's all behind us now, so let's just concentrate on giving you a damned gut birthday party, eh?'

'Yes, of course,' Josef agreed, 'but thanks again anyway.'

'No problem,' Erich smiled. 'OK, I'm going up to have a chat with Gunther before we land, which should be in around ten minutes, so buckle up. We're almost home.'

Soon enough, the wheels of the Junkers ju 52 were screeching in the winter blackness, as the bulky plane bounced along until it finally touched down on the dry landing strip. The officers were soon whisked away in a rickety scout car, and were more than pleased to be heading back to their old unit in Breslau.

When they stepped out of the car upon arrival, everything seemed a little different, and it felt as though they had been away for a very long time. They fanned out in opposite directions with their heavy kit bags over their shoulders, having agreed to meet up later in the officers' mess. Josef kicked his door open and threw his bag down onto his narrow single bunk, before dropping into his chair and tugging at his dirty boots. As he did so, the door was flung open, and he was confronted by the image of the ginger beast clutching a bottle of Zekt.

'Hey Prinz, you look like shit, man,' Uri said. 'How are you, mein Afrikan freund?'

'Uri, did you really have to come barging in like that?' Josef asked. 'You scared me half to death!'

'Ah, come here and give me a big hug,' Uri demanded, picking Josef up off the floor like a rag doll. 'I've missed you, man. I've really missed you!'

'And I've missed you, too, you big tree,' Josef laughed. 'Now, put me down before you break something.'

'Get some glasses, Josef. I want to celebrate something.'

'No need. A simple handshake will do just fine.'

'Not because of you, you idiot. I want you to drink a toast to me and mein Honig.'

'You've lost me. Honig?'

'Ja, Honig. Mein neu fraulein. Her real name is Emmy – Emmy Kirche.'

'Oh, I see.'

Josef went over to his locker and found a small cup and a wine glass, and placed them on top of his desk. He then snatched the bottle of bubbly from under Uri's arm, popped the cork and began to pour.

'Hey, what are you doing, man?' Uri interrupted. 'I'll not drink champers from a damned cup!'

'Oh really?' Josef smirked. 'Is this the big hard soldat, who says he can lay in mud for up to a week when out in the field?'

'Ja, that's right, and I'm still not drinking from that cup.'

'Fine, I'll have the cup and you have the glass. How does that sound?'

'Much better. Anyway, that cup has a crack in it, you know.'

'Shut up, Uri, and let's drink the damned toast. Right then, to Emmy, or Honig and, uh... and may you have many children. Now, I don't wish to sound rude, but could you please get out of here. It feels like I've been in this same uniform for a month.'

'Ja, I'll go, but I thought we were freunde. I thought you would want to know more about Honig, but it looks like I was wrong, eh?'

'Gott damn it, Uri, wait a minute. Of course, I want to know all about her. Please, sit down and tell me. I really want to know.'

'OK, this won't take long. I know you've had a long journey.'

'Hey, don't worry yourself. Just take your time. It's like you said, we're gut freunde, recht?'

'Ja, sehr gut freunde.'

'Well, go on then. I'm all ears.' Josef sat back into his chair with his arms folded, waiting for Uri to finish guzzling from the half-empty bottle.

'I tell you, Josef,' Uri began, wiping his mouth on his sleeve, 'you really want to see this woman. She's really something else, man.'

'Where did you meet her?'

'Right here in Breslau. She's the personal secretary to Kommandant Siltz in Lodz. You've met him, ja?'

'Yes, he's a grade one Nazi. A right bastard.'

'Yeah, what's neu about that?'

'So, what does she look like, and where's she from?'

'She looks like an angel, truly. She's got long black hair that's like silk, and beautifully soft, creamy skin. She's from Melsbach, you know, Koblenz.'

'You know, it sounds like your describing mein Monika.'

'Nein, nein, she's nothing like her. She's got class and elegance.'

'You really know how to ruin a gut freundshiff, don't you, Uri? I think you're a little drunk, so maybe I should walk you back to your room. Come on, you giant ox.'

By the time Josef had got Uri tucked safely into bed, it was too late for him to meet up with the others in the mess hall, so he decided it would be best if he, too, were to get some shut eye, and retired to his own quarters. The following morning, he was out on the rifle range with his old pal, Feldwebel Schmidt, who was desperately trying to instruct the lads on their shooting skills, when Oberleutnant Viktor Pech appeared suddenly at the side of the gallery.

'Josef!' Viktor cheered. 'Welcome back.'

'Why, Viktor, it's gut to see you again,' Josef said. 'Sorry that I couldn't make it to the officers' mess last night. I ended up having to put Uri to bed.'

'Oh, that's alright. Uri told me all about it this morning. He seems to think that he might have upset you last night, but can't remember why?'

'We all say stupid things when we're drunk, Viktor. Anyway, why are you here? Surely, it's not to discuss Uri and his bad behaviour, is it?'

'You're quite right, I'm not here for that. I've come to tell you that you're to report to Herr Hauptmann Weise once you've finished here. Don't worry, it's nothing bad, I can assure you.'

'Ah, then I take it you know what it is all about, then?'

'That's correct, but I'm not going to tell you. You can find out for yourself.'

'Jawohl, Herr Oberleutnant Pech!' Josef shouted, clicking his heels together.

'Oh, shut up, man,' Victor laughed, turning to leave. 'Just get yourself over to his office when you're ready.'

'Are you in trouble, Herr Leutnant?' Schmidt asked, having overheard only part of the conversation.

'Not at all, Schmidt,' Josef said, 'or at least I don't think so anyway. Tell the men to continue firing.' He paced up and down the line of soldiers lying on their stomachs, with his right arm behind his back as he yelled out orders and advice. 'Hold the butt of the rifle tight into your shoulder, Gruber,' he told one man, 'and then gently squeeze the trigger. Adjust your gun site, Manfried, and Private Klotz, never point your rifle at the man next to you while reloading!'

He then stood back and asked Feldwebel Schmidt to take over while he reported to Hauptman Weise.

'Yes, come in,' Weise called, prompting Josef to enter his office. 'Ah, Herzog, you got the message from Pech, then?'

'Yes, Herr Hauptmann.'

'Gut, please sit down. How was your journey back to Breslau?'

'Not too bad, sir. I'm just glad to be back.'

'Yes, of course, and it's gut to have you back. Now, I've asked to see you this morning because I have some gut news for you.'

'Gut news, sir?'

'Yes, very gut news, Herzog. Do you remember our conversation at the Hastlers' New Year's Eve party?'

'Uh, vaguely, sir.'

'Do you remember me saying that the Herr Major and I would do everything within our power to get back your laurels?'

'Oh yes, I do remember that, sir.'

Weise pushed a small, dark green leather box across his desk, along with an oval-shaped black wound badge. Josef sat rigid and dumbstruck as he stared down at the awards.

'Well, go on, open it,' Weise said, pointing to the box. 'You've certainly earned it, man.'

Josef gently pulled the domed case over, and then placed his wound badge next to it. On the lid of the case, a silver Iron Cross was stamped, and beneath it, also in silver, was the date of the battle, 23.11.39, a day that he would always reflect on with bittersweet emotion. He carefully pressed a small brass button on the rim of the case, clicking it open. The underside of the lid was lined with a fine, thin white silk, and had a gold Iron Cross stamped in its centre. The bottom of the case was also lined, but with a plush red velvet that housed a heavy black Iron Cross, edged in thin silver. In its magnetic centre sat an embossed black swastika set at an angle, and directly beneath it were the raised numbers, 1939.

'Well, don't just stare at them, man,' Weise chuckled. 'Put them on!'

Josef got up slowly and stood at the edge of the desk, pausing for a moment before carefully removing the Iron Cross from its box and nervously pinning it to his left breast pocket. He then reached down and picked up the wound badge, which he attached just below the Iron Cross.

'I don't know what to say, sir,' he said.

'You don't have to say anything, Herzog. Just wear them with pride, and congratuliere.'

'Thank you very much, sir,' Josef said, leaning over the desk and shaking Weise by the hand. 'It's a pity mein vater isn't here to see this, sir. I'm sure he would have been very proud of me.'

'Yes, I'm sure he would have been. Anyway, here are your certificates. Please keep them safe, because they're your only proof of ownership, verstehen?'

'Yes, and thank you again, sir.'

'Don't thank me, Herzog. Like I said, you earned them.'

They saluted each other, and then Josef returned to the rifle range, where he proudly showed off his awards to Schmidt, who also offered his congratulations. He then decided to leave the range, and made his way back to his office to sort out his new duty rosters. He sat behind his old rickety desk to start work, but was disturbed by a loud knock at the door.

'Egon!' he said, as his friend entered the room. 'You old warhorse, how are you, man?'

'Not as gut as you, it would appear,' Egon said. 'Stand up and let me look at you.'

Josef got to his feet and stood rigid, pulling his tunic down smartly.

'Well, look at you,' Egon smirked. 'I see Weise has given you your birthday present early, eh?'

'Hardly a present, alter junger. I earned it, remember?'

'But of course, Herr Oberst, and I'm sure you will take every opportunity to keep reminding me of that fact.'

'Oh, be quiet and grab a chair. You know, it seems like an age since I last saw you. Anything happened lately?'

'No, you've missed nothing. Life in the army camp can be boring. Unless, that is, someone decides to throw a big party.'

'Don't worry,' Josef laughed, 'the party's on, and of course you're invited.'

'Naturlich, but if it's not too much trouble, could I ask where and when?'

'It's tomorrow at twenty-hundred hours, in the officers' mess hall – damph!'

'Was ist los? I know you've left it a little late to tell me, but I can still make it, you know.'

'That wasn't aimed at you, you arse. It's Monika. I've forgotten to tell her.'

'Well, in that case, don't you think you should pick up the telephone and call her?'

'Don't worry yourself, Egon. I'll do it as soon as you get out of here.'

'OK, OK, I'm going. Don't take it out on me, just because you forgot to tell your girlfriend.'

'Yes, you're right, I'm sorry. Still, if you really wouldn't mind-'

'Hey, no problem,' Egon cut him off, taking the hint, 'I'm out of here.'

Josef waited until Egon had left the office before taking a cigarette from the small metal box on his desk. He lit the long, white filter tip and then reluctantly lifted the old black bakelite telephone receiver, but when he asked the operator to quickly put him through to the Hastlers' residence, he was stunned to hear Colonel Hastler's voice on the other end of the line.

'Ja?' Hastler answered.

'Oh, hello Herr Oberst,' Josef panicked, 'sorry to disturb you, sir.

It's Leutnant Herzog here.'

'Ah, Herzog,' Hastler said amiably, 'what can I do for you?'

'Well, sir, I was wondering if you would be so kind as to put Monika on the line?'

'I'm afraid she's not here. She's out shopping with her mutter, I think. Can I take a message?'

'No, thank you, Herr Oberst. I'll call back later, if that is alright, sir?'

'Yes, of course. It's gut to have you back with the unit, Herzog.'

'Why thank you, Herr Oberst. I'm glad to be back, sir.'

'Yes, yes, quite. You must come over for dinner sometime. Mein frau and I would be pleased to see you again.'

'That would be a great honour, sir. I will arrange it with Monika when we next speak.'

'Sehr gut. I'll leave that with you, then. Guten tag.'

'Guten tag, Herr Oberst.'

With only one day to go, panic set in as Josef realised that he had done nothing towards organising his own birthday party. No invitations had been written out, and no provision had been made for the huge amounts of food and alcohol that would be needed to soothe the massive hunger of the War Council. In fact, he realised, he had not even bothered to find out if the officers' mess had been reserved for him. Deciding that he must do something and do it quickly if he were to save face, he locked up the office and made a mad dash over to Erich Heiter's office, hoping that he had made good on his promise to do everything that he could to help with the party. As it turned out, he need not have worried, because Erich had indeed honoured his promise, and everything was already in place. The officers' mess had been secured, and Philip had taken care of the drink situation. The only thing left to do was to write out the invitations, and so Josef, realising that there was very little time to get this done, decided to return to his office. It was too late to send out written invites, so he thought it better to simply phone all of the people that he hoped would be attending. He began to compile a list of names, and then worked his way through them, crossing them off one by one as he went along. Eventually, he had covered almost everyone, but there was still one last name on the list to be scratched off.

Monika.

He rang the Hastler household once again, and this time he was more successful. He was put straight through to Monika, who sounded a little annoyed at the last-minute invite, but was soon talked around by Josef's silk tongue. She told him that Irma would not be attending, due to her still being too distressed after her recent ordeal at the hands of Lunder. Josef understood completely, and asked Monika to pass on his best wishes to her freund, who he hoped would make a full recovery.

Having finally reached the end of his list, he replaced the receiver, only for the telephone to start ringing barely a second later. He quickly answered, and was exasperated to hear Uri on the line, imploring him to hurry over to his quarters, because there was something he urgently needed to show him. Despite Josef's initial protestations, Uri refused to take no for an answer, and demanded in no uncertain terms that he come at once. In the end, Josef caved, and after hastily buttoning up his tunic he made the walk through the maze of green camouflaged barracks, saluting everyone he met along the way. As he turned the final corner on his journey, he could see Uri waiting impatiently for him in the doorway of his quarters.

'Prinz, come quickly,' Uri whispered anxiously, 'there's something you really must see.' He led him to a small car park at the back of his billet, and stood him on the edge of the tarmac. 'Well, what do you think?' he grinned.

'What do I think?' Josef replied, somewhat bemused. 'I think I'm in a car park, Uri. I can't believe that you brought me all this way just to see a car park.'

'Calm down a moment, and just tell me what you see.'

'I see an auto, Uri. Just an auto.'

'Wrong, Prinz, it's not just an auto. It's mein auto. What do you think of her?'

'Ah yes, I remember now,' Josef said, hand on chin. 'Erich told me that you had bought a new auto, and a very nice one, too. What is it?'

'Well, I'm glad you asked. Are you ready for this? It's a Mercedes-Benz Kompressor sport Cabriolet SSK Karrosserie Papler.'

'A what?'

'Do you really want me to repeat all that?'

'Well, no, perhaps not.'

'Gut, so, would you like to take a closer look?'

'Certainly, but first, I must say, that by breaking your promise to Viktor, you have placed us all in great danger.'

'Nonsense, what are you talking about? OK, I might have spent a little cash, but it's hardly the crime of the century now, is it, man?'

'You just don't get it, do you? Oh well, come on. Show me your pride and joy.'

They walked around the back of the vehicle, and then slowly worked their way to the front while Uri gestured with his finger, pointing out some of the car's finer features, like the double spare wheels that were attached to the outside of the snub nose boot, secured by a long narrow licence plate. He patted the retractable black canvas roof affectionately, before opening the passenger side door. Josef leaned inside and filled his nostrils with the thick, rich aroma of the new oxblood-coloured leather interior. The car was a black lacquered two door coupe with a long concertina bonnet, complemented by the iconic Mercedes emblem which sat on the huge split chrome radiator.

'This car must have cost a fortune,' Josef remarked.

'Yes, it did,' Uri said, 'and this baby can really move, too. Under the bonnet is a seven-point-two litre engine, and when the supercharger kompressor kicks in, it can reach speeds of up to one hundred and twenty-five miles per hour. Not that I've ever tried it, obviously.'

'I should hope not. A focker wolf [1.] wouldn't give you much more. Now, is that it? There are a lot of things that I have to attend to before the party tomorrow.'

'Well, I was going to suggest that we take her out for a quick spin, but if you'd rather sit in that boring office of yours doing boring paperwork, I'll leave you to it.'

'Don't be like that, Uri. Once the party is out of the way, I'd be glad to go for a drive.'

'I'll hold you to that. If, by some chance, I don't see you tomorrow, I'll see you at the party, OK?'

'OK, see you at the party,' Josef said, as he turned to head back towards his office.

'Oh, and Prinz,' Uri called after him, 'congratuliere on winning die Eisern Kreuz, ja?'

1. Fighter plane.

CHAPTER THIRTY-EIGHT

Josef stood silently, arms folded, in the doorway of the busy mess hall, watching in amazement as Oberleutnant Viktor Pech organised his men. All of the officers were hastily repositioning furniture and hanging decorations from the walls and ceilings, while Philip and Egon each stood on tall ladders at opposite sides of the hall and struggled to put up a large banner, and Erich and Uri pushed the long tables together and covered them with crisp white table clothes. As Viktor bent down to pick up a basket of flowers, he noticed Josef standing in the doorway, and rushed over to place a hand over his mouth and push him out of the hall.

'What the hell are you doing here?' Viktor hissed. 'You're not supposed to see all of this yet!'

'I couldn't find anyone, and when I asked Gefreiter Ghetz where you were, he told me you were all here,' Josef explained. 'I'm sorry if I've messed things up for you, Viktor.'

'It's OK, I don't think anyone saw you,' Viktor said, glancing back over his shoulder. 'The party's not until eight, so you must keep out of the way until then, or else it will be ruined.'

'I understand,' Josef said. 'I'll go now. I need to get washed and changed anyway.'

'Yes, you do that, and make sure you stay away until it's time, because the lads have worked very hard on this.'

'Don't worry, I won't spoil it. See you later.'

Josef returned to his quarters and prepared for the party that was to be held in his honour. He laid out a fresh uniform on his bunk, and then rang Monika one last time before taking a long shower. She had informed him that because of Irma's regrettable situation, she would have no choice but to attend the function alone, and asked if it would be possible for her to meet him at his quarters, so that they may enter the party together. Josef thought that this was a great idea, and eagerly agreed. It was now 6.45pm, and he had just buttoned up his shirt and trousers when there was a loud bang at his door, followed by Egon entering in a bit of a fluster.

'You've got to help me,' Egon said, despair etched across his face. 'I've burst mein breeches, and I don't know what to do.'

'Gott, you really pick your moments,' Josef said, shaking his head. 'What do you expect me to do about it?'

'Well, you're much better than me with a needle and thread, so I thought that maybe you could help repair them?'

'Right, take off your trousers and throw them to me. You know what your trouble is, don't you?'

'What?'

'You're too damned fat!'

'Now steady on, alter junger. While I agree that I may like mein food, I wouldn't say that I had a problem.'

'Now, there's your problem right there – you think you don't have a problem. Gott, look at the time. I'm expecting Monika here at any moment.'

'Don' worry, I'll be out of here long before she arrives, but if you don't mind me saying, wouldn't you be better using a darker thread? That's yellow.'

'Gut Gott, man, why didn't you tell me?'

'I, uh, just did.'

'Damnph, I'll have to start again.'

Josef did end up finishing the job with plenty of time to spare, or so he thought, but then as Egon paraded up and down the room to make sure that the stitching was going to hold, he noticed a thin piece of cotton hanging loose, and instructed Egon to bend over while he removed it. He crouched down with one hand resting on on Egon's buttock and took aim with the scissors, and unfortunately, it was at this precise moment that Monika burst into the room shouting, 'Surprise!'

After some red faces and a lot of explaining, Egon hurriedly left to finish getting ready, allowing Josef to drink in Monika, who looked like a fairy tale princess in her pretty red silk party dress, which flowed down in spiralled pleats and gathered on the floor, covering her tiny red sling-backed shoes. Her shiny dark auburn hair was slightly waved, and there was a single red artificial rose carefully fixed on the left side of her head. A row of thick red beads hung around her neck, complementing her porcelain skin, while also helping to show off her low-cut cleavage. Still giggling at the scene she had walked in on, she commented that Josef looked smart and very manly in his tunic, complete with his new Iron Cross and wound badge. So impressive was his rapid rise, she added in jest, that she could possibly see him in a general's uniform before the year was out.

They walked out of his quarters arm in arm, and Josef made Monika promise not to reveal what she had witnessed with him and Egon under pain of death. As they approached the officers' mess, they could hear the muffled sounds of music and laughter, and Josef hesitated for a moment before pushing open the door and stepping inside. The room was bright, busy and smoky, with lots of red streamers hanging from the ceiling, and directly in front of them dangled a large grey banner which ran from one side of the room to the other, bearing the words, 'Happy 21st birthday, Josef,' in blue and white water colours. To the left were rows of tables covered in white cloth, where a wide variety of food, fruit and drink had been laid out, while on the opposite side of the hall were neatly arranged tables and chairs, also draped in white cloth. On each table there was a silver tub of champagne on ice, positioned next to a small flickering candle mounted on an ornamental holder. At the far end of the room stood a group of three uniformed musicians: a violinist, a guitarist and accordion player. This makeshift band was crammed into the right-hand corner of the room, where they were quietly playing an old German standard, Guten Nacht My Dear. The lads had indeed done Josef proud, and they all stood and clapped as they realised that he and Monika had entered the room.

Viktor was the first to come forward and congratulate Josef on his birthday, giving him a manly hug while puffing on a thick cigar. The rest of the War Council soon followed, surrounding him and offering hearty slaps on the back. Egon, still red faced from recent events, sheepishly asked Josef and Monika to take their seats, so that the celebrations could begin in earnest.

Viktor stood in the centre of the room and called for silence, and then shouted, 'Where's the cake?' prompting Philip and Egon to run over to the opposite table and huddle together, shielding the cake from view while attempting to light twenty-one candles. After two failed attempts, they finally gave Viktor the thumbs up, following which he loudly announced, 'Glucklich geburtstag, Josef!'

Everyone clapped and cheered, 'Huah! Huah! Huah!' as Philip and Egon awkwardly lifted the huge cake, and then wobbled their way across the floor to place it gently down in front of Josef. They stood back and waited for him to say something, but instead he sat rigid in his chair, and simply stared at the cake like a startled rabbit.

'I think you're suppose to make a wish,' Monika whispered.

'Yes, make a wish and blow out the candles, man!' Uri roared.

Josef paused for a moment, still gazing down at the freshly baked cake, which was covered with thick white marzipan, and had the words, 'Glucklich Geburtstag, Herr Leutnant,' written across it in thin, light-blue sugar piping, framed by twenty-one tall matching candles. He filled his lungs with air, and then blew out all the candles in one long breath, creating a huge plumb of smoke that briefly hovered over the table. When the smoke had cleared, he looked up and was surprised to see Herr Hauptmann Weise and Herr Major Lowe standing before him, each holding small gifts in their hands.

'Here, just some cigars from me,' Weise said, smiling warmly. 'Glucklich geburtstag.'

'Why thank you, sir,' Josef said. 'I had no idea that either of you were coming tonight.'

'We're not staying long,' Lowe answered for the both of them, while handing over his gift. 'I hope you like Polish cigarettes.'

'Yes indeed, Herr Mayor, thank you. This was most unexpected.'

'Well, everyone likes a surprise on their birthday, Herzog,' Lowe said. 'Anyway, we really must be going now. Enjoy your evening, but don't be late for duty tomorrow, verstehen?' he chuckled.

Josef stood and shook hands with the two officers as they made their exit from the party, and Uri, obviously seeing this as his chance, grabbed his girlfriend by the arm and rapidly approached the top table.

'Still brown-nosing Herr Major Lowe, eh?' Uri said, announcing himself.

'What are you talking about?' Josef said defensively.

'Hey, only joking, man,' Uri laughed. 'I would like you both to meet mein fiancée, Emmy Kirche. Emmy, this is Prinz- uh, I mean, Josef, and his fiancée, Monika.'

'Ah, Honig,' Josef said, 'I've heard a lot about you. Oh,' he noticed a change in her demeanour, 'did I say something wrong?'

'Uh, I only use that name when we're alone,' Uri murmured.

'Oh, forgive me Fraulein Kirche,' Josef said. 'I meant no disrespect.'

'That's alright, Herr Leutnant,' Emmy giggled. 'I find it quite amusing that you have managed to embarrass Uri. That's not an easy thing to do, you know.'

'Yes, tell me about it,' Josef agreed. 'Would you like to sit down and join us?'

'Perhaps later,' Uri said, rubbing his hands together. 'There's still lots of booze on that table over there that needs some exploring, if you get me.'

'Yes, of course,' Josef laughed. 'Explore away, mein freund.'

The party was a complete success, with everyone who had been invited turning up. Josef pulled his chair closer to Monika's, so that they could be more intimate, and told her how much he regretted that Irma could not be with them on this special occasion. He then leaned forward and placed his arm around her, and they sat and chatted for a time before he moved his chair closer again, and he was about to give her an affectionate kiss when they were interrupted by Philip, who walked up to the table brandishing a large kitchen knife.

'The cake,' Philip shouted over the din. 'It's time to cut the cake!'

'Do I really have to?' Josef moaned. 'I feel such a fool.'

'Oh, but you must,' Monika bubbled, as she took a sip of champagne. 'It's tradition, you must cut the cake.'

'OK, fine,' Josef gave in. 'Keep me covered, Philip. I'm going in.'

Using the knife more like an axe, he began hacking his way through the cake, dissecting it into large chunks, much to the delight of Egon and Uri, who eagerly stepped forward with plates at the ready and began to argue over who should get the biggest piece. Viktor was called over to act as referee, asking the gentlemen to shake hands and refrain from using bad language in front of the ladies. The two behemoths reluctantly agreed to a ceasefire and were sent back to their respective partners, and Erich ordered the ragtag group of musicians to strike up once again. He then requested that everyone take to the dance floor and enjoy themselves.

'Fancy a dance?' Josef asked, arm extended.

'I thought you'd never ask,' Monika smiled.

'There they go,' Erich said to Viktor, as Josef and Monika went past hand in hand, 'like two people in love.'

'They are in love,' Viktor replied, 'and there's nothing wrong with that.'

'Oh, come off it. You know that in reality, they'll never be allowed to marry or have children. The state won't allow it.'

'So, what are they supposed to do, just stop loving each other? They know the risks, and I'm sure that they're fully prepared for whatever may come their way.'

'Look, you know as well as I do that they've got all the odds stacked against them. Surely, you must fear for them?'

'May I ask you something, Erich?'

'Fire away.'

'Is it your turn to get the drinks in, or mine?'

On the next table along, Egon and Philip were quietly discussing politics, and steadily getting drunk as they did so. Philip leaned across the table, struggling to hear what Egon was saying because he was beginning to slur his words.

'Did you see all those SS troupe gathering in the compound earlier today?' Egon asked.

'Yes, I did,' Philip said. 'They looked like FBK.' [1.]

'Well, some were, but the others were Leibstandarte. They were here with their leader, Oberstgruppenfuhrer Sepp Dietrich.'

'Wow, it must be serious,' Philip said. 'Why were they here?'

'They were here because... uh, what was I saying?'

'You were talking about the SS troupe. You where telling me why they were here.'

'Oh yes, the SS trupp.'

'Well, go on.'

'Right, now listen carefully, because what I'm about to tell you is top secret, verstehen?'

'Yes, yes, but tell me quickly, before you forget again.'

'OK, OK, now, what was I saying – only joking. The Leibstandarte were here to rest and refuel before setting off for Rastenburg, in East Prusser.'

'Ah, of course, die wolf's lager.' [2.]

'Correct. Der Furhrer is to visit Poland sometime tomorrow, although the exact time is not known for security reasons, you understand.'

'Yes, of course, but what I wouldn't give just to be there. I've never seen him in the flesh, so to speak.'

'Listen, you must never speak of this conversation, because if it ever got out, we could be shot.'

'Don't worry, Egon,' Philip laughed, clasping his friend by the shoulder, 'your secret is safe with me. Now, more wine?'

1. The Fuhrer's escort commando.
2. The Wolf's Lair.

The Grey Storm

CHAPTER THIRTY-NINE

Josef leaned back in his chair, totally drunk and exhausted. His tunic was unbuttoned, and his right arm dangled lifelessly, with his hand still wrapped around an empty glass. Monika was sat nearby, talking quietly with Emmy, who had also been left sitting like an army widow since Uri had passed out. The ginger beast was sat on the floor in the corner opposite the musicians, looking like a shop window mannequin with his head bowed and his legs spread-eagled. The music was still playing softly in the background, but only a few people remained on the dance floor, propping one another up as they shuffled around in tight circles.

'Wake up, Josef,' Monika said, nudging him with her elbow.

'What, was ist los?' he said, waking with a start.

'It's quite late. I have to go now.'

'Oh right, yes. Just give me a minute, and I'll walk you home.'

'No need. Mein vater has arranged for his chauffeur to pick me up at the entrance of the barracks, but you can walk me to the door, if you like.'

'No, I'll walk you to the car. It's very dark out there.'

Josef wobbled to his feet and struggled to button up his uniform. He linked arms with Monika, and then walked her to the door of the officers' mess on unsteady legs. They embraced on the small step outside, taking in the cold, fresh night air. He gently brushed back her hair and removed the single red rose, holding it tightly in his hand. He then began to kiss her lovingly on the lips, until she insisted that he return to the party, as he was the worse for drink and couldn't stand up straight. After a lengthy debate, she managed to convince him that she would be quite safe walking alone, pointing out that the army base was one of the most secure places to be, and adding that she only had to travel a short distance from the mess hall to the main gate, where her father's chauffeur would be waiting. He embraced and kissed her one more time, and then propped himself up against the doorframe for support, while waving her goodbye. He nervously watched as she slowly walked past the dimly-lit ammunition stores, and when she reached the corner she paused and looked back over her shoulder, giving him a wave and a smile before disappearing out of view. He remained out in the doorway a while longer, only returning to the party when he could no longer hear the clicking of her high-heeled shoes.

Monika navigated her way through the maze of shadowy buildings without issue, until all she had to do was walk between the last two dark barracks that lay ahead of her. However, as she began this last leg of her journey, she became aware that someone was following her. She heard the dull thud of boots hitting the ground, and instinctively knew that it was a well-built man. She was tempted to look back, but the fear was too great, so she quickened her step and pulled her shawl up over her shoulders. The noise of her three-inch stiletto shoes rebounded off the damp, dark walls and grew louder with each long stride. She was halfway past the barracks now, and could see the bright lights that would lead her to the main gate, but the heavy footsteps behind were gaining on her fast. She increased her pace yet again, but it was no use; she could almost feel his breath on the back of her neck, and she realised that she had no choice other than to reach deep down inside and muster the courage to turn and face her pursuer. Stopping dead in her tracks, she took a deep breath before turning around and finding that she need not have worried, because even in the dark, she knew this gentleman quite well.

'Why, is that you, Herr Sturmbannfuhrer?' Monika said, squinting her eyes.

'Yes, Fraulein Hastler,' Lunder said, stepping forward.

'You almost frigtened me half to death, sir!'

'Tut mir leid, fraulein,' he bowed, 'that was not my intention. I was concerned when I saw you walking alone. Herzog must think very little of you, or else he would never have allowed such a beautiful young woman like yourself to wander alone at this late hour. He should be flogged.'

'I beg your pardon, sir?'

'Oh, come on, fraulein. Surely, you must understand that these primates don't know how to treat white women. How could you possibly allow yourself to be soiled by this Afrikan? You're of gut German stock, and you should keep to your own kind. It's not too late, you know,' he reached out and seized her by the arm.

'What are you doing, sir?' she said, trying in vain to free herself from his grasp. 'Kindly take your hands off me.'

'Don't get uppity with me, schlampe,' he hissed. 'After being with him, you're nothing more than a used mattress to me. Now, come here and give to me what you gave to him.'

A violent struggle ensued, resulting in Monika being thrown to the ground.   She landed hard, banging her head against the cold ground, with her pretty red beads scattering across the shiny cobbles before coming to rest in the gutter. A thin trickle of blood began to run from the side of her mouth, but she still resisted strongly as the Major desperately ripped at her clothes in a blind frenzy. She begged him to stop, warning that she would call out for help, but he told her that if she did, he would kill her. Ignoring her pitiful pleas for help, he continued to pull at her underclothes like a man possessed, and although beginning to weaken, she somehow managed to let out a loud, blood-curdling scream!

Lunder responded by placing his hand over her mouth, but it wasn't enough to muffle the high-pitched sound as she kicked and punched to create space, so he put both hands around her throat and squeezed until she fell silent. Once she had stopped struggling, he slumped over her body, totally exhausted, before suddenly coming to his senses.

'No more hugs and kisses for you, schlampe,' he whispered, as he stood up and straightened his black uniform.

CHAPTER FORTY

After a series of loud bangs at his door, Josef was awake, albeit still somewhat groggy, half-dressed in his uniform. He opened the door and was greeted by an officer, Kapitan Runzel, holding out a piece of paper in front of him, as well as two guardsmen that were both wearing long great coats, with their large metal feld gendarme gorgets displayed proudly on their chests. They were armed with rifles that were pointed in Josef's direction.

'Are you Herr Leutnant Josef Herzog?' Runzel asked.

'You know who I am, sir,' Josef said, rubbing his eyes. 'What's this all about?'

'Just answer the question please,' Runzel said sharply.

'Yes, I am Josef Herzog.'

'Do you know who I am?'

'Yes, you're Herr Runzel, kapitan of die militarisch polizei. Now, will you please tell me what the hell is going on?'

'I'm here to place you under arrest.'

'Arrest? On what charge, sir?'

'I'm arresting you for the murder of Fraulein Monika Hastler.'

'What? Have you lost your mind?'

'I must warn you that anything you say will be written down and used as evidence against you, verstehen?'

'Herr Runzel, you're making a terrible mistake. This is a nightmare, a Gott damned nightmare! I love Monika. I would never hurt her.'

'Get yourself dressed,' Runzel said flatly. 'We're taking you into custody.'

'First, you must tell me about Monika. Where and when did this happen?'

'Everything will be fully explained to you once we arrive at HQ.'

'Will you allow me a telephone call, Herr Runzel?'

'You can use the phone at the station, Herr Leutnant, but we must move now.'

He was taken to a local police station near D Company HQ for questioning, and was placed in a cell. It was the same one he had shared with Uri when they were arrested on New Year's Eve. After a brief wait, he heard the lock being turned, and when the door opened, two guardsmen entered and told him to follow them, leading him down a long narrow corridor, which led to a tiny, dimly lit room where he found Kapitan Runzel and a junior officer sitting side by side behind a small desk.

'Please, take a seat, Herr Leutnant,' Runzel said, extending his hand. 'This is mein first officer, Herr Oberleutnant Gruber. He will be recording and witnessing everything we say, verstehen?'

'Yes, sir,' Josef said.

'Would you like to light a cigarette before we begin?' Runzel said, indicating a crushed-up packet lying in front of him on the desk.

'Nein, danke,' Josef replied nervously, as he settled himself into the hard-backed chair.

'Very, well,' Runzel said, placing the cigarettes into his top pocket. 'Now, I want you to tell me everything that happened from the moment you and Fraulein Hastler left the party.'

'We left the party, and I walked Monika to the door of the officers' mess.'

'What time was this?'

'Uh, it would have been before midnight, I think.'

'Could you be more precise please, Herzog? It's very important.'

'I'm afraid I can't. I was very drunk, you know. Listen, I want to make a telephone call.'

'Who would you like to call?'

'I would like to speak with Hauptmann Weise, sir.'

'I don't think he'd be too pleased to be woken at this unchristliche Stunde, Herzog.'

'Nevertheless, he's my commanding officer, and should thus be made fully aware of the situation, sir.'

'Yes, I suppose you're right. May I suggest that we bring him here, so that you may confer with him in person?'

'Yes, sir, that would be better.'

'Gruber, make it so,' Runzel said, and the younger officer stood and left immediately. 'Now, Herzog, I hope you have no objection to us continuing our conversation until Weise gets here?'

'I would rather wait.'

'These are just a few harmless questions, and you should have no problem answering them. That is, unless, you have something to hide?'

'I have nothing to hide, sir. I'm completely innocent.'

'Well, I'm glad to hear it. Now, let's go back to when you and Fraulein Hastler reached the door of the officers' mess.'

'OK, we went to the door and stood outside on the step for a while.'

'How long were you out there on the step?'

'We were there for about ten minutes.'

'Did anyone else see you?'

'I didn't notice. We talked for a while, and then she left to meet with her vater's chauffeur, who was waiting for her at the gate. That was the last time that I saw her.'

'Then what did you do?'

'I waited on the step until she was out of view, and then I returned to the party.'

'And you're sure that nobody saw you on the step?'

'If there was somebody there, I didn't see them, sir.'

'Is it fair to say that Fraulein Hastler was well on her way before twelve o'clock, Herzog?'

'Yes, that would be fair to say, sir.'

Suddenly, the door flew open and Hauptmann Weise strode in, wearing a full-length black leather coat, which was half off his shoulders, revealing that he was still wearing his pyjamas underneath.

'You must stop this interview at once, Runzel,' Weise ordered. 'Herzog, do not say another word.'

'Herr Hauptmann, it's gut to see you,' Runzel said.

'I wish I could say the same to you,' Weise replied angrily. 'What do you think you're playing at, interviewing a suspect without representation?'

'Herzog said that he had no problem with being interviewed, Herr Hauptmann,' Runzel answered, 'so I continued.'

'Indeed you did,' Weise spat. 'May I have some time alone with the suspect please?'

'Of course, Herr Hauptmann,' Runzel stood and made to leave.

'Take as long as you like.'

Weise waited for Runzel to close the door behind him before giving Josef some sound advice, reminding him that he must never talk without counsel. He then asked Josef to repeat everything that he had said to Runzel, listening intently and then suggesting that he get some rest. He promised that he would return later that morning with someone better versed in the law, to act as legal counsel. Josef repeatedly pleaded his innocence to Weise, who assured him that he believed him. They then shook hands, and Weise left to make the necessary arrangements.

Having been returned to his cell on Weise's orders, Josef lay in darkness on the narrow bunk with his hands behind his head, lost in deep thought as he stared up at the cracked off-white ceiling above. He eventually fell asleep, and by the time he woke up the room had filled with the bright orange glow of the morning sun, which was bursting in through the small grilled window above. It was a refreshing and beautiful sight, and he sat up and rubbed at his eyes. Maybe this is all just a bad dream, he thought, as he sat on the edge of his bunk, yawning and scratching his head, but when he looked around and took stock of his situation, the nightmare became very real. The key turned in the lock once again, and the cell door slowly creaked open. Runzel entered the room carrying a large tin tray, containing a small bowl of muesli and a tall glass of fresh orange juice. Josef looked down at his wristwatch; it was 6.00am.

'Guten morgen, Herr Leutnant,' Runzel said. 'Once you've finished your breakfast, I have orders to drive you to Breslau-Rosenthal for further questioning.'

'Breslau-what?' Josef asked.

'Rosenthal. It's a district near the River Oder, famous for its porcelain.'

'Its what?'

'China. You do know what china is, don't you?'

'Why are you taking me there?'

'You're going there because, firstly, it's considered far too dangerous for you to stay here. You're too close to the murder scene, and moreover, too close to the Hastler family. If someone were to seek retribution, you wouldn't exactly be a hard target to miss. Secondly, Rosenthal has a small, but well defended, military base, and you'll be much safer there.'

'I can't believe that anyone would want to harm me, Herr Runzel. Everyone that knows me will also know that I'm innocent.'

'That may be so, but it's our job to make sure no harm comes to you before your trial.'

'I see. Does that mean that after the trail you won't give a damn about what happens to me?'

'Eat your breakfast,' Runzel said, turning to exit, 'we leave soon.'

'Oh, Herr Runzel,' Josef called after him, 'what is happening about mein counsel?'

'Don't worry, all of that is being taken care of. Now, eat.'

At 6.30am, Runzel arrived with a two-man escort and ushered Josef along the corridor, stopping short of the main entrance while one of the guards surveyed the empty street outside, and then beckoned the others to move quickly from the doorway and into a waiting car, with its doors fully opened and the engine running. Once inside the vehicle, Runzel ordered him to lie down until they were well clear of company HQ, and despite them accelerating at speed, the drive seemed to take forever. He began to feel claustrophobic after being helped up from the floor to sit squashed between the two guards on the back seat, and his sense of uneasiness wasn't helped by the driver adjusting his mirror and staring at him suspiciously.

He craned his neck to get a better look out of the passenger window, and watched as the regular people went about their daily business, envying their freedom.

'We're here,' Runzel announced, as the car pulled up sharply outside a small stone building, which was draped in the familiar red Nazi hue.

Once again, Josef was led along a tiny corridor and into a small, dimly lit room, but this time there was only one solitary uniformed figure sitting behind the desk. The man gave a simple gesture with his hand, and the room was quickly cleared of all personnel. This fellow obviously holds great power, Josef thought.

The man was dressed in full Wehrmacht major's uniform, and was puffing on a long cigarette, which had a black holder attached to it. 'Please sit down, Josef,' he said. 'That is, if I may call you Josef?'

'Yes, that would be fine, sir,' Josef said, taking the seat opposite the major.

'Sehr gut,' the major nodded, and then pushed a small red and brown box across the table toward Josef. There was an old German imperial eagle on the front cover, with the words, Feiner Bulgarischer Zigaretten, written beneath it. [1.]

'No, thank you, sir,' Josef politely declined.

'Oh, go on, I know you smoke. They're quite gut, you know.'

'Well, I suppose one won't hurt, sir.'

'That's the spirit. It's important that you are completely at ease here. I find that always helps when I'm interviewing. Now, allow me to introduce myself. Mein naam ist Lari Koban, and I've been asked by Herr Major Lowe to represent you as your council. Die Herr Major seems to be under the impression that you are in grave danger, hence your being brought all the way out here.'

'Yes, sir, but as I have already told Herr Runzel, I have no enemies at D Company. I get on quite well with everybody there.'

'Yes, well, Herr Major Lowe agrees with you, but he tells me that it's not D Company that worries him, but rather some other outside forces.'

'Who are these outside forces, Herr Koban?'

'I am not at liberty to say at this point, you understand?'

'Of course. I must say, Herr Koban, that I am very impressed by how quickly everyone has moved since the arrest. It would appear that the Wehrmacht are much more efficient at night than they are during the day,' he laughed sardonically.

'Well, I'm glad to see you still have a sense of humour after all that has happened, but now we have to get serious. Let's start, shall we? I've read Runzel's brief report, and I must be honest with you, it does not read well.'

'Sir?'

'What I mean is, as far as Runzel is concerned, you're guilty as charged. You see, he has given me the three main ingredients for the recipe, and they are means, cause and probability.'

'I don't follow you, sir.'

'No, of course you don't. You're a Soldat, not a Detektiv, so let me break it down for you. You had the means by which to kill Fraulein Hastler. Your bare hands.'

'But I didn't kill her, sir.'

'Please don't interrupt. I'm only generalising. I'm not accusing you of anything, verstehen?'

'Sorry, sir.'

'That's OK. Here, have another cigarette. Anyway, so we have the means, now for the cause. Fraulein Hastler was a gut-looking woman and you were naturally attracted to her, but as you are ein schwarzemann, she could never have possibly been attracted to you in the same way. So, you forced yourself on her.'

'I must protest, sir,' Josef stood, furious at what he was hearing. 'This is most outrageous!'

'Please sit down and compose yourself, Josef. This is precisely the sort of situation you will find yourself in at your court martial, so start getting used to it. Now, lastly, probability. You have testified that you were both on the steps outside the officers' mess at around eleven forty-five PM, recht?'

'Yes, sir, that is correct.'

'And you say, that you were both there on the steps for about ten minutes before Fraulein Hastler left to meet with her chauffeur at the main gate, recht?'

'Yes, that's how it happened, sir.'

'And when she left you, it was around eleven fifty-five PM, recht?'

'Yes.'

'And from the time you were both on the step until the time she left, no one else saw you together, recht?'

'That is correct, sir, although there could have been somebody there, but I just simply didn't notice them.'

'These are the words of a desperate man trying to clear himself. Did you know that it has been estimated that Fraulein Hastler died between eleven fifty-five PM and midnight?'

'No, I didn't know that, sir. Why are you being so particular about time?'

'Why? Because it brings me back to the last ingredient, probability. Is it probable to say that in those precious ten minutes, you took Fraulein Hastler by force to those dark and deserted barracks, and murdered her before returning to the party just before twelve o'clock?'

'Nein! Nein! Das ist nicht treue,' Josef cried, 'nicht treue, I tell you!'

'Remember, Josef, you have said in your statement that there was no one around when you were both on the step at eleven forty-five, and that there was still no one around just before you re-entered the party.'

Josef slumped back into his chair and covered his face with his hands. Koban leaned forward and offered him another cigarette, and then lit one himself. They both sat in silence for a while, until Josef stubbed out his cigarette and said, 'I think I now understand what you mean by the three ingredients, sir. It doesn't look gut for me, does it?'

'Not from where I'm sitting, no,' Koban admitted, letting out a long sigh before adding, 'Look, are you sure you didn't see anyone while you were out there? Could anyone possibly corroborate your story?'

'I'm afraid not, sir.'

'That's a pity, Josef, a real pity. Oh, by the way, I forgot to tell you that Runzel found these at the crime scene. Do you recognise them by any chance?'

'No, sir, I don't. What are they?'

'Well, at first glance I would say that they look like rosary beads, but there's no cross attached to them. They could, however, be worry beads.'

'Worry beads?' Josef pondered. Wait! Wait, I do recognise them. Herr Sturmbannfuhrer Lunder has the very same beads. Yes, yes, I remember now. He would twirl them around in his fingers whenever he got agitated. It's Lunder, sir, he's your murderer. It all makes sense now.'

'Now hold on, Josef, do you know what you're saying? These are very serious allegations that you're making. I assume you have other witnesses who can back you up on this?'

'There's nobody that I can think of at this very moment, sir.'

'Then these allegations are worthless,' Koban sighed, leaning back into his chair and unbuttoning his collar. After a short pause he said, 'OK, I'll tell you what I'm going to do. It's a long shot, but it just might work. Firstly, I'm going to call the guard and have him take you back to your cell, where you must rest while I start to make some discreet enquires into Lunder's background. Now, if I can verify what you have told me, you may just escape the firing squad. Take it easy, and I'll get back to you.'

'When will I next see you, Herr Koban?'

'This could take a day or two, but hey, are you going anywhere?'

'I guess not.'

'Precisely, so just lay back, relax and trust me. I've got a gut feeling about this one, Josef.'

1. Finest Bulgarian Cigarettes.

CHAPTER FORTY-ONE

Josef took Koban's advice and lounged in his cell, letting the days merge into one another, but by day three he began to feel anxious about not hearing anything. In addition to the anxiety, he was also becoming bored, and desperately wished for something to happen. Then, on March 3 1940, something finally did, and it proved to be one of the most horrific days of his life. Be careful what you wish for, as the old axiom goes, because you might just get it.

The day started in the usual way, which meant being woken up at six AM by a guard striking the cell door hard with the butt of his rifle, and then shouting abuse through the small grill slot. This was followed by a breakfast consisting of a bowl of thick steaming slop, served up with a lump of hard bread, and after that came compulsory exercise, which amounted to a quick sprint around the small open court yard, before being taken back to the cell to finish the rest of the day. Josef was lying on his bunk, reading an old novel that had been left behind by the previous occupant, when suddenly he heard the sound of footsteps out in the corridor. The footsteps grew louder and louder before coming to a stop outside the cell door, followed by the rattling of keys and the turning of the lock. Josef leaped off the bed in excitement, expecting to see his counsel representative   Larry Koban, but instead found himself face to face with his old adversary, Sturmbannfuhrer Ernst Lunder, who stood in front of Josef wearing a silly grin and reeking of that same sweet, sickly aftershave he always wore. Lunder was not alone, as standing in the background were his trusty henchmen, the sinister, eyepatch-wearing Hauptsturmfuhrer Hants Wholner, along with Obersturmfuhrer Zeig Ulricher.

'What the hell are you doing here?' Josef spluttered.

'Well, that's no way to greet an alt freund who has come all this way just to see you,' Lunder smirked.

'Guards! Guards!' Josef yelled, as Wholner and Ulricher grabbed him firmly by the elbows.

'Oh, they can't hear you,' Lunder said, gently closing the metal door behind him. 'I've sent them away, so that we can have a little chat in private.'

'Wo ist mein counsel? I demand to speak with Herr Koban.'

'Unfortunately, Herr Koban can't make it today,' Lunder said. 'You see, he met with a terrible accident. He was run over yesterday by an SS staff car. That's what happens when people start looking under stones. You never should have named me, Herzog.'

'You bastard! Why did you kill Monika?'

'You're a funny fellow, aren't you?' Lunder laughed. 'I'm glad you've brought up the subject of murder, mein schwarz freund.'

'What the hell are you talking about?' Josef's heart quickened with panic, but he concealed it well.

'Well, it's murder that has brought me here today. You see, I've noticed that death seems to follow you around.'

'You're not making any sense. Why don't you just leave and no more will be said?'

'OK, I'll leave, but first know this. Your Russian freund, Uri Voss, and his fiancée Emmy Kirche are dead.'

'What? How can that be?'

'Well, I'm told they were found together in a lovers' lane, way out in the country. They were sat bolt upright in the front seat of Uri's beautiful new Mercedes sports car, with a bullet in each of their heads.'

'And why are you telling me this?'

'I'm telling you because it's your fault.'

'Now, just one minute. Don't you dare blame me for your murderous deeds. This had nothing to do with me.'

'That's were your wrong, oh hero of Olenica. If you had kept your big mouth shut, they'd all still be alive today.'

'What do you mean by "all?" Just how many people have you killed, you maniac?'

'I haven't killed anyone, Herzog, but you have.'

'Sir,' Ulricher interrupted, 'he has no idea what you're talking about. Should I have a go?'

'OK, you take over, Ulricher,' Lunder said. 'Maybe you can get through that thick gorilla skull of his.'

'Danke, Herr Sturmbannfuhrer,' Ulricher nodded. 'Well, it all reads like this, Herzog. Fraulein Hastler is dead. Voss and Kirche are dead. Koban is seriously injured and is as gut as dead. Oberleutnant Eckard Schlachter is dead. Oh, and so is your Polak freund, the Maus, or whatever his name is. Every other member of the so-called War Council is in jail, and there's a gut chance that they, too, will soon be dead. Are you getting the picture?'

'No, I'm not,' Josef said defiantly,' and I don't believe a word of it.'

'Oh, you better believe him,' Lunder said, pouring himself a glass of water from a tall pitcher that was sat on top of a small bedside table. 'What he says is completely true. I want to take you back to an incident that occurred at Kolo Station. Do you remember threatening Schlachter in front of Hauptsharfuhrer Trubel, after the shooting of a Juden frauen?'

'Yes, and what of it?'

'Well,' Lunder produced a piece of paper from his pocket, which he began to read from. 'Did you not say to Schlachter, "You won't get away with this. If you don't lower your weapon, I swear I'll make sure that everyone knows about your dirty little secret?" Well, do you remember saying this or not?'

'Yes, but I still don't know what any of this has to do with him being dead.'

'It was you, Herzog, who single-handedly brought down everyone around you with that stupid remark. It was just after you boarded the train for Lodz that Hauptsharfuhrer Trubel interrogated Schlachter regarding your comments. It took quite some time, I might tell you, but Schlachter eventually broke down under questioning and revealed everything about the theft of Gauleiter Greiser's gold.'

'Verdammnt!' Josef howled.

'I think he's finally seen the light, Herr Sturmbannfuhrer,' Ulricher sniggered.

'Indeed,' Lunder took a sip of water. 'You see, Herzog, if not for your little indiscretion, Voss and his fiancée would still be alive today, and your little War Council would not be in jail. The sad thing is that were it not for you, they probably would have pulled the whole thing off without a hitch. Can you believe that?'

'All of this still doesn't explain why you had to kill Monika, you Nazi bastard.'

'I don't have to explain anything to you, but maybe you can explain something to me,' Lunder unfolded a four-page letter and asked, 'Do you recognise this?'

'No, what is it?'

'Oh, come, come now. Surely, you must recognise your own letters? They're from the Polak, Stanizlaw Marzynek, and I must say, there is some very interesting reading in here. Ulricher, would you be so kind as to read out a passage for me? Any page will do.'

'Jawhol, Herr Sturmbannfuhrer,' Ulricher began, '"Reichfuhrer SS Heinrich Himmler has new plans to introduce a chemical pesticide called Zyklon B, which contains prussic acid, or hydrogen cyanide, through the shower ducts at Auschwitz concentration camp, in the hope that it will speed up the killings, as shooting is proving too costly, slow and messy."'

'OK, Ulricher, I've heard enough,' Lunder waved his hand. 'All you have achieved with your meddling is to put a noose around that scrawny little schwarz neck of yours. What I've found here is tantamount to high treason, and I shall look forward to witnessing you draw your last breath. What were you going to do with this information, sell it to the British?'

'I may be a lot of things to you, Lunder, but I'm no spy,' Josef said. 'I love Duetschland, and you had no right to read those letters. Also, you still haven't answered the question. Why did you kill Monika?'

'You really don't want to know the answer to that,' Lunder replied.

'I have to know, Lunder. Tell me, why did you do it?'

'Oh, very well, if you really must insist. I killed her because she was carrying your child,' Lunder said flippantly.

An eerie silence descended upon the room. Josef was clearly shaken, and his face became drained and ashen. The tension was only broken when Ulricher giggled and said, 'He didn't know. He really didn't know, sir.'

'So it would seem,' Lunder said. 'She was two weeks pregnant.'

'I don't understand,' Josef whispered, his voice quivering. 'Why did you have to kill her?'

'Isn't it obvious, mein chimpanzee freund? We simply could not allow another mongrel to be born into der Third Reich, to further bastardise our race, could we?'

Josef felt the sweat on his palms as he clenched his fists, and his rage grew and grew until he could no longer control himself. He sprung forward, breaking Ulricher and Wholner's grips, and grabbed Lunder by the throat, squeezing him to the point of nearly passing out. The two officers managed to regain their hold on him, giving Lunder time to stand and recover his composure. He straightened his crumpled black tunic and tie, and said calmly, 'So, you want a fight, eh? Well, it just so happens we have someone here you can fight with.' He raised his voice and called out, 'Heinz!'

The cell door slowly creaked open, and Josef immediately knew that he was in for a bad time as a huge figure filled the doorway. It was SS Feldwebel Heinz Bulmann, and he looked angry. Josef tried to struggle, but he was held tight by Ulricher and Wholner as the cell quickly filled with the heavy odour of Bulmann's sweaty bulk.

'Aren't you going to say hello to Heinz?' Lunder asked jovially. 'He, too, has travelled such a long way just to see you.'

'Hello Heinz,' Josef said, now resigned to his fate, 'it's gut to see you again.'

Heinz leaned forward and spat out a thick gobbet of deep green phlegm, which attached itself to the front of Josef's clean white vest, before muttering, 'It's really gut to see you, too, Herr Leutnant. You don't know how long I've waited for a return match.'

Bulmann launched a punch that landed square in the centre of Josef's stomach, doubling him over, followed by a quick uppercut that sent blood spraying from his mouth.

'Can I have a go please, sir?' Ulricher pleaded. 'It would be nice to get even for what he did to my jaw.'

'Oh alright,' Lunder grunted, folding his arms. 'I guess it's only fair that you should enjoy yourself, too, Ulricher. Go on, see if you can break his nose.'

Ulricher lifted Josef's head by his chin and aimed his fist, before smashing it hard into Josef's nose, sending him down to the floor, where he lay in a heap. Bulmann then leaped forward and began to mash his heavy black grenadier boots into Josef's torso, forcing him to cry out in excruciating pain.

'Did anyone hear it break?' Lunder asked in mock concern. 'Pick him up and do it again, just in case.'

'Jawhol, Herr Sturmbannfuhrer,' Ulricher replied with gusto, while wiping the blood from his knuckles. 'Stand up, you bastard. Come on, on your feet. That's an order!'

Summoning all of his inner strength and pride, Josef shakily rose to his feet and straightened his blood-soaked vest, before receiving another blow to the face that sent him crashing to the ground once more, only this time he didn't get back up.

'Did you hear that, sir?' Ulricher grinned. 'I think the nose is broken.'

'Ja, ja,' Lunder said, lighting a cigarette. 'Now, pick him up and place him back on his bunk.'

'He's out cold, sir,' Wohlner remarked, as he flopped Josef 's head from side to side.

'Then wake him up,' Lunder demanded. 'I have another surprise in store for him. Here,' he passed Wholner the pitcher of water from the bedside, 'this should bring him around.'

Wholner took the pitcher of water from Lunder, and then proceeded to empty it over Josef's head.

'Are you awake, Herzog?' Lunder asked sarcastically, as he stood over Josef's battered body. 'Sehr gut, but you look like you need a doktor. Well, it just so happens that we have brought one along with us. Isn't that lucky, eh? Come in, Herr Doktor, and examine your patient.'

Josef rolled slowly onto his side, clutching his ribs in agony, and stared down at the floor. He heard the footsteps of another man entering the room, followed by Lunder shouting, 'Die Herr Doktor will see you now, Herzog.'

With his vision blurred, Josef tried to focus his eyes, and he could just about make out a pair of black shiny boots on the floor in front of him. He slowly raised his head and gazed up at a smiling man in a white coat, who had a stethoscope around his neck and was holding a bulky brown leather case. The man's face seemed familiar to Josef, but he still had difficulty seeing clearly until Ulricher and Wholner raised him up and sat him on the edge of the bed. With his vision returning, he began to fill with dread and horror as he finally recognised the smiling man who stood before him.

'Hello Herr Leutnant,' Dr Schlossman said, 'it seems such a long time since I last had the pleasure of your company. I was only just getting to know you back in Olenica, when you unfortunately left without saying aufwiedersehen. Well, that's all in the past now. Here, let me take a look at that nose of yours. Don't worry, I'm not going to hurt you.'

Schlossman gently placed his fingers on either side of Josef's nose, and began to press and massage around it. After a lot of prodding he leaned forward, winked and whispered, 'I don't think it's broken,

mein freund.' He then asked Ulricher and Wholner to help him un-
dress the patient, to allow him to carry out a detailed examination.
The doctor carefully bathed and cleaned Josef's wounds, before
raising a limp arm off the bed and looking for a prominent vein.
In a weak voice, Josef asked what Schlossman was doing, and was
told that he was going to receive a mild sedative to help him sleep.
Josef started to struggle, to which Schlossman reacted by ordering
Ulricher and Wholner to hold him down while he administered a
painful jab with a long, sharp syringe. Josef fought back with all his
might, but then began to feel faint as the last of his strength slowly
drained away.

The next thing Josef knew, he was back in Wilmersdorf, sitting
on a large settee next to Monika in the living room of his parents'
house. His mother was crouched before them, pouring strong tea
into four white china cups that were perched on top of a small table
in the middle of the floor, while his father sat opposite in his easy
chair, trying to light his heavy brown pipe.

'So, Monika, Josef tells me that he has proposed to you,' his
mother said excitedly, 'is this true?'

'Why yes, Frau Herzog,' Monika beamed. 'Would you like to see
the ring?'

'But of course,' his mother replied, leaning forward to get a
better look.

Monika held out her hand, and with great delight displayed her
engagement ring. It was a solitaire, with a single small-cut diamond
set into the middle of a thin gold band.

'Oh, Monika, it's absolutely gorgeous!' his mother said. 'So,
what's next? Wedding bells, and then lots of babies?'

'Mutti, please,' Josef interjected, sensing Monika's embarrassment.

'It's OK, Josef,' Monika laughed. 'Yes, Frau Herzog, lots of babies, I hope.'

'Did you hear that, Vincent?' his mother asked.

'Well, I hope the two of you know what you're letting yourselves in for,' his father murmured, as he struggled with his pipe. 'It hasn't always been easy for your mutter and me, you know.'

'Oh, leave them alone,' his mother scolded. 'They're young and in love. Germany has changed quite a bit since we were married, Vincent, and there's a lot more tolerance now. Berlin is like the League of Nations these days, and I think this is a gut time for them to marry.'

'Yes, well, I wish I had your confidence, Gerda,' his father said. 'Things may be gut here, but I've been hearing reports of mass rioting in the streets by those brown-shirted SA thugs outside of Berlin.'

'Oh, be quiet, Vincent,' his mother said sharply. 'You're frightening Monika.'

'I'm just stating the facts, that's all. I don't trust this neu government. It's belligerent, and it's run by a lowlife despot.'

'Vincent! Don't talk like that, it's dangerous!'

'Bah, I can say what I like in mein haus. There are no Nazis hiding in the cupboards here, you know.'

'Well, I for one agree with Mutti,' Josef chuckled, folding his arms. 'Now is a gut time to marry, and I'm sure that what ever difficulties life may have in store for us, we will cope just fine, Vater.'

'Hmm,' his father grumbled, 'damned pipe. Have we any decent matches, woman?'

'I think that means your vater agrees,' his mother winked.

As they all roared with laughter, a sharp, searing pain began to flare up in the bottom of Josef's stomach, forcing him to shut his eyes tight and grimace.

When he opened his eyes again, he found himself laying flat on his back atop his tiny bunk bed. He was still in his grimy prison cell, and the pain in his stomach was growing ever more intense. He threw off the blanket and looked down at his groin, where he saw that his underpants were stained red with fresh blood. He froze for a moment, not knowing what to do, until eventually he decided to slide his hand under the elasticated waistband and carefully lift up his shorts. He saw a scarlet red bandage that had been wrapped around his genitals, and with great care he began to gently tug it to one side, before gingerly inching his fingertips under the damp wadding. He trembled with horror as his fingers touched the jagged railway line of stitches that ran down the centre of his scrotum, and he immediately knew what it meant. He had been sterilised.

Schlossman had finally got his way, finishing what he had originally set out to do back in Olenica. His resolve now completely broken, Josef pressed his forearm over his eyes and began to cry, loud and childlike, as he realised that despite the immense effort made to protect him, all of his father's fears for him had come to pass. He languished in his cell for another day, before receiving an unexpected visit from his commanding officer, Herr Hauptmann Weise, who arrived with a brown parcel tucked under his arm, containing food and cigarettes. Weise was shocked by Josef's dishevelled appearance, and asked to be briefed on exactly what had happened.

'I'm so sorry,' Weise said sincerely, once Josef had brought him up to speed. 'I came as quickly as I could, but obviously not quick enough.'

'It's not your fault, Herr Hauptmann,' Josef said. 'You couldn't have possibly foreseen this outcome.'

'That's where you're wrong, I'm afraid. You see, Herr Major

Lowe and I both knew in advance of a plot to bring you down, but we had no clear evidence – until now, that is.'

'Well, don't worry yourself, sir. I'm past caring about what may or may not happen to me at this point.'

'Come on now, Josef, let's not have anymore of this defeatist talk. We're going to get you out of here somehow, and I can assure you that when I get back to Breslau and report this hideous affair to Herr Major Lowe, plans will be put in place for your immediate release from this foul hovel.'

'Does this mean that you believe me when I say that I didn't murder Monika, sir?'

'We never believed that for one minute, Josef. Even Herr Oberst Hastler is rooting for you.'

'Well, that is gut to know, sir.'

'And don't believe any of that nonsense Lunder has told you about Uri's death being your fault. I'm in no doubt as to who is really responsible for that.'

'Lunder is right about one thing, though, sir. If I hadn't blabbed in front of Hauptsharfuhrer Trubel, none of this would have happened.'

'That's where you're wrong. Gauleiter Greiser never believed Erich's story right from the beginning, and had secretly launched his own investigation with the assistance of the V men.'

'V Men, sir?'

'Yes, the Verfungungstruppe, as they are better known. They are a highly trained and dedicated special SS police force, formed by der Fuhrer himself back in nineteen thirty-four. Their typical MO is to infiltrate targeted groups, be it in factories or open market places, often going undercover and befriending civilians and winning their confidence, in order to find out whatever it is they need to know. So, you see, it would have all come out in the end anyway.'

'And what of the War Council, sir? What is to become of them?'

'Oh, I wouldn't worry too much about the lads. We're working flat out to get them off with those ridiculous trumped up charges. They'll be fine, trust me. Right, I have to go and present a report to Herr Major Lowe, but first, I will speak with the superintendent and make him promise that no further harm will come to you while you're in his care. Now, eat the food I've brought you. It's sehr gut.'

'OK, sir,' Josef said, smiling for the first time in what felt like a long time. 'Thank you for believing in me.'

'No problem,' Weise said. 'You just get some rest, and leave the rest of it to us.'

Weise proved to be as good as his word, for within ten minutes of him leaving, the prison superintendent had given orders that Josef should be allowed to shower and then issued with a fresh change of clothes.

When Weise arrived back at D Company HQ, he immediately presented his report to Herr Major Lowe, who responded to the graphic details of torture and abuse by calling an emergency meeting of the Wehrmacht top brass. The session was chaired by General Otto von Waldman, and attended by Herr Oberst Rhone von Hastler, Herr Major Rudolf Lowe and Herr Hauptmann Ralf Weise.

CHAPTER FORTY-TWO

'Well, gentlemen, it would appear that we have a serious problem,' Waldman began. 'As you are by now all fully aware, one of our officers has become the target of a campaign of hatred, the likes of which I have never before experienced in all my years of military service. The fundamental question is, what do we do about it?'

'If I may speak, sir?' Hastler spoke up.

'Yes, fire away, Rhone,' Waldman said.

'I would first like to suggest moving Herzog to a place that is more secure, at least until we're out of the eye of this storm, sir.'

'"The eye of this storm?" I like that description, Rhone,' Waldman said. 'And by that description, I'm sure we are all aware of who this storm is, eh, gentlemen? OK, so we move him as soon as possible, but to where? Any suggestions?'

'What about keeping him here, sir?' Weise said. 'He would be right under our very noses, and we could easily monitor him.'

'Yes, that sounds like a gut idea, Ralf,' Waldman said, 'but consider this. If we can monitor him so, can the storm.'

'I see your point, sir,' Weise acknowledged.

'Gentlemen, if I may speak,' Lowe piped up. 'I can think of one place that would provide the type of security we need.'

'And could you enlighten us to the whereabouts of this place, Herr Major?' Waldman asked.

'Yes, sir,' Lowe replied. 'Belgium.'

'Belgium?'

'That is correct, sir. Belgium.'

'And would you mind tell us why, Herr Major?'

'Well, there is a huge fortress there called Bourg Leopold, which just so happens to be run by mein bruder, Jules,' Lowe explained. 'It is the perfect place for Herzog. It's both well protected and far out of the way, sir.'

'Hmm, I'm not so sure about that, Rudolf,' Waldman frowned. 'I feel that Bourg Leopold may be too far away. We need to keep Herzog close, so that we can keep an eye on him.'

'I think it's worthy of consideration, sir. If you don't mind me saying so,' Weise added.

'And I suppose the fact that Rudolf is your commanding officer has nothing to do with your agreeing with him, eh?' Waldman asked.

'Not at all, sir,' Weise laughed nervously, a little abashed. 'I'm more than confident that Komandant Steiner will look after him, sir.'

'OK, Bourg Leopold it is, then,' Waldman sighed. 'Rudolf, you will make the arrangements personally, while I try to delay Herzog's court martial hearing for as long as possible.'

'Why delay it, sir?' Lowe asked. 'We all know that Herzog is completely innocent, so why not let him stand trial?'

'Nein, nein, Rudolf,' Waldman shook his head, 'you must understand, there are no witnesses to testify as to the whereabouts of

Herzog between the time of him leaving the party and the time of his return. If he were to stand trial now, he would be executed for sure. Nein, we must delay, and let's hope that we can save this poor fellow from the eye of this terrible storm, eh, gentlemen?'

'Jawhol, Herr General,' Lowe said. 'I'll get on it right away, sir.' He stood, clicked his heels and saluted the general before leaving the room.

Within twenty-four hours of his visit from Hauptmann Weise, Josef was on his way to Bourg Leopold, a former Belgium fortress which had since become a prison. Upon arrival, he was introduced to people from all walks of life, as the place housed mostly political prisoners, like communists, or members of any parties considered to be enemies of the state. The atmosphere was a little more relaxed than the camps that Josef could have found himself in, such as Neuengamme and Ravensbruck, where the daily routine was deliberately harsh and brutal. He was placed in a moderately-sized cell, which he had to share with another inmate, who was also an officer in the Wehrmacht. The room had a small writing table that was placed under the large iron-barred window, with two single bunks on either side. In the corner, next to the thick iron door, was a large wash basin and a towel, which sat below a small cracked mirror. Alongside that, stuck up on the wall, was a well-thumbed picture of a beautiful, naked blonde model, who was straddling a hard-backed chair. She was pouting her full, deep red lips, and her head was tilted back slightly, allowing her long platinum blond hair to fall freely down the natural curve of her back.

'Do you like her?' his cellmate asked. He was staring out of the window, with his tunic wrapped around his shoulders.

'I'm sorry?' Josef replied, startled.

'The girl in the picture,' the man said. 'Do you like her?'

'Why yes,' Josef said, glancing over at the picture, 'she's very nice.'

'Well, don't touch her,' the man growled. 'She's mine, OK?'

'Sure, no problem,' Josef frowned. 'What are you in for, if you don't mind me asking?'

'I'll only tell you after you've told me.'

'OK. I'm here because I've been accused of murder.'

'And you didn't do it, right?'

'Yes, that's right!'

The man laughed bitterly. 'Do you know how many people have passed through here and said the exact same thing?'

'I'm really not that interested.'

'So, who was this person that you didn't murder?'

'She was mein fiancée.'

'Ah, so it was a crime of passion, eh?'

'I've just told you, I did not kill her.'

'Yes, of course, I remember,' he said sarcastically. 'What was she like, your fiancée?'

Josef stared down at the floor with sad eyes. 'She was tall and slim, with the silkiest auburn hair. She was beautiful. There will never be another like my Monika.'

'Monika, what a lovely name. Mein mutter's name is Monika.'

'Really?'

'No, I'm lying. The first thing you'll learn in here is, never to trust anyone. You can have that as your first lesson.'

'How can you possible find humour in a place like this?'

'Believe me, without a sense of humour, you won't last a week.'

'You still haven't told me why you're here.'

'Oh, it's very trivial, actually. I had improper relations with a young madchen.'

'That's it?'

'That's it. Oh, did I forget to mention that she was a Juden madchen?' he laughed.

'You are quite mad, sir.'

'Indeed I am, Herr Leutnant,' the man said, and then stretched out his hand and added, 'Gunther Siegfried, but you can call me Ziggy.'

'Pleased to meet you, Ziggy. I'm Josef Herzog.'

'Josef? You're not Juden, are you?'

The two men shared a laugh; the first that Josef had had in what felt like forever. Ziggy was a tall and handsome twenty-five-year-old, with slick, jet black hair that was parted broadly down the middle. He was elegant in his movements and mannerisms, looking more like a Luftwaffe pilot than a soldier, although personality-wise, he reminded Josef of his dear friend Uri. He hoped that this would help to make his incarceration seem a little more bearable.

'Where are you from, Ziggy?' Josef asked.

'I'm from the Reisholz district of Dusseldorf,' Ziggy answered. 'or what's left of it. Man, we got a gut pounding from the damned RAF. They flattened everything.'

'Why did they bomb you?'

'Oil refinaries, Josef. There are lots of oil refinaries there.'

'Judging by your uniform, I can deduce that you're an oberleutnant with the fifth Jager regiment?'

'That's correct,' Ziggy confirmed, 'but unfortunately, I've been told that I may be busted to privat, depending on the outcome of mein trial, which is due to begin very soon. You see, it's considered a great faux pas to fraternise with the enemy, especially if they're Juden.'

'Hey, you boys were at Rzhev, on the Eastern front, weren't you?'

'Yes, we were part of Army group centre.'

'So, why did they call Rzhev the meat grinder? Was it really that bad?'

'It was worse than bad. Imagine being trapped in your own personal nightmare. If there could be a living hell, it would be called Rzhev.'

'Can you explain what you mean, or is it too hard to talk about.'

'No, I can talk about it because I survived it. In nineteen forty-one, Smolensk had fallen, leaving the road to Moscow wide open, or so we thought, but the Russian General Zhukov had cleverly assembled eleven divisions against us, resulting in one of the bloodiest and fiercest battles I've ever had the misfortune to take part in. I must tell you, I feel so lucky to have ended up in this place.'

'What, you prefer prison to the Eastern front?'

'I'll never go back to Russia. I'd sooner kill myself first. You have no idea what it was like. We were only ninety-three miles away from Moscow, so near to reaching our objective, but couldn't move forward. There were Russian bodies mangled with German bodies and horses mangled with machinery. You couldn't take one step without standing on someone or something. You couldn't breathe in for the powerful stench of rotting flesh. It was too cold for flies, but there were plenty of worms and maggots.'

'It could be worse, I suppose,' Josef said, wanting to lift the mood.

'Oh, and how so?'

'Well, you could be put in front of a firing squad.'

Ziggy laughed. 'What about you?' he asked. 'I think there may also be a bullet with your name on it?'

'You're right, I'm not out of the woods yet. Mein trial date has not yet been confirmed, though. How long have you been here?'

'A year and a half.'

'And they're only just arranging your trial?' Josef asked, wide-eyed. 'How do you cope?'

'Here, I'll show you,' Ziggy said, as he walked over to his bunk and sat on the edge of the bed with his arms outstretched in front of him.

'What are you doing?'

'Going for a drive in mein car. Coming?'

'You are quite mad,' Josef chuckled, as he sat alongside him.

'Yes, you've already said that.'

'So, where are we going?'

'We're off to Dusseldorf. I'm now speeding down the Strasse.'

'This is a smooth ride, Ziggy. How long have you had her?'

'I've only had the car a few months. Can you smell the leather?'

'Now that you mention it, yes, I can.'

'Hey, do me a favour, would you?'

'Sure.'

'Shut that damned window please. It's getting a little chilly in here.'

They both laugh.

'I never knew that Dusseldorf was so beautiful,' Josef remarked. 'I could definitely see myself living here, you know.'

'Well, if you think this is nice, wait until you see where mein family live.'

'Wait, halt!'

'Was ist los?'

'There's a cat right there in front of you.'

'You catch on quick, mein herr,' Ziggy laughed. 'So, tell me, how did you end up in here?'

'I've already told you.'

'Yes, but what led to you being here?'

'Oh, it's a long story.'

'That's OK, I'm not going anywhere.'

'Good point. Well, from the first moment I arrived in Poland, I became a fascination to the SS, who were not happy to see a black officer in a German uniform. They would constantly harass me and make my life difficult, but I was always protected by the War Council.'

'The War Council?'

'They are a small group of Werhmact officers from mein company, one of whom was murdered by the SS.'

'What was his name?'

'His name was Uri, Uri Voss. They also murdered Emmy, his fiancée.'

'I'm sorry to hear that.'

'It was the SS who killed mein Monika, too, and then framed me for her murder.'

'Ah, they were not happy to see ein schwartz mann with a white woman, ja?'

'They were not happy to see ein schwartz mann with anyone.'

'Well, I'm sorry for your losses, Josef, truly I am. Hey, why don't you take over and have a drive?'

Josef enjoyed his drive with Ziggy, as it took his mind off his present situation. He knew instinctively that they would become good friends, and he thought that maybe if he were to adopt Ziggy's happy-go-lucky approach, he had a chance of surviving what could be a very long period of captivity.

There journey through Dusseldorf ended abruptly when they heard the sound of heavy boots approaching their cell door.

'Someone is coming,' Ziggy said. 'Quick, stand up and keep away from the door. They don't like you being too close to them.

They think you may attack, you know.'

The heavy cell door was then unlocked and sprung open with a clang. A small, fat guardsman with a rifle slung over his shoulder stepped into the room and called Josef's name, and then ordered him to attend the commandant's office at once. Josef nervously followed the guard through many long, narrow corridors until finally they reached a door with a dark brown plaque which read: Kmd. J. Steiner.

'Wait here,' the guard barked. He then knocked loudly before entering the room and announcing, 'Die gefanger, [1.] Herzog ist hier, Herr Kommandant.'

'Ah, yes,' said a soft voice from within, 'bring him in, would you.'

Josef entered cautiously, and found himself standing before a bald-headed man who was sat behind a broad oak desk, with his head slightly bowed as he scribbled on a piece of paper. On the wall directly behind him was a huge silver eagle, and to the side of it, in the corner of the room, a swastika flag was draped lifelessly over a pole.

The kommandant raised his head and smiled, and gestured for Josef to take a seat. 'Wilkommen, Herr Leutnant,' he said. 'Please, don't be nervous. This is just a freundlich chat, that's all. Come, sitzen.'

'Danke, Herr Kommandant,' Josef croaked.

'Please, call me Jules. Well, Josef, how are we treating you here?'

'I'm treated very well, sir.'

'Gut, gut. I have been asked to furnish you with anything you desire, apart from your release, you understand,' Jules laughed. 'Now, is there anything you need? Don't be afraid to speak up.'

'Well, uh,' Josef racked his brain, 'I could use some writing paper, sir.'

'Is that all?'

'And it would be nice to have something to read, sir.'

'Das ist nicht problem. Anything else?'

'I don't think so, sir.'

'What about musik. You like musik, don't you?'

'Yes, sir, I do.'

'Gut, then I will have a small wireless set delivered to your room. How does that sound?'

'That would be excellent, sir,' Josef said, staring at the kommandant in disbelief.

'You don't say much, do you?' Jules chuckled. 'Herr Major Lowe told me that you were a gut egg, but-'

'You know the Herr Major, sir?' Josef interrupted.

'Ah, now he wants to talk to me. Yes, to answer your question, I should think that I do know him, ja. He's mein half-bruder.'

'Oh, so that's why you're being so nice to me.'

'Ja, but keep it quiet. I don't want the other prisoners thinking I'm a soft touch, you know.'

'Yes, of course, sir.'

'Which reminds me, when you use your wireless set, make sure the volume is kept to its minimum.'

'Yes, sir. But what about mein cellmate?'

'What about him? I don't think he'll complain, as long as you allow him to listen in as well, eh?'

'Well, I don't know what to say, sir.'

'Don't say anything. Just keep your nose clean and all will be well. I'm sworn to protect you from this Lunder character, and that's just what I'm going to do.'

'You mean, you know about Lunder, sir?'

'Ja, I've been fully briefed on the situation. You may return to your cell now, and I'll have your requested items delivered to you as soon as possible.'

Josef was to be a guest at Bourg Leopold for almost four years, where he continued to share a cell with Ziggy, who maintained that he would be released any day now. General von Waldman had indeed managed to delay his court martial, but this left him in a legal limbo, since in the eyes of the law he was proven neither guilty nor innocent. He would spend much of his time reading regular army magazines, such as Die Wehrmacht or Signal, as well as the local Nazi-controlled newspapers, Das Reich and Das Blatt. Despite being glad to have something to pass the time with, he could not always rely on the accuracy of what he was reading, due to the enormous influence that Propaganda Minister Josef Goebbels had over all publications within the Reich. There weren't exactly a lot of other alternatives available to him, though.

Whenever possible, Josef would tune in the small wireless set that had been so graciously provided by Herr Jules. This gave him a window to the outside world, and he would sit for hours keeping track of events as they were unfolding, such as on 9 April 1940, when Germany invaded Norway and Denmark, issuing them with the stark warning: 'Offer no resistance or be crushed.' This was soon followed by Winston Churchill replacing Neville Chamberlain as British prime minister, and the Allies launching a land invasion of their own in Norway, on 14 April. These were the first of many key dates that Josef would record in what became his war diary.

1. Prisoner

CHAPTER FORTY-THREE

Festung [1.] Bourg Leopold

Josef lay on his bunk reading an issue of the military magazine Der Adler, [2.] which featured a picture of Reichsmarshal Hermann Goering in profile on the front cover. Goering's mousy brown hair looked shiny, and was neatly trimmed and smartly combed backwards. He wore a white military tunic adorned with gold Luftwaffe insignia, and around his neck the Knight's Cross hung proudly, with the large Pour le Merite just about visible underneath it.

Hearing the hurried footsteps of what sounded like guardsmen running past his cell, Josef hauled himself up off the bed and walked over to the door, carefully opening it and peering down the long dark corridor. He could see a group of soldiers huddled together at the far end, and while he could tell that they were muttering among themselves, he could not quite make out what they were saying. He decided to return to his bunk and switch on the radio, thinking that maybe they were talking about another allied attack on Belgium, since there had been many attempts before. He lay himself down and picked up his magazine, but before he could so much as open it, Ziggy burst into the room, red-faced and breathing heavily.

'Josef, Josef,' Ziggy panted, 'have you heard the news? Someone has tried to assassinate der Fuhrer!'

'What!' Josef couldn't believe it.

'Yes, it's true I tell you. They've tried to kill him.'

'Mein Gott, how is that even possible?' Josef wondered aloud, now sitting wide-eyed on the edge of his mattress. 'How and where did this happen?'

'Someone planted a bomb at der Wolf's Schanze in Ratsenburg, Poland.'

'Gut Gott, is he alive?'

'Yes, I believe so, thank the maker.'

'Who would do such a thing?' Josef instinctively reached for a cigarette. 'Was it the allies?'

'I don't know.'

'This is very bad, Ziggy. Have they caught anyone yet?'

'No, but I'm told that the net is tightening.'

Josef paced up and down with his hands on his head, muttering to himself. 'Everything is going wrong for us, you know,' he said, turning to Ziggy.

'How do you mean?' Ziggy asked, making his way over to the window, to look down into the crowded courtyard.

'Well, I think we're losing this war. I know we're not supposed to say that, but it's true.'

'Nonsense, man. I admit we've suffered some set backs but-'

'Be realistic, Ziggy,' Josef cut him off. 'The allies have landed in Normandy, the Amerikans are in Rome and we have been pushed out of Leningrad by the Russians.'

'These are minor setbacks, that's all. Hey, come over here and see this,' Ziggy said, pointing down into the courtyard. 'Look, some new arrivals. British airmen, I think.'

'Hmm, more prisoners,' Josef frowned. 'We must be full to capacity by now. Everyone is here. We've got the Tommys, the Poles, the Czechs, the French and the Amerikans. Who's next, the Russians?'

Ziggy laughed. 'Talking of the Amerikans,' he said, 'have you met your cousins, yet?'

'I don't understand.'

'You know, the three schwarz GIs.'

'Oh, you mean the Amerikans. Yes, I've seen them hanging around the compound. How long have they been here?'

'About two days, I think. Why don't you go down and talk to them? It's a fine day, and you could do with some fresh air, you know.'

'Why don't you go down and talk to them, if you're so interested?'

'I'd like to, but your English is far better than mine. We'll go together. What do you say, eh?'

'I wouldn't know what to say to them.'

'Oh, come on. It'll be a laugh, and I'll be right behind you.'

Against his better judgement, Josef acquiesced, and soon both he and Ziggy were winding their way along the many corridors until they eventually reached the busy courtyard. It was bright but chilly outside, and all the servicemen were huddled together according to their nationalities. Some prisoners stood with their hands in the pockets of their bomber jackets and trench coats, while others rubbed their hands together and blew on them for warmth. As the men talked, clouds of vapour poured from their mouths and rose up into the clear blue heavens. Josef paused in the doorway and rolled up his tunic collar, but Ziggy kept prodding him in the back, insisting that they move towards the small group of black Americans that were leaning against a wall at the far end of the yard.

Reluctantly, he stepped forward and manoeuvred himself gently through the maze of prisoners, before approaching the three GIs with great caution, for they were big men and looked quite menacing. As he got nearer, the man in the middle broke away from the other two and moved forward, and with his hands buried deep in his combat jacket he began to kick aimlessly at the loose shale on the ground, while the other two carried on leaning against the wall, smoking cigarettes. Josef stopped for a moment, and turned to check that Ziggy was still behind him before proceeding any further. When he turned back to face the Americans, he was shocked to fine that the man in the khaki combat jacket was now standing right in front of him, staring at him with big, round eyes.

'Hello,' Josef said weakly, extending his hand, 'my name is Lieutenant Josef Herzog.'

The man did not reply, nor did he shake Josef's hand. Instead, he continued to stare.

'Maybe he doesn't understand you?' Ziggy whispered from behind.

'Ja, and what did you say earlier? "Oh, your English is much better than mine,"' Josef hissed back over his shoulder.

'Is you an officer?' the American asked, in a deep Southern drawl.

'Uh, yes,' Josef answered, following another prod in the back from Ziggy.

'A coloured German officer?' the man asked.

'Yes, I'm a German officer,' Josef said. 'And your name is?'

'My name is Alvin, Alvin Cornell Jr. I'm a private in the United States Army, sir.'

'Well, I'm very pleased to meet you, Alvin,' Josef smiled. 'This is my friend, Lieutenant Gunther Siegfried, but you can call him

Ziggy.'

'Hi Ziggy,' Alvin said. 'Hey, listen, why don't y'all come over with me, and I'll introduce you to the brothers.'

'Oh, are you all related?' Josef asked.

'No, they're just the brothers, like you, man,' Alvin said.

'Like me?' Josef said, confused.

'Yeah, like you. You sure is a strange one,' Alvin shook his head. 'Come on, follow me.'

They walked over to 'the brothers', who were still leaning against the wall and smoking. As they approached, Josef saw the very same look of disbelief that Alvin wore when he'd spotted his officer's uniform. They were now standing upright, with their cigarettes dangling from open mouths.

'Hey fellas, lookihere,' Alvin boomed, smiling broadly. 'I've found me some new friends.'

'Well, I'll be damned,' one of the GIs stepped forward and said.

'This here is Maurice Pinkerton,' Alvin said, indicating the man who had just spoken. 'He's a private, just like me. Maurice, meet Hertzon.'

'Herzog,' Josef corrected.

'Whatever, man,' Alvin continued. 'He's a real German officer. Now, don't that beat all?'

'Don't tell him my rank, you fool,' Maurice snarled. 'He's the enemy!'

'Man, what's wrong wit' you?' Alvin frowned. 'He's a brother.'

'That ain't no brother,' Maurice said, 'that's an Uncle Tom, fool.'

'Alright, alright, that's enough, man,' the third GI, who had stood silent throughout the brief encounter, stepped in. He stretched out his hand towards Josef and Ziggy and said, 'Hi, my name's Sonny Williams. Pay no mind to Maurice. His bark is worse than his bite.'

Josef looked at the arm of Sonny's windcheater jacket, and noticed a large company division patch just below the left shoulder. It had an American Red Indian's head [3.] set inside a white, five-sided star, and below it there were three large vertical stripes.

'This guy's called Ziggy,' Alvin said, 'and the brother's called-'

'Herzog, yes, I heard,' Sonny laughed.

They talked a little until, in an attempt to ease the growing tension between Maurice and Josef, Sonny decided to walk Josef away from the small group. Unlike Maurice, Sonny seemed impressed by Josef because of the very fact that he was a black officer. He was a non-commissioned officer himself, and could appreciate the notion that black men were as qualified to lead as whites. They took off at a leisurely pace, strolling across the compound and leaving Ziggy to deal with Alvin and Maurice. A group of newly-arrived British airmen stared in disbelief, whispering frantically to one another as they watched a tall black American walk side by side with a small black German.

'So, Herzy, how did you end up on the wrong side, man?'

'What do you mean, Sergeant Williams?'

'Hey, cut the sergeant crap and call me Sonny, OK?'

'Of course, Sonny. What do you mean by "wrong side?"'

'Well, you know, how did you get hooked up with these Germans, man?'

'The same way you got hooked up with the Americans, I guess. I just joined up.'

'You tellin' me you're a real German?'

'Yes.'

'Get outta here! You're puttin me on, right?'

'Not at all. I was born in Wilmersdorf, Berlin, so I think that makes me a German, yes?'

'But your accent? You speak perfect English.'

'That is correct. Most German officers are multi-lingual.'

'Outstanding, Herzy. I think me and you is gonna get on just fine,' Sonny chuckled. They squeezed their way through a bunch of French soldiers and found themselves a quite corner of the court-yard, where they sat down together on the cold, hard ground. Josef took out a crushed packet of cigarettes from his top pocket and offered one to Sonny, who refused.

'It's OK,' Josef insisted, 'they're German, and very good.'

After a moment's consideration, Sonny reached over and took a cigarette, and then they both leaned back into the tight corner, where they puffed and laughed with great gusto.

'How come they didn't kill you, Herzy?' Sonny asked. 'Being a black man in Germany couldn't have been easy, man.'

'On the contrary,' Josef said, 'I've always been treated quite well, and been left to go about my business like everyone else. Anyway, enough about me, what about you? What part of the United States are you from?'

'I'm from a place called Tremont. It's in Ohio, but I guess that don't mean much to you, huh?'

'You're right, it doesn't. What about the other two Americans? Where are they from?'

'Who, Maurice and Alvin? Well, Maurice is from Philadelphia, you know, the city of brotherly love, and Alvin's from a place called Birmingham, that's in Alabama. Why is you asking me all these questions, man? Let's take a rain check, huh?'

'Why, the weather doesn't look that bad?'

Sonny laughed. 'You and me is got a long ways to go, man. A long ways! I'll catch you later.'

They stood up and shook hands, and then headed off in opposite directions. Josef was muttering to himself, trying to rehearse the strange new dialect he had just discovered, when suddenly he crashed to the floor, having failed to notice the RAF Pilot's boot that had been casually placed in his way.

'Get up, sambo,' an angry voice from above said, and when Josef looked up, he saw several men surrounding him. Some wore tanned leather flying jackets, and others were dressed in khaki battle fatigues.

'Corr, would you believe it, fellas,' the soldier whose boot Josef had tripped over said, roaring with laughter. 'Not only is he a sam, but he's a bleedin' jerry, too!' He stooped down and grabbed him by the collar, and then raised him up onto his feet and said, 'We're gonna give you a quick lesson in pain, my son, and when we're finished with you, we're gonna give it to the rest of your wog friends. What do you think about that, then?'

Before Josef could answer, Ziggy arrived on the scene, just in the nick of time, and shoved the soldier to one side.

'Are you alright?' Ziggy asked Josef.

'I am now, thanks,' Josef said, relieved to see him.

'Well, well, it looks like we get us two jerrys for the price of one, eh, lads?' the British soldier bellowed, as he pulled his arm back to strike Ziggy.

'I wouldn't do that if I were you,' Ziggy advised. 'Just one nod from me, and the guards patrolling these walls will open fire.'

'He's bluffin' you, John,' one of the pilots said. 'Let's do 'em.'

'Of course, your friend could be right, John,' Ziggy smiled, 'but can you afford to take that chance? You said it yourself, we're Jerrys. Surely, the guards would shoot you before they'd shoot us?'

The soldiers and airmen stood around, mumbling between themselves, until eventually one of them said, 'Come on, lads, let's just forget it. They're not worth it.'

'Thanks again, Ziggy,' Josef winked, as they watched the British depart. He put his arm around Ziggy's shoulder, and they started back towards their quarters. 'Would the guards have really shot those men?'

'I doubt it,' Ziggy said, laughing. 'They all hate me.'

The following morning, Josef and Ziggy were awakened by the din of air raid sirens, and the noise of the flak guns coming from defensive positions around the fortress.

'Verdammt RAF,' Ziggy said, eyes half-open. 'What time is it?'

'Six o'clock,' Josef replied, squinting at his wristwatch. 'Don't these guys ever sleep?'

He got up and, while dressing, switched on the small wireless set, which immediately crackled into life. As he walked over to the large washbasin, the soft background music was broken by the announcement of a special news bulletin.

'This is Deutsche radio, bringing you the voice of der Fuhrer,' the broadcaster announced. Then, in a low mumble that was almost inaudible, Adolf Hitler began to speak.

Ziggy jumped out of bed and fell to his knees, pressing his ear up hard against the radio set, while Josef simply stood frozen, as tepid water dripped from his face.

'Aside from a few minor scratches, burns and bruises, I am totally unharmed,' Hitler began. 'I take this as confirmation of my assignment from providence, to continue to pursue my life's goal as I have done hitherto. Sieg Heil.'

The soft music quickly resumed, picking up where it had left off, as if nothing had happened.

'Well, that's gut news, eh?' Josef said, breaking the silence.

'Yes, thank the maker. Where are you going?' Ziggy asked.

'Oh, just stepping out for some fresh air before breakfast. I won't be long.'

Josef made his way outside, but as he walked across the deserted compound, he soon found that he was not alone. Standing in the centre of the open prison courtyard was Alivin, scratching his head and staring up into the pre-dawn darkness.

'I see they got you out of bed, too, eh?' Josef said.

'They sure did, Herzy,' Alvin replied. 'Got a smoke?'

'Yes, here,' Josef said, reaching for his top pocket. 'They're German, I'm afraid.'

'Hey, no worries. I'm so desperate, I'd smoke ma grandma's fingers, man.'

They each lit up, and then watched as the thick white beams from the search lights stretched upwards and danced across the blue-black background, hunting for their prey. The sky flashed as though kissed by lightning, and then faded as the flak from the mighty 88-millimetre guns exploded, silhouetting the huge British Lancaster bombers as they dropped their deadly payload.

'I don't know about you, but I've seen enough of these fireworks, man,' Alvin said, pulling up his collar. 'Wanna grab some breakfast?'

'Yes, I'm starved.'

'Come with me. It's nothin' fancy – just something we've managed to steal from one of the Red Cross parcels in the guards' storehouse. You know, the stuff that was meant for us.'

They shuffled across the yard, doubled over with cold, and made their way down some steps into what looked like a disused basement. This led to a large room, lit by a single dim light bulb that swung lazily with the impact of each falling bomb, briefly lighting up different parts of the cellar as it went. The bare brick walls glistened with moisture, and there was an overwhelming smell of rot and damp. There were three small camp beds pushed up hard against the far wall, each with a single tattered army blanket thrown over it. Sonny and Maurice were sat on packing cases in the centre of the floor, leaning on a rickety table with their jackets slung over their shoulders, eating heartily from flat metal plates.

'Hey,' Sonny greeted them with a grin, 'looks like we have us a guest. Nehmen de platz,' he said, pointing down to a spare packing case.

'You speak German?' Josef said in surprise.

'Yeah.'

'Where did you learn to speak our language?'

'Why, in Tremont, of course,' Sonny chuckled.

'I don't understand."

'Tremont is part of Cleveland, and Cleveland just so happens to be home to one the US's oldest German communities.'

'I had no idea.'

'German town was formed in sixteen eighty-three by the settlers, and it was them who introduced the US to hot dogs and hambugers. So, I guess we owe you guys that much, eh?'

'I told Herzy that he could join us for breakfast, if that's ok with you guys?' Alvin said, sliding another crate up to the table.

'Sure, sure, that's fine by me,' Sonny said. 'I'm afraid this ain't no a la carte menu, Herzy, but you're welcome to join us nevertheless. Maurice, go fetch another plate,' he looked at his friend imploringly. 'Go on, man.'

Maurice grudgingly stood and walked over to what looked like a makeshift larder, which was basically an upturned packing case. With his back to the room, he began to fill a plate, before returning to the table and slamming it down hard in front of Josef. Mortified, Josef looked down at a piece of metal filled with slabs of dried corned beef, surrounded by clumps of dark congealed beans.

'So, Maurice,' Josef said, wanting to break the ice, 'Sonny tells me that you're from a place called Philadelphia?'

'That's right,' Maurice replied, 'and what of it?'

'Well, what can you tell me about it?'

'Why you askin'?'

'Don't be such a hard ass,' Sonny cut in. 'Just talk to him.'

'I'm from Camden County, New Jersey, an industrial town,' Maurice said reluctantly. 'Now, does that satisfy you?'

'Yes, thank you, Maurice,' Josef said, turning to Alvin. 'And you're from Birmingham, Alabama, is that right?'

'Sure 'nuff,' Alvin said, 'I come from a place called Bessemer, in Jefferson County, famous for steel making and stuff, you know,' he grinned.

'What's it like there?' Josef asked.

'Damned hot,' Alvin laughed. 'Where you from?'

'I come from an affluent residential place called Wilmersdorf, in Berlin,' Josef said. 'Do you know it?'

'Man, I just about know where I come from,' Alvin quipped.

Maurice broke the laughter by bringing his hand down flat onto the table with a loud bang. The GI then carefully peeled back his fingers and said, 'Gotcha, you sonofabitch,' and Josef filled with nausea as he leaned forward and discovered a squashed cockroach next to Maurice's plate.

'What's wrong wit' you, man?' Maurice said antagonistically. 'Ain't da food good enough for ya?'

'No, it's not,' Josef said matter-of-factly. 'This isn't the regular food ration that other prisoners get. Why are you eating this muck?'

'Because we're not white, that's why, fool,' Maurice spat, getting up from the table and walking away.

'But that's not right,' Josef said angrily.

'Well, that's the way it is for us coloured folks, Herzy,' Sonny said, leaning across the table and putting a hand on Josef's shoulder.

Josef rose up quickly and placed his hands on his hips, murmuring, 'I'm going to see the kommandant and complain about your food and living conditions. I swear to you, this will end today.'

On the other side of the room, Maurice began laughing derisively. 'And who's gonna listen to you, huh?'

'The kommandant,' Josef said, 'that's who.'

'Yeah, right,' Maurice snorted, 'he's really gonna take notice of you. Who the hell do you think you are anyways?'

'An officer in the German army, that's who.'

'No, you a coloured officer in the enemy's army, fool.'

'You know, I've had just about enough of you, Maurice. Ever since we met, you've been nothing but disrespectful towards me. Why?'

'Why? Because you an Uncle Tom son-of-a-bitch! Who's ever heard of a coloured officer? You're a freak and a joke. Ain't nobody gonna listen to you, man.'

'Well, we'll just see about that,' Josef said, before thanking Alvin and Sonny for their hospitality and storming out of the gloomy crypt. He then headed back to his quarters, where he intended to wait for the right moment to approach Herr Jules.

'Hey, why don't you cut the little guy some slack, Maurice?' Alvin said. 'He's OK.'

'Yeah, man, what's got into you?' Sonny added.

'Have you two both lost your senses?' Maurice asked incredulously. 'He's the enemy, man.'

'Is that the real reason why you hate him?' Sonny asked. 'Or is it something else, huh?'

'What you talkin 'bout, man?' Maurice bristled.

'You said it yourself,' Sonny added, 'who's ever heard of a colour-ed officer? Alvin's right, maybe you should cut him some slack. Who else has offered to get us out of this shit pit? Just remember that the next time you wanna go shootin' your big mouth off.'

The following morning, the three GIs were awakened by the heavy sound of boots crunching down the narrow wet steps. Two guards, both with rifles held at the ready, entered the room, followed by the kommandant, who was wearing a peaked visor cap and a long black leather coat, with a tanned gun belt and holster fastened tightly around his waist. 'Aufstehen,' one of the guards yelled, as the GIs scrambled out of their beds and lined up.

The kommandant slowly walked around the cellar, carefully inspecting everything. He then removed one of his gloves, and ran his index finger along the grimy table.

'I told ya not to trust that Uncle Tom,' Maurice whispered. 'We gon' get it now.'

'Mein Herren,' the commandant finally spoke, 'I have received a complaint about the state of your living quarters. I'm told that this place is not fit for a pig. Is this true?'

The three men exchanged furtive glances and remained silent, not knowing the right answer to give.

'Sergeant Williams,' the commandant stopped in front of Sonny, 'you are in charge here, ja?'

'Yes, sir,' Sonny nodded.

'So, I ask again. Is this true?'

'Well, sir,' Sonny faltered, forcing a nervous cough, 'that depends on your point of view, sir.'

'And what exactly is your point of view, sergeant?' Jules asked, now pacing up and down the line, with his naked hand behind his back.

'I think it could be better, sir,' Sonny said, steeling himself for the obligatory slap, which didn't come.

'Very well,' the commandant said, 'collect your personal belongings, you're moving out. Guards, put them in C Block. Guten morgen, mein herren.'

The commandant put his glove back on and quickly marched out, slamming the door behind him.

The Americans howled and cheered as they hurriedly gathered up as much luggage as they could carry. C Block was in the west wing of the fortress, and was considered plush compared to where they'd been sleeping. The room that they were assigned was well above ground level, and was warm and dry. It had a small, barred window that looked out onto the perimeter of the fort, and beneath it was a sheer drop of around 30ft, making it virtually impossible to escape. There were proper wooden bunks with clean blankets, and a washbasin and towel in the corner. At around midday, Josef came to see how they were settling in, entering the room with a small parcel hidden behind his back.

'Josef, you son-of-a-gun,' Alvin hailed, 'you did it.'

'He sure did,' Sonny smiled.

Silence fell upon them as Maurice rose from his bunk and stalked slowly over towards Josef, but the tension was quickly broken when he awkwardly extended his hand in friendship. 'I was wrong 'bout you, man,' he said, 'and I'm sorry. I don't know if these words will-'

'Hey, forget it,' Josef cut him off, giggling with enjoyment at the scene. 'It don't mean nothin', man.'

'Would you get a load of this guy,' Maurice laughed, pulling Josef in for a bear-like hug. 'He's already startin' to talk like us.'

Josef placed the parcel down on the nearest bunk and opened it, allowing the contents to spill out onto the bed. Everyone gathered around and began to trawl through the swag. There was a small pouch of fresh coffee and sugar, two tins of peaches, a bar of German chocolate, two apples and a packet of American cigarettes, and they were all soon brewing up and munching on the rare delicacies.

'So, Sonny, are you married – got any kids?' Josef quizzed.

'Yep,' Sonny said, and reached deep into his breast pocket and produced a couple of small, well-thumbed black and white photos, 'this here is my wife, Darlene. Ain't she the prettiest thang?'

'Why yes, she certainly is,' Josef said, pulling the photograph closer to his face.

'And this is my eight-year-old son, Carlton.'

'He looks just like you.'

'Why, thank you. And this is my ten-year-old daughter, Cheyenne.'

'Cheyenne?'

'Yeah, you know, like the red Indian. You see, when she was first born, she had this long black hair, and everyone said she looked like Pocahontas, so we named her Cheyenne.'

'I think that's a beautiful name,' Josef said, and then turned to Maurice and Alivin. 'What about you guys? Any children?'

'Man,' Alvin laughed, 'we ain't even got no girl friends back home.'

'Hey, speak for yourself, fool,' Maurice said. 'I got me a girl back home, and she's waitin' for me.'

'Why havent ya mentioned her before?' Alvin asked.

'I don't have to tell you nothin', ya hear?'

'What's her name?' Sonny chimed in.

'Say what?' Maurice said.

'What's your girlfriend's name?' Sonny persisted.

'Uh, Maureen,' Maurice said unconvincingly. 'Yeah, that's it. Her name is Maureen.'

Everybody laughed.

Josef spent the majority of what would be his last four days at Bourg Leopold with the Americans, and in that short time he came to learn everything there was to know about Sonny, Alvin and Maurice. He didn't realise it then, but this seemingly innocuous knowledge would later save his life.

According to reports on the wireless, the British 2nd army in France, commanded by Lt General Sir Miles Dempsey, along with the British 11th armoured division, had dashed southwards from Caen towards Falaise. The US 15th corps had already closed in on the so-called Falaise Pocket, making the proceeding days a living hell for the German divisions that were trapped in the area, facing constant poundings by the US 90th artillery division, in and around the Argenta district. This drove General Gunther von Kluger to declare, 'The war is lost,' before killing himself with a cyanide pill. SS Obergruppenfuhrer Sepp Dietrich narrowly escaped with the first SS Panzer corps, with the help of Brigadefuhrer Kurt Meyer's 12th SS Hitler Youth division, who sacrificed themselves by holding open the Falaise Gap before the Canadians and US 5th Corps can close it, taking 50,000 Germans prisoner and burying a further 10,000.

Josef would vividly remember that it was 9.30am on 19 August 1943, and he was lying on his bunk, tuning the wireless while Ziggy sat polishing his long black boots, when suddenly, through the crackling of the airwaves, they heard news of an uprising in Paris.

'Hey, turn that up,' Ziggy said, squatting on his haunches over a small brown whistling box on the floor.

'You see, I told you we were losing,' Josef said, 'but you wouldn't listen to me.'

'Oh, just shut up and let me listen, would you?' Ziggy snapped.

Josef could see real fear in his friend's eyes, and so decided to do as he was asked, slumping back down onto his mattress with his arms folded behind his head. A monotone voice announced, 'Die attack is being led by FFI [4.] partisans against General Dietrich von Choltitz's men. Die General, who commands some twenty thousand troops, including an armoured Waffen SS unit, is involved in vicious street fighting in Paris, France. He is desperately trying to contain the growing unruly mob, who have taken to ambushing his troops and using guerrilla tactics, sniping from balconies and bedroom windows. Ende.'

The commentary was quickly followed by a blurring rendition of the NSDAP [5.] anthem, Horst-Wessel-Lied.

Ziggy sat on the edge of Josef's bed, with his back arched and his shoulders rounded. He ran his fingers through his thick, jet black hair and said quietly, 'I think that maybe you're right, Josef. We are losing this war. I just didn't want to believe it. The Allies are tightening their grip on us. The reality is that they have us surrounded on all fronts, and are now closing in fast.'

Josef switched off the wireless, and they both sat in silent contemplation until they were disturbed by a quiet knock on the door, which was highly unusual, as normally the guards would bang loudly using the butts of their rifles. Josef got up off his bed and approached the door cautiously, trying unsuccessfully to look through the small spy hole and see who was there.

'Open it,' Ziggy said in a hushed voice.

Josef turned the handle and slowly swung the door sprung open, and was shocked to find that standing before him was none other than Major Rudolf Lowe. 'Well, Herzog, are you going to let me in?' the major asked, chuckling.

'But of course, forgive me, Herr Major,' Josef said, mouth agape. 'This is so unexpected, sir.' He hurriedly straightened the top cover on his bunk and added, 'Please, sit down, sir.'

Lowe lifted the tails of his long black leather coat and then made himself comfortable on the bed. 'No doubt you're wondering why I'm here?' he asked.

'Well, it's a bit of a shock, sir,' Josef said.

'Yes, of course, and I won't keep you in suspense. I have some gut news and some bad news. Which do you want to hear first?'

'Uh, the gut news first, sir.'

'The gut news is that I've come here to grant you a pardon.'

'You mean I'm free to leave this place?'

'Yes, but here's the bad news. It's on the condition that you volunteer yourself for a very dangerous mission. If you should survive this mission, you will be released from your unofficial sentence. Believe me, Herzog, this was the only way I could get you off those trumped up charges.'

'I appreciate that, Herr Major, but what exactly is this dangerous mission?'

'This could take some time to explain, but I'll try and make it as simple as I can.'

The Major dug deep into his trench coat pocket and produced a packet of cigarettes, and offered them around before lighting one himself. 'You know that the war is going badly for us, don't you?' he asked. 'Well, there's an SS Sturmbannfuhrer named Otto Skorzeny, who's come up with a bold plan that may help to swing the balance of the war back in our favour, and although the plan is very risky, it just might work. He intends to infiltrate the invading Amerikan armies by sending around twenty thousand English-speaking Germans to get in among them, dressed in Amerikan uniforms, to create havoc and confusion in their flanks. If nothing else, it should at least slow down their advance, giving us enough time to regroup and coordinate a massive counterattack. Now, what do you think?'

'Truly impressive, sir,' Josef nodded, 'if it works that is.'

'Well, if it works, you'll be a free mann. It's as simple as that,' Lowe said. 'Will you do it?'

'Do I have time to think about it, sir?'

'I'm afraid not. I have a staff car waiting outside, so it's either yes or no.'

'What about Ziggy? Can he come, too?'

'I'm sorry, Josef, but I can only take you.'

'Do it, Josef,' Ziggy said, grinning with excitement. 'From what you've told me about yourself, you're like a black cat with nine lives, so take a chance. You can make it out of this.'

Josef stared down at the floor, allowing himself a moment's thought, and within minutes he was in the back seat of a staff car with Major Lowe, heading off at top speed. He had sold his soul to the devil in a bid for freedom, and in a sick twist of fate, had switched allegiances from Werhmact to SS, like an animal cornered. Humans will do anything to survive.

1. Fortress.

2. The Eagle.

3. Second infantry.

4. Free French.

5. Nationalist Socialist German Labour Party.

CHAPTER FORTY-FOUR

Der Waffen SS Junkerschulen, [1.] Braunschweig

It had begun to grow dark by the time Josef and Major Lowe pulled up outside an SS checkpoint, manned by two armed guards stood on either side of a thick, round chevron barrier, which had a large sign placed in the centre, bearing the words Eintritt Verboten in broad, black gothic letters. The guards were both dressed in the sinister black uniforms of the SS, comprising shiny black boots, black jodhpurs and black tunics, with broad red swastika bands on their left upper arms. They also wore thick white ceremonial belts and white chest straps with matching gloves, smart black ties with starched white collars and shiny black helmets. The guard on the left stepped forward and peered suspiciously into the back of the vehicle, and then ordered the major to lower his window.

'Kennkarten bitte,' the round, acne-faced guard grunted, staring at Josef.

'Here we go, Herzog,' Lowe sighed, as he delved into his top pocket and produced a small grey card. On one side, in thick black ink, were the words Deutsches Reich, printed above a large black eagle clutching a round swastika.

'Bitte, warten sie hier, Herr Major,' the guard said, snatching the card and then turning and marching over to a small wooden sentry box. He picked up a black field telephone and began cranking it, all the while keeping his eyes firmly fixed on the staff car.

'Damned Shultz Staffeln,' Lowe said. 'I apologise for dumping you in among this rabble, Herzog, but it was the only way to get you out.'

'Oh, that's alright, Herr Major,' Josef said. 'It truly feels gut to be a free mann again.'

The guard returned to the car and handed Major Lowe his identity card back, and then shouted, 'Offen!' to which the other guard responded by leaning on a white counterweight block at the end of the beam. Slowly, the barrier began to lift, allowing them through.

The car's headlights followed a sharp curve in the road, which led them to the lit entrance of the Junkerschulen. There were huge black monoliths on either side of the stone steps that led up to the main entrance, which was also guarded by two black-uniformed soldiers. On the front of each monolith were the familiar white SS lightning bolts, etched beneath two limp red flags. Josef and the major were met on the steps by a tall, thin, fresh-faced man, dressed in a plain dark military boiler suit showing no trace of insignia, which made it difficult to tell what rank he held. 'Folgen mich, mein herren,' were the only words he spoke before he'd led them to their destination.

Once through the main entrance, the first thing to greet the two officers was a huge stone eagle, which was perched atop an oblong stone block, with its head turned to the left and its wings spread wide, as if ready for flight. Chiselled into the stone beneath its large talons were the words, Blut und Boden. [2.] They turned right and walked down a short corridor, before coming to a halt outside a white-panelled door.

'Bitte, warten sie hier,' the tall man said, and then disappeared through the door, closing it hard behind him. On the wall was a large picture frame, which held a verse of gothic writing on a plain white background. Josef moved in closer, seeing that it read: People who want to live must fight, and people who are not willing to fight in this world of eternal conflict do not deserve to live.

The door swung open once again, and the tall man beckoned them inside. They entered into a large living room, with heavy, draped red velvet curtains and matching tiebacks, and a floor that was covered with a thick, patterned red carpet. A black grand piano was neatly tucked into the far corner, and evenly spaced along the walls were small white statuettes of naked women, holding baskets of fruit high above their heads. Two officers in full SS uniform stood in front of a huge fireplace, which looked as though it hadn't seen a flame since the day it was built, smoking cigars.

'Ah, gentlemen,' one of the men greeted, 'please, sit down and make yourselves comfortable. A drink?'

'Cognac, danke, Herr Sturmbannfuhrer,' Lowe answered.

'And you, Viscount?' the sturmbannfuhrer smiled.

'I'll have the same, danke, sir,' Josef replied.

'From this moment on, you will only speak in English, Herzog,' the sturmbannfuhrer said, 'is that understood?'

'Yes, sir,' Josef answered.

'Very good, old chap,' the sturmbannfuhrer grinned, and then sauntered over to the drinks cabinet and took out a stubby decanter and a couple of chunky crystal glasses. 'Forgive me please, gentlemen,' he said while he poured, 'my name is Otto Skorzeny, and this gentleman here is Captain Kurt Pizer.'

Both Josef and Major Lowe nodded respectfully.

'Herzog, I take it that you have been fully briefed by Major Lowe on the way here?' Skorzeny asked.

'Yes, sir,' Josef said.

'Very good,' Skorzeny smiled. 'You, Herzog, are truly a gift from the gods, did you know that?'

'No, sir.'

'You are unique, and that uniqueness is what will make this daring mission work. The Fuhrer has asked me to come up with a plan that will help us turn the tide of this war, but it will require nerves of steel and a stiff resolve if it's to have any chance of success. Have you ever met the Fuhrer, Herzog?'

'No, sir.'

'No, of course you haven't. He has the gift of looking deep into a man's soul, you know. I've been in his presence when generals have come to him exhausted and on the verge of mental breakdown, saying that they cannot go on – saying that they cannot do what is expected of them, and do you know what happens?'

'No, sir.'

'He picks them up and turns them around. Yes, I have seen this with my own eyes. He embraces them, he takes them in his arms and reassures them in a calm, low voice, and when he's finished, do you know what happens?'

'No, sir.'

'They stand to attention, click their heels and say, "Yes, I will give it another try, my Furhrer," and then they march out. That is the power our leader has over others, and now he has turned his attention to me.' Skorzany walked over to Josef and placed his hand on his shoulder before adding, 'This mission must not fail, Herzog, for I have given the Fuhrer my word, do you understand?'

'Yes, sir, I understand.'

'It's not just my neck that's on the line here, it's the whole of the nation, so I have devised a cunning plot, and with your help, I believe we can pull this off. Now, what do you think about that?'

'It must work and it will work, sir.'

'That's the spirit,' Skorzeny beamed, and then turned to Lowe. 'You see, Major, it's the youth that will prevail and save this nation.'

'Yes, Herr Strumbannfurher,' Major Lowe agreed.

'Herzog will make the perfect American Soldier,' Skorzeny smiled. 'No one will ever doubt his authenticity. He speaks excellent English and American, I'm told.'

'You've obviously done your homework, Herr Sturmbannfuhrer,' Lowe chuckled.

'Oh yes, I know everything about Herzog,' Skorzeny said. 'In fact, I know everything about everything. Prost!' He gently touched their glasses with his, and soon they were relaxed, all smoking the mild panatela cigars he offered around.

Skorzeny was a tall and handsome man with an infectious smile, who looked more like a Hollywood movie star than a soldier. He had well groomed black hair, a pencil moustache and perfect white teeth, and the old duelling scar that ran down the left side of his face did nothing to distract from his good looks. He was smartly dressed and heavily decorated, having been awarded the Iron Cross and a promotion to captain in 1942. Then, in September 1943, he was awarded the Knights Cross for his daring rescue of Benito Mussolini from Hotle Campo, in the Italian Gran Sasso mountains. His next mission had been to fly to Budapest and prevent the Hungarian regent, Admiral Horthy, from signing a peace deal with Stalin, earning him the German Cross in gold. It was because of those deeds that he had been labelled 'the most dangerous man in Europe' by the Allies. Skorzeny had learned from the master himself, using long dialogue and personal contact to gain people's favour, and Josef was now beguiled by him. Not only did the young leutnant agree with the plan, he was wholeheartedly committed to it.

'So, Herzog, what do you think of the plan?' Skorzeny asked, repositioning himself in his chair and giving Josef a deep, searching look.

'Well, sir, it's certainly unique,' Josef replied, meeting Skorzeny's gaze. 'What are the chances of its success?'

'The chances are favourable, Lieutenant,' Skorzeny said, 'and they will be increased if I can get more men like you.'

'I take it that you mean men of my ethnic origin, sir?'

'Correct. As I sit here and look at you, I see an American, or an Englishman, or-'

'An African, sir?'

'Correct,' Skorzeny nodded, as he shifted onto the edge of his seat, pointing with his index finger.

'But with respect, sir, I know of no other minorities within our armed forces.'

Skorzeny slumped back into his chair, his enthusiasm momentarily diminished, before he suddenly sprang back into life and declared, 'You're right, of course, Herzog, but I do have you. If used the right way, you could be more potent than a whole legion of my best men. Now, it is getting late, gentlemen. I want to thank you, Major Lowe, for bringing Herzog to me. Captain Pizer will show you to your quarters, Herzog. Make sure you get some rest. We rise early here.'

They stood, saluted and shook hands, and then Pizer led Josef out of the room and through a maze of corridors. It was 10.30pm, and everywhere was quiet and deserted, save for a few male cleaners that were waxing the marble floors, and wiping the huge portraits and busts of the Fuhrer that were spaced along the way.

'Here we are, Lieutenant,' Pizer said, gesturing with an open palm, 'your quarters. We rise at five-thirty AM for breakfast, and then assemble at six for the start of die Kameradschaftag. [3.] Goodnight.'

Josef turned a silver handle and pushed open the door, finding a room that was small and sparsely furnished with a single bed, a tall locker and a small bureau, and serviced by one tiny window. Josef looked inside the locker and found a plain dark boiler suit, which looked to be roughly his size, hanging on a rail, and beneath it, on the floor of the locker, a pair of black plimsolls that were also in his size. Skorzeny really has done his homework, he thought, as he went over to the bureau and lifted the lid to find a copy of Gauleiter Julius Streicher's anti-Semitic newspaper, Der Sturm. [4.] Beneath that was an old, well-thumbed magazine, presumably left by the previous occupant, which he picked up and sat on the edge of the bed to read. On the front cover was a drawing of a group of Hitler Youth, who were gathered around a huge bonfire, waving their swastika flags and giving the Nazi salute while watching books and other literature being burned, sending plumes of black smoke high up into the air. The heading above the picture read: Deutsches Jugendfest, sonnabend den 30. Juni 1934, and below was the caption: Fordert die Deutsche Jugend, durch den kauf des festabzeichens. [5.]

Josef's heart felt heavy, for this brought back the memories of Kristallnacht, which had seen the burning of property and all literature connected with the Jewish society. He didn't bother to open the magazine, and instead decided to simply get a good night's rest, in order to be ready for the events of the following day.

At precisely 5.30am, Hauptmann Kurt Pizer arrived at Josef's door, to make sure that he was awake. 'Lieutenant?' he called. 'Excuse me, comrade.'

'Oh, Captain,' Josef replied. 'Please, come in.'

'Did you have a good night's sleep, sir?' Pizer asked.

'Yes, thank you,' Josef said. 'I'd offer you a seat, but I don't appear to have one.'

'That's OK, Lieutenant,' Pizer laughed, 'comfort is not really a consideration here. It is said that to be a good soldier, one must first experience discomfort, like our dear Fuhrer did during his early years of struggle.'

'Of course,' Josef nodded.

'I see the boiler suit fits.'

'Yes, though I don't think this colour is me. What do you think?'

Pizer laughed again. 'Don't worry, you'll get used to it. Plimsolls fit OK?'

'Oh yes, they're fine. I was wondering, though, why the strange dress code?'

'The idea is that everyone should be equal. In here, we are all kameraden. Right, let's go to breakfast, shall we?'

They entered the mess hall, which was a large, featureless room filled with wide, square tables that each seated six boiler-suited teenagers. Josef took a seat with the elders, and waited for his meal to be brought to him by one of the young kameraden. Most of the young cadets sat stoney-faced and looked only straight ahead, although a few did dare to glance at Josef out the corner of their eye. He could only assume that the men seated at his table were all officers, but even as he stared deep into their grey, emotionless faces for signs of authority, he found that he couldn't be sure.

'Tee oder kaffee, kamerad?' a young boy croaked, as he struggled to hold a huge silver tray to his chest.

'Uh, tea please,' Josef said with a smile.

'"Tee, kamerad," is the reply, comrade,' Pizer winked.

'Of course, forgive me,' Josef laughed wryly, finding it odd to speak English among Germans who didn't understand it. 'So, tell me, why are all these young people here?'

'They're here because they are our future, comrade,' Pizer explained. 'The youth are brought in from all over Germany – Berlin, Munich, Hamburg and as far away as Vienna.'

'And what do they do here?'

'Well, they're taught the basic skills of mechanics, welding and aircraft building, and spend at least one hundred and sixty hours on weapons training, learning how to use heavy machine guns and artillery, along with radios and signal communications. They also have to spend one week on the assembly line, at the MAN tank factory in Augsberg-Nurnberg.'

'It seems like a lot for their young minds to take in, don't you think?'

'Oh, I disagree, comrade. Over four hundred officers a year graduate from der Junkerschulen, and go on to bigger and better things. So, we must be doing something right, eh?'

'I take your point, comrade. Last night, you said that we would be attending die kameradschaftag after breakfast, is that correct?'

'Yes, comrade, that is correct. Why do you ask?'

'Oh, no specific reason. I was just wondering what it was all about.'

'Well, basically, it's an indoctrination into our ideology.'

'A what?'

Pizer simply laughed. 'You'll understand when we get there,

comrade. Trust me.'

Breakfast amounted to a plate of cold sausage and dry bread, and a small pot of jam. Everyone tucked in eagerly, and when they were almost finished, one of the elders stood up and took the centre of the floor to make an announcement.

'What's going on now, comrade?' Josef asked, bemused.

'Oh, it's only the kamerad fuhrer,' Pizer said. 'He always gives a little speech just before we start the day. Shush now, listen.'

A tall man with short, greying hair, wearing exactly the same drab dark boiler suit as the rest, nodded slightly to another man, who was seated at a table in the opposite corner, next to an old gramophone. The man at the gramophone quickly raised its heavy black arm, letting the chrome stylus head fall onto a thick black 78-inch vinyl disc. The record zipped and crackled into life, and the coned brass horn vibrated with the sounds of drums, trumpets and trombones, signalling the introduction of the infamous Horst-Wessel-Lied. Immediately, everyone present stood to attention, and began to join in heartily with the first two verses.

The flag high, the ranks closed solid,
SA marches with silent, firm step,
Comrades, the red front and rear action are exhausted,
Marching in spirit with our ranks.

The street free, the brown battalions,
The street free, the storm troopers,
Millions full of hope look on at the swastika,
The day for freedom and for bread sings on.

It was the unofficial national anthem of Hitler's Germany, and commemorated Horst Wessel, a twenty-three-year-old SA storm trooper who was allegedly murdered by the Berlin Communist front, back in 1930. Josef could not help but show his ignorance as he tried to follow along with the group, quietly mumbling the wrong words and placing his hand to his mouth to muffle the little nervous coughs that were escaping. He somehow managed to stumble his way through another two verses, before they all sat down again to listen to the morning's address.

'Guten morgen, kameraden,' the kamerad fuhrer began. 'I would firstly like to remind you all of the three main principles of this Junkerschulen. Eins, physical fitness. Zwei, character training. Finally, drei, weapons training. These must be remembered and practised at all times. In here, we are all bruder und kameraden. Trust is paramount. There are no locked doors here, and personal belongings can be left out at all times. If I can't trust you with mein ausrustung, [6.] how could I trust you with mein life?'

'Jawhol, kamerad fuhrer!' the impressionable youngsters roared in unison.

'Very well, aufstehen,' the kamerad fuhrer said, giving them leave to depart.

The boys all stood to attention and then marched out smartly in single file, to begin their daily work programme.

Is this to be the new Germany? Josef thought, finding the sight most disturbing. They're nothing more than mindless automatons. He realised with a shudder that this was more than just a military academy, it was a huge brainwashing factory, designed with the single purpose of spewing out thousands of perfect citizens for the Reich.

Josef and Pizer tagged onto the back of the line of marching youth, following them into a larger room that was filled with rows of prearranged seats. At the front, behind a wooden lectern, stood one of the elders, and behind him hung a huge map with thick red swirls dashed across it, pointing to key locations that were heavily circled off. The little kameraden stood rigid in front of the empty chairs, waiting for the command to sit, which came as soon as Josef and Pizer cleared the doorway on entering the room. They sat quietly at the back, and watched as the kamerad fuhrer repositioned his paperwork and got ready to deliver his monologue. Josef could not help but notice a large pale-blue poster on the wall to his right, featuring the faded face of Adolf Hitler, blown up such that it almost filled the entire space. Superimposed over it was the slightly turned face of a young blond boy, wearing a brown open-necked shirt, with a black tie and toggle and a black leather chest strap, which ran diagonally from his shoulder to his waist. A thick headline at the top of the poster read: Jugend Dient Dem Fuhrer, and along the bottom ran the words, Alle Zehnjahrigen in Die HJ. [7.]

The man behind the lectern coughed, and then began his speech. 'Kameraden,' he screeched, in a thin voice, 'these are dangerous times for Germany. As I speak to you now, the Allied forces are closing in, and if they continue their push, we will soon be fighting on our own soil.' He turned to the map behind him, and with a sweeping wave of his arm, indicated the areas of interest. 'The red lines represent the enemy, while the black circles mark our positions. Since nineteen-forty, we've been steadily losing ground. Nijmegen, Arnhem and Rotterdam have all fallen, and now France is on the verge of going the same way. The Second Panzer division and the Twenty-Sixth Volksgrenadier division, supported by Panzer Lehr, are making preparations to surround the US One Hundred-and-First Airborne Division, and the US Tenth Armoured Division at Bastogne and Noville. Our airborne battle group, Peiper, are readying for parachute drops near Elsenborn and Malmedy, both of which are presently held by the US First and US Thirtieth divisions. We are moving up the Twelfth and Twenty-Seventh Volksgrenadier divisions, as well as the First, Third and Twelfth SS Panzer divisions, and the Third Parachute Division, which will dislodge the enemies from their positions. Victory is at hand, but it is the duty of every able-bodied mann to fight and, if necessary, die for der Varterland. Remember your oath to our Fuhrer. With the will of God, we shall vanquish our enemies.'

The oath, Josef thought, remembering back to 1938, when he was stood to attention on a cold, wet parade ground in Leipzig, with his right hand held in the air, repeating back every word that was spoken by his commanding officer. I hereby swear by almighty God that I will honour and obey the Fuhrer of the German Reich and the German people, Adolf Hitler, as commander-in-chief of the army, unconditionally, and will serve him like a good soldier, and be prepared to sacrifice my life at all times in the service of this oath.

He was suddenly jolted back to reality by the sound of rapturous applause and the stamping of feet on the bare wooden floor, as everyone began to slowly shuffle out of the room. Josef stood and faced Pizer, who was smiling at him while pointing the way with his hand.

'Right, comrade, let's go to work,' the captain said. 'I hope you're ready for an intense training course.'

'Oh yes, I work better under pressure, comrade,' Josef said confidently. 'But, where exactly are you taking me?'

'To zimmer drei, [8.] a place for special operations. Don't worry, I'll be with you throughout the training.'

They stepped out into the fresh morning air, and paused to allow a small company of Hitler Youth members to march past. At the head of the formation were three drummer boys, bashing loudly on their large, deep drums, while being led by a tall, thin youth, who proudly carried a banner bearing the words, Hitler Youth Twelfth SS Division. Little flecks of snow began to float down and dance aimlessly in the gentle crosswind, as the troop, wearing brown shirts and black shorts, with black leather chest straps and belts, crunched forward and then stopped, forming two neat rows. Standing shoulder to shoulder, the boys linked arms and placed their right hands on their large silver belt buckles. On the left side of their belts hung a long black ceremonial dagger, and on their left upper arms were red and white, diamond-shaped swastikas. Despite being scantily clad in just their black shorts and white knee socks, they seemed blissfully impervious to the weather, which was beginning to turn very cold.

'Come now, comrade,' Pizer said, placing his hand on Josef's shoulder, 'we mustn't be late.'

They crossed the small parade ground and entered a thick, grey-walled building on the other side. Josef kept himself one step behind Pizer as he cautiously followed him into a crowded, smoke-filled room that was full of laughing American GIs, all lining up in front of a long, narrow table, where they were collecting various pieces of kit from a boiler-suited man.

'What's going on here, comrade?' Josef asked Pizer.

'Pick up your gear from the table,' Pizer said, 'and then I'll explain.'

'Ah, kamerad,' the boiler-suited man at the table said happily, as Josef approached, 'I have just the thing for you.' He stooped down beneath the table and produced an American army uniform that looked strangely familiar. He placed it down gently, and winked as Josef leaned forward to get a better look.

On the top left arm of the khaki jacket was an embroidered division patch, which featured an American Red Indian's head that was set inside a white five-sided star on a black background. Yes, Josef thought, I recognise this alright. 'American Second Infantry Division,' he said under his breath, lifting up the garment and inspecting it closely.

'Why don't you try it on, kamerad,' the man suggested. 'I think you'll find that it's your size.'

'I don't understand,' Josef said, turning to Pizer.

'We thought it important to place you in an American unit that you already knew well,' Pizer explained.

'You're talking about the Americans at Bourg Leopold?' Josef asked in disbelief.

'Correct,' Pizer nodded. 'You did spend quite a bit of time with them, remember?'

'Well, yes.'

'So, it made perfect sense to place you with Sergeant Williams's division.'

'Yes, of course. You guys really have thought of everything, haven't you?'

'Yes.'

'And all these men here, they're not real Americans, are they?'

'No, everyone here is German. Come, let's collect the rest of your uniform.'

They shuffled further along the table, stopping at a second boiler-suited man, who was carefully laying out individual pieces of uniforms, and calling out each one for another man, seated nearby, to record on a thick ledger.

'One M-one helmet with netting,' the man handling the uniform said, pointing to each item in turn. 'Remember to keep the chinstrap tucked into the netting, as it's rarely worn in combat. One brown knitted, woollen stiff-brimmed cap, or "beanie," as an American would call it. This is to be worn under the helmet, remember that. One pair of olive drab trousers. One pair of web leggings, to be laced up on the outside, with this strap passing under the boot. One pair of standard issue light tan ankle boots, with rubber soles. One M-four gas mask, with waterbottle and ammunition belt. One M-one carbine rifle, with twenty-round magazine and spare double canvas magazine, to be strapped to the butt of the rifle.' He did a quick double-check, silently mouthing everything to himself once more. 'OK, I think that covers everything. Now, take your place in the centre of the room with the others. Die sturmbannfuhrer is about to brief you all.'

1. Officer candidate school.

2. Blood and soil.

3. Comrades day.

4. The Storm.

5. Germany's youth festival, Saturday, 30 June 1934, demands the german youth through the purchase of the festival decorations.

6. Equipment.

7. Youth serve the fuhrer. All ten-year-olds in the Hitler Youth.

8. Room Three.

CHAPTER FORTY-FIVE

Josef and Pizer lined up with the rest of the men and waited patiently for Sturmbannfuhrer Otto Skorzeny, who soon entered the room and took up his position at the front. He stood straight as an arrow, with his arms behind his back, and paused to observe the crowd for a moment before speaking.

'Comrades,' Skorzeny began, 'I feel a real sense of pride as I stand here among you, for it is today that we make history. We are about to enact a plan that is so new and so daring, it will shock the whole world. I won't lie to you about the dangers of this mission. It is extremely risky, and many of you may not return, but remember this. If successful, it will change the present state of the war, and surely bring us a much-needed victory. Now, is there anyone here with tank experience?'

A few hands went up around the room, and Skorzeny pointed with his finger to each individual in turn, calling out, 'Yes, you,' like a statesman at question time. 'What kind of experience do you have, comrade?' he asked.

'I've driven a Panzer mark three, sir,' a soldier replied.

'Good, and you?' Skorzeny asked another.

'I've spent a little time in a Panther, sir,'

'Hmm, a serious tank, eh?' Skorzeny nodded. 'And you, in the middle row?'

'A Tiger mark six, sir.'

'Oh, you've driven one of the big boys, eh? And you?' Skorzeny pointed to a man at the back.

'A Stug three, sir.'

'Very well,' Skorzeny said, before arriving at Josef. 'Ah, and finally you, my exotic friend.'

Josef gave a small cough, and said quietly, 'A Hetzer self-propelled, sir.'

'That's not a tank, it's a pea shooter,' Skorzeny cried, and then let out a huge belly laugh that the rest of the men immediately joined in with.

'Bastards,' Josef muttered under his breath, seething.

Pizer turned to him and grinned. 'They're only playing with you, comrade,' he said reassuringly.

'Alright,' Skorzeny bellowed, indicating that he wanted quiet, 'that's the pep talk over with. Now, let's get down to some serious training, shall we? If you'll take yourselves outside, I have something to show you.'

The men lined up immediately and marched out in single file. It had stopped snowing since the previous night's downpour, and everywhere outside was crisp and white. The men stood in two straight lines with their backs to the special operations building, quietly chatting amongst themselves, but then fell silent as the clattering sound of tank tracks grew louder until, seemingly to everyone's surprise, an American Sherman tank rounded the corner and came to a squeaky halt in front of them.

Skorzeny stepped forward and placed himself in between the tank and his men, and began his address. 'Now, men, as you can see, this is an American tank. It's a Sherman M-four, built by the Chrysler company in Detroit, USA, and was recently captured near St Vith, in Belgium. It has a nine-cylinder radial engine, which will give you a top speed of twenty-six miles per hour, and a five-speed synchromesh transmission. The tank holds a five-man crew of driver, gunner, loader, machine gunner and commander. There is a seventy-five-millimetre kanon mounted on a three hundred and six-ty-degree turning turret, which has three inches of frontal armour and two inches of side armour. Please be aware that the frontal armour plating on this tank is only two-and-a-half inches thick, with even less for side protection. Now, I want you all to get familiar with this tank, because it's the same one that you'll be using when you're sent in to infiltrate the enemy. Once you're through, you will abandon the vehicle and set about your task, which is to create disruption and confusion, and then bring back intelligence reports on any enemy key positions, is that clear? OK, climb aboard and familiarise yourselves with the machine. I can't emphasise enough that time is of the utmost importance. It is our intention to send you out as soon as possible, so learn fast, gentlemen.'

Over the next two days, the comrades practised driving the Sherman and loading and firing its seventy-five-millimetre canon and machine gun. Then, on the third day, they studied maps of the enemy terrain, with each group given different tasks and objectives. Josef's team, however, were mysteriously kept in the dark about certain aspects of their mission, and were told that for security reasons, they would only be fully briefed once they had reach their destination, Monschau, on the German-Belgian border.

On the fourth day, at 4.00am, Josef's group were flown from

Braunschweig to the German border town Aachen, wearing full US army kit, and then from there they were driven by truck to Monschau. A strong shaft of sunlight broke through the dark grey clouds as the men began to tumble out from the back of the truck, to be faced by an impressive row of US Jeeps and Sherman tanks, neatly lined up with their seventy-five-millimetre canons facing upwards. It was a sight which brought home to Josef the true reality of what he was about to embark upon, and he began to feel butterflies gathering in his stomach when, suddenly, Hauptmann Kurt Pizer appeared from behind one of the Shermans, wearing a uniform from the 9th US Infantry Division.

'What are you doing here, sir?' Josef asked, having not expected to see him again until the mission was complete.

'Didn't they tell you?' Pizer said with a smile. 'I'm going with you on this mission. Is there a problem?'

'Why no, not at all. I'm really glad to see you.'

'Good. The three GIs over there will make up the rest of our crew, and that Sherman they're leaning against is ours. Come on, I'll introduce you to them.'

As they made their way over, Josef saw that the tank showed signs of light battle damage and was covered in mud, with an unconvincing camouflage net that had been hastily thrown over it. Pizer pointed out that the tank must have come all the way from Normandy, because of a strange device that was attached to its front. Indeed, across the bottom ran an iron girder with five thick prongs welded onto it. This had been nicknamed the 'hedge chopper' by the Allies, who had successfully used it to punch holes through the dense hedgerows that would appear only too often across the vast open countrysides of Europe, slowing their relentless advance.

The crew jumped to attention and saluted as the two officers neared, and a slim blond man at the front grinned, as he slapped the side of the tank as if it were an old girlfriend and said, 'our tank, sir,' drawing a burst of laughter from the rest of the crew.

'Well,' Pizer said, grinning back, 'I may as well start with this fellow first. The comedian is Bruno, and behind him are Christin and Konrad.'

The men eagerly shook hands with Josef, and then Pizer gave the order to mount up. Bruno took the driver's seat, and Josef sat at the machine gun alongside him. Pizer, Konrad and Christin occupied the turret, with Pizer acting as commander and Christin and Konrad serving as main gunner and loader respectively. Pizer stood erect, peering out of the open cupola, and put on his brown leather skullcap, complete with headphones and throat microphone, before shouting out the order to move.

The engine revved, and soon the tank was filled with its deafening roar, as a total of fifteen Shermans began to carefully roll out of Monschau in single file, with each of them heading for different locations at Elsenborn, Malmedy, Stoumont, Trois-Ponts and Spa. Firstly, though, they would have to navigate through the heavily armed US 9th Division.

Pizer battened down the hatch cover, and sat nervously looking through the periscope as they approached the enemy. He needn't have worried too much, however, since the first group of authentic American GIs that they came upon simply waved them through cheerfully.

'Christ,' Bruno giggled, 'that was easy.'

'It's not over yet,' Pizer reminded him. 'We've still got to get past those Shermans over there.'

'Shit, I didn't see those,' Bruno said.

'It's OK, just slow down a little as we approach,' Pizer advised.

Bruno awkwardly crunched through the gears like a learner driver, causing the tank to buck before it slowed as they reached the two staggered tanks that were partially blocking their way. Once they had stopped, Pizer popped the hatch and leaned out to speak with one of the American tank commanders.

'Hey there, how's it goin?' Pizer called, speaking English in a very passable American accent.

'Hi,' the commander from the first tank answered jovially, 'where have you guys come from?'

'Oh, just been doing a little recon near Monschau. God damned weather. Will it ever stop snowing?'

'Yeah, I know what you mean. Sure wish I was stateside.'

'Yeah, me too.'

'So, where you boys headin' to?'

'Uh, some place called Sart. Do you know it?'

'Yeah, but it's at least sixty kilometres from here, man.'

'Well, we'd better get movin', then.'

'Yeah, see you around, buddy.'

Bruno wasted no time in hitting the accelerator and weaving his way through the maze of artillery, trucks and men of the 9th In-fantry. They had dealt successfully with their first enemy encounter, and once they were far enough out of sight, decided to pull over for a well-deserved rest, scrambling out of the iron fortress and sitting along a white grassy verge.

'I must say, Kurt, it was pretty impressive the way you handled those Americans back there,' Josef said. 'They never suspected a thing, did they?'

'That's right, but let's not get too complacent,' Pizer warned, 'it's still early days. Pass me the map, Christin. Let's see where we are.'

Bruno filled the space next to Josef that Christin vacated, and began chomping on an American chocolate bar that he'd found at the bottom of the tank. He offered a piece to Josef, asking, 'Are you married, Lieutenant?'

'Uh, no,' Josef replied, caught off guard. He'd assumed that, like Pizer, all of the crew would have known about his past.

'Girlfriend?'

'Did have, but she was killed some years back.'

'Oh, I'm sorry to hear that, Lieutenant.'

'It's OK, Bruno. It was a long time ago. What about you?'

'I have a wife and young baby boy,' Bruno said, digging deep into his jacket and producing a small, crumpled black and white photograph. 'Here, that's Lisa, holding little Bruno in her arms.'

'He looks just like you,' Josef laughed, but inside, his heart filled with pain. He slumped down, reflecting on what might have been with him and Monika. He would never know what it was like to be married or to hold a child in his arms, all thanks to Lunder and Schlossman. His hatred for them was hard to contain.

'Gather round please, gentlemen,' Pizer said. 'I want to show you where we are and where we're going.' He smoothed out the map on top of the tank, and pressed his finger down onto a specific point. 'We are here, four miles into what's known as the Hohn Venn. It's a wide strip of land, for want of a better term, separating us from our goal, which is this area here,' he tapped the map. 'Spa.'

'I thought you said that we were going to a place called Sart?' Josef asked.

'I did,' Pizer said, 'but you never reveal your true intentions to the enemy.'

'Yes, of course,' Josef said, feeling a little embarrassed, 'forgive me.'

Pizer laughed. 'That's OK.'

'What's so important about this area, sir?' Christin asked.

'Well, army intelligence tells us that the town of Spa is where the Americans have a massive fuel dump, and it's up to us to find and destroy it.'

'So, that's why we were kept in the dark about this mission,' Josef said.

'That's correct,' Pizer nodded, 'and now that you are all fully briefed, I suggest we get moving. We've still a long way to go, and it will be getting dark soon.'

They clambered back on board and took up their battle positions. Josef checked his 30-calibre machine gun, while Bruno fired up the engine and gripped the two control levers. They were on the move again, but then night fell quickly, forcing them to stop after advancing just three and a half miles. Bruno backed the tank into a hedgerow, and due to the weather, they had to sleep in their seats, which proved to be very uncomfortable.

The following morning, they were stood around the tank, chatting and finishing breakfast before moving off, when Konrad went to take a leak in the hedgerow. He was halfway through relieving himself when he heard a strange noise coming from the other side of the hedges, and when he pushed through to see what it was, he was astonished to find a whole company of Americans moving toward him.

'Amerikans! Amerikans!' he cried, as he raced back to his comrades, panting.

'Shush, you idiot,' Pizer hissed, pushing him up against the tank. 'Do you want to get us all killed? Speak English.'

'Sorry, sir,' Konrad said, switching languages, 'but there are so many of them out there.'

'Alright,' Pizer said, 'just calm down and tell me where they are.'

'On the other side of the hedgerow. They've got tanks, half-tracks and many Soldaten – I mean soldiers, sir.'

'Right, everybody back on board,' Pizer ordered. 'Bruno, start the engine and let's get out of here, fast.'

It was too late, however, as the long muzzle of a Sherman tank soon appeared, sending the hedges crashing down before them. Three tanks and two half-tracks thundered through the gap, followed by a line of infantry. The lead tank pulled over and stopped, and Josef watched in horror through the front periscope as an officer alighted and calmy approached them. He could tell by the shoulder epaulettes that this man was a major, and his throat went dry and his hands were clammy and shaking as he wondered if Pizer would be able to pull this off. The other Americans they'd met were only privates, but this was much different, and much more dangerous.

Pizer opened the hatch and saluted, but before the American could speak, his driver shouted, 'Major Wright, General Clarke is on the telephone, sir.'

'OK, tell him I'll call him back,' the Major replied, and then turned back to face Pizer. 'What are you doing parked here, commander?'

'We were just about to shove off when you arrived, sir.' Pizer answered.

'You still haven't answered my question, trooper,' the major said sharply. 'What are you doing here?'

'I've gotta level with you, sir. We're on a special mission, sir.'

'I see. And I suppose you can't tell me what that mission is, huh, commander?'

'That's right, sir. You know how it is.'

'I sure do, but you can tell me which outfit you're with, can't you?'

'I'm afraid not, sir. You see it's-'

'Don't tell me. Top secret.'

'You got it, sir,' Pizer laughed, doing well to mask his terror.

'Well, this is most unusual, commander, but I suppose I have no choice but to let you get under way.'

'Yes, sir. Right away, sir.'

Pizer brought the microphone to his mouth and ordered Bruno to pull away, slowly. They were roughly halfway to Spa, but it felt as though their objective was a thousand miles off. They trundled on at full speed, hoping to put as much distance between themselves and the major as possible, but fate was to deal them another heavy blow. They were running desperately low on fuel, and would have to stop to refill very soon.

'Sergeant Murray, get me Division on the line, will you?' Major Wright asked, as he watched the Sherman disappear over the snowy horizon.

'Sure thing, Major,' Murray said. 'Is there a problem, sir?'

'Not if you can answer me a couple of simple question.'

'OK, shoot.'

'What's a Sherman tank doing right here, with a commander who's wearing a Ninth Infantry uniform, and who uses the Navy phrase shove off?'

'I don't know, sir.'

'Neither do I, sergeant. Now, patch me through, will you?'

The Sherman began to cough and splutter, and then finally ground to a halt.

'It's no good, sir,' Bruno shouted. 'She's dead.'

'Damn it,' Kurt cursed. 'OK, I'm getting out. I'll have to study the map.'

After hopping out of the vehicle, he began to nervously scan the map until he found a small village, Les Arsins, which was only four miles away, dead ahead. If only we could find more fuel, he thought. Just enough to get us to Les Arsins.

He climbed back inside and organised the men, telling Bruno to check the fuel cans on board, and ordering the rest of the crew to fan out and search for any wrecked vehicles, in the hope that there could be a spare fuel can to be found. Looking at his map once more, his overriding concern was just how far back Major Wright was likely to be.

'Sir,' Bruno called, triumphantly holding a fuel can high in the air, 'I've found one.'

'Good work, Bruno,' Kurt sighed with relief.

'I'm afraid it's not much, sir,' Bruno admitted.

'Yes, but it's a start,' Kurt said. 'Quickly, call back the rest of the crew.'

He began to tip the precious liquid into the tank, but after only a few spurts, it was gone. The rest of the men returned having managed to find another can, which held roughly the same amount as the first, and now they had just enough fuel to get them to Les Arsins. They set off immediately.

He had calculated that Wright's forces would still be a good six miles behind, giving him and his crew a fighting chance. He ordered Bruno to press on at full speed, all the while leaning out of his cupola and peering back with his field glasses as they went. 'Keep going, Bruno,' he screamed into the headset. 'I can see the town. Put your foot down, man.'

'She's overheating,' he heard Herzog shouting back. 'We need to slow down.'

'Nein, nein,' Kurt insisted, 'wir mussen.'

'Speak English, remember, sir?' Konrad piped up sarcastically.

At around 3.30pm, they limped into Les Arsins, which, according to the map, was three and a half kilometres east of Spa. They parked as far away from the American attachment as they thought was possible without causing suspicion, and then all jumped out and began to stretch their legs gratefully. However, no sooner had they got the blood circulating again than an American jeep roared up and screeched to a halt alongside them.

'Leave the talking to me,' Kurt said quietly, before striding over to meet the officer who had leaped out of the jeep to confront them. 'Good afternoon, captain.'

'Afternoon,' the American answered. 'You the commander, here?'

'Yes, sir,' Kurt said.

'OK, listen up. We've just got a report of some kind of enemy infiltration. Germans dressed as American GIs, can you believe that?'

'Gee, you're kidding me, right?'

'I wish I was, commander. Division say that the Eighty-Second Airborne, along with Thirty Division, have killed a whole platoon of 'em up near Trois-Ponts and Malmedy.'

'No shit?'

'Yeah, so you guys be on the lookout for anything suspicious. Apparently, they don't speak good English, and that's what tripped 'em up, so be on your toes, understand?'

'Sure thing, Captain,' Kurt said with a salute. He waited for the jeep to race away before returning to his men. 'We better get fuelled up and get out of here as quick as possible.'

'Das schweinhunde,' Konrad said.

'Shut up, Konrad, and get looking for that fuel,' Kurt ordered, in no mood for chatter.

'How can you be so calm, sir?' Bruno asked. 'Didn't you hear what he just said? They've killed all of our men.'

'Yes, I know, and there's nothing we can do to bring them back, so get looking for that damned fuel,' Kurt said impatiently. 'Josef, come over here. I need to speak with you.'

'Sure, what's up Kurt?' Herzog asked, following him over to a spot where the crew wouldn't be able to hear them.

'Look, you and I are the only officers in this crew, so it's vital that you show your full support when I have to make the hard decisions, OK?'

'Of course, that goes without saying.'

'Good. Now, I need you to act as morale officer. It will be your responsibility to keep the lads' spirits up, and judging by what may lie ahead, I can only guess that you'll be working flat out. Do you think you can handle it?'

'No problem, sir.'

'Skorzeny was right when he said that you were the best man for this job. Come on, let's find some fuel and get the hell out of here. It'll be dark in a couple of hours.'

The crew did a fine job of scavenging the odd fuel can or two from here and there, sometimes from right under the noses of un-suspecting US tank commanders, and once Kurt was satisfied that they had enough to get them to Berlin and back, they set off for the small town of Spa, 75km south-east of Liege.

Progress was slow in the fading light, and eventually they had no choice but to stop. They pulled off the main track and found themselves a small clearing among a group of trees, which was as good a spot as any to set-up camp. Bruno made a small fire using some spare gasoline, and then balanced a helmet filled with water on top of the bright orange flame to make tea for everyone. The crew huddled around the makeshift brazier, vigorously rubbing their hands together for warmth. Kurt sat some distance away from the rest of the crew.

'Christin, go get the K rations from the tank, would you?' Kurt asked.

The K ration was the creation of Professor Ansel Keys, designed for American GIs serving in the Great War. It was, theoretically at least, an all-in-one package, providing breakfast, lunch and dinner.

'Right away, sir,' Christin said.

'Come, Josef, sit here with me,' Kurt said, beckoning Herzog to move closer.

'Thank you, Kurt,' Herzog smiled. 'It's quite mild tonight, don't you think?'

'Yes,' Kurt agreed, albeit rather absently, 'quite mild.'

If it seemed to the men that Kurt was acting distant, it was because his mind was indeed somewhere far way, as he stared down at the hard ground, thinking of his wife.

'Kurt, I'm really afraid this time,' she'd said, upon hearing about his latest mission. 'Why does it always have to be you? Can't they just give you a desk job at head quarters?'

'Don't be silly, darling,' he'd laughed. 'I'm a combat soldat. This is what I do. You knew the risks when you married me, remember?'

'Yes, but knowing something and actually experiencing it are two very different things.'

'Look, Julianna, everything's going to be alright, trust me.'

'But what if something were to happen to you, and it could, you know. What about me and little Adolf?'

'Look, nothing's going to happen to me, verstehen?'

'Oh, don't talk to me like one of your soldaten. I'm not some stupid schule madchen that you can just boss around, you know.'

'Well, if that's the way you're going to be about it, you can just sit there and sulk. I'm going out for a walk.'

'That's just typical of you, isn't it? Walk away, like you always do. Go on, get out!'

'Anyone for K rations?' Bruno asked, throwing a large packet into each of their laps.

Kurt blinked as he returned from his reverie. He watched with amusement as Herzog pulled awkwardly at the foil wrapper with his teeth, and then bit down hard on the dried high protein biscuit.

'Ugh, that tastes foul,' the young lieutenant complained. 'How can anyone eat this rubbish?'

'You better get used to it,' Kurt laughed. 'It's all we've got until we reach Spa.'

'Well, if this is all we've got, I'd rather starve,' Herzog said, tossing the K bar to one side.

'Don't be stupid, Josef. If you don't eat that, you'll have to eat spiders. We'll probably be travelling all day tomorrow, and I need everyone sharp. You're no good to me if you collapse, so eat. And yes, that's an order.'

'Very well, but it's under protest.'

'Your protest is noted, but if I may be serious for a moment, I'd like to know what made you sign up for such a dangerous mission?'

'You surprise me, Kurt. I thought you knew everything about me?'

'Just because I'm SS doesn't mean I know your mother's maiden name, you know.'

'Understood, sir.'

'So, why did you sign up?'

'Truthfully, I had no real choice in the matter. It was either sign up or spend the rest of the war in prison. If I survive this, I gain my freedom. It's as simple as that. What about you? Why are you here?'

'Oh, you know how it is, for honour and country. They wanted me and I said yes. It's an old SS thing, you know. Obedience and honour, et cetera. But, to be completely honest with you, this is going to be my last mission.'

'What do you mean?'

'I've done a lot of bad things in the name of National Socialisim, and up until recently, everything they'd said had been right, but now all I see are bureaucrats getting fatter on corrupt gains, while we get weaker doing their fighting. Skorzeny has promised me a quiet desk job if I come out of this alive, and that's just what I intend to do.'

'It sounds like Skorzeny has offered us both the same contract.'

'Oh, he's a clever man alright.'

'Give me some insight into this mysterious organisation?'

'I'm afraid I don't follow.'

'Well, you know, what makes you guys tick?'

'You make me sound like an old grandfather clock.'

'Oh, come on, you know what I mean.'

'Yes, well, how should I put it,' Kurt paused to consider his answer. 'You have a strong belief and you follow it.'

'And that's it?'

'Yes.'

'I have strong beliefs, too, but I would never consider joining the SS.'

'That's just as well, since they wouldn't have you.'

'Come on, Kurt.'

'OK, look. Before you can become a member of the Shultz Staffeln, you have to prove your Aryan lineage, which must to go back for at least one hundred and seventy-five years. It must be pure and unbroken, otherwise you don't get in, and that's basically it.'

'Surely, there's more to it than that?'

'Well, I shouldn't be telling you all this, but then, I suppose you are classed as one of us now.'

'Yes, I'm one of you, so please go on,' Herzog said, lighting a cigarette. He seemed to be hanging on Kurt's every word.

'The Reichfuhrer, SS Heinrich Himmler, has given us top secret orders. Orders that give only SS servicemen, married or single, the right to mate with any eligible Aryan female regardless of her status. The idea is to create as many of the "master race" as possible.' Kurt paused for a moment, and then playfully turned the silver SS honour ring around on his little finger before adding, 'We're all given maps that detail the locations of all the ancestral Nordic burial grounds, too.'

'Why's that?'

'So that we can mate on top of the old great warriors, of course.'

'I'm afraid you've lost me there.'

'The logic behind it being that if we have sex on the graves of the old warriors, the children conceived there will inherit the souls of the great ones.'

'I don't think I want to hear any more. Thank you, Kurt.'

'Ah, the great ones,' Kurt said, as he struggled to his feet and puffed his chest out. 'Do you know your German history, Josef?'

'Why yes, I was top of the class when I-'

'Teutobuger Wald, Josef. That's where it all began. Tell me what you know of it.'

'Well, Teutoburger Forest was where the Germanic tribes joined together and defeated the former Roman Proconsul, Varus.'

'Correct. Publius Quinctilius Varus foolishly demanded tribute from the tribesmen, but they refused to pay, and with the help of Arminius, a true Aryan, they were led into battle and massacred twenty-thousand Roman soldiers, and sent Varus's head back to Augustus. This was the beginning of the Teutonic order. Have you ever heard of Lebensborn, Josef?'

'No… well, I don't think so anyway. What is it?'

'It's a programme that was devised by Himmler, back in December thirty-five, to increase the birth rate of racially sound babies. Under this programme, illegitimacy is no longer a stigma, and the unmarried mother has the same status as the married mother. Contraception and abortion are forbidden, and anyone caught practising either is severely punished. Lebensborn gives the SS man the right to mate with the young girls from the BDM, [1.] and once they fall pregnant, they're put into special clinics and we are absolved of any parental responsibility.'

'But, what happens to the children?'

'Most of the girls keep them, while others give them up for adoption. The unwanted babies are passed on to suitable Aryan families, unless they should turn out to be handicapped for any reason, in which case they're sent off to an institution and never seen again.'

'Mein gott, you mean they're murdered?'

'I didn't say that. You must understand that this is a massive programme. We're losing thousands of soldaten every week, and eventually they'll have to be replaced.'

'Yes, I agree, but not like this. It's inhuman. There has to be another way, surely.'

'This is the way, Josef. Der Furhrer wants to see the swastika flag flying all over the world. It's a question of numbers.'

'But even if you were to get every BDM girl pregnant, you still wouldn't have enough babies.'

'Yes, that's why SIPO [2.] have kidnapped at least forty-thousand children off the streets, to add to the fifty-thousand taken by your colleagues in die Wehrmacht from Ruthenia, and the twenty-thousand from Poland's Zamosc region.'

'You almost had me there,' Herzog chuckled after a moment's thought. 'This is all a big joke, right?'

'Do I look like I'm joking?'

Herzog sat rigid, the smile having now dropped from his face.

Kurt sat back down, feeling very pleased with himself as he continued his righteous sermon. 'All those homes that were destroyed during the invasion of Poland, and every other country for that matter, where did you think the displaced children went?'

'They went into camps,' Herzog said. 'I know this. I was there.'

'And who runs the camps?'

'How the hell should I know?'

'We do, Herzog.'

'By we, I take it you mean the SS?'

'Precisely. We bring them in through the front gate, and if they're lucky enough to resemble Aryans, we spirit them away out the back. We give them new passports and papers, and then send them to their new parents back in Germany, where they are subjected to six months of hard Nazi indoctrination. Now, what do you think about that?'

'You know, Kurt, every time I think I've heard it all, I get hit with an even bigger stick. You and your kind make me sick to my stomach, and if we should somehow survive this mission, I never want to set eyes on you again.'

'Well, I'm sorry you feel that way. I'd hoped that by the end of this, we might have become friends.'

'It's getting late. I think I'll turn in now.'

'Yes, perhaps you're right. We have a long, hard day ahead of us,' Kurt stood and stretched his weary limbs. 'Oh, and Josef, if we should be fortunate enough to see combat together, you'd do well to watch your back. Nasty things can happen in the confusion of battle.'

Josef awoke to the aroma of freshly cooked food.

'Breakfast, kamerad?' Bruno asked, leaning into the open cupola with a tin plate in his hand.

'Hey, that smells really good,' Josef said, pulling himself up through the hatch. 'How did you know that I like fried potato cakes?'

'A good chef always knows his customers,' Bruno laughed. 'Come on out of there and join the rest of the crew.'

Josef awkwardly climbed down from the tank and walked over to the hot brazier, and unthinkingly took a seat next to Pizer, who had just finished mopping his plate with the last of his bread.

'Glad you could make it,' Pizer said. 'I hope you can eat quickly, because we're moving out of here right now.'

'Damn, why didn't anyone wake me earlier?' Josef asked.

'Kurt said that you looked just like a little baby, curled up with your thumb in your mouth,' Christin giggled. 'So, we decided to let you sleep.'

'I think it's light enough to travel now,' Kurt said, after letting out a long belch. 'You all know the drill, let's roll. Bruno, fire up the engine. Everyone else to battle positions.'

Pizer urged caution, and ordered Bruno to maintain a slower pace than normal. He explained to the crew that although the town of Spa was only three and a half kilometres away, they would have to navigate through two major enemy outposts to get there. On their right, to the north, was the US 5th Corp, heavily armed with field artillery, and on their left, to the south, was the more worrying US 18th Airborne Corps, which posed a real threat. Pizer soon broke the solemn atmosphere by cracking a joke, likening the situation to a huge ham sandwich, with them in the middle.

'Well, so far so good. How long until we reach the outskirts, Josef?' Pizer asked.

'About another hour, sir,' Josef said. 'It would be less if we used the main road, sir.'

'No, it's better to keep a low profile. It's done us no harm so far. Bruno, stay on this course. I'm going top side.'

Pizer popped open the hatch, allowing the cold air and snow to rush in, and leaned out of the cupola. He fumbled awkwardly to find the field glasses that were hanging around his neck, before pressing them up against his pale white face and scanning all around, loudly calling out everything that he could see. 'All clear behind us, and nothing but trees and fields to the north,' he reported. 'I can see some enemy movement to the south. Must be the US Eighteenth Airborne, but they're too far away to be a problem. Gentlemen, I see the town of Spa, dead ahead.'

1. Bund Deutscher Madel (League of German girls). Female equivalent of Hitler Youth.

2. Sicherheitspolizei. Security service, commanded by Reinhardt Heydrich.

CHAPTER FORTY-SIX

A mighty cheer rang around the tank, as Pizer lowered himself back inside and closed the hatch. He ordered Bruno to break out at full speed and get them onto the main road, which would lead them straight into the well-fortified town. At 9.20am, they rolled into Spa virtually unopposed, and after a brief chat with the checkpoint guards, they slowly drove into the town centre. They found them-selves a quiet narrow side street to reverse into, and then parked up.

'Right, I want you all to split up and perform a thorough recon. Fish around for any information that may lead us to the fuel dump, but for God's sake, be discreet. Report back here to me at, let's say, ten-thirty AM.'

The men spread out and began to walk off in different directions. Bruno decided to check out the small church on the next block, while Christiin approached a group of soldiers that were stood talk-ing next to a large army truck. Konrad headed for the perimeter of the town, hoping to meet and speak with the locals.

Josef, on the other hand, went straight to the small barbershop just across the street from where the tank was parked. He gingerly walked in and sat down in an empty chair next to a white GI, who turned and stared at him in disbelief. The barber, a small, round balding gentleman wearing a white overall, approached him with a pair of scissors in his hand, saying in broken English, 'Can I help you, sir?'

'Yeah, man,' Josef said, in his best American accent, 'I'd like a hair cut. Real slick, like.'

'Slick?' the barber asked.

'Yeah, you know, like, real close.'

'Ah, I see,' the barber said. 'But, uh, I've never cut hair like yours before, sir.'

'Hey, no problem,' Josef said. 'Just treat me like any other Joe, OK?' He then turned to the shocked-looking soldier sat next to him and grinned. 'Hell of a war, eh, Mac?'

Back on the side street, Kurt was sitting on the front of his tank, reading a map, when he heard the loud roar of military vehicles. He slowly peered over the top of the large, flapping map, to find to his horror that none other than Major Wright was leaning out of the lead tank, shouting orders. He quickly covered his face, waiting until the last half-track had clattered past before jumping into the tank and closing the hatch.

Josef had also spied the major as he drove by the barbershop window, and had leaped out of his chair with his hair half done, before hurriedly paying the barber and leaving without waiting for his change. He watched from the pavement as Wright parked his three tanks and two half-tracks outside an old church, and then ordered his armed crews out.

'Kurt, Kurt, open up,' Josef yelled, as he banged on the side of the tank, 'it's me, Josef.' The lid popped open, and he tumbled in on top of Pizer.

'You'll never guess who I've just seen,' Josef said breathlessly.

'I know, I know,' Pizer replied in an agitated voice. 'I saw him, too.'

'What are we going to do?'

'I don't know, let me think. What time is it?'

'Ten-twenty.'

'Damn, where is everyone? You'll have to get back out and check around.'

'But I've only just got in.'

'You don't have to walk about, if that's what's bothering you. Just take a quick look around the corner and tell me what you see.'

'OK, but I've got a bad feeling about this.'

Josef climbed back out and jumped down onto the slush-covered cobbles, and then crept over to the corner of the street and craned his neck around. He could see Christin, who was halfway down on the opposite side of the road, standing next to a US army truck with his arms folded as he calmly chatted to a group of GIs. This made Josef smile wryly, but this was soon wiped from his face when he looked towards the church.

'They've got Bruno,' he said, as he climbed back into the tank.

'Who has?' Pizer asked.

'Major Wright and his men. They've got him surrounded and pinned up against the church wall. What should we do?'

Before Pizer could answer, there was a tapping on the side of the tank. It was an ashen-faced Christin. 'They've got Bruno,' he said.

'Yes, I know,' Pizer snapped. 'Where the hell is Konrad?'

'The Americans must have him,' Josef said. 'We've got to do something, Kurt. We're like sitting ducks out here.'

'Yes, OK, right,' Pizer mumbled, his mind clearly racing. 'Josef, you start the engine, and Christin, you man the machine gun.'

'What about Bruno and Konrad?' Christin asked. 'Are we just going to leave them?'

'I've no choice, Christin,' Pizer said. 'We must complete our mission. Did anyone discover the whereabouts of the fuel dump?'

'Is that all you care about?' Josef growled. 'You're just going to leave those two men to their fate. Is that it?'

'Yes, that's it,' Pizer replied. 'What else would you have me do?'

'I don't know, perhaps create some kind of diversionary tactic,' Josef suggested. 'At least try something.'

'What, and risk everyone's lives else, too?' Pizer asked.

'I don't know,' Josef sighed, shrugging his shoulders.

'That's right, you don't know,' Pizer said. 'So, why don't you just shut up and drive the damned tank.'

'Maybe Kurt's right,' Christin said. 'We can't help them now. Better to move on, eh?'

'Hmm, well it seems I've been out-voted,' Josef said. 'By the way, I know where your precious fuel dump is, if you're still interested?'

'Yes, of course I'm interested,' Pizer cried. 'Where is it?'

'Well, the good news is, it's only six kilometres south of Spa,' Josef said.

'And the bad news?'

'The bad news is, we've got to drive through Major Wright's unit to reach it.'

'Verdammt,' Pizer cursed, unfolding his map and poring over it for several minutes. 'Right, this is what we'll do,' he finally said. 'We'll double back on ourselves and swing left around Spa, and then on to the target. Josef, start up the engine and let's move quickly. It's only a matter of time before Bruno or Konrad crack under interrogation and reveal our plans to the Americans.'

Josef carefully manoeuvred the tank out onto the main road, and then slowly turned left, heading back the way they had come. Pizer hugged the tiny periscope, looking for any sudden enemy movement as they crawled out of the town. Once clear, Josef opened up the throttle and drove at full speed along the outskirts of Spa, desperately scanning the hedgerows and flat, white open landscapes, hoping to catch sight of Konrad, but unfortunately he was nowhere to be found. After an hour they finally came to within half a kilometre of the lightly defended fuel dump, and Pizer ordered a halt while he considered how best to proceed. He decided that the quickest and safest way to destroy the dump would be to fire one or two shots from the 75mm canon, and so began to organise the firing crew accordingly. Christin would load the gun while Josef fired it, with Pizer acting as range finder, calling out coordinates.

Christin awkwardly picked up a heavy shell and placed it into the open breech, and then slammed it shut while Josef sat nervously with his finger on the firing trigger.

'Ready, sir,' Christin said.

'Prepare to fire on my command,' Pizer said.

Suddenly, there came a huge bang from directly behind them, so intense that it rocked the vehicle tank from side to side. Earth and smoke rose up in a thick black and white plume, and hovered overhead.

'Wait,' Josef shouted, 'enemy convoy to the right.'

Pizer popped the hatch and lifted his field glasses, desperately turning the small adjusting wheel to magnify the images in front of him. 'No, no, it can't be,' he said.

'What is it, Kurt?' Christin shouted over the noise of the struggling engine.

'It's Major Wright,' Pizer exclaimed.

'Are you sure?' Josef asked.

'Yes, I'm sure,' Pizer said. 'I need you back in position, Josef.'

'But, how can you be so certain it's him?'

'Well, Josef, do you know anyone else who has three Shermans and two half-tracks?'

'Oh, then it's him alright. What are we going to do?'

'Shoot back, of course. Christin, spin the turret as fast as you can. Josef, when you hear the first shot, I want you to hit that accelerator and drive like a man possessed.'

There was a deafening bang as the 75mm cannon recoiled, spewing out its deadly shell and rocking the tank once again. A thick, strong choking smell of cordite rose up and quickly filled the confined metal space.

'Missed!' Kurt screeched. 'Let's get out of here fast,' he ordered, tapping Josef on the shoulder with his boot.

Josef used every every fibre of muscle to propel the huge 30-ton iron monster through the hedgerows and thickets, as they raced away from their dogged foe. What he didn't realise at the time was that he was driving straight into the arms of the US 18th Airborne Corps, who were positioned some 26km west of Stoumont.

The weather was turning bad, as beautiful thick flakes of snow began to fall, making it difficult for Josef to see through the periscope. He opened the small hatch cover to get a better view, wincing as he raised his hand up to protect himself from the bitterly cold wind that immediately assailed him.

'Why are we slowing down?' Pizer demanded.

'I don't know,' Josef replied. 'There must be something wrong with the engine.'

'Damn,' Pizer said, scratching his head. 'It must have been the shell that exploded behind us back at the fuel dump. OK, pull over.'

'Great, now what are we supposed to do?' Christin asked.

'Stop complaining for a start,' Pizer said. 'Both of you, grab your gear. We're going to have to make a run for it.'

'What!' Christin said. 'Have you seen how deep that snow is? We'll never survive.'

'We won't survive if we stay here,' Josef said, 'that's for sure.'

'Josef's right,' Pizer said. 'Come on, out.'

They picked up as much food, water, ammunition and medical supplies as they could carry, and then set off across the vast white landscape. They walked for two hours in the deep snow, with Josef at the rear, covering their tracks with a fallen branch, before they eventually had to stop due to cold and fatigue. Pizer suggested that they rest under a nearby group of trees, and have something to eat before starting the next leg of their journey. They wouldn't be able stay for long, though, as the night was drawing in fast. Josef scanned the horizon with Kurt's field glasses while chewing on a piece of American chocolate, leaving Kurt and Christin to sit with their backs up against a couple of thick poplar trees, taking cover from the howling gusts of wind that rattled through the full swaying branches, as they tried to eat with trembling hands. After they'd rested for twenty minutes or so, Kurt gave the order to move out, and Josef picked up his heavy green rucksack and struggled to get it up onto his shoulders, and then began to march forward, bent double and facing the wind, with the others close behind him.

The light was fading quickly, and they couldn't see more than a few feet in front of them. Josef begged Kurt to let them stop, but the commander refused, until eventually Josef came to abrupt halt, after spotting what looked to be tall, shadowy figures in the distance.

'Americans,' Christin called out, sending them all diving for cover in the soft snow.

'How many?' Kurt whispered.

'About eight of them, I reckon,' Josef said.

'And they're getting closer,' Christin added.

'OK, listen,' Kurt said, 'we're going to have to split up if there's to be any chance of escape. Josef, you break left across the open ground, and Christin, you break right and get yourself through the treeline.'

'And what about you?' Josef asked.

'Don't worry about me,' Kurt said, 'I'll back track.'

'Where do we meet up?' Christin asked.

'We don't,' Kurt said grimly. 'There's no time to draw up a plan. It's every man for himself, I'm afraid. Just try to head north-east, back towards our own lines, verstehen?'

'Right,' Josef nodded, 'gut gluck to you both.'

'And you, Josef,' Kurt smiled. 'See you back at the camp, eh?'

They all saluted one another, and then scrambled off in opposite directions. Josef swung left, as ordered, but soon got lost in the black and white blizzard, and after wandering around aimlessly for an hour, he walked right into the very people he'd been trying to avoid. Before him stood five soldiers from the US 18th Airborne Corps, fully armed with rifles and sub-machine guns.

'Halt!' one of the Americans commanded, stepping forward with his rifle pointed at Josef's chest. 'Put your hands up and keep 'em where I can see em, buddy.'

Josef immediately raised his hands, moving a bit too quickly for the nervous soldier, who responded by yelling, 'If you so much as twitch, I swear to God, I'll shoot ya.'

CHAPTER FORTY-SEVEN

Josef didn't speak, and offered no resistance as the corporal methodically went through his kit bag, jacket and pockets, searching for concealed weapons and a form of identification, while another soldier stood shining a bright light into his face, making him squint.

'So, what do you got, Sarge?' the soldier with the flashlight asked.

'Well, according to these papers, he's with Second Division,' the sergeant said.

'Second Division? Aren't they somewhere near Monschau?'

'Yeah, they sure are, Murphy. What you doin' one hundred kilometres from where you're supposed to be, boy?' the Sergeant drawled, and then produced a plug of tobacco from deep within his pocket. He bit off a wad and began chewing on it, occasionally spitting some out.

Josef's throat went dry, as he tried desperately to think of a suitable explanation. 'Well, you see, Sarge, it's like this,' he began. 'Me and some other guys were put in a Sherman and told to drive to a place called Sart. It's somewhere near a place called Spa, do you know it?'

'Sure, I know it, but why did you have to drive all this way, boy?'

'I don't know, sir,' Josef said, 'and that's the truth.'

'Well, you'd better figure it out soon, boy,' the sergeant warned, 'because my trigger finger's gettin' awful tired.'

'Honestly, sir, I really don't know,' Josef insisted. 'You see, it was top secret, and our CO got killed before we found out what we were supposed to be doing, sir.'

'So, how many more of ya, boy?'

'Uh, another two, sir, but we all got lost in this blizzard.'

'Are you buyin' any of this crap, Murphy?'

'No, Sarge,' Murphy shook his head.

'Neither am I,' the sergeant said. 'Come on, boy. I'm takin' you to see Captain Richie.'

The next thing Josef knew, he was being bundled into the back of an open-topped jeep and driven at speed to the 18th Airborne divisional stockade, 120km east of Brussels. The vehicle bounced and slithered across the thick snowy embankments, with its headlights casting ghostly silver shadows on the trees and bushes. As they reached flat, open ground, the jeep accelerated, and Josef was tossed from side to side as they pitched and rolled across the barren countryside. He fell against the hard muzzle of the corporal's M1 carbine rifle, which provided a constant reminder of the fact that he was once again a prisoner.

It was 8.30pm when they arrived at the massive barricaded fortress, and it had just stopped snowing. Josef was ordered out of the jeep at gunpoint before being taken to a small, plain room, containing nothing but two wooden chairs positioned on opposite sides of a large wooden table. He was told to sit and wait for the CO, and he didn't have to wait long, as within minutes the door had swung open and an officer had entered the room, followed by the arresting

Sergeant. The man, who was presumably the CO, sat down and lit a cigarette before opening Josef's identity book, quickly scanning through the pages and then placing it down on the table in front of him.

'Allow me to introduce myself,' the CO said. 'I'm Captain Richie, and this is Sergeant Jones, who I believe you already know?'

'Yes, sir,' Josef said.

'OK, now why don't you begin by tellin' me who you are, son?'

'Beggin' your pardon, sir, but you know who I am,' Josef said. 'You have my papers, sir.'

'Well, indulge me anyway.'

'My name is Private Maurice J Pinkerton. Serial number six-two-three-four-five-nine-seven-one, Second Infantry Division, United States Army, sir.'

'And where you from, son?'

'I'm from Philadelphia, sir.'

'Philadelphia?'

'Yes, sir. You know, the city of brotherly love.'

'You married, son?'

'Yes, sir.'

'What's your wife's name?'

'Darlene, sir.'

'Any kids?'

'Yes, sir. Got two of 'em, sir.'

'What are their names?'

'Carlton and Cheyenne, sir.'

'Cheyenne?'

'Yes, sir. When my daughter was born, she had this long black hair, and everyone said she looked like Pocahontas. So, we called her Cheyenne, sir.'

'Hmm, you're along way from Monschau, private. Why?'

'As I explained to Sergeant Jones, sir, it's top secret.'

'Indeed. Are you aware that there's been a plot to send German troops dressed as American GIs into key areas such as this one, private?'

'No, sir.'

'Well, there is such a plot. So, you can understand our concerns when someone just turns up out of the blue, eh?'

'Why yes, I do, sir, but what I'm tellin' you is the truth.'

Captain Richie took Sergeant Jones to one side and whispered, 'The boy's story sits straight with me, Sergeant.'

'With respect, sir, I think he's a lying son-of-a-bitch-goddamnkraut. I just know it. Back in Louisiana, my brother and I would go gator hunting on that big old bayou. We'd sit still silent in Papa's rickety old boat and just listen. Suddenly, I'd get this real bad feeling deep in my gut, you know, and I just knew that gator was near. Oh, he's a Kraut alright.'

'You can't be sure of that, Sergeant.'

'He's a German, and I'll prove it to ya,' Jones looked to Josef, eyes blazing. 'Who was president of the United States before Franklin D Roosevelt?'

'Herbert Hoover, sir,' Josef answered.

'And before him?'

'Calvin Coolidge, sir.'

'Who designed the Stars and Stripes?'

'Betsy Ross, sir.'

'OK, well how tall is the Empire State Building?'

'Uh-'

'Gotcha!'

'Alright, Jones, knock it off,' Richie said. 'This could go on all night. Listen up, Pinkerton, it's too late to confirm your story to-night, but I'll be on to divisional head quarters first thing in the morning. Have you got a problem with that?'

'No, not at all, sir.'

'Good. You'll be placed in custody until this situation can be resolved one way or another. Jones, take him away.'

Josef was marched to a cramped, four-by-seven holding cell, barely big enough room to hold a single bunk. There were no windows, and the only source of light came from a single dim bulb which hung limply from the wooden ceiling.

The door banged shut behind him, and Josef got under the rough brown blanket and lay staring up at the ceiling, watching a small black fly repeatedly attempt to land on the hot naked light bulb. His heart was heavy, as he realised that he would probably be lined up against a cold, damp wall and shot for espionage in the morning. His bid for freedom had failed, but what else could he have done, keep languishing in that dusty cell back at Bourg Leopold? Surely, it had been worth the risk, if only it had paid off.

He lay back on his bunk with his arm across his face, wondering what had become of his tank crew. How many made it back to Germany, and how many were dead? There was a clinking sound coming from his cell door, and he turned to find Sergeant Jones with his face pressed up hard against the door, tapping a long dagger against the iron bars and wearing a menacing expression upon his face.

'Hey boy,' the sergeant said, spitting a small black plug of tobac-co onto Josef's bunk, 'back home, we would have just strung you up from the nearest tree, no trial and no cell. If I find out that you is a goddamn German spy, I'll tear you a new black asshole with this here blade, you hear me, boy?'

'Yes, sir,' Josef said.

Jones started to walk away, but then stopped and turned back. 'Oh, and by the way,' he said. 'Out here, we also hang spies, and I'll make sure that I'm the one kickin' the chair away. Just think on that, ya hear me, boy?'

'Yes, sir,' Josef said again, pulling the blanket over his head and plunging himself into darkness.

It wasn't long before he could see the ghosts of his tank crew; the last image being of Christin heading away from him to the right, towards the white treeline, and then disappearing into the black night. Did he survive, or was he, too, captured by the Americans? Was he being held somewhere nearby, and what about Kurt? Was he right to double back on himself, or should he have kept them all together? As for Bruno, left pinned to a church wall, surrounded by Major Wright and his men, did they shoot him as a spy? Konrad had last been seen somewhere on the edge of town, but what did it matter anyway? The mission to blow up the massive fuel dump in Spa was a complete failure.

Josef soon fell into fitful sleep until, sometime in the early hours, he was awoken by a light tapping at his cell door. He slowly opened his eyes, half expecting to see Sergeant Jones stood there with his dagger again. He could just make out the shadowy outline of someone's head peering through the iron bars of the door, and, squinting in the darkness, he checked his wristwatch; it was 3.30am. He got up from his bed and cautiously approached the door.

'Josef, it's me, Kurt,' came a whisper from the other side.

'Kurt, what are you doing here?' Josef asked, half-believing that he must be dreaming. 'You should be miles away by now.'

'I've come to get you out. Stand back.'

Josef stood back and waited for what seemed like an age, as Kurt struggled with a large set of keys, bashing each one into the large brass lock and rattling it, and all the while trying to keep the noise to a minimum. Eventually, there was a loud click and the door creaked open. Kurt was now in, standing opposite Josef in the cramped, narrow space.

'How the hell did you find me?' Josef asked.

'Get dressed and I'll tell you,' Kurt said, and then recited his story as Josef fumbled in the semi-darkness, looking for his boots and coat. 'When I broke away from you and Christin, I found an old motorcycle in a disused barn, and came back to look for you both. I arrived just as you were being taken away by the Amerikans, so I followed.'

'Well, thank Gott you did, because I don't think they bought my story,' Josef said. 'How did you get past the guards?'

'Let's just say, there are a couple of bodies getting cold out there. Hurry up, and let's get out of here before we're discovered.'

Josef tied his bootlaces and followed Kurt out of the cell. The strong light in the corridor stung his eyes, but he quickly regained focus as they passed the blood-stained corpses of the American guards, who Kurt had left lying face down on the floor, still clutching their rifles.

'Stop gawking and get a move on,' Kurt hissed.

'How did you kill them?' Josef asked.

'With a knife, if you must know. Now, can we get going?'

'Yes, of course. Sorry, Kurt.'

'Ja, well, you'd think you'd never seen a dead body before. What the hell did they do to you?'

'They didn't hurt me, if that's what you mean. I haven't woken up properly yet, that's all.'

'Then wake up and grab that rifle. I can't believe that I came back for you, and now you're trying to get us both killed.'

'I'm alright now, really,' Josef said, peeling the guard's clammy, cold fingers from his weapon. 'Why did you come back for me?'

'Because, you're all I've got left.'

'Hey Kurt, I'm sorry for what I said to you a couple of days ago.'

'What, you mean I don't make you sick anymore?' Kurt laughed sardonically. 'It's OK, I'm the one who should apologise. You were right, the SS are a pretty sick bunch, but one can change, you know?'

Kurt approached the front door on his tiptoes, and peeked around the corner before signalling for Josef to follow. Both men then ran and skidded across the crisp, white compound and mounted the waiting motorcycle, with Josef sitting on the back, clutching Kurt's waist, as they drove off into the cold night with the headlamp switched off.

Der Waffen SS Junkerschulen, Braunschweg, Germany.

Two days after their daring escape, Josef and Kurt entered Sturmbannfuhrer Otto Skorzeny's office, still somewhat bedraggled following their long, arduous journey, and stood to attention while he sat with his back to them. After a time, Skorzeny slowly turned his high-backed brown leather chair around to face the room. There was a look of sadness to him, as he gazed down at his trembling hands, twiddling his thumbs nervously.

'The war is not going too well for us, gentlemen,' he said in a low voice. 'We've lost the Belgian port of Antwerp to Montgomery's Twenty-First Army, and we've also been kicked out of Greece. The German town of Aachen has fallen to the Amerikans, and the battleship Tirpitz has been sunk at Tromso, Norway, with the loss of all hands. Twelve-hundred-and-four crewmen, who went down singing Deutschland Uber Alles.'

'We had no idea it was that bad, sir,' Kurt said.

'Well, it is, Herr Hauptmann,' Skorzeny replied. 'I sent twenty-thousand men out on a crazy, wild adventure, and only two came back, yourself and mein exotisch freund, Viscount Herzog. I will, of course, apologise to der Furhrer in person for this most disastrous and foolhardy mission. It was a cunning attempt, though, wasn't it?'

'Sir, you can't possibly blame yourself,' Kurt argued. 'It was we who failed, not you.'

'Kind words, Herr Hauptmann, but you couldn't be more wrong,' Skorzeny shook his head sadly. 'You see, it was I who came up with the plan, therefore it is I who must now fall on mein sword, dear freunde. Damph, if only it had worked. It really would have been something to tell your grandchildren, eh? They would have talked about it long after we were dead and gone, but it was not to be.'

'What now, sir?' Josef asked, his voice shaking.

'What now?' Skorzeny repeated. 'Well, for me I don't know, but for you there's still a chance of honour.'

'Sir?'

'A chance for honour in combat. The two of you are to join a neu Panzer regiment. You're off to the Ardennes, once you're fully rested. With the Amerikans now rapidly advancing across German soil, we have to fight like we have never fought before. To survive, we must win the battle for the Ardennes, or face total annihilation.'

'Can we pull this one off, sir?' Kurt asked.

'With gut men like yourself and Herzog, it might be possible,' Skorzeny smiled. 'Now, get washed up and enjoy a hot meal. You're both going to be very busy over the next few weeks.'

Less than forty-eight hours later, they were flown out to the city of Bonn, and then driven by car to a town called Hellenthal, 35km east of Elsenborn, which was to be their objective. They joined up with the Third Panzer Grenadier Division, commanded by Sepp Dietrich's 6th SS Panzer Army, who were positioned 27km north-east of Monschau.

A strange feeling came over Josef as he stepped out of the barracks wearing his new black Panzer uniform. It consisted of a black forage cap and a smartly ironed khaki shirt and black tie, under a short, tight-fitting black jacket, which was fastened at the waist with a thick black leather belt and large silver buckle. On either side of his wide-neck collar sat a large, ominous silver skull inside a large white-piped square. Beneath his broad, sweeping single lapel hung the Iron Cross and black Wound Badge. He was now officially a Panzer crewman, and was placed in a new Panther auf D tank, under the command of Hauptmann Kurt Pizer.

The Panther auf D was a good, reliable machine powered by a V-12 Maybach engine, with a top speed of 28mph. Its unique feature was the six armoured glass slits around the edge of the cupola that afforded its crew a full 360-degree field of vision in battle. It boasted two periscopes and was armed with a 75mm cannon, while being protected by three-inch frontal armour, one-and-a-half-inch side armour and three inches of turret armour, giving it an overall weight of 44 tons.

Four German armies, all commanded by the 70-year-old Field Marshal Karl von Rundstedt, stretched across a massive 120km front, which started in the north, near Monschau, with Obergruppenfuhrer Sepp Dietrich's 6th SS Panzer Army, followed by General Hasso von Manteuffel's 5th Panzers. Next came Field Marshal Walther Model's Army Group B, and then lastly, to the south near Echternach, on the Luxembourg border, was the Seventh Army, commanded by the 47-year-old General Erich von Brandenberger.

On 16 December 1944, the Battle of the Bulge began, with the Germans launching their initial attack at 5.30am. The plan was for Manteuffel's 5th Army and Dietrich's 6th Army to break through the Ardennes Forest, repeating what they had done back in 1940, and then go on to the Meuse, but this time they were only given for-ty-eight hours to carry out the immense task. The 6th Army would then cross the Meuse, north of Liege, and go forward to recapture Antwerp, while the 5th Army headed for Namur and Brussels. They would then both attack the communication and supply lines of the entire Allied 12th and 21st armies, with Brandenberger's 7th Army covering the whole operation from the south.

The battle got off to a good start for the Germans, and by 17 De-cember, Manteuffel's 5th Panzers had completely surrounded the US 14th and 106th cavalry groups, forcing the surrender of 7,000 men before taking the small town of Setz, 20km east of St Vith. That same day, Standartenfuhrer Peiper's 1st SS Panzer Division took the town of Stavelot, some 25km south of Malmedy, while other German units closed in on Houffalize and Bastogne. On 18 December, the 18th Volksgrenadier Division, under the command of General Luchts, attacked St Vith, and established a circle around the Americans on the Schnee Eifel, but by the next day, Peiper's battle group were being pushed back out of Stavelot by the US 30th Division, with the help of Allied fighter bombers. When the Americans eventually retook the town, they found evidence of atrocities that were carried out against the civilian population. Men, women and children had been machine gunned in cold blood, and for no justifiable reason, as there was no evidence of collaboration or guerrilla activity in the town.

When the time came for Josef's 3rd Panzer Grenadier Division to make its mark in this fluid battle, they moved to attack the US

99th Division, which stood between them and their objective, Elsenborn. They were supported to the north by the 277th Volksgrenadier Division, whose job was to attack the US 2nd Division near Monschau, while the 12th SS Panzer Division attacked the town of Bullingen, to the south. Third Panzer did indeed collide with the US 99th, who put up fierce resistance, but after a long and bitter fight, 3rd Panzer broke through and linked up with the 12th at Elsenborn, and they both swung south to take on the mighty US 1st division, near Malmedy.

It was at this stage in the battle, while Josef and the rest of the crew were held up in a woodland area doing minor repairs on their tank, that he got the biggest shock of his life. He noticed a VI Tiger Tank parked in a small clearing opposite, with two white cross keys painted inside the white outline of a shield on the front of its four-inch Krupp armour, denoting the Leibstandarte SS Adolf Hitler. It also had the numbers 333 painted across the side of its huge turret. The cupola was open, and a man was starting to clamber out, wearing a black beret, headphones and throat microphone. Josef froze and his heart began quicken, as the tank commander leaped down onto the crunchy white ground and straightened up. This was a man who he knew very well; it was his old nemesis, Sturmbannfuhrer Ernst Lunder. To the surprise of his fellow crewmen, Josef immediately dived for cover behind their tank, peering out and watching intently as Lunder stretched and yawned, and then stepped forward, stooping under the massive 88mm turret canon. He walked the short distance across to the Panther tank with a wide grin on his face and began chatting happily with the crew, totally oblivious to Josef's presence. That was until Kurt Pizer appeared and asked for his right-hand man. Everyone turned and looked to the rear of the tank, and knowing that the game was up, Josef reluctantly emerged.

'Well, well, well,' Lunder sniggered, hands on hips, 'if it isn't Herr Leutnant Viscount Josef Herzog. Congratuliere on your release from prison. If I'd known you were being deployed to a Panzer regiment, I most certainly would have requested for you to join me. It's much safer in a Tiger, you know.'

'That may be so, Herr Sturmbannfuhrer,' Josef answered haughtily, 'but I'll chance my luck in the Panther, if it's all the same to you.'

Lunder's face reddened. 'I'll see you in battle, Herzog. A' tout a' l' heure,' he spluttered in badly-spoken French, as he marched back towards his 56-ton metal beast.

'Arrivederci,' Josef mumbled under his breath.

'What did he mean when he said, "see you in battle?"' Kurt asked.

'I've no idea,' Josef said.

The crew reboarded their Panther tank, and then continued south to engage the US 1st Infantry Division, stationed near Malmedy. Manteuffel's 12th SS Panzer Division were just ahead of them, beginning simultaneous attacks on Malmedy and Stavelot, and then, after narrowly missing the US 30th Division, turning for Trois-Ponts and Stoumont. There was a distinct feeling of deja vu as Josef and his crew trundled over the old ground, and crazy thoughts began to fill his head. He eagerly scanned through the tiny, thick glass slits of the cupola, wondering if he would catch sight of his lost comrades, Konrad and Bruno. It was a strange feeling to be driving back to places that could so easily have been his own burial ground. He owed his life to Kurt, which was something he would never forget, and he hoped that maybe one day, somehow, he would be able to repay his debt.

The Germans had done well to speedily capture their enemies' positions, taking them almost on the march. Lt General Heinz Lammerding's 2nd SS Panzer Division, Das Reich, had pushed as far west as Dinant, but all of that was soon to change. The Allies had regrouped and formed a massive V-shaped front stretching 140km, starting at Eupen, in the north, and finishing at Luxembourg, in the south, where the US 12th Corps was ensconced with its satellite armies, the 4th, 5th, 9th, 10th, 26th and 80th divisions.

On 16 January 1945, the Germans began to retreat, as Field Marshal Montgomery and General Courtney Hodge's 21st Army closed in on Malmedy, Stavelot, Rochefort and Houffalize, while at the same time, from the south, General George S Patton's 3rd US Army closed in on Bastogne and Wiltz.

CHAPTER FORTY-EIGHT

Alt Hattlich, Belgium (25km East of Eupen).

At last, it had stopped snowing, and Josef could now see far into the distance, way across the flat, open expanse of no man's land. Staring nervously through his field glasses, he watched as the Americans just beyond the second ridge organised their tanks and artillery ahead of launching their attack. New orders had come in to fall back to Eupen and regroup, and then head north at full speed to halt the Allied advance on the German town of Aachen. However, the field grey columns were no longer retreating; they were practically running.

'Friedrich, can you get anymore speed out of this piece of shit?' Kurt shouted desperately.

'We're going flat out, sir,' the driver replied.

'Well, it's not enough. I need more distance. The Amerikans have launched their attack,' Kurt said.

'We could always get out and push,' Josef said, having developed a real taste for gallows humour.

'This isn't the time to be a smart arse,' Kurt snapped.

'You're right, I'm sorry,' Josef said. 'Hey, we've got company. It's a Sherman. Look, one-hundred-and-twenty-degrees to the right.'

'I see him,' Kurt answered. 'Do you have him, Thomsen?'

'Yes, sir, he's just come into the scope.'

'OK, stop here, Friedrich,' Kurt ordered.

'Is that wise, sir?' Friedrich asked.

'Just stop, will you?'

'Kurt, I've been meaning to ask you something,' Josef said.

'Not now, Josef,' Kurt said. 'Thomsen, is he within range yet?'

'Almost, sir,' the gunner replied.

'Why are we the only tank with a red stripe on the turret?' Josef decided to ask anyway.

'What!' Kurt barked.

'He's in range now, sir,' Thomsen confirmed.

'Yes, fire when ready,' Kurt ordered. 'Now, what the hell are you talking about, Josef?'

'Does it not strike you as being a little odd that we are the only tank in the entire regiment with a single red stripe on the turret?'

'Direct hit, sir,' Thomsen cheered. 'Chritus, she's gone up like a blowtorch! Do you think we'll go the same way, sir?'

'No, of course not,' Kurt said. 'Shut up, Thomsen, you're scaring the children.'

'So, Kurt, what do you think about the stripe?' Josef repeated the question.

'I don't give a damph about the stripe. Friedrich, get us out of here, quickly.'

'There's something wrong here, Kurt,' Josef said. 'I'm telling you.'

'Look, we're in the middle of a shooting gallery here, and the last thing I'm gong to worry about right now the tank's paint job. So, if you'll excuse me, I have a battle to fight.'

'There are enemy tanks everywhere, sir,' Friedrich said.

'It's OK, just stay calm,' Thomsen said. 'Kurt, I've got a new target. A Firefly, ten degrees left.'

'Take the shot.'

'What's a Firefly?' Josef asked.

'It's just a Sherman, but with a bigger gun,' Kurt explained. 'Don't get too close, Friedrich.'

'Got him, sir,' Thomsen announced triumphantly.

'Gut shooting, Thomsen.'

'Thank you, sir.'

Mein Gott, the crewmen have bailed out, and they're on fire,' Josef said, watching in horror through the field glasses. 'Kurt, they're on fire!'

'Be quiet,' Kurt said.

'Poor bastards,' Friedrich said.

'And that goes for you, too,' Kurt looked disapprovingly at the driver. 'Let's get moving. There's nothing for us here.'

They zigzagged through the mangled, burnt-out wreckages of tanks and personnel carriers, crunching over the charred remains of their fallen comrades and enemies alike, as stiff, twisted bodies lay strewn over the green and white battlefield, now punctuated with fresh black mortar holes. Ahead of them were high rocky hills, and beyond those waited deep, open crevices, ideal for ambushes.

Kurt had secretly confided to Josef that he was now sickened by war and totally exhausted, yearning for die heimat more and more each day. He knew that the long, hard struggle was almost over, and that Germany was finally losing its unholy crusade. He told him how he desperately wanted to desert once back on German soil, but dared not, fearing that he would be branded a coward and defeatist. On top of that, such acts carried the death penalty, and were rigorously enforced by the so-called 'Flying Court Martials', who roamed the German towns and cities looking for anyone who had been reported missing by either the army, the SS or local citizens. They had powers of summary execution, which meant that after a very brief hearing they could administer punishment on the spot. The victim or victims were often put up against a wall and shot, or hanged from the nearest tree, depending on what was deemed most convenient at that time.

Eupen was now in sight, but just as they thought they were out of danger, a huge explosion rocked the tank. A missile strike from an American hand-held bazooka had damaged the left tank track, thus immobilising the vehicle. Josef peppered the surrounding area with rapid machine gun fire, in an attempt at providing cover while Kurt and Thomsen got out to inspect the broken track, only for Allied ground forces to kill them both instantly. Josef continued to fire from his crouched position until all of his ammunition was spent, and Friedrich climbed up into the turret, taking control of the 75mm cannon and firing off as many shots as he could, but it was too little, too late. Within seconds, a 10-ton, twelve-seater American M-3 halftrack approached, carrying six troopers and a mounted, air-cooled 30-calibre machine gun. They sprayed the side of the tank with bullets, causing metal splinters to break off inside the turret and blind Friedrich in both eyes, and leaving Josef with no other choice but to pop the hatch and surrender. He awkwardly dismounted, guiding a wailing Friedrich along behind him, and then stood erect as the machine gunner zeroed in on them. Expecting to be executed on the spot, he gripped his comrade tightly and closed his eyes.

He heard the burst of machine gun fire, but he felt no pain. Slowly, he opened his eyes, and found to his surprise that all six American soldiers lay dead. A moment later, he watched in amazement as a massive, three-and-a-half-ton, eight-seater Zugkraftwagen burst through the hedgerow, with its three-and-a-half-litre Maybach engine racing at full throttle. Four men wearing German uniforms were laughing loudly, as they leaned out of the vehicle with their Schmeisser machine pistols firing indiscriminately in all directions. Without a second thought, Josef immediately pulled Friedrich to the ground and covered his head with both arms, hoping to protect himself from ricocheting bullets. Then, everything fell quiet, and Josef recognised a friendly, familiar voice coming from somewhere above.

'Well, isn't that typical. I've come all this way to meet the hero of Olenica, and what do I find? He's covered in dust, with his arse in the air.'

Josef carefully raised his head and, shielding his eyes from the strong sunlight, asked himself if what he was seeing could really be true. Standing before him were Viktor Pech, Egon Binder, Philip Grinburger and Erich Heiter, AKA the War Council.

'What's wrong, Josef?' Egon asked. 'Cat got your tongue?'

'Yes, speak up,' Viktor said, grinning broadly. 'You didn't think we'd leave you out here on your own, did you? Zuzamman immer, remember?'

'Yes, together always, I remember,' Josef croaked. 'How on earth did you guys ever find me?'

'It's a long story, and I'll gladly tell it to you once we're out of here,' Viktor said, placing a hand on Josef's shoulder. 'But first, let's see if we can get this tank track repaired, eh?'

Within the hour, they had mended the tank track and buried

their fallen comrades, and after a brief sermon orated by Viktor, Josef and Friedrich reboarded the tank, followed by the rest of the War Council, but not before they'd stripped the Zugkraftwagen of its munitions and supplies. They reached Eupen just before dark, and checked into a small military barracks that lay on the outskirts of the town. The medics attended to Friedrich's wounds, while the rest of the crew took hot baths and helped themselves to fresh food and beer that was on offer in the officers' mess. Later that night, they retired to a small lounge area to relax, smoke cigars and catch up.

'Did you hear about Uri and Emmy, Josef?' Egon asked.

'I heard something, but I'd like to know what you know first.'

'Well,' Egon continued, 'Uri and his fiancée were found in a quiet country lane, where both had been executed by a single shot to the back of the head.'

'Yes, that matches up with what I've already been told.'

'You mean you knew about this?' Viktor asked.

'Yes,' Josef nodded.

'But, how could you know?'

'Lunder told me, when I was in prison.'

'And you believed him?'

'Yes, I did,' Josef said firmly. 'He also murdered mein counsel, Larry Koban, and Monika, too.'

'Gut Gott, man! If that's true, how do you feel about it?' Philip asked.

Josef took a deep breath and lowered his head. His mind was full of guilt and remorse, and it was like he was back in that cramped cell, with Lunder's face pressed up hard against his own, jeering and spitting venom. Josef's palms were wet and his throat was dry. 'Let's change the subject,' he suggested. 'So, Viktor, when are you going to tell me about how you guys came to be halfway between Alt Hattlich and Eupen?'

'Well, it's a long story,' Viktor said, 'and one that you may find hard to believe.'

'Try me.'

'Very well. From the moment you first enlisted at the Kriegshule Academie back in Leipzeg, you became part of a most barbaric and sadistic experiment.'

'Experiment?'

'That's right. Herr Hauptmann Weise and Herr Major Lowe had long suspected that something was going on, but until recently, they had no real proof. Their agents in the SD and Abwehr spent months on a top secret undercover investigation, and eventually obtained a small but important piece of information, which was passed on by a colleague in SIPO. This led them to a man called Fischer. Dr Eugen Fischer, to be precise.

Josef sat bolt upright in his chair, frozen like a startled rabbit in the beam of a car headlamp. The frothy beer from his Steiner dribbled slowly down his chin, before settling on his immaculately pressed tunic.

'I've heard of this man,' he said. 'Isn't he a leading geneticist?'

'Why yes, he is,' Viktor frowned. 'How could you have possibly known that?'

'Let's just say that I know someone who knows him. Please, continue.'

'Fischer was convinced that because of your ethnic origins-'

'Being black, you mean?'

'Well, yes. Because you're black, he didn't think that you would be able to hold a position of command over your white superiors, nor gain their respect, but you proved him wrong with your success in Olenica. This left Fischer with no other choice but to enact Plan B.'

'Which was?'

'Lunder, Ulricher and Wholner. Their job was, and still is, to bring you down because you've become too successsful. Once Weise and Lowe had proof of this, they immediately had us released from prison and gave us a simple brief: bring back Herzog. Believe me, you're in mortal danger as long as you stay here, Josef. Fischer has given Lunder the order to kill you on sight, thus bringing this ghastly experiment to a bloody conclusion.'

'What you have just said has chilled me to the bone,' Josef said, after a moment of quiet contemplation. 'I really do appreciate what the War Council, as well as our commanders, have done for me so far, but I don't expect anyone to sacrifice his own life just for me. You should all leave now, while you still can.'

'Don't be silly, you're part of our brotherhood,' Viktor said. 'You're War Council. You're Wehrmacht. You're one of us.'

'Oh, stop it, Viktor. You'll have me crying in a minute.' Josef laughed, trying to force down the lump that was rising in his throat.

'Well, you know what I mean,' Viktor said, playfully punching Josef in the shoulder.

'Yes, I know what you mean,' Josef grinned. 'By the way, you still haven't told me how you found me in the middle of a battlefield filled with German tanks?'

'Oh, that part was easy,' Viktor winked. 'All we had to do was look for a Panther auf D with a single red stripe on the turret.'

'Gut Gott, that's why we had the stripe. I knew there was a reason for it. I just knew it.'

'Yes, that was Lowe's idea. Quite clever, I thought. Anyway, we rest tonight, and then at first light we head for Aachen. Weise has ordered that once we get there, we make our own way out and then disappear into the heart of Germany. We lay low until after the war, and then, hopefully, return to normal life, and help rebuild what's left of der Vaterland.'

'It's true, then,' Josef said quietly. 'We really are losing the war?'

A sombre silence fell upon them.

After what felt like only a few hours' sleep, Josef was woken up by Egon and told to get dressed. The remaining members of the War Countil all enjoyed a light breakfast together, cooked by Erich Heiter, and then boarded the Panther tank and rolled off into the inky-blue blackness that was just starting to brighten. Josef was given the command, since he was the only man present with full tank experience, and he felt a sense of pride as he leaned out of the cupola, scanning the road ahead through a set of field glasses. Viktor acted as both machine gunner and radio operator, while Egon struggled to stuff himself into the narrow driver's seat. Erich manned the cannon with the help of Philip, who was charged with supplying the heavy armour-piercing shells.

They hadn't travelled far when Josef screamed the order to stop, and Egon panicked and pressed the breaks too hard, forcing the tank to rock back and forth, sending Erich and Philip sprawling forward in a most ungracious manner. Everything went quiet as Egon, Viktor and Josef watched eagerly from their individual vantage points, observing the long, thick muzzle of a tank appearing on the horizon, followed by its wide, dark iron body. The noise from the broad metal tracks was deafening, and the ground began to shake beneath them.

'Is it one of ours?' Erich asked.

'I don't know,' Viktor said shakily, 'but it's big. Very big!'

'Everyone, man your stations, quickly,' Josef commanded, with an urgency in his voice that dissipated as the massive vehicle drew nearer. 'It's OK, it's a King Tiger. It's one of ours.'

'Thank Gott,' Egon sighed with relief. 'How big is that thing?'

'I don't know,' Josef puffed his cheeks. 'but I can tell you that it weighs sixty-seven tons and cost eight-hundred-thousand Reich marks to build. That's the price of three fighter planes.'

'No shit,' Egon whistled. 'With that kind of weaponry, we can't possibly lose.'

Josef gave the Tiger crew a high wave, and then they were on their way again, clattering through the rough open countryside. They hadn't travelled far, however, before they came into contact with the enemy.

'I've got two sightings,' Viktor called out anxiously. 'First target, twenty degrees left. Looks like a Tiger. Second target, one-hundred-and-thirty degrees right. Not sure what it is.'

'Verstanden, I'm on it,' Josef grunted, as he leaned out of the cupola with his field glasses. 'First target is Amerikan, not German. It's a… mein Gott, it's a Pershing! Don't take your eyes off it, Egon. It can outrun us and outgun us. Second target is a Tiger. Stay on course, Egon. The Tiger will take care of the Amerikans.'

'Josef, why is the Tiger pointing its kanon at us?' Erich asked, as he peered through the turret's master sight.

'I don't know, but let's throw a sharp right here, just to be on the safe side. Head for that small clump of trees over there, Egon. No, wait. Wait! I see a white plume of smoke there.' Josef felt his stomach drop as he realised what was happening. 'The Tiger has just fired at us,' he shouted down into the open turret. 'Quick, Egon, speed her up!'

The Panther charged forward, bouncing over huge craters and

tossing the crew around like rag dolls. There was a bright orange flash, followed by a loud explosion that sounded as though it came from very close by, but thankfully everyone was unhurt. As a result of Josef's quick thinking, they were now partially protected by a few flimsy elm trees, and the Tiger turned its attention towards the heavy Pershing M26, known as the tank killer, because of its 90mm cannon. She was more than a match for the fearsome 42-ton Tiger, and they were soon engaged in a duel of immense firepower.

Large chunks of black earth were thrown up high into the air, followed by huge clouds of gas and steam, as each side probed its target with armour-piercing shells. The battling tanks eventually became obscured from view as more and more rounds fell, sending a thick curtain of grey and white cordite rolling across the open plain. This gave the Panther crew time to recover, and while Erich and Philip struggled to pick up the shell casings and other paraphernalia from the bottom of the tank, Josef pressed his field glasses to his face and focussed on the Tiger. Why would they fire on their own men? he wondered. Was it mistaken identity, caused by the fog of war? No, there had to be another reason.

He turned the adjusting wheel of his field glasses until the image of the Tiger tank became clear. He paused for a moment, and then gasped. The mist began to subside, and he could see the Tiger's bulky metal turret slowly turning to the left, ready to engage the Pershing one last time. Any doubts or questions he might have had about why they were attacked were now completely removed from his mind, as painted on the side of the Tiger's turret were the large white numbers 333. It was Lunder.

Every fibre in Josef's body was screaming, Go after him, but he knew that he had to stay calm and consider the lives of his crewmen. This wasn't the War Council's fight; it was between him and Lunder, and there could only be one outcome. Josef's heart ached with terror, his forehead glistened with sweat and his stomach churned, filling him with nausea. If he had gone to charm school, he would have come top of the class. His father had told him to always be polite and courteous whenever he was in company, and reminded him that he was different to others. He told his son that he would have to work much harder than his peers if he was to succeed and become accepted by the Nazis. However, everyone he'd met since joining the Wehrmacht had quickly warmed to him; that is, until he came across the SS. He'd tried to act the perfect gentleman when first introducing himself to Major Lunder at the Christmas dance, but had quickly realised that it would take a lot more than his natural charm to win over such a man. In the twisted mind of Lunder, everyone touched by Josef was marked for death, and one by one they would disappear, never to be seen again.

Enough is enough, Josef said to himself, realising that now was the time to save what was left of the War Council, lest they be destroyed forever. He thought for one last time of Monika – beautiful Monika – and of his dear mother, and then gritted his teeth, as fear turned to anger, and nausea became rage.

'Everyone out of the tank, now!' he bellowed at the top of his voice.

'Was ist los?' Viktor asked.

'You're all in great danger,' Josef said. 'It's Lunder who is commanding the Tiger. If you don't escape now, you're all dead men!'

'We're not leaving without you,' Erich said, looking down at Viktor and Egon, 'are we lads?'

'You must,' Josef implored. 'You can't stay here. Go now, while the Tiger is distracted by the Pershing.'

'And what about you?' Philip asked. 'What are you planning?'

'Oh, don't worry about me,' Josef said. 'I'll drive the tank out into open ground and create a diversion. That should give you enough time to slip away.'

'No, Erich is right,' Viktor said, gesturing to the rest of the group. 'We were sent here to rescue you, and that's exactly what were going to do. Egon, fire her up, and let's put that Amerikan out of commission, eh,?'

'This is madness,' Erich cried. 'We can't take on a Pershing in this old piece of shit!'

'You just keep watch with those binoculars,' Viktor ordered. 'How many shells do we have left?'

'Seven,' Philip answered.

'We'll have to make each one count, then,' Viktor said.

'Contact!' Josef called out. 'They're still firing at each other.'

'Egon, get as close as you dare,' Viktor instructed. 'Hopefully, we can hit the Amerikans before they know what's happened. How are we doing up there, Josef?'

'Lunder's just scored a direct hit on the Pershing, but she's still functional.'

'Are we within range, Erich?'

'Yes, Viktor.'

'Then let him have it.'

The Panther recoiled violently as the shot was launched, and everyone fell silent as they waited for a report from Josef, who was straining his eyes through the field glasses.

'It bounced off,' Josef yelled in disbelief. 'Quick, reload. She's turning towards us.'

'OK, keep calm, lads,' Viktor said. 'Are we ready, Erich?'

'Yes, Viktor.'

'Fire!'

'We missed!' Josef lamented. 'Now both tanks are training their guns on us. I told you, you should have got out when you had the chance.'

'Make ready for another shot, Erich,' Viktor ordered.

'I fear it may be too late for that,' Josef said.

'It's your call as tank commander,' Viktor said. 'Who do you wish to fire on, Lunder or the Amerikans?'

The seconds were ticking away, and Josef had to make a decision. Should he fire on Lunder, who was, after all, out to kill him, or the Americans, who were also out to kill him?

'Josef!' Victor shouted.

'Yes, yes, OK,' Josef sighed. 'Fire at the Amerikans. Do it now!'

The Panther belched out another round, and as the shell was propelled forward, it was answered by two deafening reports.

The crew sat motionless, and the atmosphere in the tank was that of calm resolve as the metal around them began to melt. There was an unbearable surge of heat, which made their skins blister and their bodies swell until they popped, hissing in their own juices. They all died at their stations, with their withered, blackened arms raised up to their contorted faces. The War Council had perished just two kilometres from Aachen, entombed in their iron sepulchre having lived and died by their motto, 'Zuzammen immer!'

As for the crew of the Tiger tank, they had to withdraw from the battlefield, badly damaged by the Pershing. Lunder would later take out his service pistol and shoot Ulricher dead for celebrating too loudly the demise of Herzog and his crew. He then turned to Wholner and, with sadness in his eyes, declared, 'We have killed some gut men here today, and don't you forget it.'

APPENDIX

List of Concentration Camps (given by Stanizlaw to Josef, p.33)

In Poland: Auschwitz, Lwow, Belsec, Sobibor, Treblinka, Kulmhof, Chelmno and Krakow-Plaszow.

In Germany: Flossenburge, Ravensbruck, Buchenwald, Bergen-Belsen, Dachau, Sachsenhausen, Dora-nordhausen, Oranienburg, Papenburg, Landsberg, Theresienstadt, Torgau, Grossrosen, Natzweiler and Neuengamme.

In Austria: Mauthausen.

Josef's War Diary (p.172)

10 May 1940. Germany launches an offensive in the west, codenamed Operation Fall Gelb, [1.] attacking France, Belgium and Holland. Belgium, who have been on a war footing since 1939, have mobilised 90,000 men, and while this is a mostly conscripted force, it nevertheless fights with great tenacity and courage until, on 11 May, a general retreat is ordered following defeat to the new German way of fighting, the blitzkrieg. [2.] Meanwhile, General Kurt Student, a fighter pilot during World War One, springs into action and drops 4,000 of his Fallschrimjager [3.] across Holland, and suffers only light casualties (180 Germns killed) in the process. On 14 May, the Dutch surrender.

25 May 1940. A general rescue is launched to evacuate the BEF [4.] and its French allies from the northern port of Dunkirk, France. An

estimated 338, 226 men are transported to safety between 26 May and 3 June, using an estimated 950 assorted ships and small craft, coordinated by Vice-Admiral Sir Bertram Ramsey, working from a room that has been cut deep into a cliff to hold a dynamo, hence the mission's code name, Operation Dynamo. Controversially, it is only when the last British soldiers are aboard that the order is finally given to allow the allied French, numbering some 53,000, to also be evacuated, causing great resentment in France. As the convoys cross the Channel, they are constantly harassed from the air by the Luftwaffe, and attacked at sea by Unter-boots and Eil-boots. [5.] Three destroyers and a passenger ship are sunk and four other ships badly damaged, in addition to 177 British aircraft that are lost during the nine days it takes to complete the crossing. The RAF's pounding of Dunkirk saves many lives, as the palls of smoke created by their bombs provide cover from enemy attack. This prompts Churchill to give his famous speech to Parliament on 4 June, declaring, 'Wars are not won by evacuations, but there was victory inside this deliverance which should be noted. It was gained by the Royal Air Force.'

2 June 1940. The Allies withdraw from Norway and, citing heavy losses, Admiral Ramsey bans the daytime crossing of all warships, leaving only civilian vessels and ferries to continue Operation Dynamo. However, parliament later orders Ramsey to continue with the crossings, and the following night his ships evacuate a further 27,000 French.

9 June 1940. The German offensive in France begins with the capture of Elbeuf, followed by Reims on 11 June and Chalons-sur-Marne 12 June. By 13 June, Evreux has also fallen, and the

next day the Germans are in Paris, Troyes and Chaumont. The following week sees Dijon, Pontarlier, Briare, Rennes, Saumur, Brest, Cherbourg, Nantes, Vichy and Lyon taken.

21 June 1940. Mussolini allies with Hitler and declares war on France, and the next day France signs an armistice agreement with both Germany and Italy.

25 June 1940. Following the capture of Royan and Angouleme, France is officially occupied.

28 June 1940. General Charles de Gaulle is officially recognised as the leader of the Free French by the British government. Two days later, Churchill receives news that the Germans have captured Guernsey and the Channel Islands.

3 July 1940. The Royal Navy bombards the French fleet at Mers-el-Kebir. The next day, Italian troops occupy Abyssinia, and establish frontier posts in Sudan.

10 July 1940. The Battle of Britain begins. The skies over Britain are filled with zigzagging white vapour trails, and are peppered with the black dots of enemy and friendly fighters spewing out their bright red tracers against the powder blue background.

16 July 1940. Adolf Hitler issues a directive for the preparation of Operation Sea Lion, the invasion of Britain. Hitler hatches a plan with the help of Admiral Raeder, commander in chief of the German Navy, which would involve a massive amphibious assault, beginning on the shores of France and spreading across

the channel to Britain. It would start with the 9th army and 8th corps departing from Le Harve, followed by the 38th corps and army group A from Etaples and Boulogne, the 7th corps and 16th army from Calais, and then, finally, the 13th corps from Dunkirk, Ostend, Rotterdam and Antwerp. However, by 31 July, Raeder has disclosed to Hitler that the necessary naval preparations would not be concluded before 15 September.

Walter Schellenberge, an SS functionary, presents the Sonderfahndungsliste GB, [6.] comprised of some 2,820 British subjects and European exiles that are to be arrested if the landings are successful. The list also includes institutions, establishments, writers, journalists, publishers and financiers that are of particular interest to the Nazis. The Einsatzgruppen, [7.] under the command of SS Standartenfuhrer [8.] Dr Franz Six, are to quickly follow up after the landings and establish bases in London, Bristol, Birmingham, Manchester, Liverpool and Edinburgh. Included on the SS arrest list are such names as Winston Churhill, Anthony Eden, Noel Coward, HG Wells, EM Forster, Aldous Huxley, Violet Bonham Carter, Victor Gollancz and Bernard Baruch.

7 September 1940. Britain reels with terror as the Germans begin their Blitz campaign, designed to break and weaken the spirit of the population. However, the plan backfires in that it serves to stiffen the British resolve.

12 September 1940. Italy invades Egypt via Libya.

16 September 1940. United States passes Selective Training and Service Act.

2 October 1940. Hitler orders that all planned measures for Operation Sea Lion should largely be dismantled, and Churchill delivers a speech to the defeated French nation: 'Good night then, sleep together. Strength till the morning, for the morning will come. Brightly will it shine on the brave and few. Kindly on all who suffer for the cause, vive le France.'

28 October 1940. Italy invades Greece via Albania.

5 November 1940. Roosevelt wins a third term as US president.

14 November 1940. Heavy German air raid on Coventry, England.

9 December 1940. British forces defeat Italian opposition at Sidi Barrani, Egypt.

18 December 1940. Hitler issues a directive for the invasion of Russia.

6 January 1941. President Roosevelt delivers four speeches to United States Congress, but Americans remain disinclined towards war.

19 January 1941. Britain launches its East African Campaign.

22 January 1941. British and Australian troops enter Tobruk, forming a garrison of around 35,000 men.

6 February 1941. The British capture Benghazi, Lybia.

11 February 1941. Field Marshal Erwin Rommel arrives in Libya.

1 March 1941. The Free French enter Kufrain Fezzan.

17 April 1941. Yugoslavia surrenders to Germany.

10 May 1941. Reichminister Rudolf Hess, Hitler's deputy leader of the Nazi Party, bizarrely decides to fly to Scotland on a clandestine solo peacemaking mission. He crash-lands his Messerschmitt aircraft, and is immediately placed under arrest and spends the rest of his life in prison.

16 May 1941. The East African Campaign ends when Italy surrenders at Amba Alagi, Ethiopia.

20 May 1941. German paratroopers land in Crete, bringing 500 transport aircraft and 72 gliders, supported by 500 bombers and fighters. The 7th parachute division, 1st parachute assault regiment and the 5th mountain division are dropped over Malene and Canea on the west coast of the island, and Retimo and Heraklion in the centre. All parachute units sustain heavy losses during the descent and landings, forcing Student to send in his last reserves

21 May 1941. The Germans succeed in capturing the prized Airfield at Malene, with 1,742 British and Commonwealth troops killed or missing, 2,225 wounded and 11,370 captured. The Royal Navy incurs losses of 2,000 killed and 183 wounded, while an estimated 7,000 Germans are killed. The Fallschrimjager would never fly another mission after this, and were converted into army group G following a direct order from Hitler.

24 May 1941. The German battleship Bismarck sinks the battle cruiser HMS Hood. The Bismarck was under the command of Admiral Gunther Lutjens, and was first sighted and then engaged by the Hood, along with the damaged HMS Prince of Wales, in the Denmark Strait. Despite taking considerable damage and leaking fuel following an earlier torpedo attack, launched by the British carrier HMS Victorious, the Bismarck still packs a deadly punch. Only three sailors survive after a so-called 'lucky hit' on the Hood's munitions, which totally obliterates the vessel. She was one of the world's largest pre-war ships and sank within one-and-a-half minutes, taking 1,416 officers and men down with her.

27 May 1941. The Bismarck's steering is wrecked by a torpedo bomber from the HMS Ark Royal, and the ship is then pursued by the British fleet under the command of Admiral Sir John Tovey. On the morning of the torpedo attack, Tovey positions his squadron to approach the Bismarck from the east, so that she would be clearly visible while silhouetted against the horizon. At 08.47am, the Rodney opens fire, and is quickly joined by the King George V. At 08.49am, the Bismarck returns fire on the Rodney, and at 08.54am, the heavy cruiser Norfolk opens fire and is later joined by the Dorsetshire, which attacks at 09.04am. At 09.31am, the Bismarck fires her last salvo while receiving multiple hits at point-blank range, but she refuses to sink and continues to fly her ensign, showing no sign of capitulation.

This defiance gives Tovey no choice but to move in for the kill, but first he orders the Rodney and the King George V to retire, due to their low fuel and lack of torpedos. Tovey then gives the Dorsetshire permission to finish off the Bismarck with her three remaining torpedos, but as if to cheat the hangman, Captain Ernst Lindermann lays demolition charges in the turbine room and orders his men to abandon ship. At 10.39am, the Bismarck sinks with her colours still flying. Out of a full complement of 2,222 crewmen, only 115 are saved.

1 June 1941. The British are forced to withdraw from Crete.

22 June 1941. Germany invades Russia, crossing the Bug River. Benito Mussolini, not wanting to be left out, also declares war on Russia.

7 July 1941. US troops receive a British garrison in Iceland.

31 October 1941. The USS Reuben James is sunk in the Atlantic by a German U-boat. The Reuben James was a Great War destroyer, Clemson class. She was escorting ships 965km west of Eire when she was spotted by U.562, who immediately launched torpedos and sunk her, causing the loss of 115 crewmen. This action ended America's policy of isolation.

18 November 1941. The British North African offensive, code-named 'Crusader,' begins with the battle of Sidi Rezegh, in the western desert. The plan is for the 8th army's armoured corps to push through Rommel's besieged Tobruck, while the infantry advances along the coast. The Allies would then meet up and break-out by the Tobruck garrison, before sweeping westwards across eastern Libya. Sidi Rezegh is a ridge some 32km southeast of Tobruck, and stands between the Allies and the besieged port. The British and first South African division fight hard for possession of the ridge, but the Afrika Corps and the Italian Ariete pummel and

partly destroy the South African brigade, and the battle becomes known as Totensonntag (Sunday of the dead).

23 November 1941. General Sir Alan Cunningham, alarmed at the heavy losses (17,700 casualties), suggests to his commander in chief, Field Marshal Sir Claude Auchinleck, that they should withdraw. Major-General Neil Richie is immediately brought in to replace Cunningham, and the battle rages on.

Rommel decides to relieve his post at Bardia and Halfaya Pass, Egypt, with the intention of retaking Sidi Rezegh 1 December, but he is again driven off because of high casualties (24,500, plus 13,000 captured).

19 November 1941. HMAS Sydney is sunk. Originally named Phaeton, she was transferred upon completion to the Australian Navy in 1938. She distinguished herself by sinking the Italian cruiser, Bartolomeo Colleoni, off Crete in July 1940, only to be disabled by gunfire and torpedo attacks from the German auxiliary cruiser Kormoran, in the southwestern Pacific. She is last seen on fire and drifting away from the sinking Kormoran. One dead crewman is eventually picked up after a month in the water, but no other bodies are ever found.

6 December 1941. Britain declares war on Finland, Hungary and Romania.

7 December 1941. Japan attacks Pearl Harbour, and then declares war on United States. US declares war on Japan the next day.

10 December 1941. The Prince of Wales and the Repulse are

sunk off Malaya. They were ordered to Singapore in October, to act as a deterrent to the Japanese, and were to have been joined by the carrier Indomitable before she was damaged after running aground in the British West Indies. Admiral Tom Philips has the command, and orders the ships to Kuantan to prevent a landing by the Japanese, but when they arrive, they find that no landings have taken place. However, a Japanese submarine is sighted, and at 12.33pm, the Repulse is sunk, followed by the Prince of Wales at 13.20pm. Admiral Philips is killed, along with 840 of his men.

11 December 1941. Germany and Italy declare war on United States.

17 December 1941. The Japanese land in British Borneo.

18 December 1941. Adolf Hitler appoints himself commander in Chief after Field Marshal Walter von Brauchitsch resigns.

26 January 1942. US troops arrive in Northern Ireland.

11 February 1942. Operation Cerberus sees German battle ships escape from Brest, France. Adolf Hitler gives the order to dispatch two battle cruisers, the Scharnhorst and the Gneisenau, plus the heavy cruiser the Prinz Eugen, to Norway from Brest, via the English Channel. The mission is considered so dangerous that Admiral Raeder refuses to take responsibility for it. However, the German fleet manages to slip through the British naval defence, causing a huge outcry from the British government and public.

10 April 1942. President Roosevelt announces that US forces are

to be sent to Greenland.

14 April 1942. Bourg Leopold becomes a transit camp for British and black-American prisoners of war.

16 April 1942. Malta is awarded the George Cross, after the British Mediterranean island colony, with a population of just 270,000, under its Governor, Lt General William Dobbie, refuses to capitulate despite intense air bombardment. Malta is vital to the British war effort, as it contains seven airfields and is the only harbour between Gibraltar and Alexandria, making it critical to British air and sea operations. Malta holds, but its citizens suffer from malnutrition, scabies and a Typhoid epidemic, leaving 1,493 dead and 3,764 wounded.

20 May 1942. The British withdraw from Burma.

22 May 1942. Mexico declares war on Japan and Germany.

26 May 1942. Rommel attacks Gazala.

30 May 1942. The RAF begins its thousand-bomb raid. Due to heavy daytime losses, Air Chief Marshal Sir Arthur Harris devises a plan to deliver a knockout blow to the Germans, by launching a massive air raid that will flatten and destroy the cities of Cologne, Bremen and Essen, the latter being home to the giant Krupp steel works. Harris also wrongly believes that the raid will lower German morale.

9 June 1942. Hitler avenges the assassination of Obergruppen-

fuhrer SS [9.] Reinhard Heydrich, Himmler's deputy, by carrying out massacres at Lidice and Lezaky in Prague, Czechoslovakia. Heydrich was ambushed and fatally injured when a hand grenade tossed by Czech agents trained by the SOE [10.] exploded inside his open-topped staff car. The end result is 198 Czech men shot and 184 women sent to Ravensbruck, plus the abduction of 98 children.

21 June 1942. Tobruck falls to Rommel.

1 July 1942. Battle of El-Alamain begins. This is to be the first of two battles fought for the possession of an Egyptian desert railway halt, situated some 95km west of Alexandria. On the 1 and 2 July, Field Marshal Sir Claude Auchenleck successfully prevents Rommel's Panzer tanks from breaking out through their defensive lines near Ruweisat Ridge, when Rommel makes a bid to conquer Egypt and seize the Suez Canal. Rommel tries this again at Alam Halfa in September, but is once more unsuccessful.

4 July 1942. Arctic Convoy PQ 17 is ordered to scatter and suffers heavy losses. This route was designed to ship materials – in this instance, containing 4.43m tons – from the UK to various Icelandic ports, to aid the Soviet war effort via the Norwegian and Barents seas. The Admiralty become aware of an impending attack on PQ 17, and respond by drawing up an elaborate plan to safeguard the convoy by giving it a close escort of destroyers and small vessels, while a cruiser sits well behind. ULTRA [11.] intelligence reveals that the battleship Tirpitz, the cruisers Admiral Hipper and Admiral Scheer, and possibly the pocket battleship Lutzow [12.] are, along with a force of destroyers, about to attack the convoy.

Admiral Sir Dudley Pound controversially orders the convoy to scatter, and then orders its escorts to return. The result is devastating, as U-boats and bombers pounce, leaving only 11 of 37 vessels to reach their destination. Estimated losses include 3,850 trucks and vehicles, 2,500 aircraft, 430 tanks and 153 seamen. Admiral Pound later dies of a brain tumour while still in office.

19 August 1942. Churchill risks a major raid on the French coast, with the aim of seizing and briefly holding the port of Dieppe with a force of 5000 Canadians, 1000 British and 50 American rangers, but the attack is a disaster. The Germans react quickly and attack the convoy by sea and air, and out of the 5000 troops that make it ashore, at least half are killed or captured.

22 October 1942. UK call-up age is lowered to 18 years.

24 October 1942. Second Battle of El-Alamain. The 8th army, now under the commanded of Lt General Bernard Montgomery, gains the upperhand, and by 4 November pierces Rommel's defences, forcing him to retreat into Tunisia.

27 November 1942. The French fleet is scuttled at Toulon, as aside from those units needed for security, the fleet is to be demobilised under German and Italian control. However, following the bombardment of the fleet by the British at Mers-el-Kebir, the order is only partially implemented.

23 January 1943. The British enter Tripoli.

26 January 1943. The Fezzan campaign ends, as the Free French

reach Tripoli. The campaign involves multiple incursions during the crossing of Italian-held desert in Libya by de Gaulle's Free French, led by Colonel Philippe Leclerc, who is based at Fort Lamy. His force is comprised of Tirailleur, Senegalais and Chad infantry, along with the camel mounted groupe, Nomade de Tibesti. Fourteen bombers, who later become known as the Lorraine Squadron, support them. Chad, where the campaigns are launched from, is the only Free French territory adjacent to Axis soil in Italian-occupied Libya.

On 22 January, Leclerc overcomes stiff opposition at Mirza, but captures it before entering Tripoli. After travailing 2,575km from Chad, Leclerc and his men become part of Montgomery's 8th army, to be known as L Force.

27 January 1943. The 8th USAAF mounts its first air raid on Wilhelmshaven, Germany.

2 February 1943. German forces are captured at Stalingrad.

13 February 1943. The first Chindit operation is launched into Burma. Brigadier 'Orde' Wingate leads the Chindits, who take their name from the stone winged lions that guard Buddhist temples, known as Chinthe. The chief principles of the Chindits are surprise, mobility and the use of aircraft in the role of artillery. At Wingate's disposal is the 13th King's Liverpool Regiment, 3rd Gorkha rifles, No.142 Commando Company and the 2nd Burma rifles. Wingate launches Operation Loincloth, and divides his units into eight self-contained columns. One of them is to cut the railway south of Wuntho, before marching 400km across Japanese-occupied northern Burma, to link up with the second

group under Wingate. This cuts the railway further north, near Nanken, before crossing the Irra Waddy River, where both groups then combine to sever the Mandalay-Lashio railway. Hard fighting ensues on 24 March, and Wingate orders his men to disperse and make their own way back to Burma. This takes many weeks, and out of 3,000 troops involved, only 2,182 return.

19 February 1943. The Battle of Kasserine Pass begins. In this, a crucial stage of the North Africa Campaign, Rommel launches a counterstrike to prevent Eisenhower's Allies from reaching the central Tunisian coast by splitting the forces in two. The first phase of this causes the Allies to withdraw to the western Dorsale Mountains, in order to protect their flank.

Lt General Lloyd Fredendall gives Colonel Robert Stark orders to hold the pass, which he does, but that same night Rommel switches the attack north-westwards, and by the next afternoon his assault group, along with the Italian armoured division and infantry, is through and heading for Tebessa, Algeria, while the 10th Panzer division strikes out for Thala, Tunisia. Rommel is suddenly ordered away from Tebessa and goes on to Le Kaf, where heavy fighting rages in the midst of a rain storm. The wet ground makes it difficult for the Panzers, and Rommel has to withdraw his forces. The pass is reoccupied by the Americans, but only following heavy losses of men and materials, prompting Eisenhower to replace Fredendall with General George S Paton.

13 May 1943. The Axis forces capitulate in North Afirca.

16 May 1943. The RAF dam buster's breech the Mohne and Eder dams. It is left to 617 squadron, an elite unit, to breach the dams in

the Ruhr valley, which is a primary industrial area. The Mohne and the Sorpe provide a large proportion of the Ruhr's water needs, while the Eder, the largest target, helps maintain the navigable waters of the Weser river and Mittellands canal. A canister-shaped bomb invented by Barns Wallis has to be dropped from 18m (60ft) above the water, before it bounces and detonates against the dam wall. Eight out of the 19 bombers sent on the mission are lost, and Wing Commander Guy Wilson receives the Victoria Cross for his efforts. However, despite the mission being a success, the Mohne and Eder dams are repaired and fully operational again by October 1943.

24 May 1943. German U-boats withdraw from the north Atlantic.

5 July 1943. Operation Citadel, the battle for the Russian city of Kursk, commences. After the fall of Stalingrad and the recapture of Kharkiv by Field Marshal Erich von Manstein, the German high command formulates Operation Citadel, only for the Russians to build eight concentric circles of defence by the time the offensive is launched. The 9th army, under the command of General Gunther von Kluge, attacks from the north, while the 4th Panzer army, under Manstein, attacks from the south. The 9th penetrates six miles, losing 25,000 men, 200 tanks and 200 aircraft, while Manstein's Panzers gain some 25 miles, but also suffer great losses, with 10,000 killed and 350 tanks destroyed. The Russians launch their counteroffensive in the north against Kursk 12 July, and by 23 July the Germans are back were they started.

Manstein withdraws without orders to the Dnieper, from the scene that becomes known as the greatest tank battle of the war, involving two million men, 6,000 tanks and 4,000 aircraft. This is to be a turning point that results in the Germans fighting largely in retreat.

10 July 1943. The Allies land in Sicily, Italy.

24 July 1943. RAF launch air raid over Hamburg, Germany.

25 July 1943. Mussolini resigns and is then arrested. King Victor Emmanual, with the support of the Italian army high command, dismisses and jails Musolini, and replaces him with Marshal Pietro Badoglio.

17 August 1943. The Axis resistance ends in Sicily. The RAF bombs Peenemunde, while the 8th USAAF bombs Schweinfurt, which is home to five ball bearing factories and is vital to the German war machine. The Americans dispatch 376 bombers in total. On the first raid, 230 are sent to Schweinfurt and 146 to nearby Regensburg; 147 planes are destroyed on the first raid, and on the second, 60 are destroyed and 142 badly damaged. All raids deep into Germany are temporarily suspended.

The RAF launch raids on Peenemunde a few hours after Schweinfurt and Regensburge. It is while the RAF are performing an aerial reconnaissance over Peenemunde that they discover a rocket and trailer, and soon gather intelligence that a V-2 rocket programme is being developed. The RAF loses 290 crew and 44 bombers, while the Luftwaffe loses 120 crew and 12 fighters.

3 September 1943. The Allies land on the Italian mainland.

8 September 1943. Italy announces her surrender. Mussolini is

rescued by Colonel Otto Skorzeny and his Fallschrimjager, on the orders of Adolf Hitler.

9 September 1943. The allies land at Salerno, Italy.

10 September 1943. Germany occupies Rome and much of northern Italy.

19 September 1943. German forces evacuate Sardinia.

13 October 1943. Italy declares war on Germany.

24 December 1943. Major General Dwight D. Eisenhower is named as supreme commander of the Normandy landings.

26 December 1943. The German battleship Scharnhort is sunk. She is sailing for the Arctic, to attack convoy JW55B off the North Cape, but is driven off by Admiral Sir Bruce Fraser's fleet. The retreat is covertly tracked by radar, before being confronted by Fraser's heavy squadron. At 17.22pm, the Scharnhorst signals that she is surrounded, and being attacked by shells and torpedoes. At 17.45pm she is sunk, and of a full complement of 2,000 crewmen, only 36 survive.

22 January 1944. The Allies land at Anzio, Italy, with a plan to cut German communications between Rome and Cassino. On 21 January, Field Marshal Sir Harold Alexander, along with General Mark Clark, who is commanding the American 5th army, had made an amphibious assault. Their aim had been to break through the Gustav line by launching two simultaneous attacks;

one at Cassino, and the other by sea at Anzio. It is hoped that by cutting the German 10th army's lines of communication, they would force Field Marshal Kesselring to order the evacuation of the Gustav line, allowing the armies at Anzio and Cassino to join and then march to Rome.

The attack at Cassino does succeed in attracting the German reserves, only for US Major General John P. Lucas to fail to take advantage of the German weakness at Anzio by not pressing an advance. Lucas finally tries to break out 30 January, but finds that the Germans have reorganised themselves. By 15 February, the Germans have gathered enough strength to penetrate deep into his positions, before being halted by desperate American counterattacks on 19 February. With Lucas now relieved, an allied breakout succeeds on 23 May, led by General Lucian Truscott.

27 January 1943. The siege at Leningrad ends.

1 February 1943. The creation of the French Forces of the Interior unifies most resistance movements in France, and the first Battle of Monte Cassino begins.

14 February 1943. Second Battle of Monte Cassino.

20 February 1943. The Anglo-US air offensives against Germany begin. This is the code name given to a coordinated six-day offensive launched by the RAF and the US Strategic Air Force, comprised of 8th, 9th and 15th USAAF, utilising 3,800 long-range fighters and 2,351 British bombers. Collectively, they drop some 20,000 tons onto German fighter factories and associated industries. The British fly by night and the Americans fly by day, and as

a result of this operation, German fighter production is put back two months. American losses: 254 aircraft and 28 fighters. British losses: 157 aircraft.

15 March 1943. Third Battle of Monte Cassino.

11 May 1943. Fourth battle for Monte Cassino.

4 June 1943. US troops enter Rome.

6 June 1943. Operation Overlord begins, and Allies land at Normandy.

13 June 1943. Start of the V-1 bombardment over England. The FZG-76, known as the V-1, is a mid-winged monoplane driven by a pulsating flow duct motor, which carries an 1,870-pound explosive warhead and travels at 350 mph, with a range of 130 miles. Development of this device began in June 1942, at the research station Peenemunde, and by March 1944 they had produced 35,000 units, of which 9,251 are fired against Britain, while 4,621 are destroyed by the RAF. Of the 6,551 fired at Antwerp, 2,455 are intercepted and destroyed.

16 June 1943. The Free French land on the Italian island, Elba.

18 July 1943. Operation Goodwood is launched, and the 21st Panzer division are heavily bombarded from the air.

1. Yellow case.
2. Lightning war.

3. Paratroopers.

4. British Expeditionary Force.

5. Submarines and fast boats.

6. Special wanted criminal list (Great Britain).

7. Mobile killing squad.

8. Colonel.

9. General.

10. Special operations executive.

11. Intelligence agency.

12. Originally named the Deutschland, this ship had its name changed to Lutzow on the orders of Adolf Hitler, who feared that it would be a bad omen for Germany if she were ever sunk.

BIBLIOGRAPHY

Macdonald. C. The Battle of the Bulge, London. 1984.

Henry. C, & Hillelm. Children of the SS, London. 1976.

'Tirpitz, V1 & V2 Rockets,' Encyclopaedia of WW2

Wegner. B, The Waffen SS Organization: Ideology & Function, TR. R. Webster, Oxford. 1990.

Michel. H, Paris Resistant, Paris. 1982

Bradford. E, Siege Malta: 1940-43, London. 1985.

MacDonald. C, The Lost Battle: Crete 1941, London. 1993.

Funk. A. L, Hidden Ally, Dragoon, New York. 1992.

'Anzio,' Encyclopaedia of WW2.

'Big Week,' The Oxford Companion WW2.

Gooch. J, Musolini: the Downfall

Schweinfurt, Air Raids, New York. 1978.

Middlebrook. M, The Peenemunde Raids, London. 1982.

Schenk. P, Invasion of England 1940, London. 1990.

Fairley. J, Remember Arnheim, Aldershot. 1978.

Wiggan. R, Operation Freshman, London. 1986.

Brickhill. P, The Dam Busters, Rev, Edn, London. 1977.

The Kursk Battle (3rd Impression), Bison books ltd. 1981.

Carfrae. C, Chindit Column, London. 1985.

The Imperial War Museum, Operation Sea Lion [Einsatzgruppen]: the Black Book, London. 1989.

Harman. N, Dunkirk: the Necessary Myth, London, 1980.

Bison books ltd., Diepp.

Laurent Mirouze, Europa Militaria No.2.

Brian L Davis, German Uniforms & Insignia 1933-1945.

Beevor. A, Blitzkreig Stalingrad, London. 1998.

Teutoburger Wald: www.Ibdb.Com/tmdisplaybattle

Home 8: Inet.tele.dk/aaaa/Skorzeny. Htm
Waffen SS-Junkerschulen: www.wssob.com/training.html
Horstwessel: Iespana.es/horstwessel/horsingles. Htm
Lodz: www.yad-vashem.org.il/exhibitions/temporary exhibitions/childsplay/lexicon/1
Joe Louis: www.cmgww.com/sports/Louis/bio html
Home. Att. Net/~Berliner-Ultrasonic/Mercedes. Html
www.WhiteHouse.gov/history/Presidents

All characters in this book, except for those who are named below, are fictitious. Any similarity to actual persons living or dead is purely coincidental:

Erich von Brandenberger. LT. Gen.
Joannes Blaskowitzs. Gen.
Fedor von Bock. Gen.
W. Bortnowski. Gen.
Stefan Dalp-Biernacki. Gen.
Hans Beibow. Gauleiter.
Dietrich von Choltitz. Gen.
Josef 'Sepp' Dietrich. LT. Gen.
Kazimierz Fabrycy. Gen.
Czeslaw Mlot-Fijalkowski. Maj Gen.
Eugen Fischer. Dr. Geneticist.
Albrecht Forster. Gauleiter.
Hans Frank. Gauleiter.
Arthur Greiser. Gauleiter.
Hermann Goering. Reich Marshal.
Josef Goebbels. Propaganda Minister.

Hershal Grunschman. Civilian.

Reinardt Heydrich. LT. Gen.

Heinrich Himmler. Reich Fuhrer.

Adolf Hitler. Dictator.

Tadeusz Kutrzeba. Gen.

Gunther von Kluge. Gen.

Kucher. Gen.

Lucts. Gen.

Heinz Lammerding. LT. Gen.

Siegmund List. Gen.

Walter Model. Field Marshal.

Hasso von Manteuffel. LT. Gen.

Lili Marleen. Actress.

Benito Mussolini. Dictator.

Emil Przedrzymirski. Gen.

Joachim Peiper. LT. Colonel.

Mordechai Zurawski. Ghetto Leader.

Juliusz Rommel. Gen.

Gerd von Rundstedt. Field Marshal.

Walther Reichenau. Gen.

Ernst von Rath. Diplomat.

Antoni Szyling. Gen.

Stanizlaw Skwarczyriski. Gen.

Julius Streicher. Gauleiter.

Max Schmeling. Boxer.

Otto Skorzeny. LT. Colonel.

Quinctilius Varus. Proconsul.

Horst Wessel. Storm Trooper.

Acknowledgements:

Hans Hauck.
Thomas Holzhauser.
Hilarius Gilges.
Elizabeth Morton.
Betti Friedrich.
Julietta Hillerkus.
Adolf Hilllerkus.
Ma ma Boholles.
Werner Egiomue.
Theodor Michael.
Julianna Michael.
James Michael.
Johnny Voste.
Johnny Williams.
Josef Nassy.
Gupha Voss.
Moise Shewa.
David Okuefuna.
Brian Bovell.

Printed in Great
Britain
by Amazon